J.M. Hall is an author, playwright and deputy head of a primary school. His plays have been produced in theatres across the UK as well as for radio, the most recent being *Trust*, starring Julie Hesmondhalgh on BBC Radio 4. His first novel, *A Spoonful of Murder*, is about retired primary school teachers who turn to sleuthing.

A Spoonful of Murder

J.M. HALL

avon.

Published by AVON
A division of HarperCollins*Publishers*
1 London Bridge Street
London SE1 9GF

www.harpercollins.co.uk

HarperCollins*Publishers*
1st Floor, Watermarque Building, Ringsend Road
Dublin 4, Ireland

A Paperback Original 2022
1
First published in Great Britain by HarperCollins*Publishers* 2022

A catalogue copy of this book is available from the British Library.

ISBN: 978-0-00-850961-3

Typeset in Bembo by Palimpsest Book Production Limited, Falkirk, Stirlingshire

Printed and Bound in the UK using
100% Renewable Electricity at CPI Group (UK) Ltd

MIX
Paper from
responsible sources
FSC™ C007454

To Judith

CHAPTER ONE

An old friend is met and unwanted cake is given.

Quite simply, being involved in a murder was something they would never have set out to do. As Thelma said afterwards, everything that happened was (in the beginning at any rate) the sort of thing that was part and parcel of living in a small town. Something happened, then something else, and then something else on top of that. Pat going into the bank in Thirsk, not Ripon, Liz bumping into Paula that morning in Tesco.

And the first of those events happened because it was on Thursdays when they had their 'coffee o'clock' sessions at the Thirsk Garden Centre café. Not a Wednesday because that was Thelma's all-day stint at the charity shop and not a Friday because that was when Pat liked to go to the Farm Shop and Liz picked up her grandson from school. And, by unspoken agreement, neither a Monday or a Tuesday because those days were the beginning of the week and the feeling was that it was good to meet as the week was winding down. This feeling was one that harked back to their days teaching at St Barnabus's Primary School when Friday morning break times were marked with a feeling of anticipation plus chocolate digestives. Days when life built up to the weekend; two welcome days away from powder paint and star jumps, sponge prints and cursive flicks.

Since they'd all been retired (Pat two years, Thelma and Liz four), it had to be said the weekends had somewhat lost that special quality – that snatched, hallowed glow. Truth be told the days even held a certain . . . sameness – Sundays, Tuesdays, Thursdays – a sameness to be fought against with book groups and Keep Fit classes and stints in the charity shop. Fought against but not admitted to.

Hence coffee o'clock every Thursday in the café at Thirsk Garden Centre (good parking, well away from the tourists).

And if it hadn't been a Thursday . . . if it hadn't been the garden centre café . . . they wouldn't have met Topsy and KellyAnne and, crucially, Thelma wouldn't have come across Topsy crying in the toilets, which they all agreed was really the start of things.

So: a Thursday morning in the Thirsk Garden Centre café, about eleven thirty. A dreary, dripping late February day when a wet winter at last seemed to be fading into an equally damp spring and the 'Get Set For The Season!' displays really had their work cut out to project an image of change and cheer. Half-hearted sleet smeared the café windows and everything everywhere seemed wet – sopping wet, dark and dripping. Great mirrored slabs of water lay in the flat fields round the town, roads and lanes were marked with flood warning signs and the café had a distinct smell of damp coats and cough sweets.

The place was about two-thirds full with (as Pat invariably said) People of a Certain Age. Daughters taking their parents out for coffee, the odd silent married couple glumly demolishing a full English and, most commonly, friends like themselves: coffee, cake and catching up.

Ensconced at their favourite table (the round one in the far corner, well away from the self-clear trolley and the Edinburgh Woollen Mill), they had so far that morning caught up with their various news: Pat's youngest, Liam, and his first girlfriend – yes, a nice enough sounding girl, but apparently some sort of

2

poet with one of those Celtic tattoos round her upper arm – and whether this may or may not derail Liam from his A levels and his chances of getting in to do Structural Engineering at Durham. ('Bless,' said Liz. 'Never mind "Bless",' said Pat, 'it's grades he needs to focus on, not Celtic poets.') Then there was Liz's grandson Jacob who, despite being in the most sought-after school in Boroughbridge, with the most sought-after teacher in school (the five-star Mrs Bell), was industriously working his way through every scrap of special needs support going. Plus there were increasingly persistent episodes of what Liz termed 'The Meltdowns'. The latest worrying news on this subject, related by Liz with her trademark frown, were worrying allusions from the school about the possibility of certain avenues Regrettably Being Explored.

They were winding their session down, discussing the latest saga of the executive head of their old school and her new personalized number plates (*which says everything there is to be said about the academy system,* was Thelma's dark comment) when Liz said brightly and suddenly, 'It's Topsy,' almost as if discussion of their former workplace had somehow conjured their one-time colleague into existence.

Thelma and Pat scanned the café. Thelma expected to see competent, if a trifle sombre, features – features that perfectly matched the no-nonsense handwriting in children's reading records (*Read with SOME fluency. PLEASE try and finish this book at home*). Pat instinctively checked her bust, smoothed her wavy, hennaed hair, and adjusted her floaty bright scarf, remembering as clearly as if she'd just heard it, the grunt of disapproval in the back of the throat, which had accompanied so many of the things she had done in front of Topsy over the years: liberal use of glitter, impressions of the school secretary, overenthusiastic renditions of 'We're Going on a Bear Hunt'.

The person they saw first was not Topsy but KellyAnne, Topsy's only daughter, once a golden-haired princess, now somewhat older, somewhat larger, with her mother's set sombre Yorkshire

3

face but still the princess trappings (pink Chanel coat, Michael Kors handbag, the golden locks obviously done somewhere a sight more expensive than Curl Up and Di, the salon they all used). She was scanning the busyish room for an empty table. Thelma, who had a thing about old black and white films, was immediately put in mind of Bette Davis; she could almost see the think bubble forming above KellyAnne's head with the words 'what a dump'.

And standing next to KellyAnne, a figure, arm being clutched like a child on a crossing, a stooped figure . . . an impression of bewilderment, a flushed face slightly shaking, looking belligerently around as if she was wondering where she was and just what was expected of her. Then the face suddenly clicked into focus and they both saw in it the once efficient if formidable features of their former nursery nurse, Topsy Joy. Her name had always reminded Pat (who had a habit of assigning people titles and names) of something out of a children's picture book – 'Topsy Joy at the Park' . . . 'Topsy Joy at the seaside'. Maybe that was why Topsy could be such a tartar to compensate for any wrong impression that might have been given by her name.

When KellyAnne heard Liz and saw the three of them all sitting there, her face smoothed out into sudden sunny lines of relief, almost as if she had expected them to be there and had been looking for them.

'Look who it is,' she said, brightly giving Topsy a slight shake. 'Mother, look who it is.' She smiled radiantly across at them; something about her brightness, about the deliberate nature of her words to Topsy gave an impression of their being underlined in pink highlighter pen. The three exchanged surreptitious glances; that was not how one spoke to Topsy, not ever. But then Topsy didn't seem aware of much at all; she scanned them vaguely as KellyAnne gently led her over.

'Now then.' Liz stood up. But Topsy took a step back from the slight smiling figure in the green cardigan, peering at the greying short hair, the frown lines, as if trying to bring to mind some buried memory. 'Long time no see', said Liz with less certainty.

It had in fact been over eighteen months since they'd seen her at Gordon's funeral, since they'd stood huddled together in Baldersby churchyard, Topsy's face a set mask and KellyAnne somehow reduced to the dimensions of a shrunken child.

'We've just come for a run out. Blow away the old cobwebs,' said KellyAnne. 'Haven't we, Mother?' There it was again, the warm, cheerful but deliberate tone and, they all noticed, with a definite weary edge. They all looked at Topsy who looked back like someone straining to complete a Sudoku and annoyed at the interruption.

The moment was cheerfully blasted with a sudden burst of a gutsy-sounding ballad (which only Pat identified as Aretha Franklin). There was something almost feverish in the way KellyAnne scrabbled in the Michael Kors handbag and dived on the bright pink phone.

'Ladies, I have *got* to take this,' she said in grave, regretful tones that implied it was at least a minor member of the royal family calling. 'I'll not be two seconds.'

KellyAnne was right; she wasn't two seconds, she was in fact thirty-three and a half minutes. Thinking about it afterwards each of them felt she had somewhat foisted her mother on them. (*Not that we minded. Poor love. She needed the break,* Liz said later to Pat. *Well she certainly got it,* said Pat.) And yes, of course none of them minded, not really, but it was undeniably a rather fraught thirty-three minutes that followed.

It wasn't at all that they weren't pleased to see Topsy, but equally it very much wasn't as Liz kept saying brightly, 'Just like old times.' That Topsy was having difficulties was something apparent from the get-go. For a start the conversation was sticky – there was no other word for it – with comments and questions made to Topsy being met by puzzled silence. It felt a bit like

5

talking to someone on a bad phone line; as if Topsy hadn't heard or simply hadn't understood perfectly clear remarks about their various children, their holidays, their various tussles with the new Aldi, stiff knees and leaky guttering.

And then there were the comments Topsy made herself. About Gordon, her late husband, made in the present tense as if he was simply at the golf club as opposed to Baldersby churchyard. Mentions of KellyAnne as though she were still at school – and then other, more random comments about unsafe garden walls and people coming to the house, comments that didn't quite make any sense. Pat showed a tendency to put Topsy right; experience, however, had taught both Liz (with Derek's mother) and Thelma (with Auntie Irene) otherwise. Listening to Pat's bright corrections, Thelma remembered Auntie Irene's insistence that Uncle Bill (deceased) had just nipped down to the allotment and how her mother's initially almost angry contradictions had over time morphed into a weary 'Has he, Irene?'

Talking about St Barnabus's was a bit better, though it was obvious Topsy hadn't a clue the school had become an academy (or for that matter what an academy was), plus she seemed to be under the impression that Thelma had yet to retire even though she'd been the one to present her with the cafetiere at that final assembly.

And then, aside from the difficulty of conversation, there was the fact they were now a good twenty-five minutes beyond their usual time. Liz (shooting covert but agonized glances at her watch) needed to pick up Jacob's tea and also wanted to give the bedding plants section a quick once-over. Thelma was to cover Verna at the charity shop and Pat half had in her mind a session in Harrogate tempting herself in Country Casuals. The other half – more than half – was considering getting home early enough to give Liam's bedroom a quick check to see if there was any evidence of shenanigans with the Celtic poet.

And there was something else. Something that had turned

6

coffee o'clock from its usual point of stability in the week into something rather cold and insecure. The illness that was undoubtedly creeping over Topsy was something they'd all seen at various times in grandparents, then parents, people at church, ex-colleagues and – increasingly now – the partners and the friends of contemporaries. Something they realized was one of the uncomfortable possibilities of growing old, and a possibility that they all now needed to face. If dementia could happen to Topsy, capable no-nonsense Topsy, who could scour her way through a pile of dirty paint palettes quicker than anyone in Blue Base, it could certainly happen to them.

So all in all it was a relief when KellyAnne reappeared (Sorry, ladies!) with a sunny gust of self-absolving laughter that denied the thirty-three minutes and the bulging Edinburgh Woollen Mill carrier bag. The absence had obviously done her good; she seemed a lot happier, like the spring displays, shinier, smilier, brighter . . . She carried with her a tray, with more coffee for everyone, plus five great pink Baldersby Cherry Rascals.

'This is a day for cake, ladies!' she pronounced cheerily. 'Cake, Mother!' She put the tray down and gave Topsy a sudden tight hug from behind that brought tears to Thelma's eyes. Whatever the future held for Topsy, it also held KellyAnne to help her through it.

None of the three actually wanted the cake. Thelma was full of toastie, Pat suffering from her usual post-cake-calorie guilt; Liz stared in frank horror at hers. Plus, of course, the whole coffee and cake thing was awkward because it meant they all had to stay longer still. And even with KellyAnne's brightly dominating presence, the conversation wasn't really much easier than it had been. It wasn't as though they'd ever really had that much to do with KellyAnne; throughout their years working alongside Topsy they'd been spectators to the story of her life: Muffin the pony, the private school, then another when the first didn't work out owing to various 'issues' meaning that exam grades were never what they could be. And then starting up as a beautician, funded by her parents, then working as part-owner of a stables, again funded by Gordon and Topsy. Then the married (and after meeting KellyAnne, rapidly divorced) vet from Richmond; that wedding with the string quartet and the ice sculpture. And the whole timeline liberally peppered with – as Pat put it – 'designer this, that and the other'.

As they sat there and the café filled up with the lunchtime rush, KellyAnne asked them all a lot of bright questions, which only really showed that she knew them about as well as they knew her (Liz had one son, not two daughters; Pat had never been much of a gardener; and where KellyAnne got the idea that Thelma followed rugby league was anyone's guess). There were occasional interjections from Topsy, some that made sense, some that didn't; each of these was treated in the same way by her daughter: a warm smile, a covering of her hand with hers and a significant grimace at the other three. Talking about KellyAnne was a bit more successful. She was between jobs now, the last lot having been 'frankly taking the pee eye ess ess', but was doing a bit of work for her friend Ness who ran a property business. No one liked to ask whether the vet from Richmond was still on the scene; but as if reading their minds she said, 'Of course Stuart and I are no more,' and smiled regretfully round at them.

'I'm sorry,' said Thelma.

KellyAnne shook her head with a philosophical shrug. 'You know how it is when you love someone but you just love them too much to stay together without a lot of pain?' she said.

They all nodded though none of them actually did. Pat fleetingly wondered whether throwing Rod's boxers across the room and snapping 'We do have a dirty linen basket' qualified. 'Is there anyone else on the scene?' she asked. KellyAnne smiled with a look that could only be described as coy.

'You know how it is,' she said. 'You have to kiss one helluva lot of frogs before you find your prince.'

'And of course he came to the house.' Topsy spoke abruptly. They all looked at her.

'What's that, my love?' said Liz.

'A few of them. They came to the house. Different times. Gordon said he'd sorted it. I just wish he'd told me.' She began crumbling her Baldersby Rascal with a frown of concentration. 'Financial misnomers, that's what he kept saying.'

'Mother, we don't need to go into all this now.' KellyAnne spoke gently but very firmly. The tone was less bright and held a distinct edge of steel; the weary element in her voice indicated this wasn't the first time they'd had this exchange. Topsy ignored her but kept frowning down at the plate of crumbs. 'Financial misnomers,' she said truculently.

Liz and Pat were looking at her, trying to make sense of this sudden interruption. Thelma, however, happened to be looking at KellyAnne and it was she who saw the princess features slip; replaced by another look altogether, something infinitely older and sadder and mournful with a haunted quality that reminded her of the time when Muffin the pony had to be put down.

'It's so sad.' KellyAnne dropped her voice, virtually mouthing the words. 'It's falling apart so fast. It's no life for her.'

The three looked sympathetic. There didn't seem to be much they could say.

All in all it was an undeniable relief when five minutes later Liz finally shook her head and said, 'Tesco calls,' in regretful but firm tones; Pat and Thelma then were likewise able to make their excuses, leaving Topsy and KellyAnne at the round table in the corner surrounded by the wreckage of the coffee cups and barely touched pink cakes.

Topsy Joy at the garden centre, thought Pat looking back with a sudden painful pang of pity.

9

CHAPTER TWO

There are tears and disturbing words in the garden centre toilets.

Thelma didn't leave immediately like the other two, texting Verna to say she'd be a bit late. Browsing around the Edinburgh Woollen Mill gave her five much-needed minutes to occupy her mind with nothing more taxing than pastel knitwear and tartan boxes of shortbread.

The encounter with Topsy had shaken her; she'd had no idea she wasn't well. But then life tended to be like that with people you used to work with – you lost touch. Oh, you'd make optimistic promises to meet up – promises for the most part never kept – and then you'd bump into them from time to time, in car parks, in cinema queues and you'd make those promises all over again – and you'd assume they were all right . . . and largely they *would* be all right and so the years would go by until, of course, the time came when they *wouldn't* be all right.

And then of course there was the far darker question that the encounter had prompted: what did the future hold for herself and Teddy, childless as they were? She remembered KellyAnne's tight loving hug and despite everything felt a pang of envy. Topsy had someone.

Dear God, she thought by a pile of half-price cardigans, inhaling the calming smell of new knitwear. *Bless Topsy and bless KellyAnne. Thank you for KellyAnne looking after her mother. Please give her strength and look after them. And if there's anything I can do to help, show me.*

But there was no answer except a waitress from the café calling out, 'Tuna jacket,' in forlorn, unanswered tones. God, it seemed, was managing just fine and needed no help from Thelma. She sighed and looked at the cardigan in front of her, a cheery shade of yellow.

A lemon yellow cardigan, the wool grubby and unwashed . . .

She came to with a burnt shock – time to go.

On her way out she retired for what Pat would term 'a security wee' in the ladies' room (smoked glass mirrors, bowls of potpourri, classy brown wall tiles: one of the reasons they all liked the place so much). Washing her hands with the lilac-coloured gel, she gazed into the mirror: the sensible glasses, the short brown hair, the slightly jowly cheeks . . . would these too, one day, lapse into something frowning and trembling and unfocused? There it was again – that sudden painful panic, that grave question that was never very far from her mind.

At that moment the door opened, interrupting her thoughts, and Topsy herself came in. Thelma was about to make some cheerful comment along the lines of 'long time, no see' when she realized that Topsy was crying; fat helpless tears spilling down her cheeks and splashing on her chin.

'Topsy, whatever is it?'

Topsy looked at her blankly.

'Topsy, it's Thelma.'

'It's all such a blimmin' muddle,' said, almost crossly, accepting Thelma's proffered tissue. 'A complete shambles.'

'Things can be.' Thelma's voice was soothing.

'I didn't know,' said Topsy crossly, scrubbing at her eyes with a hanky. 'They came to the house. And then I thought they were who they said they were.'

'Sometimes things happen that take us by surprise,' said Thelma calmly. She put a comforting hand on Topsy's arm – surprisingly thin and frail through the raincoat and cardigan. 'I'll find KellyAnne. She'll be wondering where you've got to.'

'. . . writing me, ringing me. Financial misnomers, that's what was said. And then coming to the house. All different times. Black van parked out front. She said I shouldn't have let them in but Gordon was the one who sent them, not me.' Again Topsy shook her head, her voice unsteady.

'You can't be too careful these days,' said Thelma.

'I heard . . . what it was that was being said.' Topsy took a deep gusty breath and with an effort gained some control over her voice. 'He thought I was asleep but I wasn't.' And now there was something different about her tone.

'What was that?' asked Thelma.

But Topsy seemed to have tailed off and was absorbed in rubbing lilac gel into her hands.

'*It'd be better all round if she was dead,*' she said suddenly. 'That's what was said.'

'I'm sorry?' said Thelma, taken aback.

'He thought I was asleep.' Topsy's tone suggested she was weary of the subject and annoyed with Thelma for having brought it up.

'If who was dead?' asked Thelma gently.

Topsy didn't seem to want to answer. 'That's the question they're asking,' she said, looking at herself in the mirror. For a moment the features seemed to strengthen; momentarily the ghost of the old Topsy was there. 'People need to be getting a grip,' she declared.

At that moment KellyAnne herself burst into the toilet, a pink-scented force of nature.

'There you are, Mother,' she said, brightly pouncing on her mother and steering her to the door.

'Your mother's been a bit distressed,' began Thelma.

She wanted to say more but KellyAnne interrupted her with a bark of 'Bless', giving Topsy a clumsy one-armed hug as she propelled her to the door.

There she paused.

'It breaks your heart, Thelma, honest to God. I tell you something.' She spoke over Topsy's shoulder, dropping her voice. 'She hates being like this. Don't tell me she doesn't.'

And before Thelma quite knew what was happening, she was left alone in the toilet, frowning into the smoked glass.

In the back room of the St Catherine's Hospice charity shop, Thelma inhaled the smell of clothes for the second time that day, only this time the smell was stale and used. As she snapped on disposable gloves and began decanting clothes from collection bags into three piles (wash, recycle, bin), she had the mental time and space to process the morning's events; what Topsy had said in the ladies' bothered her.

It'd be better all round if she was dead . . .

He thought I was asleep.

Who was 'he'?

But then it wasn't so much the words themselves as Topsy's emotional state as she spoke them: helpless, confused. And yes, Topsy was obviously ill, but Thelma's experience had shown her that dementia often tended to make people more of what they were. The grumpy got grumpier, the nervous got more nervous. There was Carmen the dinner lady, whose uncle had been big on the infamous Melmerby wife-swapping scene; when he got ill, well, who could forget that awful incident in Thirsk marketplace?

'Lord and Father,' said Thelma, 'Lord and Father who said, "Cast all your anxieties upon me," what should I do – if anything – about Topsy and her distress?'

Trying to find an inner stillness, she let various courses of action run through her mind: telling someone, not telling someone, asking advice. The trouble was she didn't know.

And the answer came to her as surely as if it had been written on the cover of the creased copy of *Fifty Shades of Grey* by her left elbow.

Go round and see her. Find out more.

She stood up with an armful of clothes for the recycling; she'd go on Monday. But not on her own. In all the time she'd known Topsy, their relationship, though cordial enough, had never quite gelled into friendship. But then Liz – nervous, hard-working Liz – that was a different matter. There had always been a closeness between the two. As Topsy herself had been wont to say: 'Me and this little lady, we go *way back*.'

Yes, she would need to go with Liz, thought Thelma, looking through a sad collection of rather damp summer tops.

But what to tell her? Topsy thought someone wanted her dead? She had a sudden vivid rush of memories of Liz's horrified reactions to various crises over the years. And, after all, the whole thing might be just some muddle along with all of Topsy's other muddles. It could all just be, as her mother used to say, something and nothing.

CHAPTER THREE

A visit doesn't follow imagined possibilities,
modern technology is discussed and memories
of a teenage heart-throb are evoked.

The drizzle was stirring lazily into steady rain the following Monday as Liz pulled up in front of Gordon and Topsy's house, a box of flapjacks wedged on the back seat. Gortops – Gordon and Topsy's house – was an angular grass-fronted building (christened *Rainton South* by Pat owing to its slight resemblance to a motorway service station) set back from the road at the edge of wide flat fields, giving onto a view of the Hambleton Hills. As she scanned the road for the reassuring sight of Thelma's mussel-blue Fiat, Liz's worried mind anticipated and rehearsed various possibilities to report back to Pat: Topsy failing to recognize them (It's so sad) or perhaps Topsy somehow miraculously sharper, better defined in her thinking (It must be something to do with being on home ground).

However, the uneasiness she was feeling wasn't solely to do with Topsy's condition; the fact was, going round to each other's houses simply wasn't something they had ever really done in all their years of working together. As with most of her colleagues, virtually all of their socializing (with the exception of the Christmas night out), all their sharing of life and death, hopes

15

and worries, ailing relatives, trips to Crete, new conservatories had been done from the circle of olive-green staffroom chairs, or whilst waiting for the photocopier, or clutching mugs of coffee whilst on playground duty.

She looked at her watch. She'd agreed to meet Thelma here at half ten. It was now nearly twenty-five to eleven. The only vehicle parked up on the wet verge was a black van, faded, slumped low on its wheels, almost as if it was trying to avoid drawing attention to itself. This added a new element to the morning's catalogue of uneasy possibilities – being ticked off in case she'd blocked the driver in – but even as she looked, the van sidled off with a hiss through the gathering puddles. She craned her head round – still no sign of Thelma. As if in answer to her thoughts her phone made a raspberry noise. (She really must get Jacob to reset the text alert back to its previous restrained *ping*.)

RUNNING APP 17 MINS LATE APOLOGIES T.

Seventeen minutes from when? Now, or half past? Should she wait? A sudden rattle of rain on the roof decided her; she had come to see her friend and see her she would. She paused a moment, hands pressing into the wheel at ten and two, breathing in like she'd taught herself. She found in life doing one's duty often involved moments like these – a breathing in, a steeling of oneself – as Pat put it, getting a grip.

Grip duly got, she put on the steering wheel lock, locked the car (going back twice to check), looking – as she did – hopefully back down the road for any sign of the neat blue Fiat, before pushing open the large five-bar gate.

The front garden was tatty.

To Liz, a seasoned gardener, the fact registered as surely as a sharp tap on the shoulder. True, it was hardly the best time of year, but even so there was clear evidence of ongoing and engrained neglect; the bushes needed cutting right back, the lawn was matted with slimy moss, the edges blurring into flower beds

16

cluttered with weeds, the whole thing unkempt as a food-stained cardigan. She knew from conversations over the years that neither Topsy nor Gordon had been great gardeners – but there had been a man who came in twice a month to keep up with the basics. She remembered the last time she had seen the garden (Gordon's wake: outside caterers and a fish pâté that had set Derek's stomach off for days); it had been bright, almost lurid with pink and white phlox and hydrangeas. And now . . . had the man been discontinued? Why? Walking up the gravelled approach the unkempt garden made Liz uneasy as surely as if there had been a notice: *Beware – Tatty garden – All Is Not Well.*

And then there *was* a notice. Uncompromising, black print in a plastic wallet, letters slightly rainbow-smudged with damp, pinned to the wood of Gortops: *No Cold Callers, Police Aware.* Liz paused, unsure, the flapjacks sliding inside the box. Police aware? She looked around, with more than half a mind to go back to the car and wait for Thelma. Finger out to ring the doorbell, she had words fluttering ready at the back of her mouth should Topsy identify her as a cold caller.

But it wasn't Topsy who answered Liz's oh-so-tentative-wishing-she-could-wait-for-Thelma ring. As the A-harmonic chimes (Milan Cathedral apparently) faded away there was a sudden belligerent rattle, a shout of 'I told you to piss off' and the door opened with force revealing KellyAnne standing there, face a cold, aggressive mask, which on seeing Liz backing nervously away, Tupperware brandished, immediately slipped into something much warmer. 'I am so sorry!' Liz found herself enveloped in a bosomy Dior-scented hug. 'Liz, my love: I am at sixes, sevens and blumin' twenty-twos this morning.'

Propelled through the doorway, the first thing Liz saw was a young man lying on the hall floor fiddling intently with a cream box from which a number of black wires emerged, connecting up to the telephone. His phone buzzed and he gave a sort of nervous twitch, slapped his pocket and pulled the phone out.

'Sorry,' he said, looking up at Liz and KellyAnne with earnest brown eyes. 'I've got to reply to this. Two secs.'

When Liz was a girl she'd had a poster from *Jackie* magazine on her wardrobe door – David Essex lying full length on a fluffy rug. His eyes seemed to stare directly out of the poster, intense, vulnerable, straight into the young Liz's psyche. Seeing this young man lying on Topsy's Dunelm rug amidst the tangle of wires brought the memory of that poster flaring vividly back.

'Don't let us interrupt you.' KellyAnne sounded exasperated.

'Sorry,' he said again but her annoyance didn't stop his texting, only made it the more frantic. Embarrassed at this sudden tension, Liz turned away and found herself looking at the collection of framed studio prints of KellyAnne across the years: from golden-haired toddler to studio-posed adult. There she was aged five as a snowflake in the Christmas play (*The Lonely Robin* . . . the hoo-ha because she hadn't got the part of the robin!); there she was as a gap-toothed seven-year-old (that time she'd used Topsy's lip gloss to apply fake spots to pretend she was ill!); there she was as a decidedly smouldering teenager holding the head of Muffin the pony (just before meeting the vet from Richmond).

'Okay, done!' The young man (he could be no more than eighteen or nineteen) sounded apologetic and eager and desperate for forgiveness all in two gasped words as he turned his attention back to the phone. 'Okay,' he said, 'it somehow got unplugged.'

'No prizes for guessing who did that.' KellyAnne raised her eyebrows, inviting the world to join in with the unspoken words: *Here we go again*.

'It just needs resetting,' said the man, turning those brown eyes toward the box of wires.

'All I need to know, Lloret, is will it go back to stopping any thieving bastard who wants to ring up on spec?' KellyAnne seemed to have forgotten her annoyance; in fact she was sounding almost flippant as she stood looking down at the supine form, hands on hips, driving one pink stiletto into the carpet. She was looking even more pink today: pink lips matching pink top (designer no doubt), fuchsia skirt. Had she had her hair touched up?

'When people ring they get a recorded message . . .' the young man (what had she said his name was? Larry? Lorry?) seemed mesmerized by the pink heel twisting into the carpet by his head. '"If you're family or friends press three; if you're a cold caller please hang up." There's some issues with people ringing from abroad but otherwise it does the job. It cuts out all the computer-generated calls.'

At this, his phone shivered again, like a buzzing wasp.

'Sorry,' he said, again, snatching it out of his pocket. 'Sorry. I've got to reply to this.'

Liz glanced nervously across at KellyAnne, fearful of another flash of bad temper, but she wasn't even looking at him lying there frenetically texting. Instead she was looking fixedly out at the steady rain, her face devoid of expression. There was something there in that look . . . something bleak . . . something lost. Again, Liz was reminded of that terrible day when Muffin the pony had had to be put down. It had been towards the end of the summer holiday and she and Topsy had been setting up the classroom for the new term. Topsy had brought KellyAnne with her and the girl had done nothing but sit hunched in the book corner with that same lost, fixed stare. Liz bit her lip. It must be so hard for KellyAnne with Topsy. Vividly she remembered the days of Derek's mother when it seemed every five minutes there was some new crisis or another.

'There, done,' said the man, running an apologetic hand through his mousy-coloured hair.

'As long as it can stop any thieving bastard who feels like ringing up my mother on spec, that's all I need to know,' said KellyAnne again, but her words now lacked energy. Liz looked at her curiously. Thieving bastard? That didn't sound good. What was this all about?

'Language.' Topsy had appeared in the doorway of the lounge in a too bright pink cardigan Liz recognized from the Edinburgh Woollen Mill sale rail. 'You're not too big for me to wash your mouth out with soap and water, young lady.' Liz smiled – this was the Topsy she'd known for over thirty years.

KellyAnne sighed. 'We're sorting out your telephone, Mother. I did tell you.' She still sounded tired. 'You can't be unplugging it. Just leave it alone.'

Topsy surveyed the white box with deep suspicion. 'There's always another new blumin' gizmo,' she said grumpily.

Again, Liz found herself smiling. How many times, how many *many* times had she heard Topsy, the archetypal Luddite, make that comment over the years? Interactive whiteboards, laptops, screen projectors, even going back to the dear old defunct Banda machine with its purple carbon sheets and intoxicating fluid – each and all uniformly and dismissively labelled as 'blumin' gizmos'.

Now she was looking with equal suspicion at the young man. 'I see he's here again,' she said sourly.

'Just make sure you leave the box alone, Mother,' said KellyAnne. Topsy made one of her trademark grunts of disapproval in the back of her throat, which her daughter ignored. 'Anyway, look who's come to see you.'

Looking at Liz properly for the first time, that confused look flashed across Topsy's face, that 'where am I supposed to be, what am I supposed to be doing?' look. 'You remember Liz,' KellyAnne continued encouragingly. 'We saw her the other day at the garden centre.'

'And Thelma,' said Liz hurriedly, realizing it was the first chance she'd had to speak. 'Thelma's coming as well, if that's all right.'

'Isn't that nice, Mum?' said KellyAnne. 'Liz and Thelma come to see you.' At the sound of the two names, the confusion flick-ered and faded and once again there was the old Topsy, now giving that look she used to give Liz when the last of the red poster paper had gone.

'Well you can tell his nibs I *can't* come in to work because she won't let me,' she said. 'She' was all too obviously KellyAnne (who accordingly rolled her eyes). 'His nibs' was Topsy's name for Mr Hargreaves, Liz's first head teacher at St Barnabus's, now peacefully in his grave for some thirteen years. 'She's only gone and taken my car keys.'

'We talked about this, Mother.' KellyAnne's tone indicated this was well-worn territory. 'You go through to the lounge, Liz, and I'll bring in the coffee. It's nearly tablet time.'

'No it's not,' said Topsy challengingly. KellyAnne smiled ruefully at Liz, as if to say 'see what I have to put up with'.

'That should do it,' said the young man (Lorraine? Surely not) as if no one had spoken. He sat up, smiling enthusiastically in a way that made Liz aware of just how brown those eyes were; again the image of David Essex came to her. She brought herself up – these were not exactly appropriate thoughts to be having. But then, she reflected, following Topsy into the living room, the visit was not exactly living up to any of the possibilities she'd considered earlier.

CHAPTER FOUR

There is bad coffee
and a dismissal of unwanted catalogues.

Squashing down thoughts of David Essex, Liz followed Topsy through to the living room with its view of stretching, wet fields and the distant swell of the moors. The long, light room was clean – that was immediately apparent. The rose-coloured carpet ruled with straight hoover sweeps. The faint smell of a rose-scented polish triggered in Liz's mind an image of a determined figure with pink rubber gloves – Paula, one-time caretaker at St Barnabus's, and now Topsy's cleaner.

Topsy stood by the window staring out at the forlorn garden. 'It's all getting a right mess.' She sighed.

Liz cast an appraising eye over the straggly borders and unkempt grass. 'Does your chappy not still come in?' she said.

Topsy shrugged off the question. 'Gordon says he'll get it done. I say that's all very well but when? He's always at that blumin' golf club.' She turned to Liz. 'You've not seen him today, have you?'

'I only just got here,' said Liz cheerfully. It was just like it had been with Derek's mother.

'He'll be at that golf club,' said Topsy again, sitting down in what was obviously a favourite chair facing the flat-screen TV.

Liz followed suit. And now she looked round the living room more closely, Topsy's vulnerability was apparent. Everywhere was the evidence of her comfy life with Gordon: his leather recliner and golfing trophies, the pictures of gaudy sunsets, photos of themselves on various cruise ships and hotel balconies. But now overlaying all that was the life of Topsy the Widow: her increasing struggles, piles of magazines and correspondence spilling over the coffee table and across the sofa, items of knitwear over the backs of chairs – clutter that at one time Topsy would not have countenanced for a moment. And then dotted all round the room, on tables and surfaces, were incongruous knick-knacks: Perspex swans, false flowers in rainbow vases, no less than three of the cheapest-possible-looking carriage clocks, swirling and twirling away on the mantelpiece – a plethora of cheap ugly things, things that the old Topsy would have wasted no time dispatching to the next school tombola.

'Tablet time, Mother.' KellyAnne had suddenly reappeared, singing out the words with a forced cheeriness. *It must be a constant rollercoaster for her, poor lass,* thought Liz. Obviously things had been sorted with the telephone man; there was no sign of the supine figure from the hall floor.

Topsy jolted upright. 'Is it?' she said. 'You're a bit early!'

'No, I'm not,' said KellyAnne patiently. She was brandishing a glass of water and a Dossette box, a pretty plastic thing with drawers in different rainbow colours. *Perfect for paperclips,* thought Liz.

But Topsy was looking past the proffered object. 'Where's that other gizmo?' she said.

For an answer KellyAnne smiled and rattled the Dossette box. 'Here.' She put the glass of water down on the rosewood coffee table, which slopped drips that KellyAnne wiped up with her pink sleeve. How Liz longed to put a coaster under the glass.

'We're back on this then, are we?' Frowning carefully, Topsy reached for the box. 'Sunday . . .' she said tentatively.

'Mother, it's Monday.' KellyAnne's voice was firm but gentle.

'Is it?' Topsy frowned at her suspiciously. There was something challenging in her voice.

'Yes, my love.' KellyAnne smiled. 'And it's very, very important you only take Monday's tablets.'

'Monday?' Topsy didn't sound convinced but she carefully counted out the tablets from the translucent lemon drawer. 'That's for my ticker, that's my waterworks and that's because apparently I'm going doolally tap.' She clicked loudly in the back of her throat.

'If I don't tell her she forgets,' said KellyAnne in a sad aside to Liz. 'Or takes two lots at once.'

Topsy swallowed the last tablet and held the glass out to KellyAnne with a grudging look of confidence and trust; KellyAnne smiled at her mother with an exasperated weariness. 'There we go, my love,' she said.

Looking round, Liz's eyes lighted upon the envelopes on the coffee table, covered in urgent red stencilled writing. *Free gift!* screamed one. *This exclusive luxury limited edition carriage clock – yours to own!*

The source of the knick-knacks, thought Liz with a frown.

'Mother,' KellyAnne sighed. 'I told you, don't open that stuff.'

'There's some good things in there.' Topsy sounded defensive, truculent like a child caught doing wrong and Liz felt a sudden urge to take hold of her hand. KellyAnne seemed about to say more but the moment was broken by the A-harmonic chimes of Milan Cathedral. KellyAnne froze, her face a set mask. 'It'd better not be that builder back again,' she said.

'It'll be Thelma most like,' Liz called after her, but KellyAnne had gone, whisking the envelopes away with her.

'I'm so sorry I got held up.' Thelma sat down having first moved two cardigans, a *Hello!* magazine and a copy of the *Ripon Gazette*. 'It's the new alarm system at the charity shop.' Here she could have gone on at some length about how – after years of

24

three padlocks and the comfortable conviction No One Would Bother Robbing a Charity Shop – the new charity commission guidelines meant all stores needed security systems, and how the duly installed system at the shop seemed to require some sort of doctorate to operate and was prone to warbling shrilly at the least provocation. But one look at Topsy told her she'd be wasting her breath. She sat down, realized she'd sat on something and retrieved what looked like a velour hot water bottle covered in a poisonous shade of lime. 'My,' she said. 'This is bright.'

'It comes with the post,' said Topsy, looking furtively at the door. 'There's some good stuff in there.' From down the side of the chair she produced yet another envelope, this one a vivid shade of lavender.

'There's some toxic shite, pardon my French.' KellyAnne had appeared silently carrying a tray of coffee. There was a shrill, almost hysterical edge to her voice and with a brisk, practised gesture she seized the envelope from her mother and tore it decisively in two.

There was a shocked silence. Liz clutched the arms of her chair as if she was on a white-knuckle ride. Topsy stared down mutinously at the cups, her bottom lip showing the suspicion of a tremble.

'It's your father sends for it,' she said defensively.

'Well we've enough carriage clocks, thank you,' said KellyAnne, her voice suddenly, alarmingly cracking; her eyes brimming with tears. She passed the back of her hand across her brow and closed her eyes, tears smudging her eyelashes. 'Sorry,' she said. 'I'm sorry, Mum. But I've said and said and said . . .'

But Topsy shrugged her off. Envelopes apparently forgotten, she was frowning at the coffee tray.

'These are the wrong cups.' She gestured at the cups, brown Hornsea Pottery. 'It's the green ones for visitors.'

'It's not a visitor, it's Liz and Thelma.' KellyAnne had recovered her composure but her voice was dry and tired out as she left the room. Liz and Thelma looked at the coffee; it was the colour of the puddles in the drive.

There was a pause, broken as the three carriage clocks simultaneously emitted tinny battery chimes.

'Well,' said Liz into the sudden silence, still clutching the arms of her chair, 'isn't this nice?'

'Indeed,' said Thelma. 'It's lovely to see you.'

And sipping the tasteless coffee they began asking Topsy questions, calm gentle questions – the daffodils, the weather, the carpet. Years of doing joint parents' evenings had taught them an easy duality, and it was undoubtedly so much easier with two of them there. Whatever gently thrown conversational balls Topsy missed the other could catch, alleviating much of that awkward stickiness. And gradually, bit by bit, Topsy began responding, sometimes with a nod, sometimes a smile, sometimes a whole sentence. Like an old PC warming up, the conversation began to come to life as together they reached round and over and past the bits of Topsy's brain that were no longer connecting to the real Topsy, the no-nonsense Topsy they had shared their working life with for the best part of twenty years. There were things that were a blank mystery and some things that sounded frankly bonkers. Now and then the whole conversation ground to a halt, but Liz and Thelma would patiently pick up the threads and try again.

And then of course there were the many things that Topsy did remember. By the time they were onto shared reminisces of that horrendous Year Two trip to Filey Brigg (winding roads and a forgotten sick bucket), there were more and more and longer and longer glimpses of the old Topsy, the rolling of the eyes, the staccato chuckle. The tension had all but gone, and despite the rain there was a weak sun turning the wet fields silver and casting the sudden arc of a watery rainbow over Sutton Bank.

Then suddenly, and mid-sentence, with the abruptness of the sun going behind a cloud, Topsy began to nod, head gently slumping down on the pink cardigan, mouth slightly open as if in protest. Liz and Thelma exchanged glances. Now was obviously the time to go. Should they wake her to say goodbye?

'She does this.' Yet again KellyAnne had entered unheard. On cue they stood up, with their coats.

'Liz and Thelma have got to go now, Mum,' said KellyAnne gently. There was no response save a small, rasping snore.

Liz smiled at the frail figure in a cardigan that was way too bright for her. She felt a sudden swell in her eyes and sinuses and wanted to give her a hug, but then this was Topsy and there were some things you just didn't do.

'I'll see you soon,' she said.

CHAPTER FIVE

A sad story is told and more bad coffee is drunk.

Liz and Thelma had intended to head straight off but KellyAnne seemed to take it for granted they'd follow her into the kitchen (sparkling clean, scent of something citric, more evidence of Paula's handiwork).

'She'll sleep for a bit now, bless her heart.' Without asking, KellyAnne refilled their coffee cups. (Thelma recalled the unasked-for cakes at the garden centre.) 'We can have a proper catch-up.'

Neither of them was at all sure what KellyAnne's idea of a 'proper catch-up' entailed but they both had similar suspicions – that KellyAnne could well be going to ask something of them. Get Topsy's shopping perhaps, maybe come and sit with her sometimes. None of which they minded, not as such – but after the casual foisting of her mother on them at the garden centre, both were aware there was potential in the situation for their being (as Pat would say) 'royally dumped on from a great height'. Thelma frowned, annoyed with herself at such thoughts – after all she had asked God to show her a way to help both Topsy and KellyAnne. Here was a caring daughter doing her best in what were undoubtedly very trying circumstances, and she, Thelma, would help in any way she could.

Liz, on the other hand, just wanted to leave. She had found the morning unsettling to say the least and all she wanted to do was go back home, tune in to the Radio York Friday phone-in and catch up with the ironing. And maybe do the Intermediate Sudoku in the *Ripon Gazette*, to prove that whatever the future had in store that here, today, there was nothing wrong with her mind. So it was with mixed feelings the pair perched at the kitchen counter (the granite worktops, how well they remem-bered the saga of *them* being fitted!) and reluctantly sipped their (still tasteless) coffee. But it seemed all KellyAnne wanted to do was talk. And talk.

Anecdote by anecdote the sad story took shape – how some six months after Gordon's death, Topsy had started asking where he was, even to the extent of driving herself to the golf club to look for him. How various people, with tactful voices, brought KellyAnne more and more tales of assorted mistakes, mistakes Topsy had made, which grew more and more apparent and inconvenient. Keys lost, timings muddled, meals burnt, doors left unlocked. Not that KellyAnne minded as such (At the end of the day when all's said and done she's my mum) but you could love someone and still find something a ball ache (Pardon my French). They'd finally managed to penetrate the labyrinthine system that was the Hambleton Memory Clinic (twice they forgot her appointments) but by the time the clinic had finally given them a diagnosis – 'an Alzheimer's related condition' (what-ever that means when it's at home) – it was a good few months after everyone else knew that something was seriously amiss. And by then Topsy was in a state where she was vulnerable to everyone and everything – increasingly prone to wandering here, there and everywhere even after her car keys had been taken away.

Take her tablets, a case in point: just now hadn't Liz seen how she, KellyAnne, had to stand over her to remind her to take them? Yes, sometimes she was fine, but other times . . . And if KellyAnne couldn't be there at tablet time (I've got a life too), she had to ring her to talk her through the tablet taking (step by step). There was of course Paula (that woman is a walking saint) but there was only so much between them they could do.

'It breaks my heart, honest to God.' KellyAnne took an enormous needy gulp of her coffee. 'Every day there's something else. Something she's lost. It's like she's falling to bits in front of my eyes.' She shook her head and looked at the ceiling and it occurred to both Liz and Thelma that a proper catch-up was indeed what KellyAnne needed.

'Can't you get carers in?' Liz asked, remembering the Honeysuckle nurses who came to Derek's mother before she went into Webster House; cheerful, energetic ladies in their lilac overalls.

'Have you seen how much those people charge, Liz?' KellyAnne shook her head. 'We're talking a grand, grand and a half a month . . .' Thelma was puzzled at this. What with the haulage business and various investments, there had always been money and plenty of it where Topsy and Gordon were concerned. The granite work surfaces hadn't left much change out of twenty thousand. Had something happened?

'Anyway, it's gone beyond that.' KellyAnne bit into a white chocolate cookie. 'Or if it hasn't yet it soon will be. She needs to be somewhere safe, bless her. The other week, when I managed to get her back indoors from the bus stop at half past eleven at night, I thought to myself: *Enough is enough.*'

'There's some lovely care homes out there,' said Liz tentatively.

'Absolutely,' said Thelma, though she avoided such places with an almost superstitious dread if she could. KellyAnne nodded enthusiastically through another gulp of the coffee.

'I've a stack of brochures. A stack. Cinemas, hairdressers, manicures, trips out. I tell you, ladies, I wouldn't mind moving into one myself.' She smiled, but it was a sad, tired smile. 'But you know the worst thing about all this? Mum knows. Don't tell me she doesn't know something's wrong. She hates it. She said the other day, "I don't like being like this." And like I say, there's only so much I can do.' KellyAnne was staring fixedly at the brown coffee cup. Once again, Liz was reminded of the demise of Muffin the pony.

'I need to protect her.' There was a distinct crack in her voice. 'I need to protect my poor old mum.'

And it was then that KellyAnne told Liz and Thelma all about the thieving bastards.

Since Topsy had been, as KellyAnne put it, 'going off to La La Land', Topsy had been the recipient of more and more unwelcome attention. Like the builder – contracted by Gordon before he died – invited in by Topsy and before they knew it presenting them with a bill for hundreds of pounds' worth of work.

And the people from Gateshead who kept on ringing up, pestering them about solar panels. Even the Ryedale tea man, who was unloading jumbo packs of breakfast tea and gift sets on almost a weekly basis. Not to mention the seemingly infinite number of mail order firms targeting Topsy with promises of prize draw bonanzas and a complete avalanche of plastic crap (pardon my French again). Here they were shown no less than three bulging carrier bags of confiscated mail.

However, this wasn't the worst of it. Not by a long chalk.

Some months previously Topsy had been rung by a man with a Scottish accent who introduced himself as a member of the fraud team from her bank, the Royal York. The call had been taken by Paula, and on learning he was not in fact speaking to Topsy, the man had rung off.

But he must have called back. From what KellyAnne could ascertain he'd said something about fraud in her savings account, but that Topsy wasn't to say anything about this to anyone.

'Which she didn't!' KellyAnne had slammed the brown Hornsea Pottery coffee jug down on the counter with a sudden angry force that made Thelma's car keys jingle. 'That's what hurts most of all. Not a blumin' word.'

31

From what KellyAnne could gather, he'd rung back at least twice and told Topsy that to keep her money safe she needed to move it to a new secure account.

In spite of Topsy's obedient silence, however, KellyAnne had got wind something was amiss and had rung the bank herself, finally getting through (after twenty-seven and a half minutes on hold!) to a bright-sounding someone or other who couldn't, obviously, give out details but logged the call and promised to 'look into it'.

In the meantime the man had rung Topsy again, this time with a complex series of instructions.

'How she managed to bloody well follow them is the mystery.' KellyAnne scrabbled in her handbag, producing an envelope promising Mrs Tapsy Boy of Rainton the Ultimate Dream Holiday, the back of which was covered in Topsy's once capable but now shaky handwriting: *Transfer via CHAPS payment to Royal York Bank . . . if asked say for property . . .*

'And she did it. She bloody well did it.' At this point her voice had quavered up and Liz instinctively took her plump beringed hand as bright tears splashed down the pink cheeks, soaking Thelma's tissue.

'She walked into the bank – the bank she'd been going into for years – and they let her do it. All her savings – 475 grand – nearly everything she has. Transferred out.'

'He wasn't from the bank?' Liz's mouth was a little 'o' of horror.

'Was he bollocks. He was some bastarding crook . . . pardon my French.'

'And the money's gone?' asked Thelma.

'All of it,' said KellyAnne bitterly. 'Gone. In the blink of a bloody eye. My poor mum. My poor, poor mum.'

CHAPTER SIX

A fraud is discussed and unnecessary plans are made.

'What, so the bank just let her?' Pat was angrily incredulous. Thelma nodded; she'd been doing her homework.

'The bank has an obligation to honour the customer's wishes, though they will robustly challenge if in any doubt.'

It was the following Thursday. Again, their favourite table, another set of coffee cups and plates in front of them.

'Even if the wishes are obviously bonkers?' Pat couldn't believe the injustice of it.

'It even turns out the cashier knew her,' said Liz dolefully. 'She used to go to St Barnabus's. Before your time. She was in our class about fifteen years ago. Mandy Pinder.'

'Only she's not Pinder now,' said Thelma. 'She married someone with a Polish name who wasn't Polish . . .'

'Quiet little thing,' said Liz. 'Rather staring face.'

'An absolute passion for My Little Pony dolls,' said Thelma.

'And this Mandy Pinder, she just let Topsy do it?' asked Pat. She could not get her head round this.

'She never was a great one for initiative,' said Thelma.

'No wonder KellyAnne was upset.' Pat was upset herself, almost too shocked to continue with her Hambleton lardy.

Liz nodded sadly, remembering – with a mental wince and a

clenching of knuckles – the ripping of the envelopes. 'Apparently it's more common than you'd think,' she said.

Thelma drew from her handbag a printout from the *Yorkshire Post* website: *£160 billion lost to banking fraud,* the headline read.

Pat scanned the article. 'I cannot believe the banks just let it happen,' she said.

'Apparently they have "training",' said Thelma, smoothing and refolding the clipping.

They all paused. There had been no need for those verbal inverted commas; the mere mention of that word brought to mind various incidents during their time teaching: lukewarm coffee, uninspiring PowerPoints, people speaking in sing-song voices as soporific as horse tranquillizers.

'But surely,' said Pat, '*surely*, if she spoke to the bank, *explained*, you know, that her mum's not well. Said about the, you know, Alzheimer's . . .'

Liz shook her head mournfully. KellyAnne had been down that road. With bells on. She'd told them in exhaustive detail of a prolonged toing and froing of correspondence – shrill and accusatory on KellyAnne's part, bland and passively uncooperative on the bank's. At the end of the day, the Royal York Bank was very sorry for the family and their circumstances but there was nothing further that could be done; KellyAnne should get used to the fact the money was gone and not coming back. The financial ombudsman had been duly referred to and, after two months, had said much the same thing as the Bank, only in a wordier way. But then, of course, the financial ombudsman received its funding from the banks, so – as Thelma put it – No Mystery There.

And that was that.

'The fact is,' said Thelma, 'Topsy *did* transfer the money across.'

'You're not telling me they didn't notice she was going a bit funny though.' Pat was feeling knotted up and yet couldn't seem to stop herself taking a bite of the Hambleton lardy.

'Apparently Mandy Pinder says she did offer a challenge,' said Liz. 'But had absolutely no idea there was anything amiss.'

'How can she have challenged her if she had no idea anything was amiss?' said Pat, taking another unwanted bite.

'Of course, she'd have been used to Topsy telling her what to do,' said Thelma thoughtfully. They paused for a moment, each with their own vivid memory of Topsy's brand of 'telling people what to do'; perhaps some sympathy was to be had for Mandy Pinder-as-was after all.

'It all boils down to Topsy's word against the bank's,' said Liz with a forlorn 'that's the way it is' sigh.

She set her cup down with a comforting ceramic chink. It was raining yet again; they could all hear the subdued rattling undercurrent on the steel roof. From where they sat they could see a Mother's Day display, splodges of pinks, yellows and duck-egg blues looking flimsy and insubstantial against the backdrop of grey skies beyond steamed-up windows. 'And *all* the money's gone?' said Pat. 'All of Gordon's shares and whatnots?'

'Apparently it was all moved across into Topsy's account when he died, to make it easier for her,' said Thelma.

They sipped their coffee and considered the family who had always had so much: the timeshare in the Algarve, KellyAnne's driving lessons and the series of top-of-the-range cars, that wedding to the Richmond vet at Lotherton Hall. (Who could forget that string quartet playing 'My Heart Will Go On'?) Topsy could have reasonably expected a comfortable old age, KellyAnne too, come to that. And now nothing.

'Of course, there's always the house,' said Pat. 'That must be worth a fair whack.'

'But the money from that will be needed for Topsy. When the time comes,' said Thelma. They all knew what 'the time' was. The bright glossy brochures piled on the granite work surfaces. The overwarm buildings with cheerful vases of flowers and organized activities, mushy vegetables and plastic jugs of water. All of that would easily soak up the price of a house, even in a place like Rainton. Old age these days seemed to need as much investment and capital as starting up a business. Thelma looked sombrely outside to the car park, trying to drive her own dark thoughts away.

'At least selling the house will provide the money for Topsy's care,' said Liz finally.

'All that money,' said Pat again.

'That's why they had to let the gardener go. They can't even afford carers to look in on Topsy. They can only just afford Paula,' said Liz.

'In some ways we should be thankful.' They both looked at Thelma. Her ability to see something positive in a generally dire situation was legendary, but surely even she would have her work cut out to find a silver lining in this instance. 'I've been reading up a bit about this. And you do hear of cases where, when the deed is done, the plan is to make sure, well . . . backs are covered.' She made a discreet but graphic gesture, drawing her teaspoon across her throat.

The other two looked askance. 'But the money's all gone,' said Liz, with a tinge of panic. 'Why would anyone – you know?' Not willing to say the words, she pointed at Thelma's teaspoon.

'The money *has*, but not the *person* who took it,' said Thelma.

'Topsy did say,' said Pat slowly, 'she did say about people coming to the house. She said it a few times.'

'She said it again when we were there,' said Liz with a worried frown. 'And KellyAnne said they'd had no end of bother with people. Even the Ryedale tea man.'

At that point Thelma could have added what Topsy said in the toilets. Topsy's voice came back to her, as it did a few times every day.

It'd be better all round if she was dead . . .

But she didn't. She hadn't mentioned it to anyone except God, who presumably already knew. Looking at her friends, she even regretted saying what she had just now. What had started as an effort to look on the bright side had transmuted into something ominous and worrying. Liz already had that wide-eyed look about her that always meant trouble. Even Pat was looking uneasy.

And then, across the room, a waitress dropped a plate and began loudly apologizing to the world, as an urn hissed, as if in sympathy. The moment passed and she gratefully let the world of the café reassert itself around her.

'She obviously needs our support,' was all she said.

'I'm going to look in on her again,' said Liz with energy. 'Maybe bring her here next time.'

Driving away from the garden centre in the leaden drizzle, Thelma realized with some surprise that in spite of everything, she actually felt a bit easier in her mind. She had wanted to know more. And now more was known. The story about the scam more than explained Topsy's tears and emotions. It even made a kind of muddled sense of those disturbing words. How natural, how very *very* natural, would it have been for KellyAnne, in the first shock of discovery, to have said something along those exact lines? But Thelma had seen so clearly KellyAnne's feelings for her mother – the memory of that sudden hug came back solid and reassuring. And the mysterious 'he' who thought Topsy was asleep? That could have been anyone – maybe even Gordon in Topsy's muddled mind.

So despite the troubling conversation they'd just had, she didn't seriously believe Topsy was in any real danger; the money was gone and she was certain Topsy wouldn't have any idea who the fraudster was. In the cases she'd researched no one did. No one ever seemed to be brought to book; very often the criminals were not even in the country. KellyAnne seemed to be keeping more than a watchful eye on her mother and now she herself would be coming over to help. Monday in fact. Verna was training a new volunteer and could easily spare her for a morning as long as that dratted alarm didn't play silly beggars.

But, as it happened, her plans were unnecessary.

By the following Monday, Topsy was dead.

CHAPTER SEVEN

There is sad news, an unexpected visit and a disquieting disclosure.

It is said that good news travels fast; the truth is, in towns like Thirsk and Ripon, bad news travels considerably faster. By the time KellyAnne had rung Liz on the Monday and told her, in congested tones, that her mum had passed away, Liz had already had a phone call from her friend Jan, Pat had been texted by Nat from the Montessori nursery in Rainton, and Thelma had heard the news via the chaplain from the Friary Hospital.

Besides which, KellyAnne herself had posted a picture on her Facebook page of her hugging a resigned-looking Topsy captioned: *To my darling mum, my bezzie mate, sleep well, all my love KellyAnne.*

Slightly at odds with the tones of this posting was the fact that when Topsy had died, KellyAnne had apparently been away on a mini-break in Portugal; immediately below the post announcing the death were images of KellyAnne from the previous day in an improbably aquamarine-coloured pool drinking an equally improbably coloured cocktail.

'It would have been quick – that's what they said to KellyAnne,' said Liz. She said the words firmly, as if she'd said them many times before, which she had, to herself. Outside the café windows, cars were spectral shapes in a freezing fog, scarves and gloves and hats were stowed in various coat pockets and handbags. There was something very comforting about being sat at their usual table that morning.

'Gone just like that,' said Pat. She sighed in a hasty effort to soften the abruptness of her words. She took a lot of comfort from that – the quickness. When she'd first started teaching in Bradford, in that heady time of dirndl skirts and never-ending sex with Rod in that attic bedsit in Manningham, there'd been a school nurse who used to regularly bang on about 'quality death'. 'Gone just like that,' she was wont to say. At the time, Pat had thought it all rather ghoulish, but as she grew older – as she'd seen her share of hospices, hospital wards and overheated sick rooms – she was beginning to see the sense in the words and even take comfort from them.

Thelma said nothing.

'And at least she was in her home, in her chair,' said Liz. She found that a great source of comfort, the fact Topsy had been found in her chair facing the flat-screen rather than sprawled out at the foot of the stairs, or even – heaven forbid – slumped naked in the shower.

'Did KellyAnne say what it was?' asked Thelma. They all knew what the 'it' was she was referring to.

'Heart most likely,' said Liz. It was what she hoped was true. In these frightening days of dementias and seemingly infinitesimal forms of cancer, the heart giving out somehow had a safe, old-fashioned quality – a throwback to the days when elderly people declined, became confused, then died in their sleep. Died in their sleep. Hardly anyone seemed to do that these days, and yet it seemed that Topsy had done just that. 'She was on digoxin like Derek's mother. I saw the box when she took the tablets that time.'

'But KellyAnne didn't actually say it was her heart?' Thelma was stirring her coffee.

'She was getting on, bless her,' observed Pat.

'I don't know if she was *that* old,' said Thelma.

In fact, none of them were quite sure exactly how old Topsy had been. Maybe her seventies? They seemed to remember a big birthday – a trip to New York with photos of Topsy and Gordon in Central Park – but then that might have been a wedding anniversary. Topsy herself had never been one for birthdays; come April 26 each year she'd slapped down a plate of Kit-Kats and Penguins on the staffroom table in a way that had positively discouraged any discussion of her age.

'It can get you like that,' said Pat, 'the heart.' She looked at her half-finished Ryedale jam fancy. No two ways about it – she absolutely needed to cut down.

Thelma stirred her coffee. 'But KellyAnne didn't actually *say* it was her heart?' she said again.

'I don't think they know yet,' said Liz. 'But what else could it be?'

Thelma didn't answer and the question was left hanging in the air between them. There was something about the way Thelma was pushing her spoon round and round her cup that suddenly put Pat in mind of the time at school when Marguerite the SEN coordinator had had a Thing with the man who came to fix the photocopier. Dan his name was, milky grey eyes and one of those medallions got up to look like a razor blade. Wife, three kids, at least half Marguerite's age. With an effort Pat pulled her mind back to the present to join the discussion of the most likely where and when of Topsy's funeral. Presumably Baldersby, like Gordon, but how long from now?

But later on, however, in the middle of cooking the evening meal (ham hock tagliatelle: an Angela Hartnett midweek supper) an image of her friend quietly stirring her coffee came back to her.

It had been Thelma who had first noticed how many times the photocopier had seemed to mysteriously break down.

* * *

It was a couple of days later when KellyAnne rang Liz again, just as Liz was wrestling with one of Jacob's fitted Batmobile sheets.

'I was going to call you,' she said, slightly guilty, phoned jammed under her chin as she attempted to fold the black and yellow crumples. It was true. Each day she'd had it in her mind she really *must* ring KellyAnne but she'd always managed to find something else to do. Part of it was to do with that feeling people often get with the recently bereaved: the possibility that the wrong word could shatter them into emotional chaos, a chaos you then had some responsibility for supporting. But there was another part – a sharp, raw memory of a frowning slight figure in a too-bright cardigan nodding off to the world with the gentlest of snores – which had made the whole idea of a phone call one that was easy to lose amongst the tasks of the day.

But KellyAnne wasn't for listening. Her voice was bright, brittle and brisk as she said how she'd made a start on clearing out her mum's things and had come across one or two bits and bats that were school-related that she didn't have the heart to chuck away, that possibly Liz could find a use for? Maybe Liz could look in some time?

'Yes, of course,' said Liz. She had it in mind to say something about how sorry she was, a tactful variation of what she'd said to Derek, to Tim, to Joyce-across-the-road: perhaps it was all for the best. But again, KellyAnne was speaking.

'Liz, my love,' she said. 'Just a heads up.' She paused and there was something about the pause that made Liz leave the Batmobile to its own devices and sit down.

'The police said they might give you a call.' Now her voice was careful and measured.

'The *police*?' Liz's mind did a guilty double take, scanning her visit to Gortops for anything that might warrant a police visit. Her parking?

'They're just asking some questions about Mum's tablets.'

'Her tablets?' Liz's mind was hearing the words but struggling to see the sense behind them.

'They seem to think there might have been some sort of mix-up. I mean you saw how muddled she was.' There was something very insistent, almost desperate, about KellyAnne's voice. Liz got the feeling tears weren't so far away. 'You were there – you *saw* how she got muddled up.'

'I did,' said Liz obediently.

'So you will come over for the box? In the next few days?' Her voice trembled slightly and there was suddenly something of a lost little girl in her tones.

'Of course I will,' said Liz.

'And all that with her pills – it's all probably nothing,' said KellyAnne.

'Of course,' said Liz, more to comfort KellyAnne, she realized later, than because she entirely believed it.

It was a few days after that when the police called, by which time Liz had allowed the whole uneasy conversation to be subsumed by the day to day: edging the borders, a knock in the washing machine, worries about Jacob. (Surely he hadn't *really* set light to a Great Fire of London display?) It was ten past eight on a raw, grey Friday morning and she was dutifully trying to make headway with the book for book group. Book group was organized by her friend Jan, the literacy coordinator from St Barnabus's; one of those friends who exploded periodically into your life, telling you what you *should* be doing: eight hours' sleep a night, some obscure series on Netflix that *must* be watched, some neck exercise that would do wonders for your posture.

And one of the things Liz really should do was to expand and nurture her third-age mind in ways that Sudoku apparently didn't even touch – hence book group. Quite what good her mind was being done she wasn't exactly sure. She couldn't say she'd really liked any of the books they'd read (a lot of accounts involving various oppressed and distressed people finding beauty in adversity); the one she was struggling through at the moment – *Broken Biscuits* – was a 'harrowing true account' set in 1970s Carlisle and she wasn't enjoying it one little bit.

So it was with a twinge of relief that she looked up at the sound of two rings on her doorbell. Only a twinge, however. There was something about the twin blasts that gave rise to a slight flutter of alarm. It was too early for the post, Joyce-across-the-road never rang more than a cheerful once and if it had been Derek forgetting his keys again there would have been multiple blasts accompanied by a volley of panicky knocks and shouts through the letter box. The sight of two figures through the frosted glass increased the flutter to a flap. When she opened it and saw two police officers – one uniform, one plain clothes – it was the starting pistol for panic that had Derek dead of a heart attack, Tim in a multi-car pile-up and Jacob hospitalized with some unspecified childhood fever.

'Mrs Newsome?' said Plain Clothes. 'DC Donna Dolby, North Yorkshire CID. We understand you knew a Mrs Topsy Joy. Have you got a minute?'

As DC Donna checked her notes and the uniformed officer introduced herself as PC Trish and tried to make her iPad work, Liz regarded the pair of them. Her main impression of PC Trish was her truly horrendous cold (pray God this would not get passed via her to Derek; he was only just nicely over that last chest do). That and the unflattering neon tabard thingy she wore. DC Donna – blonde hair, a bit all over the place and in need of the roots doing – wore a coat, blouse and trousers, shades of navy, black and grey that could only be described as 'sensible'.

The icebreaker proved to be the garden. DC Donna had commented, with admiring noises, on the array of shrubs and plants emerging from the winter damp, just showing the beginnings of their annual cycle of colour with the first egg-yellow crocuses and a small spray of hellebore (a cycle lovingly, carefully and meticulously planned by Liz). It turned out she had just bought a place over near Richmond and was grappling with a garden for the first time. Liz (who knew all about the soil in Richmond, having a cousin over that way) was able to recommend various plants and shrubs and garden centres; by the time they sat down with cups of coffee (plus a glass of water for PC Trish to take a Flu-away) she was feeling almost relaxed. Almost. The periodic growl and hiss of the radio fixed to PC Trish's belt plus her grim tutting struggles with the Ipad as she recorded everything Liz said reminded her this was much more than a social visit to chat about soil acidity.

There was a silence broken only by the hiss of PC Trish's Flu-Away tablet dissolving.

'Now,' said DC Donna, her tone turning from animation to duty, 'Mrs Joy. I believe you saw her take some medication?'

'That's what it kept coming back to,' said Liz. 'Every verse end, Topsy taking her tablets.'

It was later that morning, approaching lunchtime. On the table in front of them was the unsettling presence of a business card bearing the North Yorkshire Police logo: DC Donna Dolby. They were sat at a different table from their favourite one. Indeed they'd been lucky to get a table at all, what with the lunchtime rush and a coachload of American tourists who'd just visited the James Herriot Experience. The combination of the unfamiliar crowds, the view of the stacker (full of used crockery), the unfamiliar table – all this combined to make Liz feel disorientated and insecure, and suddenly very weary. And her friends had been so kind, dropping everything (Pat's aquarobics, Thelma's turn on coffee at Knit'n'Natter) – but now, here with them both, she felt tired of it all and wanted nothing more than to be back at home, curled up on the sofa. Not with *Broken Biscuits* but the Sudoku, and perhaps something comforting about property or baking on in the background.

'And what did you say to them?' Thelma was stirring her coffee.

'What I'd seen. How she counted them out and took them. How she got the days mixed up. They kept asking about her muddling her tablets.'

'Which she did.' Pat sounded a tad impatient; she couldn't see what the drama was and felt the whole thing could be filed away in that well-stuffed drawer in her mind labelled 'Liz Overreacting'. She took a bite of her scone realizing as she did that she wasn't enjoying it.

Liz frowned in distress. 'Only I'd not seen that. Not muddling the tablets, only her muddling up the days. There's a difference.'

'How?' said Pat.

'Presumably it'd be the same tablets, *whatever* day she took,' said Thelma.

'And, odds on, she did get them mixed up,' said Pat. 'We all saw how she was.' She really wished she hadn't started that scone, but she couldn't find the willpower to stop. There was something curiously addictive about the tang of the raspberry jam.

Liz frowned, trying to gather her blurry, uncomfortable thoughts, a cold snake of feeling slithering elusively in and out of her mind. A group of brightly dressed New York-sounding matrons were less than enamoured with the view of the pylons and the cattle mart. 'This is just not my idea of traditional York-*sheer*,' one kept saying.

'You see I tried telling them about all the other stuff,' Liz frowned as she recalled the visit. 'The solar panel people . . . the bank fraud. But I could tell they weren't interested.'

'How though?' asked Pat.

'The garden. Every time I mentioned other stuff, DC Donna kept looking out of the window at the garden. But as soon as we were back on those blessed tablets she was all eyes and ears.'

'So they must think the tablets are important,' said Thelma.

'They are if she took too many,' said Pat.

'That's just it.' Something in Liz's sharp tone made three American matrons look curiously across to their table. '*That's* what's been bothering me.'

'Go on,' prompted Thelma.

'I felt . . .' She paused, frowning up at the metal lampshades got up to look like old wash pails. The other two waited, remembering past planning meetings, sat round one of those little tables in Thelma's classroom. Liz sometimes struggled making her point, but the points – when she eventually made them – were always valid ones.

'I felt like they were wanting me to say something in particular, something that they wanted to hear. The way they asked about Topsy, and her muddling the days and the times, I just got the feeling it'd have been the easiest thing in the world to say "yes". She could easily have got it all mixed up and taken too many tablets.'

'Surely she could have?' Pat pushed her plate away. The fruit scone sat heavy; with every bite she'd thought more and more about the missed aquarobics class.

'Topsy was always so careful though. Remember the laminating pouches?' They all did. Topsy kept them in a cupboard and knew *exactly* how many were there. Woe betide anyone who helped themselves. 'It just wouldn't be like her to take all her pills in one go, no matter how muddled up she was. She might muddle up the *days*, but not the tablets.'

'What if she'd forgotten she'd taken them and took two lots, even three lots?' Pat didn't have such fond memories of Topsy and laminating pouches.

'There was something about the way she opened the Dossette box.' Liz half shut her eyes as if picturing the scene. 'Counted them out. It felt like it was something she had to get right.' In her mind she could hear that grumpy voice:

That's for my ticker, that's my waterworks and that's because appar-ently I'm going doolally tap.

'It just doesn't sit right.' She sighed and shook her head.

There didn't seem much more to be said. The American matrons were stridently leaving behind wrecked tables with the remains of jacket potatoes and paninis, looking forward to 'some gen-u-ine Yorksheer' (Fountains Abbey and Emmerdale Farm). Suddenly everything seemed a little sad and weary. Despite having talked things through with her friends, Liz felt something important had been left unsaid. She just wasn't sure what. 'It just all doesn't sit right somehow,' she said again, taking her coat off the back of the chair.

'No doubt the police will look into it,' said Pat, a trifle impatiently, reaching for her car keys. If she left in the next five minutes she could retrieve some of the day's wrecked timetable.

Thelma looked at her friends; it literally was now or never. And although it was undoubtedly as right a moment as there would be, still she hesitated, knowing what she was going to say would upset, disturb and confuse.

'Actually . . .' she said.

There was something in the tone of her voice that made the other two pause and sit back down. 'Actually, Topsy told me she thought someone wanted her dead.'

CHAPTER EIGHT

The perception of love causes worry and there is tension in the Royal York Bank.

She had to repeat the words some five times, and even then the other two had great difficulty comprehending what it was she was saying. 'You're *sure* that's what she actually said,' Liz kept saying, looking more and more distressed every time.

'It's probably all just a muddle, bless her,' Pat kept saying, but it sounded like she was trying to convince herself more than her friends.

'Did you tell KellyAnne?' asked Liz.

'I've only told the two of you,' said Thelma.

'You haven't told the police then?' said Pat.

'No,' said Thelma. A large part of her, a very large part, wanted more than anything else in the world to say yes it could all have just been some muddle.

But she couldn't.

'Perhaps it was just KellyAnne who said it,' said Pat. 'I mean she was obviously upset when she found out about the fraud. Who wouldn't be? And when you're upset you say all manner of things.'

'Except Topsy said "he".' Thelma stirred her coffee. 'She was very precise about that. *He* thought I was asleep. Which implies someone other than KellyAnne.'

'Do you not think you should tell the police?' said Liz.

'It's not much to go on,' said Thelma. 'The words of a confused old lady.' She hadn't intended the words to come out quite so abruptly.

'A confused old lady who's just died.' Liz sounded indignant.

'You already tried telling them,' said Thelma gently.

'Not that someone wanted her dead!' She sounded distressed now, her hands tight claws clutching her handbag. What on earth would she say when she drove over to Rainton to see KellyAnne?

'I'm saying they'd need a bit more to go on,' said Thelma.

'Remember Rod's lock-up?' said Pat. They all did, that time when Rod's tool store had been broken into and several thousand pounds' worth of equipment taken. There had been witnesses and CCTV footage and even half a registration number taken, yet due to a combination of circumstances and manpower, the crime was deemed unsolvable and filed away wherever unexplained misdemeanours were filed away.

By unspoken agreement they stood up and put on their coats. Something cold had entered their world, something cold and alien, something Thelma recognized as surely as she would a smell.

Evil.

'She was confused and she was muddled.' Driving away from the garden centre Pat realized she was repeating the words over and over again under her breath like a sort of mantra. Topsy, being murdered? Surely – *surely* – the whole thing could be dismissed as a combination of Liz overreacting and Thelma putting two and two together and making five.

She shook her head impatiently as she slowed for the roundabout. That was the fourth aquarobics class in a row she'd now missed and she couldn't remember the last time she'd been to Keep Fit. That new sage top, which had fitted fine when bought just before Christmas, was definitely tighter than was comfortable.

She sucked in her tummy and thought of the fruit scone. Why oh why had she continued eating it?

Plus she had more important things on her mind. Her son Liam.

Or more specifically her son Liam in love. For in love he most definitely was. She was sure of this fact for three reasons.

1) His clothes. Normally his choice of non-school attire was one of three or four T-shirts each bearing some caustic legend. (It's not sarcasm, it's an allergic reaction to your stupidity.) Over the past few days, however, these had been abruptly replaced by slogan-free polo shirts in softer shades of blue and purple. Plus, he'd washed his jeans. Washed them *himself*, as opposed to leaving them coiled like some venomous snake on the floor of his bedroom.

2) His singing in the bathroom. Normally when scraping at the patchy fluff on his chin and sideburns, there were variations of something toneless with barely discernible lyrics about rebellion, misunderstanding and general struggle. These (like the clothes) had been replaced by something more tuneful; this morning she was sure she'd caught a snatch of Abba.

3) His attitude to her and Rod. This was the big one. Normally his relations with them were polite, though barely deferential and seasoned with sarcastic phrases; she was known as Nigella's Lurve Child (shortened to *Mu-um* when food, clean clothes or the checking of patches of sore skin were required). Rod was Thirsk's Self-Made Man (TSMM for short). Collectively they were referred to as 'Parentage'. But now? Only yesterday he'd come behind her as she cooked, rested his chin on her head as she braised chicken in tarragon, and said, 'This smells amazing.'

All of this brought back clear memories of how she, herself, had been when she met Rod. The singing, tick; the clothes, tick (that cheesecloth blouse!). This – put together with recent and increasingly frequent appearances of India the Celtic poet (She's not a poet, Mum, she's a Performance Rapper) led her to the inescapable conclusion he was definitely in love . . . which was great but . . .

But.

Somehow with her youngest son, everything seemed to be more of a big deal than with the other two. Why, Pat wasn't exactly sure, it just seemed he was a child who seemed to struggle more . . . And whereas Andrew and Justin seemed to lumber their way amiably enough through childhood illnesses, exams, acne and girlfriends, Liam somehow hadn't managed to take them in his stride. His chicken pox had resulted in a spell in hospital, frequently during exams he'd been found sleepwalking and there hadn't seemed to be any girlfriends, at least no one significant. And now? Of course, it was great he was in love, of course.

But. Durham in the autumn – that hard-won place to study Structural Engineering. She remembered how it had been when she met Rod, fortunately towards the end of her time at college, but even so, there was that disastrous teaching practice when nothing seemed to matter as much as him and his MG Midget. If she'd met him earlier in the course, or before . . . she'd certainly have thrown everything to one side and been glad to do so. And Liam? One of her dark three-thirty-a.m. fears was of a certain trailer park the far side of Boroughbridge. Liam and someone – the Celtic poet-rapper? – and a baby. Celtic Poet didn't seem to be going to university. She was apparently too busy 'sorting her head out' (whatever that might mean), which involved moving to Manchester. Or Nottingham. Somewhere where it was 'at'. (The implication being that Durham was definitely not where it was at. And what if where it was 'at' ended up being a trailer park in Boroughbridge?)

But, she didn't *know*. As Thelma always said, what she needed were facts. Which was why she needed to get home pronto. She needed to give his room the once-over for condoms . . . or maybe even put a pack in? The plan for the day had been aquarobics, bank in Ripon to pay in cheques, Farm Shop for ingredients for supper, which would have left ample time for a fact-finding tour of Liam's room. But all this nonsense about Topsy had put paid to that.

Murdered! She was confused and muddled! Once again she found herself shaking her head, as if trying to rid herself of an irritant. Breathing slowly she allowed herself to explore the thought. The truth was confused and muddled were the very last adjectives she'd have replied to her one-time colleague. But, she thought grimly driving away down York Road, she had to remember Topsy was *ill*. And besides she had her own concerns. Pausing at the junction with Sutton Road, Pat reviewed jobs and time. Certain things were no longer possible but she knew whatever she did or didn't do, it was vital that tonight when Rod said, 'Did you manage to get to the bank?' she was able to reply, 'Of course.' She did a series of rapid calculations of typical traffic, probable queue lengths and likely parking spaces with a speed that would have startled any corporate project manager but came as second nature to your average primary school teacher with a family home to run.

The Farm Shop was a no-go; that was obvious. But if she went to the bank here in Thirsk – as opposed to Ripon – she could try that new Aldi. It'd certainly have the ingredients for one of her standbys; anything missed could be mopped up at the Tesco Express and she should still have time enough for a once-over of Liam's room. After all there was no hard-and-fast reason why it had to be the Ripon branch. A bank was a bank. It was just that Ripon was where all those years ago Mr Riley had given them their first loan and it had become her habit to pay cheques in there. And as for aquarobics – she discreetly pulled at the new sage top – she could always go on Rod's exercise bike and catch up with *Homes under the Hammer*. (She knew whilst she'd certainly do the latter, she'd almost certainly give the former a miss.)

Which is how come she came to see what she saw in the bank.

There was a longer queue in the Royal York Bank than she'd anticipated; moreover there seemed to be no movement in said queue whatsoever. At two of the counters – not so much proper counters but those silly desk arrangements they had these days – complex transactions appeared to be going on and at a third, a startlingly tanned girl was on the phone. The woman in the queue directly in front of Pat exuded an impatience that would have been apparent from the parallel set of shoulder blades under her raincoat even if it hadn't been punctuated by a series of sighs and tuts as she waited. 'Woman on a mission' Pat christened her as she watched her hand clenching round the strap of her shoulder bag, trying not to let the woman's tuts affect her own growing tension.

And still the queue was showing no signs of moving. At two of the tills with people serving, there appeared to be negotiations as involved and protracted as those of a grandmaster chess match. On one of them was a rather jolly-looking black girl who punctuated every fresh interaction and comment with cheery bursts of laughter. At the third till the girl was still on the phone. Now she looked at her properly, Pat could tell that this phone call was something that shouldn't be happening. Could tell by the nervous side-to-side movement of the girl's rather startlingly silvery-blue eye-shadowed eyes, the way she had her hand cupped over her mouth, the rapid, almost furtive way she was talking. She seemed to be having some sort of disagreement; at one point she shook her head vigorously as if trying to make something go away.

'No way should she be on the phone making personal calls.' It was as if the man behind her in the queue could read her thoughts. Irritated, she looked at her watch: ten past. She'd have

53

to cut out Aldi altogether and fall back on defrosted Lamb Henry if things didn't get a shift on.

'Come on.' Woman on a Mission's forceful undertone was clearly audible. In an effort to stay calm, Pat focused her attention on the various signs round the branch. Images showing, as the tasteful lilac words sang out, *People living life,* whilst letting the Royal York Bank *worry about all the rest.* Living life in the eyes of the Royal York Bank appeared to consist of elegant people wearing pastel sweaters whilst walking down white beaches, clinking champagne flutes, all sophisticated smiles as they paced on treadmills. The sight of the lithe silver-haired woman in a rose-coloured leotard made her wince anew; first thing she'd do when she got in was move Rod's shirts from where they were all currently hanging on the exercise bike. She pulled in her tummy but the sage top continued its unflattering pressure.

To take her mind off the uncomfortable thought, she turned her attention to some homemade signs sitting incongruously amongst the others. *Save our Branch,* one poster bleated. *Say no to branch closures.* Of course, she'd read about this in the *Ripon Gazette,* how branches – Thirsk, Boroughbridge, Ripon – were losing custom due to the growth of online banking. Something Pat (now in her tenth minute of queuing) could well understand were it not for the fact that the thought of online banking always made her deeply uneasy. One read about these frauds and scams all the time. Mind you, as that business with Topsy had shown, apparently you weren't much safer in a bank.

Topsy.

The memory of the conversation in the garden centre came back with a cold unwelcome jolt. (She was confused and muddled!) But wait a minute . . . She looked round, realization dawning. Wasn't *this* the branch where Topsy had actually made that fateful transaction? She felt uneasy, half expecting to see shadowy figures with mobile phones peering from behind the display boards looking for someone to scam.

'I'm sorry?' A deep slam of a voice cut across her uneasy thoughts, hers and everyone else's in the branch, judging by the way all heads swivelled to the counter. It was Woman on a Mission; her voice stronger and deeper and more heavily Yorkshire than Pat would have guessed from the cardigan and Cath Kidston bag. She was being served by Silver Eyes, now off the phone. 'Can I just say, I find your manner extremely offensive.'

What on earth had Silver Eyes said to her? She was now staring blankly up at the woman; her bronze face slightly reddened, making an unfortunate contrast to all the eye make-up. 'I'm very sorry.' Was that bored tone just her normal way of speaking? If so, that was very unfortunate. 'I didn't mean to be rude.'

'Well you were and you are. Bloody rude. Now you've finally finished your call.'

Now the jolly cashier (*Jo Tyler – Happy to help!* according to her name badge) came bustling up. Pat couldn't hear exactly what was being said but the tone was unmistakable: oil on troubled waters. But Woman on a Mission was having none of it.

'I demand to see the manager.' Her knuckles shone white round her strap.

'She'll be lucky.' Pat turned and saw silver hair tied back in a ponytail, plus a big tummy pushing its way out of a sweatshirt. 'Branches share them these days. He'll be in Ripon or Northallerton or somewhere.'

No manager? The bank suddenly seemed a whole lot less secure and solid to Pat. Unregulated, a bit like a classroom without a teacher. No wonder crimes happened here! She remembered Mr Riley giving them their first loan to start up the business, her and Rod like schoolchildren tiptoeing into his office. That maroon blotter on the desk and behind it on the wall an oil painting of daisies in a jar. His wife had been very prominent in the Ripon Art Society. Mr Riley would have sorted out the angry woman. Come to that, he wouldn't have countenanced the cashier being on the phone and he'd certainly have done something to stop Topsy handing all her money over to some crook.

'Total ingrained incompetence.' Woman on a Mission said and with that stalked out of the branch. Ingrained incompetence. Pat didn't like the sound of that one bit. But then she did feel a stab of pity for the cashier whose redness had deepened and was now joined with tears, making the eye make-up even more unfortunate. She was being hugged by the jolly cashier. 'Never mind, Mandy,' Pat heard her say. 'Zumba it out tonight then Pals of Pinot.'

Jo Tyler Happy to Help went back to her own till, but as she did shot Silver Eyes a look, a swift powerful look, a look that was . . . What was the word? Charged.

Then she smiled encouragingly for Pat to move forward, the look so completely erased that Pat wondered if she'd imagined it.

As she walked to the till she caught sight of Silver Eyes' name tag: *Mandy Szafranska, Happy to Help*. Mandy Szafranska. Thelma's voice in her head was as clear as if she'd been stood at her shoulder: *Only she's not Pinder now. Married someone with a Polish name who wasn't Polish*.

So this, then, was the actual infamous enabler of Topsy's fraud. *Ingrained incompetence*. The words sang out in Pat's head. Just who had Mandy Pinder-as-was been on the phone to when she was meant to be serving? 'I'm very sorry about the wait, madam.' Jo Happy to Help smiled warmly. 'What can I do for you?'

Pat handed over the cheques, but uneasily. She had an unshakeable feeling the money she was paying over – the money that would fund Liam in Durham and so much more – was simply not safe in the hands of these people.

Without giving herself time to think she spoke.

'I couldn't help overhearing just now,' she said. Jo's face froze over a shade and the smile faded down a few notches.

'Zumba.' Unconsciously Pat pulled at the sage top. 'I've been looking for a good class.'

CHAPTER NINE

*Once again predictions prove very different
from reality, medication is discussed and confusing
scenarios are challenged.*

Thelma's words stayed with Liz throughout the afternoon, a chilly undercurrent to the tasks and encounters of the day (finishing another chapter of *Broken Biscuits*, thinning the perennials, reassuring her daughter-in-law Leoni that a Pupil Referral Unit was only for older children). Once the day was done, however, and she was lying in bed, there was nothing to stop those words surging back with full unsettling force.

Topsy said someone wanted her dead.

Once again the darkness was punctuated by unsettling bursts of rain rattling against the windows in a way that matched the bursts and rattles of her thoughts as they swelled and surged round the same things: the tablets, Topsy taking the tablets, the rainbow-coloured Dossette box. When she did sleep she kept on starting herself awake from panicky jumbles of dreams about lost keys and missed trains, her mind coming back to that same thing: Topsy saying someone wanted her dead.

Driving past flat grey fields to Rainton the next day, she wondered what on earth she was to say to KellyAnne. She had hoped the plan to collect Topsy's things could be quietly dropped but KellyAnne had again rung. A large – a very large – part of her had wanted to find some excuse and cry off from going (even now she was more than half tempted to stop the car and do a three-point turn on the puddled lane) but KellyAnne had sounded so insistent on the phone . . . insistent with that trace of something else . . . Fear? Plus there was a small, stubborn part of Liz's thinking, a part reflected in a tightness round her mouth and a whiteness as her knuckles gripped the wheel, that kept her driving on.

In her mind was a hope – vague but nevertheless strong – that when she saw her, these horrible worries would be somehow put to rest. Quite how, she wasn't sure, but she had a vision of herself sitting at the granite worktop in the kitchen of Gortops drinking tasteless coffee and KellyAnne saying or doing something that would make Liz think, *Of course*, and drive home, heart and mind lightened with enough energy to face more chapters of *Broken Biscuits*.

However, as with her previous visit, reality proved very different from her predictions.

The first deviation from this wishful vision came as she pulled up outside Gortops and found herself experiencing a powerful sense of déjà vu that took a her second or two to process. Parked in front of the house once again was a faded black van. Only this time there was a man stood in front of it, uncertainly scanning the house as if summoning up the courage to go in. He obviously belonged with the van. He had the same air about him, the same slumped, faded look, quilted jacket, polo shirt, washed-out jeans, and he clutched what looked like an old-fashioned Filofax. He had eyes that had apologetic wrinkles round them, she noticed.

She remembered last time – something about a builder who was owed a lot of money for some work Gordon had commissioned? KellyAnne had been none too pleased. She remembered that cold face when she'd opened the door. Was this the same chap? For a moment she stayed in the car, more than half tempted to drive off, but then she gave herself a mental shake and told herself to get a grip. She got out of the car, retrieving the Tupperware box of baking she'd brought (the second of the things she could more or less successfully bake: a Victoria sponge. Only no icing, merely a sober, respectful dusting of icing sugar, suitable for a time of mourning).

The man turned round as Liz approached. Looking at him from closer quarters she had a sense of recognition. He put her in mind of someone; she wasn't sure for the moment exactly who, but whoever it was she felt it was someone with bad associations.

'Are you going in there?' He spoke with a rather nasal, confiding tone.

'I am,' said Liz. Who was it he reminded her of? A friend of Tim's? The man looked worriedly back at the frontage of Gortops as if it were an intricate puzzle to be solved.

'I know the lady's passed on,' he said. 'But it's just she owes me some money.'

Liz frowned. What on earth to say? Surely he didn't expect her to be responsible for getting his payment?

'Can I help you?' The voice that cut across Liz's worried thoughts was friendly but there was enough question and challenge in the sunny tones to make them both start slightly. Its owner was a slight woman with rounded shoulders. A slight overbite gave her a faintly ratty look, which wasn't helped by the curtain of mousy permed hair that hung round her head. The navy blue suit she wore was slightly on the shiny side, a bit tight in the wrong places whilst loose enough to look a bit dishevelled. As Pat would have said, it did her No Favours. 'Ness Harper, Green Grass Properties,' she said.

'They owe me some money,' said the man clutching his Filofax defensively. 'I did some work a while back and I'm owed money.'

The woman's smile was a mix of regret and steel and On

Your Bike. 'I'm sorry to have to inform you Mrs Joy passed away last week,' she said cheerfully.

'Yeah, and I'm sorry and all that.' The man sounded defensive and not a little bit petulant as if thwarted out of some promise. 'But there's still my money?'

The smile slipped not one iota. 'If you submit an invoice you'll be paid in full when the estate is settled,' she said.

And now the man's face was no longer apologetic, suddenly it looked dark and cross. Liz found herself taking a step back, alarmed at the sudden tension. 'I'm owed that money,' he said quietly.

'Then you'll get it when the estate is settled. If you'd like to leave some contact details?'

The man stared angrily at the woman. Who *was* it he reminded Liz of? Someone from Derek's work? Then all at once his posture slumped slightly in defeat and he went back to his van shaking his head, muttering about taking further steps.

'And you, sunshine,' said the woman in an undertone. She turned to Liz, smile again intact. 'You must be Liz?'

Liz faced the woman feeling very glad she *was* Liz. Floundering, she said something about being here to see KellyAnne and brandished the Victoria sponge by way of justification.

'Bless!' said the woman. 'Keep it away from me!' She gave a bark of laughter and held up a beringed hand. 'Two pounds I lost this week! Come in, you're expected.'

Following her through the front door, Liz had her second feeling of déjà vu that morning. Once again a figure was supine on the hallway, this time dismantling – or trying to dismantle – what looked like a piece of flat-pack furniture. She realized, with surprise, that this was the same youth – what was his name? – who'd been fixing the telephone when she'd called before. Just who was he? Now she looked, he had the same mousy hair as the estate agent she'd just met. Was he Ness Harper's son? And what was he doing here now?

'We met before,' said Liz. 'Though I'm afraid I've forgotten your name.' This wasn't entirely true, seeing as she hadn't properly heard it in the first place.

'Lloret,' said the man. He met her eyes and then quickly looked away. There was something uneasy in that glance.

'That's an unusual name,' said Liz politely.

'Say it to rhyme with "floret",' said Ness. 'It's a place in Spain.' There was a sudden false coy note in her voice. 'It was where a certain someone was conceived!'

Lloret flushed (as did Liz) and turned his attention to the flat-pack. There was a violent splintering sound and two sides came apart in a shower of woodchip.

'That's right, you wreck the joint,' said Ness in tones that would have sounded almost flirtatious had there not been such an obvious age gap between the two.

'It's just all a bit technical.' He looked mournfully at the heap of woodchip. How brown those eyes were! Once again memories of David Essex on the furry rug came into Liz's mind and as he bent down she caught a whiff of his shower gel, something fresh with pine.

'Give me strength,' said Ness laughing. And then, to Liz's surprise, she went up and gave Lloret a tight hug. 'What am I going to do with you, sunshine?' Liz felt half embarrassed, whilst half of her envied her inhaling the pine shower gel. Mother and son – they had to be. But why that inappropriate comment about where he'd been conceived? She shook her head. Three different people in as many minutes, and none of them KellyAnne. Liz's doubts, which she'd mentally told to calm down and be patient now, seemed to be standing, lined up, in her head, arms akimbo saying, 'Well?'

'Come on through.' Ness released him and headed off to the kitchen, moving with a confidence that set Liz's teeth on edge. She obviously knew her way round Gortops. Following her, Liz noticed KellyAnne had done a good bit more than make 'a bit of a start' on Gortops. The hallway and living room were cluttered with stuffed heavy-duty refuse sacks, each one bearing a neat sticky label: *clothes, tops, towels, linen, to keep.*

And finally there was KellyAnne in the kitchen, brisk and business-like in a pink tracksuit, emptying a cupboard of Hornsea Pottery crockery, looking up as they walked in.

'Our friend the builder was back,' said Ness. KellyAnne gave a ferocious sigh and looked at the heavens.

'Don't worry.' Ness raised one fist in a salute. 'He was no match for Ness Harper, Green Grass Properties! Little weasel.' Another annoying laugh.

'There's some right bar-stewards in the world,' said KellyAnne moving from behind the work counter. 'Hello, my love,' she said to Liz and held her for a long sad moment, before breaking and handing her a blue IKEA box marked *Mum's school stuff*.

Inside: a tangle of objects, twined, random and meaningless to most, but to Liz as poignant as if Topsy herself had put them there five minutes previously. There were Topsy's pinking shears, unarguably labelled *Property of Mrs Joy* in uncompromising permanent marker (Topsy cutting the pink and yellow rectangles for Mother's Day cards), her silver whistle on its coiled string of emerald nylon (Boys and girrrrrls, stand STILL!) and a staff photo taken at least ten years ago: Feay the Head, Liz herself – her hair thicker and darker, Pat in her burgundy period, Thelma looking exactly the same, that dinner lady who died of cancer, Marguerite (pre-disgrace). And Topsy, grimly and grudgingly smiling out at the world.

Liz felt something in her nose and throat suddenly jam, and she found herself turning her face away, looking out at the tangled sad garden as KellyAnne gripped her hand and Ness went 'Awwww bless' with another highly grating laugh. She blinked the tears that were making the grey day outside even more blurry and fumbled for a tissue.

'Get this inside you, my love.' Ness cheerfully broke the moment, handing over a coffee that was a much better colour than the previous cup she'd drunk here. 'We've all been filling up left, right and bloody centre here.'

Looking at her, Liz wondered just how long the two had been friends. She was pretty sure she'd not heard of her before, but then with KellyAnne's friends it was always hard to keep track. Ever since school there'd been a steady procession of Jades and Lils and Shazzes and Jacks – one moment as thick as thieves, the next moment bitterly and irrevocably fallen out. Thick as thieves. Liz winced at the expression and despite the warm kitchen felt a slight shiver.

She looked over at KellyAnne. Here she was, at last, sat at the granite work top with a coffee just as she thought she'd be, but with absolutely no idea of how to start any sort of conversation, let alone one that would put her mind at rest. The thought of saying *anything* about Topsy thinking someone wanted her dead seemed as remote and fantastical as Topsy herself walking into the kitchen in her Edinburgh Woollen Mill cardigan.

But as ever, grief notwithstanding, KellyAnne had no problem filling any sort of silence. As Liz sipped her coffee, clutching the whistle, KellyAnne began to talk, brightly, quickly, as if getting the words out before the emotion set in (punctuated by inter-jections and the inevitable laughs from Ness).

She'd been away for one of those mini breaks: Portugal, Thursday night to Sunday, Teesside Airport, taxi, £450 all in. It had been a spur-of-the-moment thing. (Babe, you needed it!) She could've taken Mum, of course she could, but to be perfectly honest she Needed the Break. (Absolutely!) In hindsight (a wonderful thing my love!), she should've checked Paula was okay to look in on her mum as per usual, but it was so last minute the thought never crossed her mind; it was only when she got to the Algarve she remembered Paula herself was away. She could've got someone – Ness, Liz even, anyone – to look in on her but she spoke to her mum on the phone, reminded her to take her tablets – like

63

she'd done stacks of times before – and she seemed fine – well, you know, fine for her. (She probably thought she was the one in Portugal, bless her heart!)

She'd rung on the Sunday from the airport just before flying back but there'd been no reply. Not that she'd thought much of it. There were times when her mum was watching *The Yorkshire Vet* and a bomb could have gone off and she'd have been none the wiser. She rang again when she landed. Again, no reply. It was then she should've got someone, a neighbour (or you, Liz) to look in . . .

Here emotions seemed to be finally catching up, reducing her voice to a hoarse whisper. She paused as Ness gave her a hug. (Babe, you did what any of us would have done.) Thus revived she took a deep breath for the final part of the tale. As she had driven up to the house, she had suddenly felt this cold feeling and knew – just *knew* – something was wrong. She let herself in and sure enough there Topsy was, in her chair, TV on, stone cold . . .

There was a pause and Liz realized the whistle she was clutching had turned warm; opening her hand, she saw deep pink indentations where she had gripped it. If only Ness would go.

As if reading Liz's mind, KellyAnne looked across at Ness, now respectfully wrapping brown coffee cups.

'Babe, why not do that Skype now?' she said. There was a certain amount of command in her voice. Ness immediately stood up and smiled cheerily. 'No rest for the wicked.' She laughed. Liz felt faintly surprised; for all her bossy nature, Ness Harper was surprisingly compliant when told what to do by KellyAnne. How much 'bezzie mates' were they? She watched her take her laptop and leave the room. Now, at last, she was facing her across the granite worktop. Hopefully, hopefully now would come a relief to her worries.

'So did you hear from the police?' said KellyAnne immediately after the door shut. Her tone was eager and urgent.

'I did,' said Liz. 'They came round.' She gave a truncated version of the tale she'd told Pat and Thelma. When she'd finished, KellyAnne was silent, looking at her hands clasped on the worktop.

'KellyAnne,' she said, 'I hope you don't mind me asking. Has there been some problem with the tablets?'

KellyAnne sighed, a deep, deep sigh. 'Liz,' she said, 'your guess is as good as mine.

'The police have been asking me loads about Mum's tablets. You know how it was with Mum. I said when I saw you. All over the place with her different tablets, bless her. You saw for yourself.' There was something insistent in her tone. 'I told the police how she got into these terrible muddles – how I had to remind her just to take the tablets in the drawer. I mean many's the time I had to physically stand over her to make sure she took them.'

'She had one of those boxes,' recalled Liz.

'A Dossette box. Which worked, as long as she kept to the right day . . .'

A memory played in Liz's mind. *'Sunday.'* *'It's Monday, Mother . . .'*

'The thing is, Liz . . .' KellyAnne dropped her voice and looked over her shoulder but there was no sign of either Ness or Flat-Pack Youth. 'The thing is, when I got back, I think there were more days gone than there should've been . . . and the tablets were all muddled up. Almost like the box had been dropped and the tablets just put back any old how . . . so I'm thinking, maybe she took too many or something? But at the end of the day I don't know. Anyway, the police took it away . . .'

'The Dossette box?'

'The Dossette box, the tablets, all her medication. I said to them, take it. I never want to see any of it again.'

'I suppose they have to check these things out,' said Liz. It was all beginning to make a horrible kind of sense. 'Derek's mother. Once she took a load all in one go. She ended up in the Friarage.'

'Exactly.' KellyAnne seized on the anecdote. 'That's exactly what I reckon Mum might have done, God bless her.'

'You said you rang her from Portugal to tell her to take them.'

'I did, like I always do if I'm not here. I rang her up, I said, "Remember, Mum: get the box, take Saturday's tablets – the blue and yellow, the red and yellow, and the white." The receptionist was laughing at me. I don't know what I must've sounded like.'

'And you've said all that to the police?'

'Liz, till I'm blue in the face! But at the end of the day I was three thousand miles away when she took the blumin' things so the top and bottom of it is, I just do not know.' She sighed, a sigh that seemed to come from the very bottom of her soul. 'I should have been here,' she said quietly.

Driving back, Liz felt none of the lightness of heart she'd hoped for. As she'd said to Pat and Thelma, she'd seen Topsy about to take the wrong day's tablets but not the wrong *tablets* . . . There was a difference. She didn't like it. There was something about the situation that did not sit right.

She shook her head. There seemed to be an awful lot of people on the scene at Gortops – that builder, Ness, Flat-Pack Youth (Larry?), Paula, and of course KellyAnne. Previously she'd had an image of Topsy peacefully dead, alone in her chair. But now the image seemed to have altered. She was still in her chair but on all sides she was watched by shadowy, formless figures.

But what could Liz do about it?

CHAPTER TEN

Various phone calls are made and strong coffee is craved.

'Thelma, I should've been there.' KellyAnne's voice thrilled down the phone, putting Thelma in mind of Joan Crawford in *Mildred Pierce*. 'Never mind how hard it's been, never mind how much I needed a break: bottom line, she was my mum and I wasn't there for her.'

Thelma frowned. Everything about KellyAnne's speech felt sculpted and shaped to elicit one answer from her: a comforting negative. She felt slightly guilty in not performing to cue, falling back instead on a vague tutting noise. KellyAnne, however, showed no signs of noticing the muted response. Any attempt to venture onto thin ice and ask about medication and tablets grew less and less likely as the stream of talk showed no sign of slowing or stopping.

'I ask myself again and again: is there anything I could have said or done; hand on heart, Thelma, there's nothing.'

Except possibly not go three thousand miles away without sorting out care for your mother. Thelma offered up a quick prayer of penitence at the judgemental thought. It was now nearly twenty-five past; Teddy was due back from the College Finance Committee, which invariably left him with a worried furrow, and she'd hoped to have supper well underway plus an offer of sherry by the time he walked in.

'. . . and if she *did* take the wrong tablets . . .'

Thelma sat up, thoughts of defrosting a Farm Shop lasagne temporarily banished. Wrong tablets?

'. . . thing is, Thelma, when she took them I was three thousand miles away . . .' Dramatic pause.

Thelma seized the moment. 'The police were saying to Liz something about a mix-up?' she said tentatively. 'With the tablets?'

'That's what they're saying, Thelma. Liz saw how she was with them – all over the place. But that was the thing with Mum towards the end, God bless her: her life was one big mix-up. *You* saw how she was.' Her voice shifted a tone or two up the emotional scale. Thelma opened the freezer door and surveyed the tightly packed contents. Removing a lasagne was going to be tricky one-handed.

'I mean the time was coming, no two ways about it – she wasn't safe on her own. Going out to look for Dad all hours of the day and night . . . Many's the phone call I got: "Your mum's at the bus stop." And then wandering across the fields in her slippers . . .'

Her slippers? Two casseroles and a curry fell onto the tiles with explosive force. This was news to Thelma and she wanted to ask more but now KellyAnne was on a fresh tack, talking about her mother's muddles – or rather her mother's muddles and the impact they had had on her daughter's life. Retrieving and replacing the meals, she offered up another quick prayer. She was wrong to feel so irritated; whatever had or had not happened, the girl had lost her mother.

'I mean the trip away was a sort of last chance . . . I planned when I came back – well, I was going to bite the bullet and move back in for a while.' As she was speaking, Thelma managed to check the salad drawer and write *cherry tomatoes* on the reminder board.

Twenty-two minutes now.

'I should've been there, Thelma,' said KellyAnne. The tone had changed. Joan Crawford was sliding into a lost, spoilt child and despite everything, Thelma finally felt an emotion other than frustration about supper.

'. . . and I drove up to the house, and I swear to God, Thelma, this cold feeling just came over me . . . and I knew – I *knew* – something wasn't right.'

The noise of a key in the front door made Thelma sit up. No cheery cry of 'Clergy in the building'. Bad sign.

'KellyAnne, I'm going to have to go,' she said.

'A look?' Thelma, phone cradled under her chin, scraped the remainder of the lasagne into a Tupperware container. 'What sort of look?' It was two hours later and Teddy was de-stressing in front of the snooker.

'I don't know – a look,' said Pat, curled up on the sofa, glass in one hand, phone in the other.

'Angry?' said Thelma. 'Impatient?' She put the lasagne dish into soak. Would Pat be able to tell if she gave it a go-over with the scourer whilst they were talking?

'Sort of both,' said Pat. 'Without knowing I couldn't be sure. She wasn't happy – I knew that. Whatever Mandy was up to, I reckon Jo knew about it and wasn't pleased.' She took a sip of her Merlot, rich velvety red. 'Anyway, the police'll be looking into it.'

'So are you going to go to this exercise class?' asked Thelma.

'Am I heck,' said Pat. 'What d'you think I'm going to do? Cartwheel up to her and say, "Hey, Mandy! How's tricks?"' She took another blissful sip of her wine. Tomorrow she'd start the diet proper.

'So that's three people in the house that we know about.' Liz sounded worried but trying not to sound worried, a tone Thelma knew of old. There was a pause. 'Are you there?' said Liz.

'I was just thinking,' said Thelma, loading the dishwasher.

'About what?'

Thelma didn't answer because she wasn't exactly sure – something about tablets and looks and muddled words, but also about wanting to get the kitchen done so she could catch up on *Garden Rescue* with Teddy.

At the other end of the phone Liz frowned. This was not the response she'd been wanting when she called her friend. What she wanted was for Thelma to reassure away her worries with words akin to her mother's – it was, in all probability, something and nothing.

'Of course,' said Thelma, 'the person to ask would be Paula.'

'Paula?'

'She cleaned – three times a week? She'd be the one to know about people coming and going.'

Liz frowned; this was less and less what she wanted to hear. Ask Paula?

'I'm going to have to go,' she said, finally switching on the dishwasher.

Later on, Thelma sat at the kitchen table cradling a camomile tea and wishing it were coffee. Normally she was fine with camomile tea, but tonight she craved coffee, strong instant coffee. Playground Duty Coffee as she called it, but she wanted to stand some chance of being able to sleep. Find some peace from those questions that had kept buzzing round her head all through *Garden Rescue*. Could Mandy Pinder have knowingly transferred the money to a fraudster? And what about these people at the house – the Dodgy Builder, Bossy Ness and that young man repairing phones and trashing flat-pack furniture?

She reviewed the sad sequence of events that marked the end of Topsy's life.

Bigger picture, however one looked at it, it all hung together. That wicked fraud, the subsequent upset, the dementia – it all more than explained Topsy's upsetting words at the garden centre. And then the absence of KellyAnne, that muddling of the tablets, the fatal tragic accident . . .

'Oh Lord,' she said. 'All of this makes perfect, perfect sense.' So why then was she sat there craving coffee with a strong feeling that something *didn't* make sense? And what exactly was it?

Thinking about it next day, snatching ten minutes after doing the flowers in the chilly peace of St Catherine's (the heating was never turned on unless there was a service or a group), she wondered if she'd maybe not been a bit hard on KellyAnne going abroad; at the end of the day she'd been someone doing what they wanted to, at the expense of others.

Something she knew about maybe better than anyone else.

A grubby yellow cardigan . . .

Firmly she forced her mind back to the day's jobs; she'd done the flowers (daffodils, fairly weedy, the best the market had to offer) and she was due to the charity shop in twenty minutes. If she was going to pay the paper bill before her shift, she really needed to be making a move but she somehow lacked the energy; she'd not slept at all well. She yawned, blinking, her mind for the millionth time looping and re-looping those words of Topsy's.

It'd be better all round if she was dead . . .

'Lord,' she said aloud. 'What doesn't make sense?'

She tried to still her weary mind, eyes resting on the stained-glass window behind the altar, the muted colours of Jesus reaching out his hand. It was a dark old day and no mistake, hard to believe that in the coming weeks spring sunshine might turn those panels of glass into blazing shapes of colour. Her gaze dropped down to the altar and instinctively paused. Something struck a wrong note. What was it? She looked more closely. Of course, the daffodils she'd arranged. Say daffodils and the mind expected vibrant spots of egg-yolk yellow, not these decidedly lean greenish specimens, looking odd and incongruous in the

71

dim light. It was, she reflected, strange how you could know that something was wrong without immediately realizing exactly what it was – the eye ahead of the brain.

She sat up slightly. What was it that made her think of? Something KellyAnne said . . . *I knew – something wasn't right*. KellyAnne had felt this cold certainty that something was wrong.

But *how*? How had KellyAnne realized something was wrong *before* she went into the house? What had she seen?

CHAPTER ELEVEN

A prayer of sorts is said in Tesco and various causes of indignation are shared.

Like Thelma, Liz slept badly. Going blearily round Tesco the next day (note: Jacob was now firmly OFF He-Man Croquettes and ON Arkham Turkey Melts), weaving round and among the baskets and the trolleys, the broccoli and the bread rolls, gave her some sane light-of-day perspective. So what if the police were asking questions? Wasn't that bound to happen in the case of a sudden death? And anyway, they hadn't seemed very bothered . . . She remembered DC Donna staring unconcernedly out at her emerging primroses, the watery sniffs of PC Trish (unconsciously she dropped two packets of Day & Night Nurse into the trolley). Surely the truth – and it was a truth that was much better contemplated here in Tesco at ten thirty in the morning than in the stormy small hours of the night – was that people died. And it was sometimes sudden. People, like those around her, they muddled on from week to week with their muesli and vine-ripe tomatoes and bin bags . . . and then it all stopped.

And even if Topsy had mixed up her heart tablets, surely that was all there was to it? Nothing more sinister than that. And as for all that awful business with the bank fraud, it was nothing

73

more than a coincidence, a nasty coincidence but a coincidence all the same. It all made perfect sense.

So then why this continuing cold niggle of unease?

Like Thelma before her, Liz said a prayer – a sort of prayer. Gripping the trolley handles whilst standing near the ready meals, she said to whatever power her tired mind groped towards: 'Shouldn't I let this – whatever it is – be?'

For many years Liz's view of God had been as a deity of two parts: on the one hand a benign creation celebrated with tea-towel-on-heads nativity plays at Christmas and masses of bright tissue paper at Easter; this was the God that she'd taught for thirty-six years along with frog spawn, People Who Help Us and number bonds to ten. The other part, however, was of something altogether sterner: a celestial being ready to frown in displeasure and point a disapproving finger as she snuck into the last parking space or walked on past a *Big Issue* seller. This polarized view had of late been changing – retirement, the death of her parents, that cancer scare of Derek's – and then moments of sudden beautiful peace on sunny days had made her think there might perhaps be a bit more to it than her previous simplistic notions.

But in spite of all that, at this stage in her life, she fundamentally believed any responses to questions put to the Almighty would be along the wagging-finger, thunderbolt lines. Therefore it would be fair to say she didn't immediately recognize the small figure in a vibrant turquoise jacket frowning at a pack of chicken goujons as an answer to her prayer.

Paula, one-time caretaker at St Barnabus's, latterly cleaner to Topsy, looked up, caught sight of Liz and regarded her with a total lack of surprise. 'Will you look at these?' She waved the chicken goujons in disgust. 'Gone up 50p and there's half what was in there six months ago.'

* * *

74

'Terrible,' pronounced Paula, vigorously tearing and emptying two packets of sugar into her coffee. She looked balefully round the Shopper's Oasis Café. 'Absolutely terrible, the whole thing from start to finish. But then she was, God love her, a Very Poorly Lady. I'd seen it with Mother. I knew exactly the way things were heading.'

Liz regarded the woman labelled a Walking Saint by KellyAnne with a feeling of hope. If anyone could still those uneasy niggles about Topsy, it was Paula with her trademark brand of acidic no-nonsense judgements. She herself had two overriding memories of Paula from over the years. The first: that whatever was happening in life, Paula's glass was invariably more – much more – than half empty. Whenever Liz thought of her, she had a memory of aggressively mopped floors, accompanied by bitter monologues with the invariable refrain of 'it's disgusting'. The second was of Paula's son Nigel (known from an early age as Rocky after lamping a bully twice his age) who (after a false start culminating in three months at a young offenders' institute) had found work as a stripper, a member of a massively successful local group known as 'the Northern Knights'.

In a weird contrast to her incessantly bitter world-weariness, there had been something rather touchingly innocent in Paula's attitude to her son's chosen profession; whereas most parents could reasonably be expected to show some reticence, Paula's corner of the boiler house had always been vibrant with pictures of Rocky, his perfect white smile, his improbably blue eyes, in various stages of undress. He was now, Paula informed her as they queued for coffee, working in sales – and going from strength to strength. So much so he'd invested in a fancy car from that fancy car place over in Boroughbridge. Quite how true all of this was Liz wasn't very sure, but one thing was obvious: Paula believed every word of her son's success story.

Coffee obtained, they sat down and the subject turned abruptly to Topsy.

'She should never have been left to her own devices like that. Not a lady in her condition. Never. Disgusting I call it. Not that her daughter cared a jot.'

'KellyAnne told me how much you'd done for her,' said Liz diplomatically.

'Did she also tell you how she thought I'd been nicking money and got the police on me?' Paula puffed up her shoulders and bosom in a sort of triumphant indignation, a gesture Liz knew of old.

'Surely not,' she said.

'Police comes round a day or so after – £400 had been taken from Mrs Joy's bank account; did I know anything about it? "I do not," I says. "And furthermore before you leave this house I want you to search my purse and my pockets; in fact you'd better search the whole place whilst you're about it and I can tell you what cash you will find: a jam jar full of 20p pieces for the cancer and that's it." That shut them up.'

'So some money had gone missing?'

'Taken out of her account with her cash card.'

'But surely – well, couldn't it have been Topsy herself who took the money out? She was getting very muddled.'

'She'd have had a job.' Paula smiled grimly. 'The money was taken *after* she died, on the Sunday morning they said. And it went from the cash point here, just outside.'

Liz looked out across the rainy car park at the cash point, half expecting to see some sinister figure in a red and black striped jersey and black mask queuing patiently. She looked back at Paula.

'Did they find out who took it?'

Paula snorted again. 'Turned out it hadn't been taken at all; turned out it was Milady KellyAnne getting the cards mixed up. Shame she didn't realize before she had the police knocking on my door. Shame for that matter she beggared off to the Algarve, leaving a very poorly woman all on her own. But that were all par for the course.'

Liz made a neutral tutting noise.

'I'd have been going over to see Mrs Joy myself, but our Rocky was performing in Cleethorpes so I was seeing to our Cesca and our Reuben. I'd said to KellyAnne: "KellyAnne, I am not around this weekend – I have the grandkids." But it'd obviously gone in one ear and out the other. As per usual.' She broke her Kit-Kat with a doleful snap. 'And then on the Sunday morning KellyAnne rings me up, in a right state. Couldn't get her mother to wake up. All over the place she was.' She shook her head grimly. 'If only she'd said she was swanning off to the Algarve, I'd've sorted something out; of course I would.'

'I gather the trip was all a bit last minute.'

Paula gave her trademark noise of disapproval, a cross between a snort and sniff. 'How long does it take to make one phone call?'

'She probably didn't like to bother you.'

'Never stopped her before, that one.' Paula had a look in her eyes that Liz knew only too well (that awful time with Pat and the glitter silhouettes!).

'It must have all been a bit full-on for her, what with looking after her mum,' she said.

Another snort, this one more expressive, more ireful.

A mix-up with care . . . muddled pills . . . the whole thing was starting to make tragic but understandable sense.

'It must have been so hard for KellyAnne,' she said.

'I tell you something, Liz.' Paula's tone was dark as she smoothed out the silver paper with the air of someone sharpening a blade. 'As far as her mother was concerned, Madame KellyAnne did not want to know. I was all on to get her to admit something was wrong in the first place. "KellyAnne," I'd say, "I'm worried about your ma. I went through this with Mother; I know how these things go."'

'It's a hard thing to face.'

'Doesn't get any easier by ignoring it.' Paula had never been renowned for hearing the other side of the argument. 'I'd say to her: "KellyAnne, take my advice and get your ma's name down for Lovage House." Nothing.'

'But eventually she listened?'

'Only when someone made off with all the money. Only then did she finally wake up to the fact she needed to get off that big backside of hers and do something.'

'It was terrible,' said Liz, 'all that money going like that.'

'It was me as took that first call from that little bar-steward. Of course I didn't know who it was. "Hello. Is that Mrs Joy?" he says, nice as you like, Scottish voice. "It's the fraud department of the Royal York Bank here." So I goes to get her, but by the time we got back he'd rung off. Why do that? I said to our Rocky, "I don't like this." And that Wayne from the Knights, he said it sounded like a scam so Rocky looks it all up on the Internet. So I rings Madame KellyAnne and you know what she says?' She paused for breath, Liz said nothing. Paula's questions were always purely of the rhetorical kind. '"If it's important they'll ring back."'

She shook her head with an air of one whose dire prophecies were ignored. 'Well they did that. With bells on. I says again to KellyAnne, "Your ma says the bank's been on again and they said something about her moving her money and I tell you straight up I don't like what I heard." You know how long it took her to do something? Three days.' Three fingers with hard orange nail polish rapped on the Formica table. 'Well, of course, by then it was all long gone.'

'It must have been awful for them.'

'It was for Madame KellyAnne. I don't think Mrs Joy knew what on earth was going on, poor love. I goes round – you never saw such a fuss – there's KellyAnne booing and hooing and carrying on and there's that useless friend of hers bossing her around. A complete nightmare the whole thing. And there's poor Mrs Joy, hasn't a clue. "What's happening, Paula?" she kept saying to me. "Some argy-bargy," I said. "Let's watch *Pointless*."' Paula looked down at her coffee. 'I tell you, Liz, for what it's worth, she's better off out of it. It's a horrible, horrible thing to go through and a damn sight worse if your nearest and nearest don't give a monkeys.' She sighed. 'She looked so peaceful sat there in her favourite chair.'

Abruptly all the vinegar had gone and there was a sudden waver in her voice, one that Liz could understand only too well. She put a hand on Paula's arm and together in the Shopper's Oasis Café they had a moment for Topsy.

'So you think it was all a mix-up then?' said Liz eventually.

'What else could it be?' said Paula, fumbling for a tissue in her sleeve. Was it Liz's imagination or was there a bit of a bark in her voice? 'The way she was, it's no surprise she made a lulu of taking her tablets.' She stuffed the tissue back in her sleeve. 'It was only a matter of time before something happened. There was a smoke alarm going off you know.'

'A smoke alarm?'

'That Saturday when it happened. I rang Mrs Joy when I got back from our Rocky's – I'd no idea KellyAnne was away – there it was, beeping away. I said to her: "What's happening? Is something burning?"'

'There wasn't any sign of any smoke damage was there?' asked Liz. Surely Kelly Anne would have said if there'd been a fire?

'She went off somewhere and it stopped. But the point is, she'd obviously left something burning to set it off in the first place. If it hadn't been the tablets it would have been something.' She looked out of the window at the rain-pocked car park; once again there were tears in her eyes. Liz put a hand on her arm. She was now feeling easier in her mind – very sad but definitely easier. Paula had no problem accepting the fact Topsy had muddled her tablets, and that was good enough for her. And as for those words to Thelma . . . Well, people who were ill in that way, they said things. She remembered Derek's mother insisting Val Doonican had been staying for the weekend. She took hold of her car keys – time to be making a move.

'Like leaving the back door unlocked.' Paula shook her head. 'She was always doing that. Anyone could have walked in. Just like Dusty Webster said.'

'Dusty Webster?'

'A woman as lives in the village. I saw her when I went round afterwards; she reckoned she'd maybe seen someone hanging round the place that night. She was relieved when I said it was most likely her medication.'

And just like that, the uneasy niggle was back. A cold feeling crept over the back of Liz's neck and she let go of the car keys. She was opening her mouth to ask questions but at that exact moment a cheerful voice cut across their conversation.

'Mother, I said wait in the car park.'

Liz had an impression of an improbable tan, equally improbable white teeth and a whiff of something expensive.

'I was just talking to Mrs Newsome,' said Paula. 'Rocky picks me up after my Monday shop. You remember Mrs Newsome, Rocky?'

'I do, how are you, Liz?' His easy, smiling use of her name for some reason rankled. Her mind spun back some thirty-odd years to the times that sunny smile had been used to get him out of trouble, and the floods of heartbroken tears when it didn't. That time when it transpired he'd been showing his bits behind the Portakabin in exchange for Top Trump cards.

'How are you?' said Liz with her usual feelings of faint embarrassment, unable to put from her mind the image of him ripping off some Velcroed item of clothing to wild screams and waved Prosecco bottles.

'Good, Liz, thank you. Busy but good.' His smile did slip one jot. Had he had his teeth whitened? But now she looked at him, he was showing his age. His skin, though tanned, was becoming wrinkled, presumably the legacy of the many sun lamps he spent his time under. How old was he now?

'Your mum says you're working in sales.'

'That's right. Chief buyer, big local firm.' His tone managed to imply it was something at least akin to Harvey Nicks. 'And still with the Knights.' That easy smile. 'Can't let them down after all this time.'

'Right.' Liz didn't have a clue what to say. When it came to the Northern Knights, none of her usual enquiries about people's jobs seemed very appropriate. He seemed to pick up on her unease; the smile widened and with a flourish he produced a glossy flyer. On the front were seven men dressed – or nearly dressed – in what looked like Viking outfits. *Dare you face the Northern Knights?* screamed Gothic black writing. 'You should come and see us some time. Talking of which . . .' He turned his easy smile to Paula. 'Wayne says can you do Monday, not Tuesday, as he's holding auditions Tuesday. And I need to be in Pontefract after all.'

'And I suppose you want me to have Cesca and Reuben?' Paula's grudging tone failed to conceal the fact that, as far as she was concerned, the sun rose and set with her grandchildren.

'Nice one, Mother.' He took a cereal bar out of her shopping bag and ripped it open.

'Hey, you,' said Paula in mock indignation.

'Mother, behave,' he said, picking up the bags of shopping.

After they'd gone, leaving a cereal bar wrapper and a lingering scent of aftershave, Liz found herself still sitting in the Shopper's Oasis, unwilling to move, the flyer stuffed deep into her pocket. She watched the two figures retreating across the rainy car park towards a red car that Liz knew from Jacob's last obsession but one was top of the range. The sleek red machine looked like it was meant to be driven down some palm-lined Californian boulevard, not loaded with shopping in a car park in Thirsk.

She looked at her empty coffee cup, reviewing her end of the conversation with Paula. Her fleeting moment of peace had well and truly gone and the back of her neck felt cold and stiff.

She gave herself a mental shake. *Get a grip, Liz*. The police were looking into it – that was good enough for her. It had to be and besides, she had more pressing things to be thinking about.

CHAPTER TWELVE

In which a phone call, a news report and a depiction of evil provoke similar resolutions.

The police were Looking Into It. That's what each of the three thought during the day and if their nights were visited by dreams of murky call centres, lurking figures and confused words about death, those dreams were firmly suppressed when the mornings came. But the next Saturday, for each of them, something happened so that for different reasons, their thinking changed.

For Liz the moment came whilst ironing Jacob's Bat Cave duvet cover. Her feelings of unease, after talking with Paula, had been largely shoved to the back of her mind, especially after the latest saga of her grandson's behaviour, this time over the class Easter egg competition. It wasn't so much that Jacob hadn't won – though from the many and extensive accounts Jacob had given her of the Eggman Eggmobile he'd made entirely by himself, Liz could only guess how disappointed he would have been. There'd been something else apparently, something that had triggered a full-blown meltdown, the upshot of which had been the five-star Mrs Bell talking about exploring the possibility of taking things to the Next Level – whatever that might entail. A big meeting had been called with Tim and Leoni for the next day and it was this she was worrying about as she ironed, when her mobile rang (the theme from *Spider-Man*: she must get Jacob to change it back).

'Liz, my love.' KellyAnne sounded breezy, almost buoyant. 'It's not good news, but what I'm saying to everyone is it's news I find good.'

The police, she said, had been in touch. They were still waiting for the toxicology report but most likely it had been the tablets and, having investigated, the police were of the opinion Topsy had, despite everyone's best efforts, muddled her medication and unless further information came to light they did not propose taking any further action.

'Quick and painless, Liz. And I'm not being funny or anything, but really at her age and taking everything into account, how good is that?'

Sitting next to a pile of unironed bedding after KellyAnne had rung off (love you, babe), Liz couldn't feel it was good at all. She knew she should have felt relieved. It was, after all, what she'd wanted to be told − a tragic muddle − but inside, something still felt stubbornly not right. It was like the time when the Hambleton Memory Clinic had made their first assessment of Derek's mother and pronounced there was nothing wrong with her aside from old age. She hadn't believed it then, and there was something in what KellyAnne was saying that she didn't believe now.

During the conversation she had opened her mouth a few times to say something about someone being seen hanging round the house that night but KellyAnne had been rattling on about needing to put things behind her, move on, organize the funeral (a week on Thursday if possible), maybe booking the Bay Horse in the village for the do, and then she was gone, leaving whatever doubts Liz had with Liz herself.

For Pat the moment came when she was watching Sky News with Rod a few hours after Liz had rung and told her about KellyAnne's call.

84

To be strictly accurate the news was on, rather than being consciously watched, certainly not by her. She was on the sofa next to Rod (surreptitiously pulling at yet another top that was definitely more clingy than she would have liked), flicking through one of her 'trashy magazines'. Liam (a blue-polo-shirted-Abba-singing Liam) was out with friend Luke so the house was absent of the fevered thudding bass that usually emanated from his room. And to say Rod was actually watching the news was also over-stating things somewhat. He was waiting for some football match to come on, Larson the dog prone in his lap. Rod was flitting from channel to channel, his sandy greying head focusing with equal attention – or lack of attention – on the news, *Ice Road Truckers* and some film about a group of trapped teenagers who had unaccountably started spouting blood from ears and eyes.

And now they were back on the news, which seemed only marginally less far-fetched and depressing than the blood-spouting teenagers. And so it was Pat happened to look up from an account of a soap star's disastrous flirtation with Botox (still, however, depressingly slim) to see the familiar Royal York Bank logo.

'Hang on a sec,' she said as Rod's finger flexed on the remote.

That the story was tawdry was made clear by the newsreaders ever-so-slightly disdainful tones. Not only had there been an outcry at the size of bonuses awarded to the top management at the bank – to the tune of some £450,000 – but one of said top brass, a thirty-something whizz kid, had apparently run up a bar tab of £25,000 including £5,000 on a bottle of cham-pagne. Not only that, but he'd then promptly and proudly tweeted a picture of said bar tab – a picture of which had promptly gone viral.

No one from the Royal York Bank was available for comment, said the newsreader in studied neutral tones that provoked a loud noise of disgust from Rod plus some comment along the lines they should all be shot, every last one of the fat-cat bastards. Pat made no response; she was trying to get her head round the

85

notion of £25,000 on a night out . . . *five thousand pounds* for a bottle of champagne. Her mind went back to those difficult end-of-financial-year days at St Barnabus's . . . begging for laminating pouches, buying pencils and glue sticks from Poundland with her own money.

And bonuses of £450,000.

Almost exactly the amount Topsy had lost.

For Thelma the moment came about the same time as Pat, as a result of a conversation with Teddy after the Ripon College Chaplaincy Players production of *Night Must Fall*, which had a number of Teddy's first-year students in the cast. They were walking across the college grounds in companionable silence hand in hand; at last, the rain seemed to have stopped although the grass was still soggy and puddled underfoot. The whole evening had been a welcome distraction. Earlier that day Liz had called, telling her what KellyAnne had said and, like her friend, instead of quietening her mind, the news had had the opposite effect and she'd spent much of the afternoon sat at the kitchen table polishing the brass as her thoughts had played and replayed themselves.

'What did you think of the play?' asked Teddy.

'Very entertaining.' Thelma thought of the girl who was playing the old woman. Attempting to. Face paint, a grey wig and a lot of affected stooping. Teddy took her hand. 'What did you think of Will?' Will was one of Teddy's final-year students; Thelma knew Teddy held him in the highest regard, referring to him privately as Wunderkind Will. He had played the young murderer who throttled the old lady; the look in his eye as he had done so had made Thelma distinctly uneasy.

'I thought he was very convincing.'

'Yes.' There was something in the way Teddy said that word that made Thelma stop and look at him. He sat on one of the benches, and she sat next to him, fingers still entwined. The bench was cold and damp through her coat; earlier the *Look*

North weatherman had warned that winter wasn't done with them yet and that tomorrow could bring a band of sleet and possibly snow.

'What did *you* think of Will?'

Teddy stared across the deserted college grounds, gathering his thoughts. 'It . . . disturbed me.' He fell silent and Thelma waited for him to assemble his words. 'It disturbed me just how well he understood the nature of evil.'

'He was certainly very chilling when he killed the old lady,' said Thelma.

'Not so much then . . . The lead-up to that point. What disturbed me was just how ordinary Will was able to make evil.'

As ever he put into precise words the currents of Thelma's thinking. The young man reading the paper to the old lady . . . His voice had been so . . . natural. And then – he'd casually folded up the paper – and strangled her.

'You think Will has that side to his nature?'

'We all have that side. Will is able to access it. He understands better than most that evil is . . . ordinary. Everyday. Banal even.' Teddy stood up. It really was very cold and damp.

Ordinary evil. The two words ran in Thelma's mind like the refrain of a song, as she made the bedtime drinks. The banality of evil – not like the cartoon character-style evil accompanied by moustache twirling and peals of wicked laughter, Dick Dastardly stood by the side of the road cackling with two sticks of dynamite. But ordinary. The people at work who would help themselves to packs of paper and highlighter pens on a regular basis. Mo the dinner lady who'd regularly taken a week off each July with 'her back' and was invariably to be seen at the Great Yorkshire Show. Banal acts, accompanied by slews of self-justification, as if nothing was wrong with it all.

A lemon yellow cardigan . . . It needed washing, it was grubby and stained on the sleeves . . . And a gummy smile, chocolate round the mouth . . .

Thelma checked herself, forcing her thoughts back to Topsy. That person who helped themselves to her savings. People pestering her: the solar panel people, that builder Liz had told her about. The organizations claiming she had won vast amounts of money. No moustaches, no peals of cackling laughter, just *ordinary evil*. The two words seemed to crystallize the foggy thoughts that had been growing ever since that conversation in the toilets.

It'd be better all round if she was dead . . .

And now, as far as the police were concerned, it was all just a tragic accident. She set the drinks down on the coffee table and told Teddy everything about Topsy. Teddy said nothing as he listened. Thelma chose her words, chose the order of her words, thinking and pausing as she spoke, secure in the knowledge that he wouldn't interrupt her until she finished. He then asked her a series of questions. Not with a scared or angry or worried agenda, just with the purpose of finding out facts. She answered the questions with thought and care. Finally he took her hand. 'I know you'll do the right thing,' he said.

The right thing. But what on earth was that?

Over in Borrowby Pat was telling Rod. He didn't listen as well as Teddy – at times his attention was obviously distracted by the football – but he got very animated by Pat's account of the fraud with the bank. At first he couldn't believe what he was hearing and then he proceeded to hold forth at length about the bastards who would take an old lady's money, and how the police needed to get their arses into collective gear and catch them.

'That's the thing with online banking,' he said. 'You can't trust them.'

'Thelma said they'd never be able to trace them. They could be anywhere. Not even in this country.'

'Don't you believe it.' Rod took a final swig from his can of lager. 'Seriously, it'll be someone as knew Topsy.'

Pat looked uneasily around the shadows of the living room, seeing in her mind's eye figures talking plausibly into their phones, wreathed in the purple smoke from her dreams. Rod was expounding about people who helped themselves to what wasn't theirs. Half listening to him, Pat thought about Mandy Pinder-as-was – and the look Jo had given her. She wasn't imagining it; there'd definitely been more in that look than one colleague would give another. The whole idea of going to the Zumba class as some sort of aerobic Miss Marple had seemed ridiculous in the extreme, had done from the moment she'd asked Jo about the class. What exactly was it she thought she'd do there? Samba next to Jo and Mandy and hope they'd start talking about murdering Topsy?

Now, however, with the image of shadowy callers in her mind, she began to feel differently. The image was added to by others . . . The man with the bar bill . . . those cheques paid trustingly into the bank . . . Liam going to Durham (pray God) . . . that smiling woman in the rose-coloured leotard in the bank poster . . . *Live your life, let the Royal York Bank worry about all the rest.* And Topsy, working hard all her life, left with nothing. She felt a surge of sadness for Topsy. Sadness and affection, emotions – truth be told – she'd never really felt when she was alive. And anger. Suddenly she felt very, very angry. She realized her foot had gone to sleep and stretched out. She really was in need of some sort of exercise class . . .

'So that's it.' Liz tried not to sound apologetic or defensive as she attempted to make neat, folded sense out of the duvet cover.

'I hope it is,' said Derek.

It had taken her thirty-seven minutes to tell the story, and even with his frequent interruptions for clarification she wasn't entirely sure he'd grasped all the ins and outs. Of the three husbands he'd been the one to react most, asking Liz to promise him to let it alone, it was none of her business. Of the three husbands he was the only one who could imagine his wife doing just the opposite.

'I hope it is,' he said again as he left them room.

'It is,' she said after him, knowing, however, she'd almost certainly be lying awake in the small hours wondering just who had been hanging round Gortops that night. Later on, having put the ironed Bat Cave cover back on the duvet, Liz found herself taking the blue IKEA box of Topsy's things from the wardrobe and sitting on Jacob's bed. The blades of the pinking shears were cold in her grip as she sat frowning.

Derek put his head round the door to find her looking at her phone.

'*Garden Rescue* in five minutes,' he said. Liz looked up. 'Who are you phoning,' he asked.

'I was just checking to see if I had Paula's number,' she said, trying to sound vague and unconcerned.

'Why?'

'Just to see if she'd be free for a bit of cleaning at some point.' Derek just looked at her. 'I won't bother,' she said. She put the phone in her cardie pocket and stood up.

'Probably for the best,' he said firmly.

Later when she did try, there was just a continuous tone. Paula must have changed her number. Probably for the best.

The next morning Thelma rang the police asking to speak to DC Donna Dolby. She'd duly been put through and had given her an account of the conversation with Topsy in the garden centre toilets. DC Donna thanked her for the call and said she would Look Into It. She also made it clear that people suffering from dementia often said strange and disturbing things and this comment could almost certainly be safely dismissed under this heading.

CHAPTER THIRTEEN

A witnessed transaction provokes action and a feeling of sadness is explained.

Monday morning found Liz standing by the kiosk at the front of Tesco's, her glance flitting between the gun-metal sky, the supermarket tills and three foil packs of Batman Unleashed cards she held in her hand. She knew there was a particular sort Jacob wanted, or rather didn't want, and for the life of her she couldn't remember which. She tried in her mind to recreate his precise tones. 'Batman, Grandma, but not . . .' Not what?

She gave another glance at the tills but could see no sign of the determined figure in the turquoise coat. Monday – Paula's shopping day, she remembered her saying – and it was about this time she'd bumped into her before. With no current contact number, and not wanting to ask KellyAnne, the only option seemed to be hanging round the front of Tesco where she could say she'd bumped into her by chance.

Again she looked from the cards out to the steely sky. She really did not want to be lingering, not today, not according to the *Look North* weatherman. Already, ominous spots of something between sleet or snow were beginning to fall. Ten more minutes. In the meantime, what was it to be? Arkham Avengers? Dark Knight Reborn?

And it mattered. Absolutely it mattered. She could picture her grandson's cross little face hunching down into his shoulders, outraged eyes staring out miserably at the world through those thick-framed glasses as he struggled to cope with Liz's wrong choice. And today it mattered a hundred, no a thousand, times more than usual. Earlier that morning Tim had dropped in, as he 'just happened to be passing'. Liz (who had, through Tim's work at Ackroyds, acquired a competent working knowledge of farm machinery outlets in North Yorkshire) had recognized this to be a total fabrication but had naturally said nothing, chatting pleasantly about this and that as she made coffee and found one of his favourite caramel wafer biscuits, all the time covertly watching her son as he sat at her breakfast bar with that helpless look that reminded her so much of Derek.

And, as she knew he would, in his own time he began talking, telling her more about the saga of the Easter egg competition. It wasn't so much that the Eggman Eggmobile hadn't won; what had upset Jacob had been the unfairness surrounding the winning egg. Fair meant a massive amount to Jacob – one of the many reasons Liz's heart frequently broke when she dared think of his future. The winning egg had apparently been a creation of dyed eggs, silk flowers and glitter entitled 'Eggstatic!' It all sounded decidedly saccharine to Liz, and knowing the capabilities of seven-year-old girls as she did, she had more than half a suspicion that 'Eggstatic' was the work of a parent.

This suspicion was confirmed one thousand per cent when she learnt the seven-year-old girl in question was none other than Elsie Preston-Batty, daughter of Maggie Preston-Batty (Call me Mags for goodness' sake!), parental volunteer and lynchpin of St Anne's PTA. Having observed both mother and daughter ruling the roost at various birthday parties at various play gyms, Liz had no difficulty whatsoever in understanding Jacob's outrage at the result. Fortunately he'd been restrained from outright attacking 'Eggstatic' but had gone round with one of his black clouds, which he remained under for the rest of the day, emerging only to beat three children with a metre stick when they had made fun of the Eggman Eggmobile. The upshot of all this was that a Big Meeting had been called that night by the five-star Mrs Bell and Tim wanted to ask could Liz collect Jacob so he and Leoni could attend and talk it through afterwards.

So, although long term Liz wasn't at all sure how things would turn out, with Jacob, and with Mrs Bell (who no matter how five-star she was, must surely have limits to her patience), in the short term she knew that it was vitally important he and Leoni went to that meeting in the knowledge Jacob was safe with her, and that afterwards the pair of them could go out to Curryosity for their tea and talk through whatever needed to be talked through. And it was doubly important for Jacob that he had Arkham Melts, Luna Croquettes and spaghetti hoops with two slices of unbuttered white bread and afterwards went to bed under his Batman duvet having been read *Peace at Last* (his current bedtime book) twice through.

So, Batman what? She frowned. She could, of course, buy all three but with things as they were she didn't want to be accused by Tim of spoiling him, rewarding his bad behaviour. She turned the lurid foil packets over in her hands and looked to the sky from which, to her alarm, fat specks of sleet were quickly falling. And still no sign of Paula. She sighed; time to be getting back. She cast one final glance at the cash tills.

And saw the builder who had been at Topsy's house.

Definitely him, hunched inside an indeterminate black anorak, beanie hat shrugged low on his head. He hadn't seen her. He seemed to be with an elderly lady who was wearing one of those old-fashioned plastic pixie hoods and drawing money from the till, money which she then carefully counted into his hand.

And in that instant Liz recalled exactly who the man in the slumped black van reminded her of. Mr Bettridge, parent of Sammy Bettridge, that year she and Topsy were in the Portakabin.

Of course! Mr Bettridge. The deferential manner, the weak voice trying to sound strong. Mr Bettridge, always ready to meet her eyes with an apologetic smile as he promised dinner money, trip money, oboe lesson money. Money that seldom if ever came. And then there was that unfortunate business with the petty cash at the firm where he worked. He'd be out by now, one of those open prisons she seemed to remember (taxpayer-funded holiday camps Derek called them). This man wasn't actually Mr Bettridge of course, but he bore a strong resemblance. That type of person.

She stood in the strengthening sleet watching their retreating forms, spotted with white. And there was the black van, faded and rusty as ever, rapidly gaining a gloopy white frosting. And now the old lady was getting into the van as Dodgy Builder scraped slush off the windscreen with what looked like a Tesco clubcard.

She didn't like it. It did not sit right.

What to do?

Why do you need to do anything? The voice inside her head was confident, slightly patronizing, with strong overtones of her friend Jan. It was a voice she recognized of old, the voice of common sense.

'It doesn't sit right,' she said.

What doesn't? You see a man who reminds you of someone not very nice, being given money by someone.

'By an old lady,' she said to herself. What she'd seen of her had touched something inside; there was something about her face beneath the blue plastic hood. Something trusting. Something . . . vulnerable. Like Topsy.

There could be any number of reasons, said the voice of common sense and even as it spoke, she saw the black van weaving out of the car park leaving slushy lines in its wake. Instinctively she memorized the registration number MH09 JBG (Milford Haven where cousin Diane lived, 09 the year Derek got shingles, JBG – Jan's book group), *which you should be preparing for now,* said the Jan voice. *Rather than hanging around in sleety car parks.*

Hanging around.

With a rush Paula's words again came back to her.

She reckoned she'd maybe seen someone hanging round the place that night.

What if . . . what if it had been the builder? Her mind went back to that morning stood outside Gortops. What was it he'd said? *I know the lady's passed on*. But *how*? How had he known Topsy had passed on? And what if KellyAnne for whatever reason *hadn't* made a mistake – and he had taken the money out?

Come on, get your shopping and get yourself home, said the Jan voice of common sense. *And better write that number down before you forget it,* the voice concluded indulgently.

Liz always carried an IKEA pencil in her coat pocket. Now she slapped her pockets for something to write on. There was something stiff and glossy; pulling it out the pink words challenged her: *Dare you face the Northern Knights?*

More words came back to her: Rocky's to his mother.

Can you do Monday, not Tuesday, as Wayne's holding auditions Tuesday? Monday. *Today.* Today Paula would be cleaning at Northern Knights. She scanned the flyer. There was the address, a Northallerton one, Bullamoor Road. Almost before she knew it, she was negotiating her way out of the car park.

What about the sleet? hectored the Jan voice. *What about book group? What about Jacob's tea?*

'What about them?' said Liz out loud, confident, defiant but already starting to panic about the rapidly whitening roads.

The same sleet was lacing the fields with a soggy grey as Thelma drove towards Rainton. A large part of her wished she'd stuck to the morning's plan: waxing the furniture to Classic FM. Something secure and life-affirming for a dark March day. She had hoped talking it all through with Teddy would give the matter some much-needed perspective. But her husband's words had acted not as a benediction so much as a call to action, and

95

action had won out over beeswax and Classic FM. Which was why she was now driving to Gortops to see if she could find out just what had given KellyAnne that premonition of doom. On the back seat was a jumbo roll of bin bags in case any assistance was required with clearing, which – knowing KellyAnne – was more than likely.

The wheels of her mussel-blue Fiat hissed wetly as she pulled up outside Gortops, just as a final splatter of sleet rattled against the windscreen.

The garden still looked scraggy and unkempt, but on a cheerful note a splodge of white snowdrops was emerging near the bush by the gate. Avoiding the worst of the slush, Thelma pushed open the five-bar gate and headed into the drive, earnestly scanning the garden and house. A black wheelie bin, the one for recycling, was standing slap in the middle of the drive. Something about it, alone and forlorn, brought back the memory of Topsy and her confused tears. Squashing the sudden wave of sadness, Thelma pushed the bin to the side and approached the glass frontage.

The house was empty. Thelma saw that even before she could see the empty hallway; the whole place had about it that grey, still emptiness seen in abandoned buildings and dead animals.

She peered through the glass. From here she had a clear view of the entrance hall, open staircase and – through to the right – a glimpse of the kitchen. The place had clearly been emptied. It wasn't so much the lack of furniture and fittings, it was their marks of absence, dusty, pale oblongs on the floors and walls, depressed marks in the carpets, plus the detritus of packing: a newspaper, a stray bin bag, a plastic lid. Surely it would have been better to leave some stuff in the house, so it didn't have this dead, deserted look? Or was the thought of having dealings with the property simply too painful after what had happened? Her thoughts returned to the reason for her visit: just what had KellyAnne seen that told her something was wrong?

On the mat by the front door was a whole fan of junk mail,

bright with bold lettering, that Thelma could read even at this distance: *Important Prize Draw information inside!* sang one canary-yellow envelope.

There seemed nothing more to be learnt. Thelma shivered; despite her winter boots, her feet were getting decidedly chilly. As she retraced her steps her eye was caught by the snowdrops she had noticed earlier. Looking at them now she realized one wasn't a misshapen flower; the splodge of white was, in fact, a sodden, crumpled piece of paper. No, not a piece of paper, a card, a business card. She carefully picked it up and read the name: *Oliver Harney, building and repair work.* The builder Liz had mentioned? She had just carefully wrapped the sodden scrap of card in a tissue and put it in her handbag when a voice made her look round.

'There's no one there, love.'

The speaker was lean, probably a woman in her fifties, but so bundled up was she – in anorak and man's hat – that Thelma had trouble telling. A small dog shivered patiently at her feet.

'I was looking for KellyAnne. I'm a friend of her mother's.'

'They've been gone a day or two.'

What now? Back to beeswax and Classic FM she supposed. But then she had a sudden memory of something Liz had said.

'I wonder, could you tell me where I could find a Dusty Webster?'

If Thelma had been younger – or male – the woman might not have answered so readily. As it was, she jerked her head towards a neat right angle of council houses. 'She lives down there, down Sunny Bank. But she won't be there – it's Monday.'

This was said with some significance as if it explained everything. 'Lunch club.' Her head jerked a different way. 'At the Bay Horse.'

CHAPTER FOURTEEN

A dance routine is interrupted, financial fecklessness bemoaned and a minor theft discovered.

Sitting in her car, parked up on the Bullamoor Road, Liz breathed in and out, hands pressing the wheel. The building was one she recognized; the upper floor of a small parade of shops. In years gone by it had been the premises of Dance-tastic! – a children's dance school. She remembered attending a show starring some of the children from her class. Now the cheery rainbow sign had gone, and next to the shabby door – sandwiched between a convenience store (grated windows) and the Get Stuffed Takeaway – a sober plaque confirmed this was indeed the headquarters of Northern Knights, prop. W. Hughes.

Liz took a steadying breath; she was here to see Paula, to find out anything she could about the person hanging round outside Gortops, and maybe some more about the Bettridge-style builder. The sleet was thankfully fading as she locked the car, casting a worried glance round the huddled houses of Bullamoor Road. *Are you sure you're safe to leave it here?* said the Jan voice prompting panicky visions of calling Derek (Derek, I'm in Northallerton and the car's been stolen). She checked the lock again, and then a third time before approaching the door, on which someone had written in black indelible marker: *Get 'em off*. Next to the door was one of those bell and speaker jobbies. 'I'm here to see Paula Oldroyd,' she rehearsed under her breath before pressing the bell.

There was a distant buzz but nothing else. Should she ring again? Her finger hovered over the bell but then the speaker crackled. 'I'm here to see Paula Oldroyd,' she tried to say, but before she got halfway through there was a buzz and she felt the door give under her hand. Taking a last glance at the car (Derek, I'm in Northallerton and the car's had its windows punched in) she ventured inside.

The first thing that struck her was a strong smell of damp. Immediately in front of her was a flight of stairs and on the walls of the stairway were individual photos of men, slightly faded, the Northern Knights themselves. Thor, Gunner, Bjorn . . . they stood glaring moodily out of a pale purple mist wearing sheepskin and very little leather. Some held axes, some held swords. Thor brandished a hammer. Rocky was two-thirds of the way up the stairs, Gunvar, Dark Lord of Desire, with not a trace of that easy smile as he brandished his axe, one foot on a hay bale, looking markedly younger than he had in the Shopper's Oasis Café.

At the top of the stairs was a reception area, slightly faded chairs and coffee table plus a desk and computer and, despite the trademark scent of Paula's polish, still a strong smell of damp. It all looked slightly sad and dated and a very unlikely setting for the Seven Gods of Dark Sex promised to the peoples of Cleethorpes, Gateshead, Pontefract and Castleford by the various framed posters on the wall.

There was no one about, no sign of Paula, but behind a door where she remembered the Dance-tastic! studio to be she could hear music playing, some insistent shouted words and a thumping beat.

'Hello,' she called, oh so tentatively. Was that a voice behind the door? Pushing it open she had a fleeting impression of speakers and rails of costumes before her attention was grabbed in a headlock by what was going on at the far end of the room. On the stage, where she had once watched Daisy and Claire Moretti perform 'Spring Surprise', a rather spotty youth, stark naked, was frowning with concentration whilst simultaneously waving a pair of rather grubby pants over his head and flexing at the hips so his bits flicked back and forth like a Newton's cradle.

Watching him was a man with a bored expression, which seemed to have been copied from Simon Cowell.

'I am so sorry!' Liz felt like she almost shrieked the words as she backed away to the door.

'You're all right, love.' The bored man flipped off the music. 'We're just about concluded here.' He turned to the young man who was bent over, hands on knees, panting. 'Okay, Dean, thanks a lot: kit back on, my man.'

'It's Duane, mate.' The young man smiled cheerfully and pulled on his pants as Liz tried to look anywhere but at the stage.

'That was good,' said the bored man checking his phone. 'A lot of va va voom-ski. Exactly what we need.'

'I do another to Michael Bublé,' said Duane. 'My girlfriend says it's mint.'

'Brilliant,' said the man without looking up from his phone. 'As I say we've a few more to see. Now, love.' He gestured to Liz and she followed him back into the reception area. 'I'm Wayne,' he said over his shoulder. 'I take it you've not come to audition.' He laughed at his own joke and walked over to the desk.

'No,' said Liz, trying to laugh along but failing. 'I'm looking for . . .' but the man wasn't listening.

'Come on, wake up shake up.' He slapped the computer on the side. 'It's just about had it.' He rubbed the mouse frantically on the desk. 'Hen night is it?'

'No,' said Liz. 'Nothing like that.'

The man looked at up her, comprehension dawning in his

moody eyes. 'You're here about the sunbed,' he cheerfully pronounced, clapping his hands. 'Hallelujah!'

Before Liz could disclaim any connection with any sunbed, the door opened and Duane appeared, fully clothed but, even so, it was hard for Liz to get the image of that pendulous tackle out of her mind.

'I'll be off then,' he said.

'Thanks, Darren.' Wayne didn't even look up from the computer.

'Duane,' said Duane, cheerfully enough.

'Like I say, I've a few more to see, but very impressive, mate, well done. I'll be in touch in a couple of days.'

'No probs.'

Wayne looked towards the door and the noise of Duane's feet thundering down the stairs. 'Don't call us, we'll call the shots,' he said. He smiled ruefully at Liz. 'These kids, they think it's just a case of rip off your kit and wave the old crown jewels in the air. Bit more to it than that.' He smiled, and there was the same easiness in his smile as there was in Rocky's. Liz suddenly realized that this was Thor from the pictures, minus hammer and sheepskin. Now sporting a Great North Run T-shirt with hair tied back in a ponytail, looking markedly older than his picture. 'And they all think it's El Easy Dosho.' He sighed. 'It's fiddling hard work. I tell you, I used to work in the prison before it closed. That was a breeze in the park compared to this.'

'Anyway,' said Liz. She needed to get out of here, pick up the Luna Croquettes and get back in time to get Jacob.

'The sunbed.' Wayne stood up and headed back into the studio, Liz trailing after him. 'Rocky said he'd have somewhere to store it. And I just can't have it here.' He gestured at a wardrobe-sized cardboard package, which stood in the midst of a pile of shields and plastic swords. 'Top of the range this, worth a mint imperial: if it was known that it was here we'd be broken into before you could say "no business like show business".'

'I'm not here about the sunbed,' Liz finally managed to say. 'I'm looking for Paula Oldroyd, Rocky's mum.'

'Not the sunbed?'

'I'm afraid not. Doesn't Paula work here?'

'She does, but not till tomorrow.'

'I thought the days had been swapped,' said Liz, trying to ignore the Jan voice gleefully crowing in the back of her mind.

'They were, but then something contorted and we had to switch the auditions round so we swapped back.'

Liz sighed to herself. This was, as the Jan voice was wasting no time in telling her, a complete fool's errand.

Wayne sadly regarded the offending sunbed with folded arms. 'Typical Rocky.' He sighed. 'Splashes out on a top-of-the-radius sunbed, not a thought to where it'll go. No room at his place, but that's Rocky all over, reaching for the stars without a rocket . . . "Use it here," he said. "Oh?" I said. "And who's going to pay the old leccy bill then?" I says to him, "Rocky mate, stick with Bronze and Beyond like the rest of us."'

He looked at Liz. 'You know it? Just off Malpas Road. We get group discount and everything.'

Liz sympathetically, but firmly, disavowed any knowledge of Bronze and Beyond. 'I only wanted to speak with Paula,' she said, but Wayne was in full flow.

'Rocky should be buying a house, not renting,' he said. 'That's what I did, back in the day, back when we started up. Raking in the spondoolies we were.'

Liz nodded, remembering those heady days when Paula sported designer shoes and was regularly whisked off for spa weekends in Barnard Castle.

'Seven gigs in a week, sometimes two a night.' Wayne smiled at the collection of plastic axes. 'Three houses I bought: two in Yarm and one in Thornaby. I rent them out – that's my pension plan. I said to Rocky: "Get your money into some property. Those rainy dates will come, my son. There's only so long people'll pay to see our bits." Did he listen?' He sighed and adjusted a picture of himself with what looked like a stuffed bear in a headlock. 'And I was right. Times change. Now you can see anything and everything on your phone. Now we're lucky to get Cleethorpes and Pontefract. Anyway.' He finally looked at Liz. 'If you want to get in touch with Paula, your best bet is to ring Rocky at the call centre.'

'Call centre?' Liz looked at him, puzzled.

Wayne crooked his thumb and little finger like a phone. 'Hello,' he said in fluting tones. 'This is Paragon Insurance. I understand you've recently been in a motor misdemeanour.'

So much for chief buyer, big local firm.

'I don't suppose you could let me have Paula's number yourself?' she said.

He looked at her doubtfully.

'We used to work together.' She spoke hastily. 'And just recently our friend died so I wanted to get in touch with her.'

Which was sort of true.

'Was that the lady out in Rainton?' asked Wayne.

Liz nodded.

'A sad business.' He came to a decision and got his phone out again. 'I had an aunt who had dementia, God cuddle her. It's no bloody business getting old.'

He looked reflective, suddenly much much older and sadder than his barely clad Viking alter ego, who smouldered down at them from a poster for the Victoria Theatre, Halifax. He wrote a number down on a raspberry pink Post-it Note and handed it to her. 'She was the lady who was deflowered out of all that money?'

'You heard about that?'

'Me and half Northallerton.' He smiled, and there again was the cheeky look. 'When old Ma Oldroyd has a story to tell, Has She a Story to Tell!'

Liz nodded with her own vivid memories of this.

'The day after she took that call she were in here sounding off about it. I told her, I told them both how these scams work. I said, "They ring up pretending to be the bank, tell you there's a financial misnomer, get you to transfer your money out. Poof, it's all gone."' He sighed and stood up.

'Anyway. Is there anything else, love? I'm expecting another audition in ten-ski.'

'You've been very helpful,' said Liz. She tried to banish a sudden vision of flying genitals. 'And good luck with your sunbed.'

Descending the stairs she could see a figure beyond the frosted glass of the door; presumably the next auditionee. As she opened the door the figure took a nervous step back. A wave of familiarity spread over Liz – one obviously shared by the young man who flushed to the roots of his sandy hair.

'Jeremy?' she said 'Jeremy Fairhurst?' She regarded her one-time pupil, star of the Badgers table and latterly head chorister at Ripon Cathedral.

'Hi, Mrs Newsome,' he said glibly, the blush not abating one jot. 'I'm just making a delivery.'

'Come on up, Jez-lad,' shouted Wayne from the top of the stairs. 'You're early-schmearly.'

Driving away in her thankfully intact car, Liz speculated on the twists and turns that had led these people to Bullamoor Road and the Northern Knights. Jeremy (whose mother, she remembered, had been so set on him studying law) – and then Wayne with his three-house pension plan – and Rocky with nowhere to run his sunbed and his job at the call centre. She thought of the sultry images glaring down from their wreaths of purple smoke and the older faces of Rocky and Wayne. How soon it all goes. How very soon it all goes.

Never mind that. It was the Jan voice back in full force. *It's gone two, you've no Luna Croquettes and Jacob to pick up at three in Boroughbridge.* Liz sighed and drove back towards Tesco. She should just have enough time.

Anyway, said the Jan voice bossily, *you're no further on. And you don't know any more about that dodgy builder.*

'I've Paula's number,' said Liz aloud. She patted her coat pocket. There was something else there, a shiny hard rectangle. Pulling it out at the next traffic lights she saw the Arkham Avengers cards and realized with a flush of shame she'd not paid for them.

See, said the Jan voice. *See what happens when you play silly beggars.*

CHAPTER FIFTEEN

Lunch is refused and the conclusion is reached that
taking mail from a wheelie bin doesn't constitute theft.

Thelma paused on the step leading to the entrance of the lounge
dining area at the back of the Bay Horse. There had been lunch
clubs for the elderly aplenty throughout her years with Teddy
but hitherto they'd always been something she avoided if at all
possible, especially since she'd retired. Memories of Auntie Irene's
mealtimes at Lovage House had always served to put her off the
whole notion; such occasions were an unwelcome prompt for
those dark fears regarding whatever the future might bring in
her childless old age. Mentally preparing herself now she was
taken somewhat by surprise by the swell of highly compos-mentis
laughter that suddenly emanated from the dining room. The
landlord looked up from moodily scanning the *Ripon Gazette*
and raised his eyes in the sort of expression you might expect
were there a gang of Hell's Angels in the back.

'One goes in there at one's own peril,' he said to Thelma.

There were about sixteen men and women of different ages.
Most were talking with animation; all were embarked on a plate
of roast something or other covered in a rich brown gravy. On
a table to one side was an incongruous collection of tins and
boxes of sweets stuck with lozenge-pink raffle tickets. When they
looked at Thelma the conversation paused, but it wasn't one of

those pauses in films where a stranger walks into a country pub and everyone falls silent. Here, the pause was warm and encouraging and expectant. Thelma was trying to think of some reason why on earth she could possibly want to gatecrash a lunch club, and also how to enquire about Dusty Webster when a voice said: 'Hello, Mrs Cooper.' A lady with a startling mop of auburn hair, who could have been anything between sixty and eighty, beamed in welcome. 'She used to teach our Hannah,' she announced with authority. Thelma looked as the smiling face merged with one from the past, from the part of her mind labelled 'parent'.

The speed of it all was remarkable; one moment she'd been hovering at the doorway, the next she was sat by the lady with auburn hair (Mrs Booth, mother of Hannah Booth from at least twenty-five years if not thirty years ago) accepting a ginger ale and fending off a plate of braised steak and vegetables. No one seemed at all curious as to why she was there; she knew Mrs Booth and had known Mrs Joy; for the moment that was enough and she was content to let the crackling fire return the feeling to her toes whilst thinking of ways of identifying Dusty Webster. She learnt that Hannah was now a senior midwife at a hospital in Middlesbrough. (Her mind threw up a sharp sunlit memory of three little girls flat on their backs in the home corner with dolls stuffed up their jumpers whilst a stolid little girl – Hannah – in uncompromising plaits forcefully intoned, *Push*.)

She also learnt:

- The doctors at the Cathedral medical practice were in the habit of writing off anyone over the age of sixty-five as 'old' and therefore not worth referring – a graphic account of someone called Barbara's shoulder was given as evidence to support this.

- The potholes on the lane to Dishforth were nothing less than lethal but the council Simply Were Not Interested.

- There was a man going round Baldersby selling patios; he was to be avoided at all costs.

Sitting there, as the fire crackled and spat its way round a fresh log, Thelma felt a growing sense of security. Out there were the wide flat wintry fields, giving on to a world of dodgy patio salesmen, disinterested doctors and lethal potholes; here, in this room, those things were kept at bay. Better than kept at bay, laughed into submission by Mrs Booth and her friends with their scraped-clean plates and glasses of wine and beer. The atmosphere reminded her of the staffroom back at St Barnabus's, where at playtimes and lunchtimes the bleak world was firmly banished beyond the circle of olive green chairs arranged around that worn grey carpet. The talk of dodgy patio salesmen brought to mind the soggy card tucked in her handbag.

'Do you get many door-to-door traders here?' she ventured. 'Suspicious types? I only ask because I remember Topsy saying something to me a while back.'

'It's like anywhere,' Mrs Booth said.

'It's a sight better since they put the no cold call block on the village,' said one man with authority.

'It doesn't stop them all,' said someone else in tones of doom.

'Keep your front tidy,' said an eager-looking man with an RAF tie. 'Keep the grass trimmed and try and avoid grab rails on the front door – it's the first thing they look for.' He spoke with a self-confident knowledge that had more than one pair of eyeballs rolling.

'So no cold callers but you end up face down in the lupins,' said Mrs Booth, commanding a chorus of laughter.

Thelma tried to remember what Liz had said.

'Topsy said something to me about someone in a black van? A builder?'

'Not everyone's a crook,' said the RAF man in slightly lecturing tones. Thelma scanned the rest of the faces but there was no response other than a general downcast look at the mention of Topsy's name.

'We don't half miss Mrs Joy,' said Mrs Booth.

'Come back, Topsy Joy, all is forgiven,' said someone else.

'Hey, Brian,' said a woman to RAF tie, 'remember last Christmas when she threw that meringue at you?' There were general cackles of laughter. Thelma was aware of a slight feeling of surprise. Throwing a meringue? 'You all knew her then?' she said.

'We did, my love,' said Mrs Booth, who seemed to be a sort of spokeswoman for the group. 'I remembered her because of our Hannah of course. But she started coming here after she lost her Gordon.'

'Even recently, with her illness?'

'We're all nuts here,' said someone. 'It didn't bother us.'

There was general warm laughter and cries of 'You speak for yourself.'

'Lately one of us would go and fetch her,' said Mrs Booth. 'We took it in turns.'

'I heard how difficult things were, what with her wandering around at night,' said Thelma. 'Looking for Gordon.' She could have added about her wandering across the fields in her slippers but somehow this detail seemed disloyal to Topsy's memory.

'I don't know anything about that,' said Mrs Booth. She sounded puzzled. Thelma looked round the group and saw blank looks on the other faces. 'Of course she was getting a bit forgetful, poor love.'

'Pink sixty-three,' said one man in a voice of doom uncannily like Topsy's. Everyone laughed again.

'She used to draw our raffle,' said Mrs Booth, gesturing at the rag-tag collection of tins and sweets.

'There was no arguing with Topsy Joy,' said RAF Brian.

Thelma, with her own memories of PTA raffles over the years, smiled; she could well believe it.

'Now, do you know when the funeral is?' said Mrs Booth in businesslike tones. Thelma was aware of a sense of anticipation in the group; she knew from St Catherine's what occasions these funerals could be amongst older people: times to catch up, to reminisce, underlaid by an unspoken satisfaction at having outlived the deceased.

'No, not yet. Sometime soon I'd imagine.'

'I thought you'd come to tell us.' Mrs Booth looked disappointed.

'No. Not as such.' *Here goes,* thought Thelma. 'It was just such a shock to us. Me and my friends,' she said. 'You remember Liz Newsome and Pat Taylor? We'd only seen her the week before. It seemed such a tragic accident, muddling up her pills like that.'

Now there *was* a silence like the one in films as glances were exchanged. Eventually someone spoke.

'Topsy Joy would no more muddle up her pills than I'd pole-vault over Baldersby church.' There was a general stir of agreement.

'There's a few of us,' said Mrs Booth, 'a few of us oldies – well, I can say this to you, Mrs Cooper – some of us thought something wasn't quite right about what happened.'

'Tell her, Dusty,' said someone. A nervous-looking woman in a cherry red cardigan looked at her empty plate with unhappy concentration.

'It's all right,' said Mrs Booth. 'You can trust Mrs Cooper.'

'All I'm saying,' said Cherry Cardigan, who was presumably Dusty Webster. 'All I'm saying, the night it happened . . . there was someone at the house, someone other than Mrs Joy.'

'She saw them,' said RAF tie.

'Not exactly saw,' said Dusty Webster, looking flustered.

'Let her tell it in her own way, Brian,' said Mrs Booth in a voice of absolute authority.

'I was taking Ziggy for his evening walk.'

'Dog,' chipped in Brian.

'He's a rescue,' explained Dusty Webster. 'He has set ways. He won't do his business just anywhere; his favourite place is the gate into Syke's.'

'That's the field just beyond Mrs Joy's place,' said Brian.

'Anyway it was that Saturday, the night it happened . . . about seven. I know that because I wanted to get home for *Strictly*.' The way Dusty said it had a certain defensiveness about it, as if her story had been challenged.

'Anyway I was passing the house and I saw the light go on upstairs, and that made me think as how it was my turn to call for her for lunch club only I'd a doctor's appointment for that Thursday and I'd need to get someone else to call for her. And it had been snowing – not much – like today's lot, sleety wet stuff, but enough to stick on the ground a bit. And when I looked at the house as I was passing, there was someone looking in.'

'Looking in the door?' said Thelma, trying to envisage that glass frontage.

'No, the window next to it. The one at the side, on the right. I shouted out, "You need to knock; she's a bit deaf," and they turned and looked at me. I'd have said more but Ziggy was in a hurry, so I thought when I got back I'd say something if they were still there. When I came back there was no one there. But I knew they hadn't gone away.'

The log suddenly spat, but despite the fire Thelma felt something like a shiver.

'There were footprints going to the house . . . but not coming away again.'

'Where did they go – these footprints?'

'Round the side of the house, to the back door. But like I say, they didn't come back.' Dusty Webster looked sadly down at her empty plate. 'If only I'd said something, gone and knocked on the door.'

'You weren't to know, Dusty love,' said Mrs Booth, again with that tone of authority. 'It's not your fault.'

An image from two nights previously came to Thelma, a young man casually folding his paper, reaching out and strangling an old woman.

Ordinary evil . . .

'This person,' she said. 'Do you know if it was it a man or a woman?'

'I really couldn't tell, love – probably a man, but it was that dark, and besides they were all togged up.'

'You told the police?'

At this there was general chorus of derision, which put Thelma in mind of her own experience ringing them.

'It all just goes to show,' said Brian eagerly, 'you can't be too careful. There was that woman in Topcliffe.'

'Give up about that woman in Topcliffe,' said Mrs Booth, so Thelma never learnt what it was had happened there.

Before she got in the car Thelma went back to the front of Gortops. She looked in the window to the right of the frontage; the one Dusty Webster had said someone was looking in. There was nothing in there, just a utility room with a view of the side door. Why look in there and not through the frontage? Why not, for that matter, knock at the front door? Unless . . . whoever it was didn't want Topsy to know they were there. As she walked back to the gate the noise of the shutting and locking of a door made her stop and look to the side of the house. She heard the woman before she saw her.

'I'm here at the house now.' The voice that floated round the corner sounded reedy, plaintive. 'I thought we were supposed to be meeting here? But I've got to get back to the office. Can you give me a ring?' The woman appeared round the side, juggling keys and a sheaf of mail; among them Thelma saw the yellow envelope she'd seen through the door earlier. On spotting Thelma the woman's annoyed expression was stamped over with a smile that could only be described as 'professional'.

112

'Hello,' she said. 'Can I help you? I'm afraid the house isn't quite ready for viewing yet.'

Ness. The suit, the smile, the perm – it could only be. And here she was stuffing the mail under an outstretched arm, laughing and announcing: 'Ness Harper, Green Grass Properties,' in tones of utmost confidence. Thelma explained who she was, earning herself a laugh, and a cry of 'Bless'.

'I suppose you know what happened.' Ness lowered her voice respectfully.

'That's why I'm here, to see if I could help in any way,' said Thelma. It wasn't entirely a lie she thought, picturing the roll of bin bags on the back seat of her car.

'Bless,' said Ness again. 'But it's all done, all bar the shouting. I'm just here to collect the post. The place is going up for rent, just until KellyAnne can get it on the market, bless her heart. We just need to get the place cleaned and off we all go.'

A text pinged and she feverishly scrabbled for her phone. 'Great,' she said in exasperation looking at the screen. 'Thank you very much.'

Looking up she said, 'I must fly: Thirsk office calls!' She started thumbing rapidly through the mail. 'Junk, junk, junk, junk,' she chanted, pulling one or two out and stuffing them in her bag. Opening the wheelie bin she dumped the rest inside, letting the lid fall with a conclusive thud. 'I should shred but life's too short,' she said, walking back to the gate. 'I'll tell KellyAnne I saw you.'

Thelma watched her driving away at speed; she'd certainly been in a hurry to go. What had the text said? She went back into the driveway and opened the wheelie bin, putting to one side her qualms. Stretching inside she could just about retrieve the dumped mail. How could it be stealing when it was in a bin? When she was going to make sure it was all properly shredded?

Eventually.

CHAPTER SIXTEEN

Zumba Insanity proves challenging in the extreme and emotions run high in the changing rooms.

By twenty-seven minutes past seven that same evening, Mandy Pinder-as-was (Szafranska? Scepanksa?) was nowhere to be seen amongst the ladies of the Zumba Insanity class, held in what had been the old Feed-Mix Factory off the marketplace, now expensively metamorphosed into Body Futures Gymnasium. Tucked away in what she hoped and prayed was an unobtrusive manner at the back of Exercise Space 3, Pat was beginning to ask herself just what the hell she thought she was playing at. The righteous mix of zeal, doubt and curiosity that had so fired her up when watching the news the other night had faded; sitting self-consciously on the floor she wondered if those feelings had, in fact, been more to do with her worries about Liam than any real belief there was some sort of conspiracy involving Topsy and the bank fraud.

And all that stuff about a sinister call centre with a shady operative . . . it was laughable. Plus the worries about Liam had faded too. There'd been no sign of anything remotely approaching birth control in her guilty once-over of his room that afternoon, but more importantly he seemed back to his regular laconic self. The black T-shirts were back in evidence, the music emanating from his room had reverted to its usual tuneless thump and when served a last-minute sausage pasta he'd said 'Go Nigella' in trademark world-weary tones.

Moreover he seemed droopy, sad, like the time Apollo the hamster disappeared. Whatever had been happening with the Celtic poet, it seemed to be happening no more. The only substantial worries that had stayed with her from the day were those about her figure. Whilst in his room that afternoon an unfavourable combination of wardrobe door and window had suddenly and accusingly shown her herself at an angle that was frankly appalling, and one that no amount of stomach sucking in could dispel. So here she was, with increasingly grave doubts, at the back of a class where it had to be said the atmosphere was as different from her semi-regular Keep Fit class (Mums, Bums and Tums) as it could be.

There was the room itself for a start: icy polished wood floors, a faint smell of cinnamon, stripped brick walls, the occasional gloss-painted metal pillar or girder, black and white photos of bodies contorting in various ways that made Pat wince anew at her reflection in the smoked glass doors and frantically pull her stomach in (again). This room said 'exercise' in a way that Borrowby village hall with its stacked plastic chairs and collages of friendship done by the Brownies decidedly did not.

And then there were the attendees of the class itself, minus Mandy Pinder-as-was but with Jo from the bank, her jovial nature tempered somewhat by a beautifully lithe body and very expensive leotard. But then that seemed to be the norm: lithe bodies and expensive leotards. Pat looked down at her own cobbled-together outfit. *Her* leotard definitely showing the signs of years of going through the wash with various overalls and rugby kits, her exercise tights indelibly wrinkled, her battered plastic bottle of water was the only one to be seen amongst a blooming of pink, orange and blue steel flasks. And then there was the atmosphere amongst the attendees: subdued conversations punctuated by various stretches and deep breaths, twists and flexes. No laughter to speak of.

115

Pat thought of her friend Olga from Mum, Bums and Tums. That time they'd laughed so much when attempting to Position the Core, with such disastrous consequences. Discreetly Pat checked her 'just in case' pad. And then, perhaps most alarmingly of all, there was the instructor herself. 'Call me Kate' as she'd barked, adjusting her iPhone and plugging it into some complicated-looking sound system (Pat thought fleetingly of the days of her Rosemary Conley exercise video cassette). All angles and bones and a hollow at the base of her throat you could fit a small Starbucks cup in. And that smile. That grim 'I am a professional smile' that put her so strongly in mind of that awful inspector from the last OFSTED but one. As different from Olly, the instructor at Mums, Bums and Tums, as you could get. Pat couldn't envisage 'Call me Kate' bursting into extracts from *Evita* or carolling out: 'Buttocks clenched, ladies . . . I want us cracking walnuts here!'

Call me Kate made a final adjustment and trilled out: 'Time for Zumba Insanity,' in a way that sounded like a threat rather than a call to activity.

At that moment the smoked glass door opened and Mandy, tanned face impassive, the silvery-blue eyeshadow replaced by a silvery green, walked calmly in and took the empty place by Jo. Was it Pat's imagination or did Jo seem less than pleased to see Mandy?

'Time to Zumba Insanity!' said Kate again, in a way that made it crystal clear what she thought of latecomers. Mandy's face remained blank and oblivious as the class started.

Zumba Insanity.

It certainly was.

Afterwards, Pat's overriding memory was of feeling increasingly sick, very sick, along with a tightness in her chest as she tried to snatch breaths between moves that grew ever more complex and exaggerated. Salsas, sambas and various hoppings from foot to foot that the rest of the class seemed to master with ease leaving Pat making floundering approximations and thanking God she'd chosen to go at the back.

116

Fortunately Call me Kate seemed more focused on barking out instructions in a voice that never varied in pitch or energy (did she not need to breathe, this woman?) but Pat still had this awful feeling that went right back to Mrs Heatherington at Cottingham Secondary Modern that at any moment there'd be a cry of 'You there at the back! You in the wrinkled stockings with the slipping incontinence pad!'

What on earth had she been thinking of? Any thoughts of discreetly observing Mandy had long flown away like a hat in a gale; her world shrunk down to the pair of aquamarine-clad bony buttocks in front of her flexing and springing like independent creatures and not pausing for a second (as Pat did and for considerably longer than a second) at Call me Kate's frequent cries of 'Let's take it up a notch.'

If she closed her eyes she could just – *just* – still see the blurred leering face of that bank employee waving his bar tab but he was fading rapidly into the distance. If he wanted to get pissed on five-grand bottles of champagne, let him. She tried summoning up the image of her body reflected back at her in the mirror. But this image likewise faded, to be replaced by something a bit more primal: basic survival. At the occasional thirty-second water breaks when the women fiercely glugged from their designer flasks, Pat didn't even try to reach for her bottle but simply stood, hands on knees, trying to get some breath back in her body and slow the clamouring of her heart.

By three-quarters of the way through (and boy, were her eyes glued on that clock), her mind was throwing up all sorts of stories about middle-aged people who died after sudden unwarranted exercise (that woman in Malton who'd been shovelling snow). Would Rod marry again? And a sudden, unexpected and painful pang! The thought she'd not see Liam's baby in the trailer park. Where had that come from? By the time she was in the middle of planning her funeral (purple lilies, and 'You Make Me Feel Like a Natural Woman'), Call Me Kate's cry of 'Time to cool down, ladies' felt as welcome yet unbelievable as the end of World War Two must have done.

As everyone stretched out (and Pat simply stood panting), she took the chance to look around; they all looked only slightly shinier than before. And then as Kate unclicked the iPhone they all started chatting as naturally and as easily as if they had bumped into each other in Morrisons – no, not Morrisons; judging by all the expensive brands of shampoo that were appearing out of top-of-the-range bags, it'd be M&S or that new designer deli in Ripon.

'Well done.' Call me Kate was bearing down on her with a threatening smile. 'How did you find it?'

Pat didn't like to say 'like the third circle of hell'; instead she gasped something about it being challenging.

'You'll get used to it. I was watching you.' Please God, surely not? 'You were picking it up well. A few more sessions and you'll be well away. Anyway . . .' A form sprang from Call me Kate's hand into Pat's damp grasp. 'This is to sign up for the class fulltime. The first one's free. Cash or card. We take contactless.'

As she walked away Pat looked at the form, and suffered a shock almost equal to that of the Zumba session. No wonder everyone looked like they belonged in some private box at York races. With Craig it was £16 a session and they all clubbed together to get him IKEA tokens at Christmas. Looking at Kate's prices Pat could see they'd need something considerably more than IKEA tokens; a week in the Seychelles perhaps.

She deliberately lagged back in the changing room as all the lithe forms pranced into and out of the shower in their peach and cream towels. And mirrors everywhere! Resolutely she kept her eyes on the floor. She'd had enough trauma for one night.

There was no sign of either Mandy or Jo, not that it mattered much to Pat. Any thought of observing, even spying on Mandy, seemed as remote and ridiculous as Topsy doing anything other than dying peacefully in her chair. In fact dying peacefully in her chair seemed quite an attractive option; the way her thighs were keening she'd no idea how she was going to manage those gear changes on the hill through the village. 'I feel so old,' she whispered to her reflection in the smoked-glass mirror. As the last of the sirens decanted themselves into their designer jeans, she waited for her breathing to reach an approximation of normal and tentatively stretched her legs in preparation for standing up. As she did, the door to the steam room opened and Jo and Mandy emerged. (The green eye make-up was miraculously intact; it must have some sort of tar component.) Their lockers were round the other side of the large brick partition from where Pat was sitting; she was unseen but they were not unheard.

'I'm not being *like* anything.' Jo sounded weary.

'Things are just really difficult for me at the moment.' There was a distinct whining note in Mandy's voice.

'Look,' said Jo, 'I'm not being funny or anything, I just want a night off. I just want to relax. Have a chill-out in Pals of Pinot.'

'So do I. I was just saying.'

'I just don't want to get into this.' Pat caught a scent of what she judged to be rather expensive coconut hair oil. 'All I was saying is that is the very last time I cover for you.'

'I never asked you to cover for me.'

'Okay, Mandy, I'll say it as your friend: people are asking what's up with you.'

'It's none of their business.' Mandy sounded petulant.

'People aren't stupid. They notice stuff. Look, as your friend, you've got to come clean with them, Mandy.'

'I keep telling you, it's all sorted.'

'So what were all those calls today in aid of?'

'It's all sorted.' But Mandy's voice was dropping into a whisper. 'It's just all been doing my head in.' There was a pause. 'She was in again, you know. The daughter.'

'Mrs Thing's daughter?'

'Making a big song and dance about getting money for the funeral.'

119

'Did she say anything to you?'

'Julie served her. But she was looking at me. Giving me the evil eye. I can do without it.'

'The investigation found you not to blame.' Jo had obviously said this sentence many times before.

'Well I wish someone'd tell her that.'

'Look.' Jo was sounding practical now. 'Best will in the world, the poor woman's dead. Which is very sad. But surely that's it. All done and dusted.'

'Poor Mrs Joy.' Mandy gave a sigh that sounded so desolate. 'I was always so scared of her at school.'

There was a pause whilst sprays were applied and again Pat caught a whiff of something expensive. Then Jo spoke again.

'And the other stuff . . . it *is* sorted?'

Silence.

'Mandy, is there something else? Something you're not telling me?'

'No.' But there was; if Pat could tell that then Jo surely could. There was a silence from Mandy.

'Look come on, don't cry.' Jo sounded more weary than concerned.

'My life's such shit. I can just do without it.'

'You need to tell them, love. Come clean.'

'I need this job.' Her words came out in a sharp wail. 'Look, I'm just tired. It *is* sorted. I just need to make one more call. I swear on my mother's life.'

How many times, how many *many* times, had Pat heard children, up to their neck in guilt, use those very words?

The changing room door thumped shut and she was left alone with her thoughts.

Limping to the car she was not at all sure how she felt – apart from physically torpedoed. Instead of finding answers she seemed to have found more questions: who did Mandy need to call? And just where were they? And how on earth could she find out?

CHAPTER SEVENTEEN

Speculations are aired and a night out is planned.

The white card, puckered from the rain, sat on the round table in the corner between two cups of coffee and one of herbal blend tea. *Oliver Harney,* read the text in smudged ink, followed by a blurry mobile number.

Liz jabbed at the card with an angry finger. 'He was just like Mr Bettridge,' she said. 'That type. The same weak expression, same way of staring you right in the eyes and telling you a barefaced lie.'

'But that doesn't mean he was the same as Mr Bettridge,' said Thelma gently, but Liz was on something of a roll.

'Why was the old lady giving him money? Why were they driving off together?'

'She could have been his gran, or his aunt, or a neighbour,' said Pat as she copied the number down on the back of a flyer for the Hambleton Choral Society's Spring-tacular. 'I'll see if Rod's heard of him.' She sounded a bit out of sorts, Thelma thought. And why was she wearing that plain top? It was almost dull, not Pat at all.

Pat took a sip of herbal tea and winced. How her soul longed for a mouthful of strong coffee. 'Going back to Mandy Pinder-as-was. That Jo was *really* taking her to task about something . . .'

'Something to do with work perhaps?' Again Thelma was using her most diplomatic 'devil's advocate' voice.

'"You've got to come clean" – that's what that Jo said. You don't say that about some lost biros.' She was feeling decidedly tetchy, and it wasn't just the nagging pains from her hip and the desire for caffeine. That morning, prompted by the memories of those lithe forms in the changing room, she'd taken another frank and painful look at herself in her bra and knickers; what she had seen had cast an indelible cloud of gloom over her world. The result was: coffee was out, plus anything and everything less healthy than salad, fruit and herbal tea. She'd told Rod and Liam they had to fend for themselves tonight as she wouldn't have time to cook after aquarobics and possibly a go on the exercise bike (now devoid of hanging shirts).

'And then there was that Ness.' Liz was obviously not at all interested in the doings of Mandy-Pinder-as-was. 'Laughing like a blumin' hyena, throwing her weight around. And that Flat-Pack Youth she had in tow.'

The other two looked at her. 'What Flat-Pack Youth?' said Pat.

'Lorry or whatever his name is,' said Liz. 'Wrecking the flat-pack. And he was there that other time fixing the phone. Seemed to be with Ness.'

'And of course Ness did have a key to the house,' said Thelma.

'Well she would have if she was in charge of renting the place out,' said Pat, miffed that yet again they'd moved on from Mandy Pinder-as-was. Yes, there it was, the muzzy beginnings of a caffeine-withdrawal headache.

'Plus,' continued Thelma, 'she'd obviously arranged to meet someone at the property. Someone she wanted to see. She sounded quite put out when they didn't show up.'

'So you think she was meeting up with someone to divvy up the stolen cash?' Pat hadn't meant to sound so snippy but she was feeling, frankly, disappointed. She had come along to the garden centre, yes feeling bruised and depressed, but that at least despite her lack of answers, she had something important to tell her friends. Only to find out they had their own adventures to tell and were too full of them to fully appreciate her descent into the third circle of hell at Zumba Insanity. Thelma going to Rainton and Liz (Liz!) going to the headquarters of a load of strippers (Liz!). Truth be told she was feeling upstaged. It all reminded her a bit of that time when she'd covered the climbing frame in red paper and turned it into a reading bus . . . to a similar lack of enthusiasm.

'I'm saying,' said Thelma patiently, 'that Ness, for some reason, had arranged to meet someone where they were unlikely to be disturbed.'

The words had a sobering effect.

'So you think Ness . . .' Liz paused, still trying to avoid the 'm' word, 'Ness . . . tampered with Topsy's tablets?'

'I have absolutely no idea,' said Thelma simply. 'But we have to face the possibility something happened. And if something happened, someone made it happen.'

Liz looked aghast. 'I must have another word with Paula,' she said, squashing down thoughts of what Derek would have to say. 'If anyone knows anything it'd be her.'

'She might,' said Thelma carefully. 'But would she know what she knew?'

'You mean she might miss something?' asked Pat.

'Just suppose the fraudster did know Topsy. And, as we know, when he rang the first time he got Paula. And we also know he tried again.'

'Paula didn't take any more calls,' said Liz. 'She told me.'

'She didn't take any more calls from someone *saying they were from the bank*,' said Thelma. 'So if they had called again and got Paula instead of Topsy . . .'

'They'd have pretended to be someone else,' finished Pat.

'Or even said who they were,' said Thelma. 'So if you asked Paula: "Did you pick up any more calls from the bank?" she'd say "no". But if you said: "Did you pick up any other calls?" it could well be a different picture.'

'And you think that's what happened?' asked Liz.

'I don't know,' said Thelma. 'All I know is that Paula is someone who sees what's there, but isn't so good at seeing beyond that. Remember Mr Mac.' They all did. The wonderful Mr Mac, Rocky's first employer, who could do absolutely no wrong, right up until the time he and Rocky were stopped on the A66 with a lorry load of stolen farm equipment.

Pat tried again. 'Suppose Mandy Pinder-as-was, was in cahoots with whoever took Topsy's money? Maybe even the Dodgy Builder?' She pointed at the card.

'So now you're saying Mandy tampered with Topsy's tablets?' Liz was sounding more and more alarmed.

'People can do all sorts of things when cornered,' said Pat.

'But Mandy Pinder, she knew Topsy.' Liz shook her head, blinking back a sudden image of Topsy stapling a tinsel crown round the five-year-old Mandy's head . . . Mandy standing stock-still, gazing solemnly at her white-robed, tinselled reflection in the classroom window, the image sharp against the winter gloom outside. 'She knew Topsy when she was five.'

'I bet Hitler wouldn't have done what he did at the age of five,' said Pat. Suddenly she could feel herself losing her energy towards the subject. If she were to make that later session of aquarobics she needed to leave now – not that with the way her hip was feeling she'd be able to do much more than bob gently up and down on the spot.

'Of course there was that one time . . .' They both looked at Thelma who spoke as she stirred her coffee. 'That time with the ponies.'

Liz's eyes widened in remembrance. 'That Little Pony collection.' She could still see the bagful of lilac, pink and yellow animals with their big eyes and sprays of nylon hair.

'Sean Stanbury. He did something of some description to one of them.'

'I remember.' Liz's eyes were still wide. 'He cut the hair.' She could see the spray of pink nylon hair sprayed across the classroom carpet. 'He cut the ponies' hair and she fetched him one with a trundle wheel.'

'Out cold and a cut on his temple the length of my finger. He had to go to A&E.' Thelma put her spoon down.

'But to do away with Topsy,' said Liz again; even as she said it the words sounded so false to her, so . . . Sunday night TV drama . . . This was *Thirsk* when all was said and done.

'Mandy made the transaction, and Mandy is doing something she needs to come clean about.' Pat was still feeling peeved and uninterested, even though they finally seemed to be taking on board what she was saying; right now all that felt important was getting to aquarobics.

'Of course there is one way you could find out,' said Thelma calmly. The other two looked at her. 'And that's ask her.'

She calmly returned their gaze.

'What?' said Pat. 'Just stroll up to her and say: "Excuse me, Mandy Pinder-as-was, I was just wondering, did you happen to murder your former nursery nurse after scamming her out of her money?"'

'How you'd actually do it—' Thelma was stirring her coffee again '—is for us – her former teachers – to arrange to be in the same place she is and strike up a conversation. It'd only be natural we'd mention Topsy.'

'And?' prompted Pat. 'What then?'

'And,' said Thelma, 'see what happens. People say all sorts of things, without knowing they've said them. If you see what I mean.'

They both did. Years of experience of what children had said and not said about various missing pencil cases, broken toilet seats and spilt paint had made them all experienced in divining the truth from the maelstrom of words people said when they were caught on the back foot. 'But where could we go and meet her?' asked Liz, an edge of panic in her voice. 'We can hardly do that in the bank.'

'That's the question,' said Thelma.

'Pals of Pinot.' The other two looked slightly startled at Pat's words. 'I heard Jo mention it as they were going out. It's this new wine bar in town, in what was the post office. Our Andrew's been sometimes. That's where they seem to go after Wednesday Zumba.'

'A wine bar?' said Liz unenthusiastically. Where would she park?

'So,' said Thelma, 'are we up for it?' Pat felt she could hardly say 'no', having harped on so much about Mandy; she forced herself to envisage that grinning bank official with his bar bill. In Liz's mind was Derek's serious entreaty to leave well alone – but alongside this was an image of those forlorn pinking shears nestled in their box of oddments. She nodded reluctantly and Pat raised her herbal tea in a sort of toast, then remembering what was in it, pulled a face.

CHAPTER EIGHTEEN

An offer of supper is rejected and there is a further crisis of image in the bedroom.

Pat arrived home feeling tired. She'd not made aquarobics; despite all her good intentions she'd found herself driving right on past the leisure centre. She was somewhat bothered about what she'd committed herself to with the whole wine bar business. Speculating at the garden centre over coffee (or herbal tea) was one thing – but confronting Mandy-Pinder-as-was in a wine bar? And even though her friends did seem to be taking her seriously, she couldn't escape that feeling she'd had so often with them over the years, that when it came to plans and ideas she was very much number three. Thelma was the one who made the plans, Liz had the worries that led to plans – but her ideas . . . her plans . . . The reading bus – Pumpkin Day – the Rap Nativity . . . always it seemed they'd been met with the same tepid response.

Take their response to her adventures at Zumba Insanity – if only they'd said something like 'Pat, well done', if they'd even listened properly – but their reactions, as ever, had been characteristically lukewarm. Yes, they were going to talk to Mandy Pinder, but it felt like the idea had come from Thelma rather than anything she had said or done.

127

She sighed. She felt hungry. The hollow hunger that only Day Two of a diet can bring. This was ridiculous. Dieting was one thing, starving another. And there was Rod and Liam to think of. Last night Liam had cooked up some gross-looking fish finger sandwich, and as for Rod . . . her thoughts went back to that polystyrene container with the fatty smell from Planet Kebab. And later, her sneaking into the kitchen and stuffing her face with the leftover fries, undoing all the pain and good work of the day. No matter how tight her tops were getting, they all needed a good meal.

She began collating ingredients for an Angela Hartnett midweek supper – one of Rod's favourites, venison and carrot stew. Wholesome and not really fattening, not if she used low-fat crème fraiche rather than cream. Her tired mind found huge solace in the term 'midweek supper'; there was something infinitely stable and reassuring about the words, something that cocked a definite snook at concepts like Internet fraud and murder. *Murder.* The word brought her up with a slight shock – not so much the word itself but her casual mental usage of it, as offhand and deliberate as she'd once used words like 'playdough' and 'ring binder'.

She went to the vegetable basket. No carrots. Or rather three wizened specimens coated in green fur. How had that happened? Utterly deflated she sank down again, her gaze roaming to the barista machine and past the machine to that opened bottle of Merlot on the side by the door.

Liam's jacket was hanging on the peg.

Surely Thursday wasn't one of his study afternoons? But there was his bag dumped on the flags by the grandfather clock; there were his new trainers in the jumble of family footwear. And, as if in response to her train of thoughts, Larson whined reproachfully from where he was curled up in his basket with a decidedly banished look on his face. More often than not he was to be found in Liam's room, stretched out on the broad windowsill, happily oblivious to the various thuddings emanating from his music centre. That was something else. No music. Was he in? He wasn't due back from school for another three hours if it wasn't one of his study days. Come to think about it, she was sure it was a cross-country night. Was he ill? No, she'd have heard surely. Getting her phone out she checked his status on his Facebook page – yes, there it was – cross-country, with a gloomy emoticon.

From upstairs there was a creak of floorboards and simultaneously the words formed as if in indelible Comic Sans font above Pat's head: Celtic poet. Hard on the heels of the words flashed a series of images from the past twelve hours, singing Abba in the bathroom, the splash of Rod's Aramis, a cheerful cry of 'Good morning, Thirsk' as he had sauntered downstairs that morning, images that had not properly registered until now because of her fussing about a pulled muscle and some far-fetched nonsense about phone fraud and people going round tampering with tablets.

As a mother there were some things Pat definitely wanted to know about: if a sacrifice of a hard-won university place and a trailer park in Boroughbridge were on the cards, she did not want these things coming out of the blue. Equally there were some things she had no wish to see whatsoever. Whenever there were mice in the house she'd acquired the habit of making a lot of noise before coming downstairs or entering a room to avoid seeing that unnerving blur of grey arrowing across the stone flags. Similarly, she now turned the radio on very loud, clashed a few pans on the Aga, all the time singing a Madonna song. When she considered she'd made enough noise to interruptus the most oblivious of coitus, she went up upstairs to Liam's room.

She felt a relief that left her slightly breathless (also feeling slightly foolish . . . singing like that!) to see it wasn't any tattooed Celtic poet but new-friend-Luke sprawled on the floor in a *Les Misérables* T-shirt, back against Liam's bed, a textbook in his hand whilst Liam himself typed furiously, his face an intense frown.

The window was open, letting in a muddy smell from the damp fields, mingling with scent of laundered linen Febreze. If they'd been attempting to light their farts or smoking or even experimenting with pot (ah, the dear, dead 1980s) then so what? There were worse things.

'Would you like some tea or coffee, lads?' she said, her voice bright with relief at the receding vision of the trailer park. Liam shook his head without looking at her; Luke said no thanks. And there was something in the way he said those words Pat instinctively didn't like, something she couldn't quite put her finger on, something that felt almost in the nature of a rebuff.

'I thought you said you were going to aquarobics?' Liam's voice sounded accusing.

'Something came up.' Unconsciously her hand stole into her pocket, feeling for the paper with the Dodgy Builder's number written on it. 'Anyway, I thought you were doing cross-country.'

'Why would you think that, Mother Mine?' He didn't even look up but continued typing.

'It said on your Facebook page.'

'Just because it's on Facebook it doesn't mean it's set in stone.' Liam had that weary, patient tone, a sure sign he wasn't happy about something.

'Everything going okay?' she said.

Liam didn't answer and again in Luke's oh so polite acknowledgement there was something, some . . . sharpness of tone. Sharp. It was a good word all round to describe Luke: angular features, face all lines, that pointy nose set between these dark brown, almost black eyes . . . eyes that shot and darted away rather than held a gaze, a hint of a half-smile playing on his lips. 'You're welcome to stay for supper, Luke,' she said, wanting her prickly feeling about him to be dispelled by a smile, an acknowledgement. But even as she spoke, she sensed Liam tense. Was it the word 'supper' he often teased her about? 'It's not much, just a casserole.'

'Luke's vegan, Mum,' said Liam flatly, in tones that made her feel as if she'd just tried to shove a burger in the boy's mouth.

'I could do some pasta,' she said lamely. Was pasta vegan?

'Actually I'll need to be moving when we've finished this.' Luke's words were so nakedly dismissive her feelings hardened into dislike.

This shocked her; it was a point of pride on her part that she liked Liam's friends and they liked her. 'She's not like other mums' was the comment she'd so often heard when driving teenage lads to cricket or collecting them in various states of inebriation from discos. Obviously Liam wanted her to go, but something made her stay put, some feeling she couldn't quite fathom . . . For some reason she did not like to leave her son alone with this boy. She remembered the number she'd copied down.

'If you wanted to track down a crook . . .' They both looked at her. She felt her voice falter in the face of those twin stares. 'Well a fraudster . . . someone ringing people up . . . and you had his phone number, could you do a search thing on the Internet?'

Was that a muffled laugh from Luke?

'What sort of search thing?' Liam's tone was simultaneously patient and scathing.

'You mean Google?' Now Luke's tone was oh so polite but Pat didn't miss the glance he shot at Liam.

'Isn't there a search thing you can do on the Internet?' Her Internet experience was M&S sales, flights to Malaga and finding Fleetwood Mac on YouTube. 'Where you put in some phone numbers . . . ?'

'I think she means Fetch,' said Luke. Again so deliberately polite.

'Oh right.' Liam put out a hand without even looking from the screen and Pat produced the choral society flyer from her pocket. Liam looked at the yellow paper with an incredulous expression that made her want to clatter him.

'On the back,' she said. 'Written in pen.'

'Is that all?' Again that patience. 'I need more than one number.'

'I thought you just typed it in.' She hated the defensive tone in her voice.

'Mother, it's a multi-phase search algorithm . . . the key word being *multi*. One is not multi.'

'I thought you could do it with any number.'

'Well you can't.' He turned away, the audience definitely over and there was something so dismissive about his tone. Pat felt her cheeks burning.

There was a time not so long ago if he'd turned away from her, spoken to her in that tone of voice, she'd have fired a combination of threats, punishments and maybe a quick clatter on the backside. When had that moment passed?

She didn't go downstairs; instead she went into her bedroom and sat on the bed feeling old, fat and frumpy. Her body was packing up, she'd run out of carrots and even Luke's friends didn't like her any more. Suddenly she sprung up (ow!) and flung open her wardrobe, grabbing tops and skirts and sweaters: the pinks, the blues, the oranges, the purples, the daring, the cheerful, the autumnal all piling up on the floor. Just who was she trying to kid? She was a naïve frumpy fifty-something tolerated by her son and her son's friends and she should stop dressing like she was twenty – no thirty! – years younger. The sage green top hit the top of the pile; all that was left in the wardrobe were a series of sober blues, greys and greens elasticated and X large. As she bundled up the clothes into the charity bag, a pink shoe fell to the floor.

Pink. What did that make her think of? A sudden image of KellyAnne's Facebook page, her smiling from a Portuguese swimming pool, holding a lurid pink-coloured cocktail.

Hard on the image came Liam's words: *Just because it's on Facebook it doesn't mean it's set in stone.*

CHAPTER NINETEEN

Cleaning is done under false pretences, relief is short-lived and the significance of coffee cups is considered.

Liz sat awkwardly on the uncomfortable straight-backed chair, the one she normally put folded clothes on as she did the ironing. In her hand was *Broken Biscuits*; she'd been trying to read the same paragraph (something about drugs hidden in a hostess trolley) three times now but had barely taken in a word. Her head was cocked, listening for sounds – the hum of the hoover, the hiss of polish, the no-nonsense vibration of surfaces being thoroughly dusted – or rather the absence of those sounds. It'd been quiet now for some ten minutes, which could surely only mean one thing.

Sure enough the living room door opened and in came Paula, in her trademark pink housecoat bearing a tray of two cups of coffee and two caramel wafers. 'I've done downstairs,' she announced, 'so I thought I'd make us coffee.'

'How lovely,' said Liz. She put her book down and braced herself; the time had come for the task she'd set herself.

Paula passed her a cup and a caramel wafer. 'I hope you don't mind,' she said, 'I've been in your biscuit tin.'

Liz, who knew it mattered not one jot whether she minded or not, merely smiled. 'Sit down,' she said. 'Have a breather.'

In fact Paula already had sat down, on the sofa in exactly the spot Liz craved herself. 'How's the back?' she asked.

Liz could feel herself blushing. 'You know,' she said vaguely. 'Touch and go. I'm treading carefully.' Actually there was nothing whatsoever wrong with her back, but she felt safe in the knowledge this thought would not have occurred to Paula. 'Like I said, I could feel a twinge in the garden coming on,' she said, crossing her fingers. 'And I thought "uh-oh". I daren't risk the hoover.'

'When my back goes, it *goes*,' said Paula, unwrapping her biscuit. 'I say to our Rocky, "Rocky, it's Gone." I need the heat pads bringing over and you need to tell Reuben and Cesca it's Netflix and best behaviour.'

Liz shifted somewhat guiltily in her chair. She was sure the Almighty must have some sort of thunderbolt in store for her, for her deception – not to mention Derek if he should find out – but then she reminded herself it had been Paula who rang her. 'Our Rocky says you were looking for me,' she had said almost accusingly down the phone.

Liz had been momentarily at a loss. The worries and questions about intruders and keys and dodgy builders that had been playing and replaying in her mind refused to form into words. Plus she'd remembered the words of that old insurance advert – 'we won't make a drama out of a crisis' – and the various ways over the years in which Paula had done just that. So it had seemed simplest and quickest and indeed most natural to ask Paula to do what she did best – clean, as she'd done once or twice in the past when Liz had been laid low by her back.

Which was why Liz was sitting in the most uncomfortable chair in the house feeling largely guilty.

Largely, not wholly. There was an equally prominent part of Liz's mind that desperately wanted answers from Paula, despite Thelma having spoken with Dusty Webster. Exactly what answers she wasn't sure. Come to think about it, she wasn't even very sure of the questions – but something that would make her sit up with and think 'aha!' Something to quieten Pat and her wild speculations. Something that would enable her to knock on the head their excursion to Pals of Pinot the following night.

And anyway, she told herself, Paula – having lost the income from Topsy's – would probably welcome the money.

She had considered messing the house up in some way but hadn't been able to think of any plausible way of doing this. There was no point in untidying things when Paula didn't know where anything went and Liz couldn't think of any way to make things dirty. She'd briefly considered spilling talc, but spilt talc just looked like spilt talc and anyway why would she be spilling Lily of the Valley talcum powder in her downstairs rooms?

'I see you got your royal invitation.' Paula's huffy voice broke into her thoughts. She was gesturing at the silver, grey and white card on the mantelpiece, which invited people to celebrate the life of Regina Joy at Baldersby St James Church, and, afterwards, the Bay Horse, Rainton, the following Thursday.

'Have you heard anything from KellyAnne?' asked Liz.

'I have not.' The emphasis on the words implied she neither wanted nor cared to.

'I guess she'll have a lot on with organizing the funeral,' said Liz.

'If she'd not gone swanning off to the Algarve, there wouldn't need to be no funeral.' Paula heaped sugar in her coffee. 'If only she'd said something, I'd have come over, I'd have brought our Reuben and Cesca if I'd had to.' Having seen Reuben and Cesca making short work of Reindeer Land at the garden centre last Christmas, Liz could understand why KellyAnne had possibly forgone this option. Or maybe she'd not wanted to incur one of Paula's snorts of disapproval by saying she'd gone? Or maybe she genuinely felt it was okay to leave her mother alone?

'Anyway,' said Paula, warming to her theme, 'what good does it do, telling someone what tablets to take if they're poorly like Mrs Joy was? Our Rocky was saying you could say to someone "take the small blue tablet" – but what if they don't know what the heck "blue" is any more?'

That was a thought. Topsy lacking the ability to tell which tablet was which. Liz hadn't thought of that. She remembered the careful way she'd counted them out of the Dossette box; if she'd dropped them the chances were she wouldn't have been able to tell them apart. That was something to share with Thelma and Pat. But not quite enough to call a halt to Pals of Pinot sadly. What else could she ask? She could start with Ness.

'I hear from Thelma that KellyAnne's cleared the house,' she said.

Paula looked grim. 'And cleared away two nearly full cans of my best polish with it.'

'I understand she's putting it up for rent through that friend of hers, that Ness.'

'Has she?' said Paula darkly.

'I understand she runs some sort of property rental business.'

'Property.' Paula managed to make it sound one step up from prostitution. 'In my day property were something you lived in, not swanned around waving a laptop at.'

'I understand she's been a good friend to KellyAnne. She said how she used to sit with Topsy from time to time. Keep an eye on her.'

'There's keeping an eye on someone and keeping an eye on someone.'

Liz recognized this particular tone of old; it meant some revelation – often sordid – was forthcoming. 'Oh?' she said.

Paula dropped her voice. 'All I'm saying was Mrs Joy would be sleeping a bit too heavily whenever Milady Ness had been "looking after" her.'

'You mean she drugged her?'

'I'm saying nothing.' Paula righteously pursed up her mouth as if disowning any sort of gossip. 'Don't get me wrong, it's something I was tempted to do more than once with Mother. By the

136

end I only had to walk in the room and she'd begin wailing and rocking back and forth.' She shook her head. 'I tell you something, Liz, when my time comes I'm not going through any of that. I say to our Rocky: "Give me some tablets, sit me in my favourite chair, put *Yorkshire Vet* on and let me drift off."' Another shake of the head. 'I'll never forget how it was with Mother.'

Having lived through the demise of Paula's mother at the time, Liz had no wish to do so again. Besides, she had her mental list of Topsy-related worries to work through before Paula made a start on the bathroom. 'KellyAnne was saying they'd had all sorts of trouble with salesmen and such. Not just the fraudster, but others.'

'I'm surprised she noticed, that one,' said Paula. 'Full of herself and her doings, never time to notice anything else in the world.'

'Were there any more calls?'

Paula shook her head. 'The bank only rang that one time when I was there,' she said.

'I mean did anyone else ring, wanting to talk to her?'

Again a shake of the head. 'The only person as ever rang – apart from Milady KellyAnne – were our Rocky; he knew I'd not hear my mobile if the vac was switched on.'

So much for Thelma's idea of people ringing. She tried another tack.

'There was this builder chappy when I was there. Reckoning he was owed money.'

'Shifty-looking so-and-so in a black van?' Paula looked grim.

'That's him.' Liz wondered how to make a reference to the resemblance to Mr Bettridge but decided against it; she could just imagine the tale Paula could make from such a remark.

'Seven hundred pounds he wanted for knocking down a wall!'

'That sounds a lot.'

'Especially when there was nothing wrong with it in the first place.'

'Oh?'

'Not according to our Rocky. Nothing wrong with it at all. And a right old mess he made. It was one of my days when he poled up asking for his money. I said, "Who on earth asked you to knock down that wall?" He only reckoned on it'd being Gordon who contacted him. "Really?" I said. "How? Séance?"'

'Did he get nasty?'

'Not so much nasty as mardy. Bottom lip went out, just like our Reuben. Right little weasel he was. If he'd come again he'd have felt my boot up his backside.'

Liz sipped her coffee (just how she liked it) and reviewed her list. There were a few things to worry about: Ness possibly drugging Topsy, the builder asking for money. But none of these seemed likely to lead to someone coming in and tampering with tablets. Who else was there she needed to ask about?

Paula meanwhile was on something of a roll.

'And then there was all that junk mail. The times Mrs Joy would say to me, all excited like, "Paula, I've won big money!" Disgusting.' Paula shook her head. 'I used to put it all straight in the recycling if I got to it first. With Mother, it was the first sign she was going off – answering junk mail and cold calls. I had to have a block put on the phone and the mail redirected to me.'

Of course! thought Liz. *Flat-Pack Youth.*

'Did you ever see a young man there?' she said. 'Bit of a techie? Brown eyes?'

'Him.' The words were said with a vicious emphasis that made Liz jump.

'As you know, I'm not one for talking about people.' A stock phrase of Paula's, usually followed up by a particularly stinging piece of character assassination. 'But I know his sort. Looked me full in the eyes he did. I thought, don't you try that big-eye routine with me, young man. I'm old enough to be your grandma.' She gave a grim sniff.

'Did he ever come round on his own?'

'Not that I ever saw. Just with that Ness. Once to measure up the house and once something to do with fixing the phone.'

So that was Ness, the Dodgy Builder and Flat-Pack Youth. That just left the mysterious figure. She hadn't much time; she could see Paula had finished her coffee.

'Thelma spoke to Dusty Webster about what she'd seen, someone hanging round the place.'

'She was walking the dog and reckoned someone was there,' said Paula.

'So you don't think they could have had anything to do with it?'

'To do with what?' Paula looked blank.

'Topsy muddling her tablets.'

The blank look remained. 'How can someone hanging round the house have anything to do with Mrs Joy mixing up her tablets?'

'I know it sounds far-fetched,' said Liz apologetically. 'But you hear such things.'

'It was gone seven when Dusty Webster went past,' said Paula. 'Mrs Joy always took her tablets at teatime.'

Liz was aware of a slow flush of relief starting somewhere in her chest and spreading up to her cheeks.

'Of course,' she said. '*Of course.*'

'Mrs Joy got stuff muddled,' said Paula patiently. 'Just like Mother.'

Liz nodded; it was exactly the bit of common sense she needed to hear. By the time the person was hanging around outside, Topsy had already taken her tablets. She relaxed and for a moment it was just like the old days when she'd drop into Paula's boiler house for a coffee first thing on her way to the classroom to hear the all latest goings-on.

'Anyway.' Paula stood up. 'This won't get the bathrooms done.'

'So did your Rocky find a place for his sunbed?' asked Liz.

Paula shook her head. 'That Wayne,' she said. 'Getting his

knickers in a knot. It's only till Rocky gets a new place.' She looked exasperated and Liz reflected that Paula's maxim – Rocky could do no wrong – was unchanged by the passing of the years. She remembered the Great Top Trumps scandal and Paula's insistence that Rocky only did what he did because he was told to.

'Right, back to it.' Paula picked up the tray. 'Now you be watching that back of yours, lady.' She paused in the doorway. 'It is good to talk to someone,' she said.

'I was thinking you must be missing going to Topsy's,' said Liz.

'You do get sick of the sound of your own voice.' Paula sighed. 'I was thinking: I reckon that explains all that with Mrs Joy and the cups.'

'Cups?' said Liz.

Paula smiled sadly. 'Two of them – brown cup and saucers. On the draining board they'd be, when I went round of a morning.'

'Two cups?'

'It was KellyAnne as first pointed it out – not that she was a great one for noticing anything to do in the cleaning department. It was a few weeks back and she said. "There's been cups left out, Paula . . ." I thought nothing about it, but over the next few weeks or so when I'd go round in the morning, there they'd be on the draining board – two of them, brown cups and saucers. I'd say, "Have you been having people round again, lady?"' Paula smiled fondly.

'For a neighbour maybe? Or a friend from her lunch club?' suggested Liz.

'There was never anyone coming in that I could tell.' Paula shook her head. 'No, like I say, I think she did it herself. She wanted people to come round, so she'd get cups out for them, and even though no one came she'd wash them up afterwards. What else could it be?'

'I don't know,' said Liz, not knowing but thinking of several worrying possibilities.

'There were some that morning we found her. All set out on the draining board. I remember thinking "You poor love". Put them away myself I did. Anyway.' She stood up. 'I can't stand here gassing.' She took the tray out leaving Liz sitting just as uncomfortably as before, only this time it was nothing to do with the chair.

CHAPTER TWENTY

Pat seeks to impress her friends and help is offered to find dreams.

About the same time Liz and Paula were having coffee, Pat was crossing the cobbles of the marketplace feeling there was something immeasurably steadying about carrying a hefty bag full of vegetables. It was hard to feel too hung up about dieting (not 'dieting', eating smart as the Yummies not Tummies website said) when you had the ingredients for at least five healthy recipes that wouldn't have you sneaking handfuls of cold fries later on. Tonight she was trying the Mushroom and Broccoli Cheat Stroganoff (105 calories a serving); she just needed to pick up some more diet crème fraiche and one-cal spray and she was all set.

Not that she was feeling totally one hundred per cent. The hip still nagged, the head was still muzzy and of course there were still the worries about Liam and whatever was going on with the Celtic poet. She wasn't exactly sure what the latest developments were but he'd gone very quiet again, with no singing of any description, no sarky comments and no one (with the exception of Larson) allowed in his room.

And of course there was all that with her friends. She knew she'd been off with them yesterday, and felt as she always did after one of her what Rod termed 'Snippy Dos'. She was a bit embarrassed at her behaviour, but underneath there was the core of something unresolved. As she queued in the Polish deli for the crème fraîche she felt could imagine the pair of them, laughing at her hare-brained speculating. If only she had something really solid and cracking to tell them when they met tomorrow at Pals of Pinot. Something to elicit a 'Well done, Pat.' Emerging from the store, she cast her eyes round the market-place for inspiration. She saw the Royal York Bank and briefly considered going in, but then the plan was for them to see Mandy Pinder-as-was tomorrow. And besides, what could she ask her in a crowded bank? Then there was the Bettridge-type builder, but she could hardly ring him. Who else? Flat-Pack Youth, Ness . . . *Ness* . . .

Hadn't Thelma said something about her office being in Thirsk? A quick chat with her might give her something to tell them tomorrow night that would make them sit up and listen.

A scan of her phone told her what she needed to know: Green Grass Properties, just off the marketplace on Millgate. How handy was that?

The windows of Green Grass Properties promised much. The various property cards were set against the backdrop of two large local vistas: Fountains Abbey in the misty dawn and a moor-scape on a glorious summer's day, complete with vibrant butterflies and buttercups. *Come home to Yorkshire,* sang a caption. The problem, as far as Pat could see, was where you'd come home to. The wrong side of Northallerton. That new faceless estate the other side of the racecourse. None of the properties looked much cop, except for Gortops. *This luxurious five-bed property with stunning views of the moors* was displayed proudly and incongruously in the midst of the two-bed terraces and estate rabbit hutches. On the door to the office was a tasteful ivory sign: *Open – to help you find your dreams!* Pat pushed the door and found a flight of carpeted stairs and a smell of something vanilla-y.

Ness was sat at her desk – her very swish desk – looking very much as Pat had imagined from her friend's descriptions. The perm, tick; the suit, tick. *Not a good look,* Pat thought (just as her friends predicted she would). Pat was wearing her black elasticated skirt, the one normally reserved for walking Larson. This was only until she could shed a pound or two. Yes, Ness was very much as described, only her graphically described laugh was missing. She looked as if Pat wasn't who she'd wanted to see coming through the door. However, quickly enough, a professional smile was slapped on and she said pleasantly enough: 'Can I help you?'

'I was just looking to get ideas,' said Pat. Like all primary school teachers she was rather good at thinking on her feet. 'My eldest finishes uni this summer; he seems to think he can just move back in. Me and his father have other ideas.'

Then there was the laugh, just as described. 'My two are at the Barbie doll stage,' said Ness, 'but when the time comes – well, let's just say it's handy having one's own rental business.' She gestured with a careless but proud hand to the dove-grey carpet tiles, the track lighting, pristine office furniture, cared-for plants and further vibrant Yorkshire landscapes. The only thing that could be said to let the place down were the rental properties themselves.

'I heard about you from my friends,' said Pat. 'Liz and Thelma? Friends of KellyAnne.'

'Oh bless!' Another peal of laughter, accompanied by a wide smile. 'Well you've come to the right place. There's some classy stuff out there.'

'I couldn't help wonder,' asked Pat. 'Why "Green Grass" agency?'

Ness smiled archly. Obviously Pat had done the right thing in asking. 'The Green Green Grass of home,' she sang, doing a sort of hand jive with two pointed fingers. 'It was my idea.' She looked pleased at her cleverness.

At that moment the phone rang and with a lunge that was almost frantic, Ness scooped up the receiver. 'Hello?' she said, something high and expectant in her voice, something that was checked when she said, 'Oh, hello' in flat, disappointed tones.

As the conversation on the phone unfolded (something about who was to go to Aldi), she smiled at Pat and pushed a contact form and folder of properties across the desk to her. Having filled in the form, Pat cast her eyes over the various properties on offer with her critical builder's wife's eye. She didn't like the look of the flashing on the Dowber Way one, and the guttering on Bank View in Sutton looked none too clever. Yes, it was as she thought. With the exception of Gortops, none of these were much cop.

Eventually Ness replaced the receiver.

'Sorry.' She laughed. 'Just the fiasco.'

Pat looked at her blankly. 'My other half.' Again Ness laughed. 'Fiasco – fiancée. Don't ask me which one he is. Because I don't know! Anyway.' She rapped the folder with hard purple nails. 'Seen anything that grabs the attention?'

'There's some fabulous places,' lied Pat. 'As I said, I'm just getting a few ideas at present.'

'It's a busy old time,' said Ness. 'Busy busy busy. They come flying in one day and flying out the next.' Pat could see that at least three of the properties in the folder had been on the books for some five months but naturally said nothing.

Anyway, enough of this, she thought. *To business.*

'So you know KellyAnne of course,' she said, looking through the folder.

'Bless her heart, yes.' Another laugh.

'Were you at school with her then?'

'Oh no! We only met last year, on a friend's hen do. Girls Unleashed and all that!'

Pat smiled; she always found it faintly depressing when women, especially women over forty, described themselves as 'girls'. 'I worked with Topsy of course,' she said.

145

Ness composed her face into something grave and reflective. 'You heard about what happened . . .' She made a discreet shape with her mouth, as if death were something shameful.

'I did. Of course, we worked together for a long time.'

'Awwww.' This time the laugh was more muted, almost sympathetic.

'I only saw her a fortnight or so before, but she did seem quite muddled.'

'Bless her heart, I'd go and sit with her sometimes, give KellyAnne a break, poor love . . .'

'That could have its moments I imagine.'

'She was asleep most of the time,' said Ness easily. 'It was later on at night when most of the fun and games happened.'

'So I gather. Wandering about, Thelma said.'

'At the bus stop, round the lanes. One time halfway across the fields, poor love. KellyAnne told me some nights she had to lock her in just to make sure she didn't go off on walkies.'

'And of course there was all that business with her mixing the tablets.'

Ness shook her head gravely. 'Not good.'

'Liz told me how she saw her muddling them up.'

'I kept all the way out of that,' said Ness decisively. 'That was all KellyAnne's department.'

Pat was wondering how to bring up the subject of hotels in the Algarve when footsteps sounded on the stairs. Instantly Ness was on the alert, rather like Larson when she opened his treats box. Into the office came a young man in a sharp suit; judging by the smell of shower gel and his wet hair he'd only recently showered. On his face was a slightly helpless expression; Pat realized with surprise it was a face she recognized.

'Well well well.' Ness almost succeeded in sounding arch and casual. 'The wanderer returns. Good evening, sir.'

But the young man was looking at Pat with frowning recognition on his face.

A large penny dropped with a very loud clang in Pat's mind. Not Lorry at all!

'It's Laurence isn't it?' Pat smiled.

'Lloret,' corrected Ness.

'You play cricket for Rievaulx XI with my son Liam. Liam Taylor.'

'Hi, Mrs Taylor, how's it going?' Lloret shot her a smile that rated high on the dazzling scale; Pat suddenly saw how long his eyelashes were against his warm brown eyes.

'I didn't know you worked here,' said Pat.

'When he's not playing cricket he's supposed to be my assistant and webmeister, which is why he's meant to be going out to view a property near Melmerby.' There was a noticeable edge to Ness's voice.

'Yeah, I'm sorry.' Lloret shrugged, a sort of bewildered, helpless shrug. 'I'm running late.'

'Did you not think of getting in touch?'

He shrugged again. 'My phone imploded. I'll go now.'

Pat felt sorry for the lad; he was obviously in some sort of bother. 'My friend Liz said she met you at Topsy's house,' she said. The change in Lloret's expression from unease to shock was striking; his eyes strayed to the stairs as if contemplating a quick exit. But before Pat had a chance to react, Ness cut in.

'Anyway,' she said. 'If you maybe want to have a think and come back nearer the time?' Pat looked blankly at her. 'Houses for your son?' Now the folder was withdrawn and there was a distinct note of dismissal in the voice. Pat stood up. There didn't seem to be much more she could learn and besides, her bladder was telling her she had an increasingly limited window in which to get home.

Getting in the car with the bag of vegetables she wondered exactly what she'd learnt. Nothing that would have much of an impact on the other two, particularly if they'd been off having their own adventures again. The only thing was the identity of

Flat-Pack Lloret: not Ness's son but her assistant. And apparently a rather unreliable assistant at that. But that was hardly worth a 'Well done, Pat.'

Driving down Millgate she remembered that sudden, startled look. She cast an eye over Green Grass Properties and noticed that the premises were now closed. (But looking forward to helping you find your dreams later!)

CHAPTER TWENTY-ONE

Roof tiles are checked and doubts are cast about wiring plus there's an incident with a cloakroom door.

Ripon, the following morning: a grey but busy Thursday, the cathedral bells briskly sounding the call for midweek prayer over the rooftops, the marketplace and the jumble of stern Victorian terraces near the college. Here ranks of wheelie bins stood at various angles by the side of the avenues and crescents; somewhere, the mechanical peeping of a reversing bin lorry punctuated the rhythmic clanging. The faded black van sidled to a stop in front of 47 College Gardens, knocking one bin and nudging another. The man driving was frowning with a helpless air, simultaneously manoeuvring the wheel, finishing a can of Red Bull and glancing at an open Filofax that was perched on the dusty dashboard. With his combed, thinning hair and ironed polo shirt his watery apologetic smile didn't merit a second glance from the dog walker who passed him as he got out of the van; if, however, they'd seen the sudden hardening of features into the appraising sweep he gave the facade of number 47 they might have thought again.

By the time the man was listening to the clanging door chimes fading away and admiring the stained-glass window in the door, the glance had been buried and replaced with the watery open smile, the Filofax tucked under one arm like the Bible of a door-to-door missionary.

The person who opened the door seemed awkwardly at odds with the neat garden and glimpses of an equally neat hallway within; the man got an impression of fussy flapping clothes, blacks and purples, cuffs and pockets, topped by a dated black and purple shawl that gave off a distinct aroma of the charity shop. Her helmet of greying hair was badly in need of a brush and overall she gave off a sense of movement – fluttering hands, shuffling feet, nervous glances. Had the words 'poor old dear' been suspended above her head they would not have been out of place. The only thing that was steady were the eyes, surprisingly steady eyes; magnified behind large thick glasses, they regarded the man as he smiled at her.

'Mrs Temple? Oliver Harney – builder. You rang me.' The man felt a sense of relief; his hunch had been right – he had a strict rule that only he initiated contact with people, but this dithering old dear, plus the glimpse of antiques in the hall behind her, proved his instincts to make an exception had been bang on.

'Oh yes, of course.' She looked vaguely but nervously over one shoulder.

'You rang about your guttering.'

'Yes, do come in.' She appeared to come to a decision and turned away, colliding with the dark wood coat stand.

'Careful there.'

'I'm always doing that. There's so much clutter.'

He would hardly describe the hall as cluttered, and the furniture was well looked after, the dark wood exuding a smell of polish – real polish he noted approvingly, not those sprays you got. A solemnly ticking grandfather clock surveyed all. Old, well preserved. Oh yes, he'd definitely been right.

'You know how it is,' said Mrs Temple, 'you buy one thing and then you buy another, and then there's things you inherit and then before you know where you are, you're cluttered up to the eyeballs.'

She seemed to be hovering, unfocused, probably losing it a bit, poor love. 'You said about your guttering?'

'Yes.' She seemed relieved. 'The back guttering. Since my husband passed away . . .' (ah – so she was on her own!). 'Well, he always took care of things like that.' She led the way through to an equally neat kitchen. An Aga, a real one, not one of those cookers got up to look like one. Classy but a bit old-fashioned for him. He was currently hankering after one of those steel and glass things you got in those Scandi-noir thrillers.

'Can I just ask . . .' he forced his tone to be deliberately casual, '. . . how you got my number?'

'I really can't quite remember.' Mrs Temple looked distressed. 'From someone that I do know . . . I can't quite remember who – Jean at church? She had some work done a while back – but was that painting?' She turned with a perplexed frown and suddenly seemed to notice where she was. The sight of the kettle seemed to steady her. 'Coffee?'

Again that smile coupled with a direct stare that transformed his rather weak-looking face into something more trustworthy, a look that had stood him in good stead so many times. 'I'd love one.'

The name Jean didn't ring a bell, but then the old dear didn't seem to know herself. It was proper coffee too, from a cafetiere. Though, truth be told, he preferred instant, didn't like the brown residue you got at the bottom. She was relaxing a bit more now, the talk coming out in a fluting stream. He had long noticed how people, older people, relaxed over coffee, telling you things about themselves. And that was when you could do business. He learnt Mrs Temple was fairly recently widowed after forty-two years of marriage, had no children (good) but supportive friends at church, and was blessed in having enough money to get by with a modicum of comfort. (Modicum. He made a discreet note in his Filofax to look the word up.)

In return he told Mrs Temple about himself. This time he

talked about the wife who worked all the hours God sent, as bright and innovative (another recently looked up word) as they came, about Phoebe his three-year-old daughter who was a proper Daddy's girl and every bit as bright as her mother, plus a new son (Carter) who was shaping after him in every way, including the way he refused to sleep through at night. A real night owl. That previous night he could only have slept two hours. At most. Emboldened by the way Mrs Temple was smiling in a distinctly misty-eyed way over the photos on his phone he said, 'I do a bit of furniture sales too.'

Without asking she poured him out another coffee. He didn't really want it, especially after the Red Bull but he was on a bit of a roll. 'You were saying about the stuff in your hall. I know what it's like – downsizing, finding it hard to get shot of stuff.' She looked uncertain but not dismissive. 'Think about it,' he said. 'If there's stuff you want shot of . . .' His words implied he was doing her something of a favour. He slugged back the last of the coffee (those brown bits!) and stood up. 'Right,' he said. 'Let the dog see the rabbit.'

The garden was – again – immaculate. (It didn't seem quite right, but the old dear obviously got someone in from her church.) Between old brick walls was an arrangement of pots, beds, trellises and benches; somewhere, the tinkle of a fountain (not such a comfortable sound after all that coffee).

'Here,' said Mrs Temple. She stopped by the single-storey back wall of the kitchen where the paving slabs were spattered with damp. She stared vaguely and nervously upwards.

'Ah.' His tone was significant. He fetched a ladder from the shed (no padlock, nice set of tools) and climbed up. 'Ah,' he said again. 'Right. You need a new length of guttering. It's shot.'

'It can be fixed?'

'No problem. Or rather that's not the problem. Have you heard of tile slippage?'

Mrs Temple hadn't. Tile slippage, he explained (using the

Filofax as a demonstration tile), caused leaks and then the guttering to bend and, as in this case, come apart. After all, as he said, you yourself would have a bit of slipping and sliding after a hundred years of North Yorkshire rainfall. To support his story he showed her a fragment of tile, which looked just like a fragment of tile, but the reverent way he held it meant that this was a whole lot more than just a bit of broken tile. The only thing to do really – and he was being honest here – the only thing that would really sort it was to take the whole lot off and start again. You could just replace a bit – but then three, four years down the line you'd be back to square one.

Mrs Temple had been punctuating his recital with soft chirps of dismay; now she said with the air of someone bracing themselves for bad news: 'How much?'

'Some rip-off merchants would charge seven to eight grand.' He wondered briefly if he'd been too blunt. Mrs Temple clasped the drainpipe and looked as though she may well pass out. 'But me – I'm not about ripping people off. I reckon I could do you a really good job for two – maybe three grand.' She relaxed, or rather her body did. Her eyes remained still and watchful, almost as if they belonged to someone else.

'Thank you,' she said.

'You need time to think. Sleep on it. I'll call you in a day or two.'

'Thank you – you've been most kind.' The words rang with sincerity – so why then did he feel a bit uneasy, as though he'd missed something important? She led the way back into the hall. He stopped suddenly (as he always did) and looked at the skirting board.

'Can I ask you a question, Mrs Temple? When did you last have your wiring redone?'

She slapped a hand to her frowning forehead. 'I forget exactly, many years ago. Mother was still with us so that takes us back to the early Nineties . . .' He knelt down and tapped the skirting board.

'Interesting,' he said.

Another soft cry of dismay from Mrs Temple. 'We won't worry about that today,' he said, standing up and giving her a frank, honest smile. 'I wonder, have you a loo?'

The downstairs cloakroom had a framed piece of embroidery on the wall. *Delight yourself in the Lord and he will give you the desires of your heart.* He washed his hands using lavender soap. Real linen towels – nice. *Why* then this feeling of unease? The house? Mrs Temple? Now he came to think about it, he wasn't sure he would actually call back – he had plenty of work, plus a sure-fire way of finding as much as he needed. Replacing roof tiles was something he'd not actually done for a few years now, and it was bound to be a real clart. But then four grand – and money from the wiring on top of that . . . The image of the Scandinavian cooker hovered enticingly somewhere in front of the embroidered picture. He realized with something of a jolt that Courtney and the baby weren't actually figuring in the images, just himself in one of those black silk dressing gowns. He finished drying his hands and reached for the handle, which was – he noted approvingly – one of those ceramic jobbies.

The door wouldn't open.

His first thought, he was turning it the wrong way. Other thoughts tumbled rapidly into his mind – the bolt, the catch, pulling not pushing – but no, the door was stuck. Or locked? He rattled the handle.

'Hello?' No response. 'Mrs Temple? The door seems to be stuck?' He hit the panel; the noise and the violence of it slightly shocked him. 'Mrs Temple?' His heart was pounding, his palms slippy with sweat. After another few seconds, his mind poised in a rollercoaster car frozen above a chasm of various unpleasant possibilities . . .

The door clicked and opened, and there was Mrs Temple, peeping like a reversing lorry, hands fluttering, apologizing. She was *so* sorry, this door was always doing that – it had happened

154

to Jean from church – and she'd been out in the garden chasing a cat from the borders and never heard her. She was always saying someone should look at it – maybe he could?

He smiled and headed towards the door. Maybe he was just being daft, one fluttery old lady and a house full of very nice antiques.

'Your Filofax.' She waved it at him; he felt a surge of annoyance, he never normally let that out of his sight. Driving away the niggle persisted but he couldn't be bothered thinking it through and turned up the radio until he was nodding to the strains of Tees FM.

When she was sure the van had gone, Thelma went upstairs and divested herself of the black and the purple creations that all went straight back in the charity bag (worn by Mrs Bramson in *Night Must Fall*). Strictly speaking that was the property of the College Chaplain Players, but it wouldn't be needed for their next production (*Ole Mrs Jenks!* – a farce set in a Spanish hotel) and it would only attract the moths. She showered and spent a good five minutes brushing her hair back into its regular glossy bob. Even now her daring felt a bit like it belonged to someone else and it was important not to dwell on the adrenalin-fuelled smugness she was aware of; facts had needed to be learnt and now she had learnt them.

'Forgive me Lord,' she said into the mirror. 'Forgive my falsehood.' Truth be told the face that stared back at her didn't look very penitent. Since her conversation with Teddy and her trip to Rainton she had felt this overwhelming need to do something. And now she had. She thought of Mrs Temple. Had she overdone it? Those hand movements? The chattering? Still lit up by the adrenalin she continued brushing her hair, remembering Blanche Dubois in that college production of *A Streetcar Named Desire* . . . how many years ago? Too many. She'd been no one's first choice for the part but two weeks before the show the first Blanche had had a row with the director (splitting up with him in the process) and Thelma had been rapidly upgraded from second neighbour. The ruckus that ensued!

She remembered the words in that review in the *Ripon Gazette* – 'raw sexuality'. Not at all the thing for a second-year trainee infant teacher in 1971. Her tutor had advised her in no uncertain terms to focus on her teaching and Teddy, whom she had been seeing for some three months by this point (amiable dates and hand holding), had suddenly become very nervous, gaunt and staring, and ended up banging on her door at 3 a.m. one morning to propose marriage.

She brought herself back to the present with a mental shake; it never did to revisit the past too much. Nevertheless whilst printing out the photos she'd taken on her phone and looking up the areas codes, she permitted herself a small smile of remembrance.

CHAPTER TWENTY-TWO

Theories are aired at Pals of Pinot,
plus an upsetting scene is witnessed.

'What I think is this.' Liz took a decisive sip of her Wine of the Week. 'I think we should go to the police and tell them everything we know. Everything.' She set her glass down firmly and looked doubtfully round Pals of Pinot. She need not have worried about noisy crowds; looking round, there couldn't have been more than seven people in what had been the old post office. Gone were the scuffed black and white tiles, the battered lemon plaster walls and the high counter behind, which Nancy Hirst had ruled for so many years with brisk tyranny; in their place were bare wooden floors, splintery low tables and equally low stools and benches, none of which were suitable for Pat's hip (still murmuring about Zumba Insanity).

'At the end of the day, they are the police and they do know what they're doing.'

The other two exchanged discreet glances.

'If the police wouldn't go after the people who did Rod's garage and that was with CCTV evidence, they're hardly going to bother about details like brown cups on draining boards.' Pat took a distasteful sip from her sparkling mineral water and looked longingly at Liz's glass. Typical Liz, upstaging her with something as dramatic as the brown cups story, and then immediately taking the wind out of everyone's sails by saying they should leave it well alone. 'It's not much for them to go on,' she said.

'Maybe that's because there's nothing much to go on,' said Liz. She shivered slightly; it was rather cold in Pals of Pinot and she was fast realizing the top she'd chosen wasn't really suitable.

All three had given considerable thought about what to wear for their expedition; it wasn't as if this was any old night out. Liz, who had convinced herself the place would be hot, crowded and packed out with young people, wore the black sparkly jumper she'd worn to Derek's niece's twenty-first — thin enough to withstand the hottest room and sparkly in the acknowledgement of some sort of occasion. Thelma had viewed the evening in much the same way as she'd viewed the visit by Oliver Harney (or Tony Ransom, as she'd learnt from another business card tucked in the Filofax) and had chosen from her own wardrobe as carefully as she'd selected the costume for Mrs Temple: a smart but sober black jacket, a white blouse and a jaunty paisley scarf that gave a nod to the fact there was a wine bar as part of the proceedings. Pat, still in a bad place on the subject of clothes, had opted for what she termed 'her safe blue', a plain but smart outfit usually reserved for trips to the doctor's or Sunday lunch with Rod's parents.

'If there were two brown cups the chances were two people were drinking from them. Topsy said a few times about people coming over to the house,' Pat said with growing animation. 'It could be someone we know or someone we don't, gaining her confidence, taking her money — and then you know . . .'

Thelma was frowning slightly. As Pat had been speaking, something had suddenly come to her, something — some detail that didn't quite sit right. But the thought eluded her, floating at the back of her mind like a half-solved crossword clue. She took a sip from her elderflower and tonic and looked round the bar. No sign yet of Mandy Pinder-as-was. The only other customers were three girls rather glumly working their way through a bottle of white; Thelma thought she recognized one of them from the pharmacy at Morrisons. One of them was telling a rather indignant story. From time to time snatches of accounts about people Turning Round and Telling Them Straight floated across to where they were sitting. Just a quiet bar in a small northern town on a Tuesday night in late March.

Liz was looking stubborn in the face of Pat's energetic speculating. 'I just think we're getting in over our heads.' This expression was recognized by both the others as a sure sign of stress, applied in the past to a whole range of situations from a new combi-boiler to an overambitious harvest assembly.

'Unless you walk into the police station dragging the culprit behind you, the police are not going to be interested. End of,' said Pat.

'What's needed here—' Thelma used her best calm and decisive voice '—are details the police would be interested in.' It was a tone they both knew, the same tone that had brought them out to this rather chilly bar.

'Such as?' said Pat.

It was then Thelma told them about her 'little encounter' with Oliver Harney/Tony Ransom. They both listened, Liz in particular looking increasingly horrified.

'I'm not being funny,' she said, 'but weren't you . . . I mean wasn't it a bit of a risk? He could've turned nasty.'

'He was hardly going to cosh me over the head for dressing up and play-acting,' said Thelma. 'Anyway I had the rape alarm in my pocket and Maureen next door on standby.'

'It just all sounds a bit risky.' How Liz wished she had done what she'd planned: say what she'd said, and then headed straight back home. She could be watching *MasterChef* by now. It was knockout week.

'Like I say, we should leave all this to people who know what they're doing.'

'This Oliver Harney had been at Topsy's at least four times that we know of. Someone needed to talk to him to find out more,' said Thelma firmly.

'And did you?' asked Pat.

'A certain amount.'

'Such as?'

'Such as I suspect everything he was telling me was a pack of lies.'

Despite herself Liz was interested. 'What makes you say that?'

'He kept going on about his baby Carter keeping him awake most of the night. But no way did he have the look of a new dad who'd only had a few hours' sleep. Remember Connor Simick's dad?' They all smiled at the memory of the snores fluting above the Year Two recorders at that Christmas concert.

'If he lies about that it's not likely he's being truthful about much else. Plus he drinks coffee.'

'So do most people,' pointed out Pat.

'Cups on the draining board,' said Thelma. As she spoke she tensed. There it was again in her mind, that ghost of a detail that was eluding her.

At that moment Pat simultaneously kicked her, nudged Liz and made shushing noises with her mouth.

'Don't look,' she hissed as if their heads were likely to swivel 180 degrees while their eyes shot out on stalks.

Thelma turned her head slightly and saw two women entering the bar: a bonny black girl who was presumably Jolly Jo, the other Mandy Pinder-as-was.

'That jacket's Chanel,' said Pat in a conspiratorial undertone.

Both Thelma and Liz recognized her instantly. Over the years they had encountered many ex-pupils; some had been instantly recognizable, fuller-grown versions of their six-year-old selves, whilst others had been more indelibly overlain by the passage of age, haircuts, glasses, wrinkles and calories. Mandy fell into the former category. Her hair was scraped back much as it had been when she was a child in a way that still presented the same shape of face, her wide-eyed, slightly blank look (embellished with bright eyeshadow). But there was something else there, some quality that had not been there twenty years ago, a quality they both momentarily struggled to put into words. *Sad,* thought Liz; Thelma, put in mind of Celia Johnson in *Brief Encounter*, plumped for *haunted*.

If Mandy had seen her ex-teachers, she hadn't recognized them; she and Jo headed for a table in another corner of the wine bar, deep in conversation. 'What do we do?' said Liz, her body tense as if she was expected to leap into action and perform a rugby tackle.

'Nothing for now,' said Thelma calmly. 'In a moment one of us can go to the bar, see them and start a conversation.'

'Go on with what you were saying about chappy,' said Pat. 'Bettridge-type builder . . .'

'Oliver Harney,' said Liz.

'Or Tony Ransom,' said Thelma.

'The outhouse roof. Does it need doing?' asked Pat.

'Does it buffalo.' Thelma set her glass on the table and told them about the subsequent inspection of said roof by Ernest Crabtree. Ernest was a handyman employed by the college since the year dot who had been 'looking after' Teddy and Thelma since they'd moved into the decrepit shell that was 47 College Gardens all those years ago. With a care that bordered on the tyrannical, he'd overseen the renovation of the house, its roof, its wiring, its walls, its damp course. Whenever there'd been a skip outside number 47 you could be sure Ernest Crabtree wouldn't be far away. When Thelma had invited him round to check out Oliver's diagnosis, emotion had for once robbed him of words. He'd had great difficulty in grasping the fact that Thelma wasn't in fact finding an alternative handyman and when he'd been told about the 'slippage' and the quote for the roof he'd had to be sat down and offered a cup of tea. When Oliver's comments about the wiring had also been relayed, the tea had to be hastily upgraded with a slug of Teddy's good whisky and he wouldn't leave until Thelma had promised repeatedly and faithfully not to let Oliver Harney anywhere near the roof, guttering, wiring and anything else belonging to number 47.

'So he was making it up.'

'From start to finish. Like baby Carter. Plus, there's this.' From her handbag she produced sheets of paper, enlarged photos showing pages from a Filofax. Scribbled on each page were a series of numbers in blue, red and green pen, some underlined, some with stars, some with question marks, scribbled in a cramped, badly formed hand.

Pat looked at the sheets. If Liam wanted more numbers to do his search engine thingy, more numbers he would get. She folded a copy and put it in her handbag.

'Have you called any?' she asked.

'Two had no answer and one had been disconnected. Two were answered by older people. When I said I'd been recommended this builder, neither of them seemed to know what I was talking about.' Liz and Pat both sensed more was coming. 'And then I called a number in Masham. I initially reached a Mrs Walker, but very quickly the phone was taken by her daughter Jennifer. I said my spiel about this builder being recommended to me. She didn't recognize the name Oliver Harney but when I mentioned a rather battered black van, her blood pressure must have gone up several points. The reaction was, shall we say, explosive.'

'Why?' said Pat. 'What had he done?'

'That I shall find out when I see her next week. I don't know if anyone fancies a run out to Masham?'

She had on her calm, determined voice again. Liz and Pat looked at each other, neither wanting to commit themselves. Pat was feeling a resurgence of inferiority. Compared to pumping Paula for information and bearding a dodgy builder, a quick chat with Ness plus the establishment of the identity of Flat-Pack Lloret seemed like small potatoes.

For Liz this all seemed to be positively charging in the opposite direction from her plan to call a halt on what they were doing. 'Borrowing' a man's Filofax to take numbers from it! She remembered how possessively Oliver Harney/Tony Ransom had clutched the battered black case and a thought struck her.

'However did you get hold of the Filofax in the first place?' she asked.

'He happened to put it down when visiting the You Know Where,' Thelma spoke calmly. 'All I had to do was photograph the relevant pages with my phone.'

'You took a chance,' said Pat.

'He had a little bit of a problem with the cloakroom door.'

'That was lucky.' Liz realized, while listening to the story, she'd drained nearly all of her wine, and was in need of another, which wasn't like her at all.

'Not really. I locked the door from the outside. Fortunately, he was in rather a hurry and didn't hear the key.'

Liz tried not to laugh, but Pat didn't. Thelma joined in, then finally Liz. The noise was the most lively sound that had been heard in Pals of Pinot that evening; the barman looked up from his phone and the three glum girls, turning, saw three ladies of a certain age were obviously enjoying some joke. Maybe an anecdote about one of their grandchildren. Only Mandy and Jo remained oblivious, deep in conversation.

'Now: the bar and Mandy Pinder.' Thelma stood up. 'What does everyone want?' But before she could stand up, a voice made them turn.

'Stop giving me a hard time.' Mandy's voice was shrill; her face an impassive mask just as it had been when Pat saw her in the bank.

'I'm just trying to help you out, Mandy.' Jo looked the very opposite of jolly.

'I can handle it, okay?'

Jo shook her head. 'I'm just about sick of this,' she said and stood up.

'Why are you being like this?' Mandy's voice rose in a wobbly out-of-control way. 'You know how hard it's been for me lately, what with Mrs Joy's daughter coming in and calling me all the names under the sun.'

'Button it,' said Jo, sharply now.

'I'm *sick* of buttoning it,' wailed Mandy. 'I made a mistake.'

'Yeah, you did, big time. And I'm not going to cover for you any more.' And with that, Jo turned and stalked out of the bar.

Mandy Pinder-as-was promptly burst into noisy sobs. Which was the cue for all sorts of things to happen: Thelma to advance with tissues, Liz to hover anxiously behind. The barman stared worriedly round in case Jo reappeared and some sort of catfight ensued whilst the three girls typed manically into their phones like court stenographers.

'Mandy,' said Thelma calmly. 'It's Mrs Cooper. From St Barnabus's, remember? Is everything all right?'

Mandy looked at her, her face blotchy but impassive. Thelma tried again. 'Can I help you?' she said.

At that moment there was a sort of tinkling whoosh and Thelma looked round, half expecting some sort of fairy to appear but the noise was merely the text alert on Mandy's phone. Still sniffing, she snatched it from her bag (her Michael Kors bag, Pat noted). Whatever drama, whatever woe, whatever calamity, it seemed everything was put on hold when people's phones went off. It was definitely the case with Mandy. Her face froze; she looked impassively round the bar and left.

CHAPTER TWENTY-THREE

*An apology is made, a tale of reckless abandon is
related and the nature of wickedness is contemplated.*

Waiting outside the Thirsk bookshop for Derek, Liz reflected on
the evening. She felt more than a little resentful about having
to witness that whole scene when she'd not even wanted to go
to the bar in the first place. All this speculation like it was a
game of Cluedo or something! She knew she was going to feel
deeply awkward at the funeral; how she'd face KellyAnne she
did not know.

She looked in the window of the bookshop, hoping to distract
herself. There was a big display – March, the month of murder!
– with an array of dramatic-looking titles. She looked away, eyes
recoiling reflexively, and turned her gaze to the other side. There
was a display of the new Julia Donaldson book, which turned
her weary thoughts back to her other worry: Jacob. The upshot
of the big meeting the other day had been new strategies to try
each day. But avenues were being exhausted and things were
looking serious. It wasn't that Mrs Bell wasn't trying her
damnedest (apparently she loved the little guy to bits), but this,
it seemed, simply wasn't stopping Jacob from having some meltdown or other on a virtually daily basis. A report card system
had been instated, which involved either Tim or Leoni (or herself

if she was picking him up) reporting to Mrs Bell for a discussion on how the day had gone. But despite all of this there'd been yet another upset today.

From out of the Darrowby Arms came a burst of laughter, which for some reason reminded her of when Tim was little and Mum and Dad used to babysit so she and Derek could go to the quiz night at the Ainderby Stoop (now that curry restaurant). Remembering those far-off days gave her a pang; when had life become so bleak? She'd always had some idea that in your sixties, life became gentler, slower – gardening and coach holidays – but none of this *upset*. Her thoughts were broken by the familiar sight of the silver Corsair with the reassuring figure of Derek sat at the wheel. She felt a flush of guilt as she recalled his earnest entreaties to leave the whole question of Topsy alone. Well, leave it alone she would; let Thelma and Pat do what they wanted.

'Good evening?' he said as they pulled away.

'So-so,' she said. 'Definitely so-so.'

'Never mind,' he said, signalling left.

'Did our Tim ring?' she said.

'No.'

She suddenly wanted to tell him she loved him but knew better than to speak whilst he was negotiating a mini roundabout.

Thelma retraced her steps to the Aldi car park, one hand in her pocket clutched around the rape alarm (yes this was Thirsk, but one never knew). The night had grown even mistier, wispy murk stealing up from the river to hang pearly across the racecourse. She would have to go easy on the drive back to Ripon.

Like Liz she'd been more than a little disturbed by both the evening's events and by Pat's eager, almost avid, analysis of them. Murder – if murder it was – wasn't something to be picked apart like a reality TV show. There were real people, real feelings. Into her mind came an image of Mandy Pinder's stare as she'd been confronted by Jo.

'Oh Lord,' she said as she crossed the smoky car park towards the reliable mussel-blue Fiat. 'Bless Mandy Pinder, bless her, hold her hand and walk alongside her, whatever trouble she may be in.'

'Mrs Cooper?' Seldom had Thelma's prayers been answered so immediately. So sudden and so close was the voice that Thelma's hand instinctively tightened around the rape alarm before registering the figure who'd appeared from behind the trolley bay. 'It is Mrs Cooper, isn't it?'

'Mandy,' she said, her voice shaky. 'You startled me. Are you all right?'

'I'm sorry,' said Mandy. 'I thought it was you, and I thought, well, I wanted to apologize.'

'Apologize? Whatever for?'

'For tonight.' Mandy's voice was faltering at Thelma's calm tones, bringing as they did the echo of far-off, safe, secure days when the worst things to face were forgotten PE kits and flunked spelling tests. 'I didn't mean to rush off but I got this text from the babysitter. And all that with me and Jo, it's just been a long day. We're both really tired.' She looked down, her fingers pleating and re-pleating her scarf (Michael Kors it looked like). 'And then there's what I said about Mrs Joy's daughter . . . You see what happened was there was this mix-up . . .'

'I heard about what happened,' said Thelma gently.

'I know she's upset and I feel terrible but honestly and truly . . .'

'Mandy, there's no need to apologize to me,' said Thelma soothingly but the flow was resumed, unstoppable, growing in pitch and speed (and shrinking in coherence).

'I never would have, never ever, I swear on my mother's life . . . but you do something, and then it's done and it can't be undone, and then you and Mrs Newsome and that other lady heard everything, and you all must think I'm terrible, but sometimes you make bad choices . . . and you do things you know, like, you shouldn't but you don't have a choice.'

'Mandy,' said Thelma firmly.

167

But at that moment there was a gently tinkling swoosh, not a fairy appearing on the parked trolleys but Mandy's phone again. Only this time Mandy didn't even look at it, instead she scanned the shadows of the car park with that impassive look. 'I've got to go,' she said and abruptly walked to what looked like a very expensive car. She didn't seem to be moving particularly fast, but the car was accelerating out of the car park before Thelma had a chance to so much as fasten her seat belt.

Getting out of the car back home (she really must put some Deep Heat on that hip), Pat was suddenly struck by the peace of the night. The mist was clearing and, round the side of the house, in the patchy milky sky, a moon was rising over the distant Pennines. It was the sort of night when it was easy to believe in the oncoming spring as a force stirring in the tangled hedge-rows and under the muddy fields. She paused, breathing in the damp night, then noticed the sit-up-and-beg bicycle, leant up against the outhouse wall.

The Celtic poet. Peaceful thoughts evaporated and the trailer park in Boroughbridge shimmered into life somewhere out across the fields. What to do? Loo first obviously, but what if she missed the Celtic poet's departure? But then, even if she did see her, what to say? Even as the thoughts chased across her mind, the back door opened.

Pat had never actually met the Celtic poet but over the weeks had built up a strong image of her. Lilac vest and almost certainly some sort of black leather jacket. Cropped hair, possibly dyed blue or maybe purple, and definitely a nose piercing. So different from this was the girl who began wrestling with an outsized padlock that Pat momentarily assumed she must be someone else. Her hair far from being cropped made a honey-coloured cross between a halo round her head and shawl down her shoulders and she wore an emerald green jacket and long skirt. She looked up and saw Pat.

'It's a lovely night,' she said, hoisting the back upright. 'I'm India, Liam's friend.'

Why oh why did life's important encounters always happen when one needed the loo?

'If you wait a sec I'll run you home,' said Pat. She suddenly felt how crumpled her safe blue always looked after a couple of hours.

'Thanks.' Celtic Poet gave a warm smile that didn't seem in anyway supercilious or patronizing. 'But I'm needing this old boneshaker tomorrow.'

'I can easily put it in the back,' said Pat.

'Thanks, but it's only five minutes. And it's good to be cycling on a night like this, y'know?' Pat did know, or rather could understand. Wise, that was the word that came to Pat. Wise. How come, she wasn't sure, seeing as India was seventeen, but the girl had a calm wisdom, which seemed to be a part of the night.

'How was your night out?' said India, fastening her jacket. From what Pat could see, her other clothes seemed properly fastened, nothing hastily done up, nothing on inside out. 'Liam said you were trying that new wine bar.'

Pat felt suddenly profoundly dissatisfied with her safe blue. 'It was okay,' she said. Not even to a child of the night with wise green eyes could Pat face unpacking the whole tired tangle of events. 'I imagine Liam's been saying no end of things about ageing women out on the tiles.'

'You know Liam,' said India laughing, a spontaneous laugh, which Pat found herself joining in with, a sudden shared moment.

You get my son, she thought. It suddenly occurred to Pat that actually plenty of people had relationships spanning home and college.

'How is he?' she said suddenly, urgently. She hadn't known she was going to say what she did until the words came blurting from her mouth.

India stopped, one foot on the gravel, one foot on the pedal, but didn't immediately answer. Then she looked at Pat. 'The Internet. It saps the soul,' India said. Her words had the air of a pronouncement and her eyes looked suddenly black and bleak. 'People say things and it's out there for everyone to see, y'know?' For a minute she looked angry, but then she shook her head. 'But Liam's got a lot of sense to see him through, and I don't know, maybe in some ways it's a good thing?' And with that she smiled in farewell, mounted the bike and was off down the gravel drive with a rattle.

The Internet saps the soul? What on earth did she mean by that? Pat wanted to stay outside a moment and ponder her encounter with this girl who was so very unlike how she'd imagined. But knew she had probably less than a minute in which to reach the downstairs cloakroom.

Comfort regained, Pat knocked on Liam's bedroom door. She never used to knock. She could date the change quite precisely; he'd moved into Andrew's old room when he went to Loughborough. Liam had put a plaque on the door − one of those *Keep Calm* ones − *Keep Calm and Go Away*. And ever since then she'd knocked.

'Yes?' The voice didn't sound very welcoming but nor did it sound like a rebuttal.

She opened the door and let her eye sweep the room for signs of baby making, though quite what these would be she wasn't exactly sure. Disrupted sheets? Discarded underwear hanging from the lampshade? But the room was sign-free and peaceful, almost as if in some way India's presence lingered. The lamp was on, and soft music played. The window was open, letting in the mild smell from the fields. Larson, prone on the window seat, turned one eye on her as if to say 'don't start'.

'How are you?' she said.

'I'm good.' He didn't turn round and she saw he'd cleared whatever he'd been doing from the computer screen. India's words came back to her − *the Internet saps the soul*.

170

'How was Pals of Pinot?' It was with weary effort he spoke.

'Eventful.' She couldn't lie but didn't want to get side-tracked by the events of the night. She hadn't been sure exactly what she was going to say; in the event only one word came out.

And then she said, 'The Internet.'

It wasn't so much his face changed as it froze, reminding her of a fox she'd nearly run over one night, jewelled eyes wide, staring into her headlights. 'What about it?' he said, trying and failing to make his voice light and unconcerned.

Pat hadn't a clue what to say next, but all at once his voice and face changed to something nearer normal.

'You mean your numbers?' And whatever his tone had signalled turned to blessed, familiar irritation. 'I've told you, I can't do anything with only two numbers.'

'Ah.' Pat was all too aware of the shake in her voice and fingers as she fumbled in her shoulder bag. Whatever had caused that frozen look in her son's face she simply couldn't face it, not just now. 'Numbers,' she said, handing him Thelma's sheets.

'And what do you want me to do with them?'

'Your search thing,' she said, having no idea herself. 'Fraud.'

He sighed and turned away. This was obviously her cue to go but Pat hadn't quite done yet.

'I saw India leaving.' As soon as she said the words they felt overbright and clumsy . . . false.

He looked at her, suddenly watchful again.

'I like her. She's a nice girl.' A pause, still that watchful look. 'Are you and her having a thing?'

Pat hated the way that yet again she just blurted the words out. But recent years had led to her belief this was a big part of motherhood to older teenagers: blurting out those things that needed blurting out.

He didn't turn round for a moment. His gaze seemed to be resting on his Gandalf poster.

'Define thing.'

'Thing. A you and her thing,' said Pat determinedly, giving the elephant in the room a firm slap on the rump.

'Maybe not in the way you're thinking.' The smile was still there. What did it mean?

What was that supposed to mean? Surely, please God no, not that awful term 'fuck buddy'. Whatever, it was now brass tacks time.

'As long as you're being careful.' She took a breath. 'You know, protection.' He met her gaze now, not unkindly. When had he developed that wispy fuzz under his chin?

'Sunblock?' he said.

'Contraception.' There, she'd said it. If a trailer park in Boroughbridge was on the cards – well, she'd said it. He was now grinning broadly. Why?

'Condoms, Dutch cap, the pill, the coil, not forgetting the old coitus interruptus,' he reeled off the list in a way that made part of her shrivel up inside.

'I don't want to know – as long as you're being careful,' she said.

'Actually, Mother Mine, we used a much more effective form.'

What was he talking about?

'She sat there.' He pointed to where Pat was. 'And I sat there.' He gestured to the sofa.

Her eyelids prickled. She had a sudden vision of him aged six in Cyberman pyjamas, coughing, one of his nasty chest coughs, big bright eyes. Still her little boy, well, in that respect. There was a sudden nasty possibility she was about to embarrass both of them. To cover the moment, Pat stooped to gather up a collection of running and cricket gear left out for the wash. Cricket.

'Lloret,' she said.

He looked at her blankly, with that doubt-inducing incomprehension that teenagers are so good at.

'Isn't that his name? Lloret something or other? In Andrew's year at school. You were on the team with him at Rievaulx last year.'

172

His head swivelled and he looked fully at her for the first time, an expression of dawning comprehension on his face. 'Lozza Whitlaw?'

'Tall lad.'

'Big brown eyes and a "please like me" look on his face.' Pat nodded. 'What about him?'

'I saw him today. He's working for a friend of KellyAnne.'

'Captain Implosion.' The comment was directed out of the window rather than said directly to her.

'Sorry?'

'It's what he's called. Great one for the ladies, our Lozza – usually more than one at a time. And when things get too much he just goes AWOL and says his phone "imploded".' Liam sketched two quotation marks in the air. Exactly the words Lloret had used at Ness's office that time. Pat noted. 'Last year at cricket, it turned he was seeing both the captain's sister and that Mrs Beesborough who does the scoring.'

'Lucy Beesborough?' Pat had a vision of floaty skirts, knitted berets and frizzy red hair; a battered Morris Minor van slapped over with various National Trust stickers.

'That's her.'

She had to get this straight – Lucy Beesborough had to be thirty-five at the very least. Wasn't there a Mr Beesborough on the scene somewhere? 'You mean this Lozza was seeing Lucy Beesborough?' she said again. 'They actually had an affair?'

Liam nodded. 'The Birds and the Beesboroughs. His bit of fun on the slide.'

'His *what?*'

'It's what Dribble said.' Dribble was a member of the cricket team, well known for his howlers. Pat continued to look bewildered as she took this in. 'He got it wrong, Mother – he meant to say "bit of fun on the *side*".'

'Yes, okay I understand,' she said. There was something about this conversation she was finding deeply uncomfortable.

'It all came to a head just before the cup match,' continued Liam. 'Big drama in the score box, Dribble has to score, Lloret goes AWOL and we got stuffed by Pateley Bridge. Thank you and goodnight, Lloret Whitlaw.'

Sitting on the bed later, mug of hot chocolate in hand (was it really only thirty-seven calories?), Pat thought about what Liam had been saying. Lucy Beesborough. She remembered times at the matches, those interminable conversations about feng shui or the shortcomings of their MP.

Then the thought hit her like a burst of caffeine.

Of course! Ness! Lloret and Ness!

That's why she'd looked so eager when there were footsteps on the stairs. That's why she'd been so keen to get rid of Pat. Her mind went back to that shut door. (Closed. But looking forward to helping you find your dreams later!) A mix of thoughts and feelings ran through Pat's mind. Ness must be at least twenty years older than the lad. That perm, that suit – and Pat's casual dismissal of them both – yet despite all that, Ness had something that attracted a young lad who was more than a bit of a dish. And how could Pat have missed it when it was there right under her nose!

She took a swig of the chocolate. (If it was only thirty-seven calories could it hurt to grate some cooking chocolate into it?) And then there was Liam. Not up to whatever with Celtic Poet (India!). But *something* was going on . . . something to do with the Internet in some way, something to do with people saying things. What things? And India had said good sense would see him through.

See him through what?

Teddy finished winding up the grandmother clock in the hall. 'Don't stay up too long,' he said. Listening to his retreating measured tread, Thelma reflected on one of the many benefits of a long marriage: knowing the other person, knowing when they wanted to talk and knowing when they wanted to be left alone with their thoughts. She sat back and tried to let the peace of the room, the lamplight, the glowing colours of the wood, subsume her mind. She knew sleep was a long way from being possible.

In the distance she could hear the chaplaincy clock striking eleven, a call for her to try and make sense of her thoughts rather than let them tear around like overexcited children. Was Topsy murdered or was it just as everyone seemed to think, just some tragic mix-up with her tablets? Not just everyone, she thought. There were the over-sixties from the lunch club. The voice came into her mind—

Topsy Joy would no more muddle up her pills than I'd pole-vault over Baldersby church.

And those other words . . .

It'd be better all round if she was dead . . .

Wait a moment. Those words. So far Thelma had been puzzling over who had said them, but who had they been said *to*? Whoever said the words would have presumably been saying them *to* someone. Who? The mysterious 'he' who had thought Topsy to be asleep?

The clock struck the quarter. She was still some way off sleep but her mind was tired and wilted at the prospect of going through things any more. Almost without thinking, her hand reached for her old, red, soft-backed prayer book, the one given her by her Grandmother Spillman, containing prayers, the Psalms and the New Testament. Many was the time that the soft cover, the silky, gilt-edged pages had given some wisdom, some insight.

The book opened at Psalm 32.

Many are the sorrows of the wicked but steadfast love surrounds the one who trusts in the Lord.

The sorrows of the wicked. Thelma nodded in satisfaction; as always she'd been given a fresh way to look at the problem. Not that she could assume each person in her thoughts was wicked – though of course they would be if they'd murdered Topsy.

But who could be said to be sorrowful?

How about Oliver Harney? She smiled momentarily as she remembered Ernest Crabtree's entreaties not to let the man anywhere near 47 College Gardens. If Oliver was inflating prices to vulnerable people, that was certainly wicked. But did it go any further than that? She remembered the cloakroom door panels trembling under his beating fists. Certainly edgy, panicky. She cast her mind back to their encounter . . . He was confident, practised. But not sorrowful? No, not sorrowful – but then neither did he strike her as someone who was particularly happy.

Who else? Ness. She remembered the tense slamming of the wheelie bin lid and her swift, almost frantic exit to Thirsk. Someone else who was not happy. And she had a strong suspicion why.

Flat-Pack Youth. Lloret or whatever his name was. She had yet to meet him, but from the way both Liz and Pat described him, he had that certain appeal that almost always led to trouble. She thought back to the last youth group leader but one. Yes, definitely trouble. But the sort of person likely to mess with someone's tablets?

And then of course there was Mandy. Of all of them, it was she who was looming largest in Thelma's thoughts. She pictured that pale face and haunted expression in the car park. And again more words, more cryptic troubling words . . .

Sometimes you make bad choices.

What bad choices?

'Oh Lord,' she said for the second time that night. 'Bless Mandy Pinder, bless her, hold her hand and walk alongside her.'

The sorrows of the wicked. All in all virtually everyone seemed to have sorrows of one kind or another. And wickedness could be so *so* ordinary. *The gummy smile . . . the hands reaching up to her . . . her hands on the handle of the pram . . .*

She gave herself a shake. She did not want to be thinking of that, not tonight. Where was she? Wickedness, ordinary wickedness, a world away from that cartoon wickedness where the villain (or villainess) cackled gleefully as they raked in the spondoolies. Spondoolies? Where on earth had she got that word from? Oh yes, Liz. No, not Liz. Liz *talking about* that Wayne from the Northern Knights. She smiled to herself. Liz going to the headquarters of a band of strippers!

Wait a minute. She frowned. For a second something had been there. But it was gone.

Of course the only truly sorrowful one in all of this was KellyAnne. She remembered that tight hug, that haunted look, and then with a suddenness that made her close her eyes and dig her nails into her palms, that old perennial black worry came back to her. Who would look after her and Teddy when the time came?

She sighed. Time to get to bed, no earthly point in sitting here waiting for what Pat always called a lightbulb moment.

Hang on.

Lightbulb.

Dusty Webster had said she'd seen a light go on upstairs when she passed the house and saw the person hanging round outside. Which meant that at half past seven Topsy was presumably *not* unconscious in her chair . . .

CHAPTER TWENTY-FOUR

The life of Topsy Joy is celebrated with
many flowers and some speculation.

The church at Baldersby St James was full for Topsy's funeral. Extra
chairs had to be put out at the sides and even then there were
people standing at the back. Liz, Pat and Thelma sat halfway down,
on the right, with Topsy's ex-colleagues from St Barnabus's: Jan and
Marguerite allowed out for the morning, Feay back specially from
the Tuscan timeshare and of course Paula, dour and grim, in a
surprisingly chic black number (Our Rocky splashed out, bless him).

As they waited, Paula offered a muttered commentary on who
was who in the packed church: the golf lot, the Rotary lot, them
from the village and the cousins with whom Topsy Never Spoke.
Thelma noted the over-sixties were out in force dotted round
the church: there was Mrs Booth, her hennaed hair under a
respectful black pill box; there was Dusty Webster looking nervously down at the glossy order of service; there was Brian, RAF
tie replaced by a black one.

KellyAnne, in something obviously expensive and black, cut
a solitary and strangely out of place figure at the front, the cousins
who never spoke all cramming in the row behind. Next to her
sat Ness (*come on, love,* thought Pat, *you're totally the wrong build
for shoulder pads*), and, next to her, looking even more lost than

KellyAnne, sat Lloret. Pat had wasted no time in whispering her speculations to Liz and Thelma and thus it was they all noted the discreet squeeze Ness gave his left buttock as the pair sat down. Lloret himself looked uneasily up at the church windows as if considering them as a means of escape.

The Victorian church had been bedecked, no other word for it, in a way that created an uneasy mix of Baldersby and Beverly Hills. Sumptuous sprays of lilies stood round on ornate iron stands, obscuring the Slimming World advert, the Twin Toilet notice and the Brownies sponsored crochet. The waxy blooms adorned the pew ends, the font and the pulpit, dropping bruised fragrant petals on the chequered black and orange floor tiles, their heavy scent battling against the usual church smells of paper, faint damp and Pledge polish.

At the front, at the foot of the pulpit steps, was a prominent easel bearing an image of Topsy looking out suspiciously on the world. Behind this was a veritable copse of flowers and it was here the white coffin with gold handles had been laid.

A lone violinist played the theme from *Schindler's List*. 'Total brouhaha or what,' muttered Paula to Liz. Liz didn't nod at this comment though she agreed with it; the music seemed especially out of place. Liz's memories of Topsy and music were of her bashing out various hymns and children's songs on the battered old piano in the school hall, or grudgingly jiggling to 'Hi Ho Silver Lining' on staff nights out.

Amongst the total brouhaha the Reverend Val could well have looked out of place, but she didn't. She gave the eulogy in grave and simple tones that made a reality of Topsy Joy, beyond the violinist, the picture and the flowers. A reality that made the congregation smile and reach for tissues in equal measure. When she announced the second hymn – 'The Lord is my Shepherd' – all the St Barnabus's lot, even Paula, smiled with their various memories of the way Topsy would dragoon the various casts of different nativity plays over the years.

'It's a hymn about God being with us each step of the way,' said the Reverend Val.

Pat looked at the backs of Ness and Lloret; they were obviously not great hymn singers. She couldn't believe she'd been so slow about what was going on with them . . . and if she'd been slow about *them*, what else had she been missing? Her thoughts spooled back to Liam, still in his mopey mood, still barely talking; this morning he'd gone for the school bus without even saying goodbye.

'He maketh me to lie down in green pastures, he leadeth me beside the still waters' sang the congregation with varying degrees of ability and enthusiasm. Pat found herself looking at Topsy's image. There was a small arch to the right eyebrow she'd never noticed before. How strange that was, considering the hundreds and thousands of times she'd seen that face. She found herself remembering another time when she'd been at her wits' end about Liam, who'd taken to sleepwalking into their bedroom and waking up with the most blood-chilling gasps and fits of coughing. She'd been sitting in her classroom, worried sick, trying to find from somewhere the where-withal to mount pictures of rainbows for a classroom display when there'd been a grudging hand on her shoulder: Topsy.

'They all go through something like this,' she'd said. Not with sympathy because Topsy didn't do sympathy, but when she'd come back from the staff meeting the rainbow pictures had all been neatly mounted ready to go up on the wall.

Yea, though I walk through the valley of the shadow of death, I will fear no evil.

Liz had done her crying for Topsy the night before, in her spare bedroom, holding the pinking shears. Now, carefully guarding her mind from any distressing speculations, she summoned up memories of their times together. That sports day when Topsy manhandled a stray dog threatening to disrupt the sack race . . . that trip to Helmsley when it didn't stop raining and Eleanor Wadden had thrown a shoe in the river . . . the reassuring hands on the shoulder, the cups of decaf, the laminating, the mounting, the sharpening of pencils.

A coughing sob made her look up to see Ness pressing a tissue into KellyAnne's fumbling hand. The poor girl looked to be in floods. She found herself remembering Topsy telling her about KellyAnne when she faked the spots with her Chanel lip gloss . . . '"I'm not well," she says. "I'm not well." And there was my favourite green vase all smashed up and hidden in the bin, and there was our KellyAnne, these lip-gloss spots all over her face. The little madam.' Topsy's face had been as soft as the play-dough she'd been rolling into fist-sized balls.

'. . . *You are with me, you will comfort me.*'

'Be with me and comfort me,' echoed Thelma in a silent prayer, trying to focus beyond the flowers and whatnot to the solid reassurance of the Victorian church. Even if Topsy was murdered, nothing could bring her back. What was done was done. In some ways wouldn't it be simplest if they could all walk away from this lily-filled building and think: that was it, that was Topsy Joy?

Out in the muddy churchyard the first hopeful dots of daffodils were appearing in the hedges and between the graves. Despite the charcoal-grey skies there was a feel of peace; the wind soughed in the trees and across the road could be heard the noise of children in Baldersby school playground. 'Topsy would like that,' said more than one person.

We all have to be laid to rest at some point, thought Thelma looking beyond the churchyard, through the trees to the stretching green fields beyond. And this point, this place, was as good as any; in fact, it was better than most.

Was there any point in her trying to find out any more?

'Must have been hundreds of pounds' worth of flowers!'

'What's going to happen to them all – that's what I'd like to know.'

'And that big picture? What were that in aid of?' At the wake in the Bay Horse the talk amongst the over-sixties was all about the church décor.

'I've never seen owt like it,' was Mrs Booth's definitive judgement.

'It was certainly different,' said Liz neutrally, hoping KellyAnne – holding court in the lounge bar – couldn't hear. She wanted to go and pay her respects but KellyAnne was surrounded by a cluster of people. The St Barnabus staff had all had to hurry back (boss's orders), Feay had gone and Liz found herself in no hurry to talk to Thelma or Pat (what was Pat thinking of, whispering that about Ness and Lloret just as the coffin was coming in?) so she'd gravitated over to the over-sixties. Like Thelma, she knew Mrs Booth of old. Brian she also knew slightly as being a bowling acquaintance of her dad's; he lived out in that bungalow on its own midway between Sharow and Dishforth.

Paula sat in another corner of the bar with more of the over-sixties. Liz could hear her knowledgeably and authoritatively reeling off a list of Topsy's medication and their various side effects to which the others were enthusiastically contributing, in the same way her Year One class used to talk about their Pokémon cards.

'Cling film's coming off, ladies and gentlemen,' called Jan Tevendale and there was a general exodus to the back room where one of her famous buffets was laid out.

Not hungry, and wanting to avoid any conversations about the effectiveness of various laxatives, Liz was left with Brian who was looking hopefully at her. It was a look Liz had seen many many times over the years, on the faces of children, usually boys, stood in the corner of the playground, maybe bouncing a ball, wanting someone to play with.

'I'm not a great one for queuing these days,' he said. 'My knee, you know.' He smiled as if confiding a secret. 'RAF 1951. Rugby. Us against RAF Feltwell. I went one way, my knee went the other.'

Liz smiled sympathetically. She had the feeling that this wasn't the first time he'd told this story. 'Let's sit down until the queue's died back a bit,' she said, remembering her dad's verdict on RAF Brian as he called him: *Nice chap but likes the sound of his own voice.*

'It means I can't do things like I used to, you know,' he said, rubbing the offending knee. 'Odd jobs and whatnot. Once upon a time I'd have been up a ladder like a shot – now I think: *Hold on, you silly old buffer, get someone in.*' From where Liz was sitting she had a view into a shadowy niche by the main door, empty apart from Mr Flat-Pack stood scrolling on his phone. As she was thinking that she must remember to call him Lloret not Lorry, Ness came and joined him. Almost against her will, Liz found herself covertly watching the pair as Brian cheerfully rambled on.

'. . . I'm lucky to find him. Talk about five-star service . . .'

There was something about the way the two of them were standing that drew Liz's attention. Was something going on as Pat seemed so sure? There had been that squeeze of the backside, but even so, she must be near twice his age. But then that didn't mean anything these days . . . Memories of Tim and the Baldersby Jezebel came to her mind. No, one never knew.

'. . . this one afternoon when he came on one of his sorties he needed some money for materials. I hadn't much on me so do you know what he did? He only took me all the way to the machine in Thirsk . . .'

Ness was talking intently, showing no signs of stopping, staring up at him, one hand clutching his sleeve. And he . . . he was looking uneasily round the alcove, eyes fixed on the various horse brasses and sepia pictures of the Dishforth hunt. *Trapped* was the word that came to Liz.

'. . . almost like the voice beyond the grave. It was about three months after the funeral . . .'

And now her hand was shaking his arm, as if trying to get

and keep his attention. He looked down at her now, uneasy . . . definitely trapped . . . and she smiled, brushed that floppy fringe away from his face.

'. . . I'm very lucky. He said another winter and I could have lost the whole roof . . .'

Suddenly Ness laughed, but there was something about that laugh that cut through to Liz's inner being . . . something sad but defiant and angry all at the same time.

Liz found herself straining to hear what was said but Brian was still in full flow: '. . . always time for a cup of tea. Fascinated by my RAF stories . . . I rather gather he's fitting me in as a special favour.'

And now Ness had turned away now as if she wasn't listening – but neither was she moving – effectively leaving Lloret stuck awkwardly where he was. 'Babe.' KellyAnne's voice cut clear across the bar, beginning to fill now as people returned with paper plates loaded with Jan Tevendale's Wensleydale and bacon quiche. 'Can you just ask at the bar about the tab?'

For a moment Ness didn't move, and then reluctantly she turned and walked to the bar taking an almighty gulp of Prosecco as she did so.

'I think it may be time to brave the buffet,' said Brian, standing stiffly up.

'You go on,' said Liz. KellyAnne, at last, was on her own; now was the time to go and pay her respects.

Thelma and Pat obviously had the same thought. It seemed natural for them to approach KellyAnne together. Thus it was they found themselves on stools in front of the leather armchair in which KellyAnne was somewhat regally ensconced, with a smile that they all felt, though gracious, was somewhat forced and artificial. The three smiled back.

'It was a memorable service.' As ever, Thelma found the exact words the other two were fumbling for.

'You did your mum proud,' said Liz.

'She's my mum,' said KellyAnne simply. 'I had to.'

'The flowers were lovely,' said Pat.

'So,' said Liz. 'How are things? I've been meaning to ring you.'

KellyAnne looked tired. 'You know. A lot to sort.'

'And have you heard any more from the police?' Liz asked.

There was a slight pause and KellyAnne looked down at her fingers entwined in her lap; it almost seemed she hadn't heard.

'Why?' The question was said mildly enough but there was something set in her face, something that reminded all three of them of her mother when something had displeased her. 'Have you heard something?'

'No, of course not.' Liz was looking worried.

'The police said to me . . .' KellyAnne painstakingly emphasized her words as if patiently repeating them in the face of sustained challenge. 'They said what happened was a tragic accident.' She looked Liz in the face. 'And if people go round implying anything different it makes everything one hundred thousand times worse.'

'I one hundred per cent did not mean anything,' said Liz earnestly, looking as if she wanted the tartan carpet of the Bay Horse to open up and swallow her. 'I'm so sorry.'

'No.' KellyAnne shut her eyes as if shutting out the pain. 'No, I'm sorry.' She opened her eyes and put a hand on Liz's arm. 'I'm so sorry, Liz. It's me. I'm just . . . I'm all over the place.'

'Of course.' Liz put a tentative hand over KellyAnne's hand.

'I just can't forget . . .' She shook her head and looked down. 'I just can't forget that when Mum was going through whatever it was she was going through, there I was, sunning myself in the bloody Algarve . . . That's what I've got to live with.'

Joan Crawford, was Thelma's irreverent thought.

There was a pause.

'I love the Algarve,' said Pat brightly with the air of one changing the subject. 'Carvoeiro . . . we went there the first holiday without the lads. It was brilliant. We always said we'd go back. Was that where you were?'

'Santorini.' KellyAnne was ostentatiously dabbing at her eyes with the tissue proffered by Liz.

'I've heard of it. We were looking at that in the brochure. Was it any good?'

'The quiet end of busy. Some nice bars.' With a smooth flourish KellyAnne checked her phone and proffered it to Pat. 'The Hotel Da Intereiza. Five-star but not in your face with it.' Pat squinted and could just about make out a white building set against an aquamarine pool, the best her eyesight could manage without glasses in the dim light of the bar.

Liz tried again. 'I've never been to Portugal, but I remember your mum and dad going one year, KellyAnne. It looked lovely. And I remember your mum . . .' she paused and her voice took on an anecdotal note that invited them to smile, '. . . your mum had this big set-to with the hotel about the pillowcases!' She stopped with the abruptness of someone who realizes they might well be saying the wrong thing, and looked anxiously at KellyAnne.

Across her face was flitting a sudden expression of something darker, sadder, something that cut right through the piled hair and make-up and added a sagging ten years to her face. Her eyes were suddenly sparkly with unshed tears and she began frantically fanning in an effort to dry them.

'We were all so sorry,' said Thelma, putting a hand on her arm.

KellyAnne nodded wordlessly.

'And that hymn!' said Pat, again with that breezy 'life goes on' tone of voice. 'How many times do I remember your mum playing that.'

'It was one of her favourites,' said KellyAnne, still flapping. 'What the vicar was saying, about walking with God . . . It made me think she and the big fella upstairs were looking down having a right old smile. She always did have a soft spot for old time music.'

Naturally Thelma didn't point out that that particular tune had been composed in the 1990s.

CHAPTER TWENTY-FIVE

Emotions run high at the wake,
and views are shared in the car park.

At the back of the Bay Horse, Pat was sat on a bench in the empty beer garden thinking about making an exit. If she went in the next twenty minutes she stood a good chance of getting home before Liam and if he'd left his computer on, as he sometimes did, she could maybe get a look at his search history. (Hopefully his password was still Lars0n12!)

A movement made her look up.

'Hello, Mrs Taylor.' Lloret was stood by the wheelie bins. His eyes strayed nervously from her towards the back door of the pub.

'I'm just getting a breath of air,' she said. She was aware of a feeling of awkwardness talking to him in light of what she guessed about Ness but then he could hardly know about her suspicions.

'It was a good funeral . . .' He paused, self-conscious at the comment. 'I mean to say it was a good occasion . . .'

'I know what you mean,' said Pat. Good wasn't exactly the word she'd have chosen.

'When I die that's the sort of funeral I want.' As he spoke for a second he looked so lost and bleak that Pat took half a step forward. *What on earth made him say something like that?*

'You're far too young to be having thoughts like that,' she said.

'We've all got to die sometime,' he said in a small voice.

'Lloret,' said Pat. 'Is everything all right?'

'So this is where you're hiding.' Ness's cheerful voice cut in before he could answer, and he looked round, rather guiltily, Pat thought. Was he meant to be helping with the wake in some way? 'Come on, sunshine, you can't hide away out here.'

Ness barely looked at Pat as she walked up to him and brushed something real or imaginary off his suit. There was such a possessive air about the way she did it that Pat half expected her to spit on her handkerchief and scrub his face.

'Hello again,' she said to Ness, somewhat annoyed at being so totally ignored.

'Hello there.' Still Ness didn't look round and there was a brittle cheerfulness in her voice that made Pat wonder how much she'd had to drink. 'Come on, mister.' She linked her arm with Lloret's.

'Actually we were just in the middle of a conversation,' said Pat. She was damned if she was going to be ignored by some missy with wonky shoulder pads. Finally Ness looked at her.

'How *is* your son?' The words were nonetheless harsh and confrontational for being enveloped in one of her ubiquitous laughs.

'Justin?' Pat felt puzzled. 'He's all right thanks. Due to turn up this weekend, no doubt with a bin bag of washing.'

Ness laughed. It wasn't a nice laugh. 'I meant the one at home.'

'Liam?'

'Ness.' There was something urgent in Lloret's voice.

'He's fine.' What was Ness going on about? How did *she* know Liam?

'I've often thought Facebook must be a nightmare. I keep my two off it. End of. If it wasn't for the business I'd keep off altogether.'

'Ness.' And now Lloret sounded angry – really angry. What on earth was going on?

'I'm just saying.' Ness tried to sound innocent but failed. But she did sound more than a bit pissed. Lloret turned and walked away.

'What?' Now Ness was trying to sound innocent, and again failing. Lloret kept walking. 'What?' she said again, following a bit unsteadily.

'You do my head in sometimes, you do,' he said, striding off across the car park with Ness tottering after him.

Pat looked after them. *Something* had happened there.

She had plenty of ideas, none of them very nice. And Facebook? What did she mean by that?

As Pat came into the bar to say goodbye to KellyAnne, she found her talking with Liz and Thelma again.

'I hear your mum's house is up for rent,' Liz was saying.

'I couldn't go back there.' KellyAnne shuddered. 'Not after . . . finding her like that.'

'It was so tragic, the whole thing.' The quick almost gushing quality in Thelma's voice was so unlike her normal measured way of speaking that Liz and Pat looked at their friend's drink to see if a whisky chaser was sat alongside the elderflower tonic. 'That time I came across to the house,' she said, 'walking in the drive, I had this . . . how can I describe it? This great wave of feeling that something wasn't right.'

'That's it, Thelma,' said KellyAnne. 'That's exactly how it was with me that morning.'

'I often find,' said Thelma, 'those feelings are grounded in fact. Your eyes see something that only registers subconsciously.'

Pat opened her mouth to speak – what was all this babble in aid of? But there was something about Thelma's manner that made her close it again.

'With your mother's house, when I went over that day, I couldn't think why I suddenly felt this sadness, and then I realized what it was: it was the wheelie bin.' KellyAnne was looking blank; she obviously wasn't following this at all. 'It wasn't stood against the wall; it was stood right in the middle of the drive. Your mother would never have left it like that. That one thing out of place – it

190

was enough to bring on this wave of sadness . . . And I was wondering, forgive me for being nosy, that morning when you came to the house . . . You said you knew something was wrong . . . I was wondering if there was something you saw? Or didn't see? Something that told your brain something was *wrong*.'

KellyAnne was staring into space.

'Maybe there was a window left open?' said Pat.

KellyAnne's faded blue eyes seemed fixed on a sepia print of the old Methodist chapel.

'Paula said she'd heard a smoke alarm the night before,' said Liz, trying to move the subject on. She wasn't at all sure what Thelma was doing but she knew she didn't like it. At her words KellyAnne's eyes seemed to abruptly focus.

'Babe,' she said. And then: 'Can someone see to her?'

The three followed her stare. Unnoticed by them, Ness had re-entered the room and was sat at the bar under the dartboard, perched on a stool, head down, rocking slightly. There was, Pat noticed, no sign of Lloret.

'Babe,' said KellyAnne again.

Ness jerked her head up, smiled woozily and raised a glass of Prosecco in an unsteady toast.

All eyes were on her; Thelma noticed Paula watching with grim enjoyment. Two of the Rotary lot approached her but she waved them back and attempted to stand, pushing herself up using the edge of a table, which promptly flipped over, taking Ness and half a dozen glasses with it.

She sat up with a wild giggle. 'Don't mind me, folks,' she said. 'I'm just wrecking the place!'

The two from the Rotary tried to help her up, but she pushed them away laughing. 'I'm good,' she said. And as they persisted, with a sudden scratching anger: 'I said I'm good.'

She stood up and faced the bar, lipstick smudged, shoe missing, shoulder pad askew. It was, Pat thought, almost impossible not to feel sympathy for her. Almost.

'Blumin' hummer,' said Ness. 'Who'd have thought it'd be here?' And then wildly, embarrassingly, she started singing: 'Tell me on a Sunday please!'

Everyone watched in a rather stunned silence. The faces ranged from shocked pity (Liz) to avid attention (Paula and the over-sixties). Still no sign of Lloret.

'Babe.' KellyAnne was advancing towards her, voice low and clam. 'Babe, I cannot be doing with this today.'

Ness's face crumpled into hot ugly sobs. KellyAnne looked over her shoulder round the bar. 'Can someone get her phone and call Craig?' she said.

This effectively marked the end of the wake. Liz unobtrusively fetched a large coffee and she and KellyAnne sat with Ness as the rest of the party took their leave. The over-sixties were amongst the last to leave and Thelma had no difficulty in predicting what the topic of conversation would be at their next gathering. Paula was left sat talking to – or more accurately at – Dusty Webster. It was one of those conversations held in a lowered voice, occasionally behind a hand; Thelma caught the odd phrase . . . *better off out of it* . . . *didn't give a monkey's* . . . KellyAnne sat on her own at the other side of the bar, sipping wine and texting moodily, showing no interest in the plight of her so-called best friend; it fell to Liz to sit with her to dispense tissues, wipes and make gentle conversation.

Standing in the car park, Thelma and Pat watched as Craig, the fiasco, a slight bearded man in a beanie hat, half carried Ness across to a muddy Land Rover as she feebly protested that she needed her own space.

'I wonder if he knows about Lloret,' said Pat. 'And that his fiasco has been involved in a lovers' tiff.'

'I think you'll find it was rather more than that,' said Thelma. 'I think Lloret might have been finishing whatever it was that was going on between them.'

Pat looked at her. 'What makes you think that?'

'Well,' she said, 'Ness is obviously very emotional.'

'She's drunk,' said Pat dismissively. She wasn't ready to share what had been hinted about Liam.

'And of course there was what she said.'

'I'm just wrecking the place?'

'Who would have thought it'd be *here*? *What* would be here? Something important obviously. And then of course there was that song.'

'Don't remind me.' Pat could still hear those discordant tones . . . *Tell Me on a Sunday*.

'It's from a Lloyd Webber musical. It's a song a woman sings when she's being finished with by her lover. About wanting to choose the place where she's to be given the news.'

Liz came outside. She looked tired and drawn. 'Well,' she said.

'I tell you what,' said Pat, 'I tell you who would have enjoyed all this, and that's Topsy.' As ever she'd irreverently hit the nail on the head. 'Anyway,' she said, 'Masham tomorrow. I'll drive. What time shall I pick everyone up?'

Liz paused as she fumbled in her black bag for her car keys. 'No,' she said. The other two looked at her. 'No,' she said again, and looked at her friends, that flinty edge in her voice. 'I'm to pick up Jacob tomorrow.'

'Is everything all right?' said Thelma.

'No, it's not.' The strength in her voice took them all by surprise, Liz included. 'It's just all this.' She shook her head as if trying to clear a buzzing noise. 'All this asking questions . . . all this upset . . . It's our friend's *funeral* . . . KellyAnne's just buried her mother for heaven's sake.'

Frowning in distress, she got into her car and drove off, watched in silence by Pat and Thelma. They looked at each other.

'Well,' said Pat. It felt like there was nothing else to be said, at least nothing that they had any energy for.

★ ★ ★

Finally alone, Thelma breathed in the cool air before getting into her car. Should she perhaps ring Liz? She thought about her friend's angry words. She could see her point of view. See it, but not share it. She realized with something of a shock that she was as sure as she could be that something untoward had happened to Topsy. And that simple as it might be for her to walk away, it was something she just couldn't do.

She breathed again, allowing the peace of the fading afternoon to surround her but even as she did so the sound of another car, with a rattling rather unhealthy engine, made her look up. A rather shabby red vehicle was manoeuvring in, one that had surely seen better days. It had big rusty dents on one side and the windows looked like they were held in place with duct tape. And behind the wheel was someone it took her a moment to recognize as Rocky. Thelma was conscious of a feeling of surprise. She'd never seen him driving such a jalopy, even in the early days of the Northern Knights when times were tough.

'Hello, young man,' she said as he got out. 'Long time no see.'

'Is my mother in there, Mrs Cooper?' His voice was downbeat in a way that put her in mind her of the aftermath of the Top Trumps scandal. He frowned at the back of the pub. 'She said she'd be in the car park,' he said, looking at his watch. 'And I'm running late.'

'She's probably talking,' said Thelma. 'Just give her a shout.'

Rocky got his phone.

'Just go in,' said Thelma.

He shook his head. 'I don't like to intrude,' he said. And then as the phone was answered: 'Mother, I'm in the car park. We need to be moving.' He sounded stressed and Thelma looked at him closely. He seemed tired. None of his usual bounce . . . and surely . . . Weren't those love bites showing on his neck above his collar?

'I'm to be in Redcar by seven,' he said, putting the phone back in his pocket.

'How is everything with your group?' asked Thelma. 'Still busy busy from the sounds of it.'

'It's not what it was, Mrs Cooper,' said Rocky. 'But needs must.' He smiled and there for a moment was the old Rocky. From his pocket he produced one of the ubiquitous flyers. 'If you ever wanted to hire us, Mrs Cooper, I could do you mate's rates.'

Thelma tried and failed to picture the faces of the church committee if she hired the Northern Knights as entertainment for the upcoming Spring Concert. 'I'll bear that in mind,' she said. 'And I hear you've branched out into sales.'

'Like I said, needs must. No spare money. Hence the old rust bucket.' He nodded toward the car, which seemed to be gently leaking something or other. 'You know what it's like when you have kids.'

Thelma didn't and Rocky, looking at his phone, didn't see the shadow that flitted across her face. 'I'll go and see if I can root out your mother,' she said.

'She said she was coming,' he said, looking impatiently at the door. Suddenly his phone blared out with some pop song. He looked at the caller and shook his head, rejecting the call.

'Did you sort your sunbed out?' asked Thelma. His head jerked up to look at her, face alert. 'Liz, Mrs Newsome, was telling me,' she said.

'Is she still here, Mrs Newsome?' He looked uneasily at the door. She shook her head. 'She left about ten minutes ago.'

Again he looked at the pub. 'The sunbed had to go back,' he said. 'Too many spondoolies. I've just not got that sort of money.' He looked at Thelma, appearing to come to some sort of decision. 'Mrs Cooper,' he said. 'How did you find Mum today?'

Thelma pictured Paula's avid attention to Ness's spectacular fall from grace. 'She seemed fine,' she said. 'It was very generous of you to buy her that lovely outfit.'

'That.' He shook his head, almost embarrassed. 'That was going dirt cheap on eBay that was. No way could I afford that normally.'

He looked at Thelma with those almost startlingly blue eyes. 'No, I'm very sorry, of course, about Mrs Joy, course I am, but if I'm perfectly honest I'm glad Mum's out of that place.'

'Oh?'

'With everything going on. I don't mean the fraud – that'd be some organized criminals, not even in the country. No . . .' He looked again at the back door of the pub and dropped his voice. 'I mean the people in the house.'

'Ness?'

He nodded. 'And others. I reckon that Kel don't know half what's been going on there. There's been bad stuff going on, Mrs Cooper.' He shook his head gravely. 'When there's financial misnomers going on people do some bad things.'

A bang of the door heralded Paula, in her chic funeral outfit. Rocky looked at the approaching grim figure.

'I tell you, Mrs Cooper,' he said, 'I'm glad she's out of it.'

Thelma stared after the dented red car as it drove out of the car park emitting a disturbing rattle. Really, so unlike his usual style of vehicle. Things must be very tough indeed.

CHAPTER TWENTY-SIX

Love and electronics achieve wonderful things in Masham.

'. . . and I tried calling a couple of times but it went straight to voicemail,' Pat said as a tractor loomed into view and Thelma changed down gear. 'Have you heard from her?'

'No,' said Thelma, continuing to drive steadily behind the tractor.

Pat yawned. She'd not had much sleep the previous night, lying in the dark worrying and wondering about Liam, about Facebook, about the good sense that was needed to see him through some unidentified trial. But she felt easier this morning as one often did on a sunny day bright with daffodils and the first bluebells. Liam had gone to school if not cheerfully, without apparent upset and her grim imaginings seemed to somehow shrivel under the morning sun. It was in all probability just some Facebook spat. Now she was thinking about Liz.

'I was wondering if I should go round and see her,' she said.

'And say what?' asked Thelma.

'I don't know. Tell her I'm sorry.'

'For what?' She calmly changed down again as the tractor slowed for a hill. Pat knew if she'd been driving she'd have revved the engine, sworn and looked for somewhere to pass. Thelma did none of these things.

'Well, she seemed upset,' said Pat.

'I suppose to Liz what we're doing *is* upsetting.' She adjusted her mirror. 'We think perhaps something happened to Topsy and we want to find out more. And to do that we have to ask questions, questions we wouldn't normally ask at times we wouldn't normally ask them. Like you finding out from KellyAnne where she was staying.'

Pat shifted in her seat. Had she been that obvious? But then this was Thelma. 'At least we know she was in the Algarve,' she said. Thelma said nothing as she changed down again as the tractor slowed to a crawl. 'I mean she'd hardly have shown me the hotel she was in if she hadn't been there.'

'Yes,' said Thelma. There was a timbre in her voice that Pat knew only too well.

'You're surely not thinking she *wasn't* in Portugal,' she said. 'The police would've checked.'

'It's probably nothing,' said Thelma.

'But?' said Pat.

'It's just that KellyAnne was very ready to show you the details of the hotel on her phone. Almost as if she was *expecting* to be asked,' said Thelma as they drove past the *Welcome to Masham* sign.

Mrs Walker lived halfway up the hill leading into Masham, on the right-hand side, before you hit the stone houses and town square proper. Surrounded by cream stucco walls with black iron gates, Ure View stood out noticeably from the other houses.

'More like Fort Knox than Masham,' said Pat, a bit unsettled by the walls and the gates; not at all what she'd expected. Neither was the intricate intercom device on the gate pillar that Thelma was trying to work.

'Hello.' Thelma spoke tentatively into the grill, which crackled in response. An electronic whirr made them both look up; a security camera was swivelling its blank face down towards them. Pat automatically adjusted her scarf (a subdued maroon creation).

The grill spluttered into life and a tentative quavery voice came out. 'Hello?'

'Mrs Walker. It's Thelma Cooper here. I rang yesterday.'

'Yes.' Silence.

'I rang you yesterday. I spoke to your daughter.'

'Yes.' A slightly different inflection on the word, otherwise nothing.

'You very kindly agreed to see me.'

Another silence. Pat shifted, she could envisage this going on all afternoon. 'Is your daughter there?' Again silence.

The whole expedition was looking very doubtful but at that moment a breathless 'hi' signified the approach of a rather plump woman in a lilac polo shirt with a mass of faded ginger hair, who was hurrying up the hill towards them.

'Jennifer Walker,' gasped the woman. 'I'm sorry, I had to wait at work until Suzanne came. Only she was running late because her car wouldn't start. Why do people always text "LOL" when they're letting you down?'

She smiled, hands on her knees, panting, face red. Jenny-in-a-Hurry, Pat christened her.

'Jenny?' said the intercom. 'Is that you?'

'Mother, I'm coming in.'

'There's a lady.'

'I know there's a lady. There's two ladies.' Jenny-in-a-Hurry fished some sort of gizmo from her pocket. 'I'm doing the gates. Don't be worried, it's only the gates.'

She pointed the gizmo, which made the gates rattle and hum into life and obediently judder open. Immediately a flurry of deep barking cascaded from somewhere round the back of the house. Thelma, not a dog lover at the best of times, shrank back towards Pat, and Pat, used to the easy-going Larson, shrank back towards Thelma. However, Jenny-in-a-Hurry merely smiled apologetically, pressed another button on the gizmo and the noise cut off abruptly mid bark.

'Fido,' she said, enjoying their reaction. 'You just can't be too careful. Any cold callers who managed to wheedle their way in think twice after a quick burst of Fido.' She pressed the button again; again another volley of deep rolling barks.

Behind the walls Ure View was just another double-fronted bungalow of the type you'd get on the edge of any town, particularly one where people were wont to retire to. The glossy blue door opened and a small old lady in a salmon-pink cardigan peered amiably out at them.

'Have you seen your father anywhere?' she said.

'He'll be somewhere around,' said her daughter easily. 'I hope you ate that sandwich I left you.' The woman looked vague and serene and Jenny-in-a-Hurry gave her a sudden hug. 'Old nuisance,' she said. 'These ladies have come to see you. Let's get the kettle on.'

Talking about it later, it was the hug that stuck in Pat and Thelma's minds, the hug and what it signified. Yes, Mrs Walker had dementia as well, at a slightly worse stage than Topsy had been. She was *just* about able to manage in her own home, but was far enough on 'that slippery slope' as Jennifer put it to make her vulnerable to anyone who came along. It was a familiar story: since her husband's death there'd been, at first, a muddling of times and places, followed by a growing confusion that latterly saw her wandering round Masham at all hours of the day and night (including the one famous occasion when she set the alarms off in the Co-op at three o'clock in the morning). But Mrs Walker was adamant: she wanted to stay in the place that had been her home for over forty years and Jennifer – living a mere five doors down the road – was equally adamant that that was what was going to happen. However, working in public health she was, as she put it, Here, There and Everywhere and there was only so much she could do.

'Much as I'd like, I can't be in two places at once,' she said, setting down a tray of tea, which Pat and Thelma both clocked was a good colour.

200

Their answer had been technology. Jenny-in-a-Hurry's son Kyle was something of an IT whizz, working for the MOD. 'Very hush hush,' said Jennifer cheerfully. 'If he told me what he did he'd have to kill me.' So Kyle had taken Ure View in hand, turning up one weekend with a mate and a van full of electronic gadgetry. The electronic gates were fitted with an intercom which, when activated, immediately relayed a picture of the caller to various devices in Jennifer's house plus her smartphone. As well as Fido (state-of-the-art speakers hidden in various shrubs), the grounds were fitted with security lights that bathed the house in tungsten brightness when any of the sensors were activated (a bugger when it came to foxes and cats, said Jennifer, but better than darkness). Inside there were smoke alarms in each room plus a series of cameras that enabled Jennifer to check on her mother at any hour of the day or night and see if she'd had a fall or was in any difficulty whatsoever. She did wear an alarm pendant around her neck but hadn't really grasped the reason for its existence.

'She thinks she won it in Bridlington in 1954,' said Jennifer.

'I do not . . .' Mrs Walker fingered the pendant fondly. 'Your father won it for me. Six ping-pong balls in a jam jar.'

Finally Mrs Walker had been tagged, a sort of ankle bracelet. If she did leave Ure View, as well as activating an alarm her presence would show up on a map on Jennifer's phone and alert her to call a willing team of friends and neighbours. 'Our own private ASBO, aren't you, Mum.'

'If you say so, dear.' Mrs Walker obviously had no idea what was being talked about.

And what could have been an intrusion, a trial . . . it all came back to that hug, the hug that said everything. *Electronic wizardry and love: together they could rule the world,* thought Pat. She wondered if Liam, Andrew and Justin would go to similar lengths for her and Rod.

Thelma's thoughts were gloomier; it took the combined efforts and energy of this whole family plus the top-secret electronic wizardry of Kyle to keep Mrs Walker safe. Who would be there for her and Teddy?

'It's all very impressive,' she said.

They were sitting in large comfy chairs in Mrs Walker's living room, big west-facing windows looking at a slope vibrant with late tulips running down to the river; the sunsets from this room must be quite a sight. Thelma could quite see why Mrs Walker wanted to stay where she was. Jenny, with what was obviously a practised gesture, scooped up a pile of mail and sorted briskly through it. 'Junk, junk, junk,' she chanted wearily, depositing it in a carrier bag. Thelma could see many of the same stencilled promises that had been on the mail she took from Topsy's bin. 'I have to keep it well away from Mother, don't I?' Mrs Walker smiled placidly at her daughter. 'She believes all this crap they tell her about big wins.'

'Thank you for seeing us,' said Thelma. 'We just wanted to ask you about a man named Oliver Harney.'

'Our man didn't call himself Oliver Harney; he called himself Tony Ransom.' Jennifer shifted in her chair and her face had undergone an abrupt change, as if an indicator above her head had flashed from cheerful to hostile. 'But from what you were saying it sounds like the same fellow.'

'We'd be very grateful for anything you could tell us,' said Pat.

'Have you been stung too?' Jennifer's complexion was becoming blotchy pink.

'We've had a couple of friends now who've been approached.' Thelma chose her words carefully. 'And we've one or two concerns.'

'You're not the police? I don't want to talk to the police.'

'We're not the police,' said Pat, a bit flattered that Jennifer thought they might be.

'Just concerned friends,' said Thelma. There was something intrinsically trustworthy in her tone and Pat saw Jennifer visibly relax. 'How did you first get in touch with him?'

Jennifer shook her head. 'He got in touch with us.'

At that moment the room was flooded with a shrill peeping noise, almost as if Jennifer's words were being bleeped out. But the noise continued. One of the smoke alarms? Both Pat and Thelma looked towards the kitchen, half expecting to see clouds of black billowing out.

'Relax.' Jennifer was laughing at their reaction; the indicator was on cheerful again. 'Tablet time, Mother.' More technology, this time in the shape of a plastic cylinder, not unlike a model flying saucer, with a small aperture from which Jennifer took three tablets.

'Marvellous gadget,' she said. 'I can fill it up with tablets days in advance; it goes off whenever you programme it to.'

'So this Oliver Harney,' said Pat. 'Or Tony Ransom.'

'You can tell your friend from me to have nothing whatsoever to do with that parasitic bastard.'

'I do wish you wouldn't use that language,' said Mrs Walker.

'How did you come across him?' asked Thelma.

'He came across us. It was not long after Dad died.'

'He's not dead – I keep telling you.' Mrs Walker looked apologetically at Pat and Thelma. 'She will keep saying he's dead. Try the allotment, I tell her.' She blinked and smiled amiably; she was beginning to sound drowsy. A side effect of her tablets?

'He turns up here at the house,' continued Jennifer. 'I wasn't here that day but he tells Mum that Dad had booked him to do some jobs on the place, work on the roof, stuff like that. And the thing was – it was just the sort of thing Dad might've done, off his own bat. One time we come back off holiday and there's a gazebo suddenly appeared.' She smiled sadly at the photo of a tanned man waving cheerily from the balcony of some apartment.

'And anyway Mum and me, we were all over the place. So when this Tony turns up one day . . . well, it feels almost like it was Dad looking out for us.

'But then he starts making a right old mess, leaving stuff all over the drive. And gradually we start noticing how plenty's getting started but not a right lot of stuff's getting finished, at least not very well. He took all the tiles off one side of the garage, goes away for the weekend, and there's a thunderstorm and bang, there's all Dad's tools gone rusty. That sort of thing.'

Thelma remembered those darting, probing eyes. The so-called tile slippage and the question mark over the wiring.

'Then we start getting these bills: £300 here, £400 there.' Her face was getting pinker, her voice becoming more shrill at the memory.

'And there's money going out of Mum's account, and it turns out he's taking her to the cash point in Ripon – not here in Masham – and getting the cash for these so-called bills.

'I tried asking him what was going on, but he were that bloody slippery, never there when I went round, never answering his mobile.' She paused. 'Then this one time when I was just leaving, I caught him. And I said, "Can I have a word?" And he said, "Can it wait?" And I said, "No, not really." And he gets out of his van . . . It's not that he actually said anything. He wasn't threatening or owt like that; he was a bit of a weed, truth be told . . . but there was *something* about him.'

Thelma remembered how the panels of the cloakroom vibrated as Oliver Harney/Tony Ransom had thumped them. She really had been a bit foolish come to think about it; she offered up a quick prayer of thanksgiving for deliverance.

'He answers everything, looks me straight in the eye, promises it'll all be done and more by the end of the week . . .'

Exactly like Mr Bettridge, thought Thelma.

'But of course by the end of the week nothing's better so I think *enough's enough*. So I take a day off work and I wait at Mum's till he comes round and I bin him off. I say, "Thank you very much, we'll pay what we owe, but we've had enough." And it all got a bit heated and I said things I probably shouldn't have and that's when he got this nasty look in his eye.'

'Like he might get violent?' said Pat.

'Worse than that – like . . . he just stood there looking, shaking his head. And if you told me he'd come back later and smash the place . . . or . . .' She broke off and looked at her dozing mother. 'Or worse . . . at that moment I'd have believed you.

'Looking back I shouldn't have even paid what I did, but I didn't want him turning up when Mum was on her own. And then of course I get someone proper in to look at what he's done – surprise surprise, it all needed doing again.'

'Did you tell anyone?'

'There was that much starting to go off with her ladyship—' she gestured to her mother '—I just couldn't face it. After all, he'd done the work and I had paid him.' She shook her head. 'But then a fortnight later, all this rubbish gets dumped in front of the house. And then a week after that, there's this big scratch on my car, car keys or something.'

Thelma remembered that time when Mr Bettridge had had the children's music lessons stopped due to non-payment of bills. And then suddenly three cars in the staff car park had something like a Stanley knife stuck into the tyres.

'He sounds an out-and-out crook.' Pat, married to a builder, felt outraged at this slur on the profession.

'But that's not all,' said Jennifer. 'I was working at a surgery in Richmond and one of the practice nurses, she happens to mention this trouble her mum was having with a builder, only he wasn't calling himself Tony Ransom, or Oliver Whatsit, but listening to her it's pretty clear it's the same guy.'

'It certainly fits a pattern,' said Thelma. They were sat in a teashop in the market square where the up-and-down honey-stoned houses with their mullioned windows seemed to drowse in the late afternoon sun. The clock had just struck three and the day was beginning to gently wind down. As they sat there the first children from school were getting into four by fours across the square.

205

It was a good place to sit and think and mull. It was atypical for a tourist teashop, with its deep red walls and dreamcatchers; the new-age music reminded Pat of places and parties she used to frequent in her pre-Rod days. The place was almost empty. Apart from themselves there was just one other couple: a man and woman. She, with an expensive-looking silvery blonde helmet of hair, was gazing dreamily out across the market square; he, in an expensive-looking jacket, was immersed in a guidebook. *Mr and Mrs Bland,* Pat thought.

She stirred her herbal tea without enthusiasm and looked longingly at the stack of rocky road arranged under a glass dome on the counter. With an effort she forced her thoughts back to rogue builders. 'Pattern?'

'The numbers I rang. Two old ladies, one moved to a home, two disconnected numbers.'

'So . . .'

'So here we have a man going under different names who seems to prey on vulnerable older people. At least two we know about: Topsy and Mrs Walker.'

'And you think . . . he killed Topsy?'

Thelma frowned. 'That doesn't fit quite so well.'

'Jennifer said she thought he could turn nasty.'

'Scratching a car, dumping rubbish, that's one thing . . . but tampering with someone's tablets? They're two totally different things. It'd be like a shoplifter suddenly becoming an armed robber . . .'

'If he was covering up the fraud?'

'But then why keep on doing dodgy building work if he had his hands on all Topsy's money?' She frowned to herself and looked out of the window.

The church clock struck the quarter and Pat had to take something of a reality check. Here they were in a teashop in Masham, talking about different forms of murder in the same tones they used to use to plan Key Stage One Sports Day. Mrs

Bland was still looking out across the square, probably planning what to cook for tea. Maybe later the Blands would watch *Canal Boat Challenge*. A calm, untroubled evening at the end of a calm, untroubled day. She brought her attention back to what Thelma was saying.

'It just doesn't fit . . .'

Thelma stopped, brought short by her own words. Suddenly it was there again, that niggle, that sense of something missed. There was plenty about Oliver Harney/Tony Ransom that didn't fit, but there had been something that afternoon – something she'd seen or heard, something *did* fit with what had happened. What? Something Jennifer had said? She ran her mind back over their conversation . . . not being in two places at once . . . the need for gadgets – the gates, the lights, the pill dispenser – and then there was all that junk mail Jennifer had confiscated, just like KellyAnne with Topsy. She thought of that bulging carrier bag still in the boot of her car. She really needed to go through it properly.

Pat interrupted her thoughts. 'So what about Lloret and Ness?'

'What about them?'

'Could they not have something to do with it?' The thought of Ness being hauled off by the police was one that gave her no small degree of satisfaction. Besides, the scenario of Ness committing the fraud and silencing Topsy was a hundred times more plausible once Lloret's technical know-how was thrown in the mix.

'Possibly.' Thelma sounded vague.

Pat had a distinct feeling her ideas were being passed over. 'She'd have done anything to hang onto him,' she said. 'Her bit of fun on the slide.' Thelma looked at her. 'It's something one of Liam's mates said,' she said, wondering how much she needed to explain. 'He got it wrong.'

Thelma said nothing but continued staring at her friend. Unnerved, Pat got up to pay. Talk about killing a joke stone dead. Truth be told she couldn't see that the afternoon had actually got them much further on. They'd suspected Oliver Harney/ Tony Ransom to be a crook and they now knew he was a crook. And as for the rest, well, if anything *had* happened, it was anyone's guess. She looked across at Thelma who was now staring out at the cobbles of the marketplace as if beholding the surface of a distant planet for the first time.

Retracing her steps she passed by Mr and Mrs Bland's table.

'You're a selfish bastard,' Mrs Bland was saying mildly, almost conversationally, to Mr Bland.

'You always have been. You're a selfish bastard and I'll sleep with who I want to.'

CHAPTER TWENTY-SEVEN

A reckoning takes place in Willow Base and anger is felt at various injustices.

About the same time Thelma and Pat were making speculations in Masham, Jacob was stood hunched in the corner of the Willow Base classroom, head hunched down into his shoulders reminding Liz vividly of Derek's mother and that time in the care home, when she'd hit a resident attempting to steal her custard cream.

'Jacob,' Mrs Bell was saying in calm, reasonable tones. 'Do you want to tell your grandma how you disrespected me and the children this afternoon?'

No reply, but his shoulders hunched even more.

Liz was feeling pretty hunched herself, still flushed with the embarrassment of being oh so tactfully summoned by Mrs Bell in front of the other parents and grandparents waiting in the chilly sunshine to collect the various members of Willow class. She'd been thinking – or rather trying resolutely not to think – about the events of yesterday. The upset, and the distress . . . Poor KellyAnne. And at her own mother's funeral! And then Mandy, the previous night . . . No, whatever was going on, whatever had happened – and everyone else seemed to think nothing untoward had taken place – she was determined to have no more to do with it.

These had been her thoughts before that sunny, tactful voice had cut across them with: 'Jacob's grandma? Could I possibly have a quick word?'

She'd looked up and seen the smiling face of the woman she knew from parent assemblies and Christmas fayres as the five-star Mrs Bell.

There'd been a perceptible stir amongst the assembled mums and grandmas and Liz was pretty sure she'd heard Mags Preston-Batty's undertone of 'here we go again'.

Following her into school she saw Mags Preston-Batty mime a telephone and Mrs Bell give a smiling thumbs up. The meaning was obvious: 'talk later'. The mateyness of the gesture made Liz feel very definitely on the outside of the sunny, cheerful community that was Willow Class – the grandmother of that terrible Jacob Newsome.

Inside the school everything – the displays, the décor, the technology – was brightly, energetically light years away from the profession she had given over thirty years to. On the walls displays reflected the very latest drives and dynamics of primary education: *British Values, Web Club, Spot the fronted adverbial!* (*This is a progressive and driven education environment,* the Ofsted report had carolled.) They showed all too clearly a profession spinning further and further forward on energized waves of change away from the job that had once been Liz's life. The only thing slightly out of place in this modern forward-looking environment was Mrs Bell herself, with her greying brown hair, cheerful make-up-free face and baggy purple jumper.

She stopped outside Willow Base classroom.

'As you may gather, "Jacob's Grandma"—' she had put light-hearted inverted commas round the name '—we've got a bit of a report system up and running, and I'm sorry to have to tell you we've had what you might term *une incidente.*' Her words were humorous and invited Liz to share in the sentiment. He'd had, she said, such a brill day – no less than three emojis earned

(Liz had made a mental note to find out just what these emojis were) – which was pretty darn good for any child. However, then . . . Mrs Bell's words became precise, carefully chosen, with a trace of sadness . . . Then in the afternoon he'd 'lost it', grown very hostile, very aggressive and – pregnant pause – destroyed another child's artwork.

'Was it Elsie Preston–Batty's?' Liz couldn't help herself.

'No.' Now Mrs Bell's sunny tone held something else, something with a hint of steel, something that told Liz she did not care for being interrupted and had no intention of telling Liz just whose picture had been destroyed. Liz, feeling suitably abashed, had found herself looking shamefaced down at her feet, fearful of getting on the wrong side of those sunny tones again.

Mrs Bell carried on. Things had gone from bad to worse. Jacob had, apparently, refused to speak to herself or her teaching assistant, refused to do any more work and had, in short, continued to be very angry and disruptive for the rest of the afternoon. And she had tried. As she had tried every single day and would go on trying. With Bells On. With a weary look that hinted just how hard she had tried, Mrs Bell talked of long late nights devising behaviour strategies for Jacob, of making charts, planning specialized work for the little man. And she wasn't going to give up, No Sirree. She told Liz more about the behaviour strategy plan drawn up with Tim and Leoni, and the contract signed by them and by Jacob himself; by which, any misdemeanours would be shared with the family and accordingly followed up at home with a withdrawal of iPad time.

Which was what she wanted Liz to do, as she understood tonight he was staying over with her.

'Of course,' said Liz cravenly.

And then Mrs Bell had opened the classroom door revealing the hunched little figure, under the watchful eye of a support assistant who was (rather grimly Liz thought) slicing paper on the guillotine. 'Welcome to creative chaos,' said Mrs Bell with a self-absolving laugh.

Liz's first thought was how like Derek's mother the cross, hunched figure looked.

The second involved Mrs Bell's classroom. Creative chaos wouldn't be how she described it.

It was, not to put too fine a point on it, a tip.

It was untidy, but not the natural ten-past-three-in-the-afternoon classroom untidiness . . . It was a deep engrained untidiness that went way beyond the flow of any one school day, an untidiness that had evolved over days and weeks and months.

Everywhere there were piles of things, heaped on every available surface: sheets, folders, exercise books. Nothing seemed to be organized. There was no system to the piles. Dog-eared green books were stacked against rings binders, which were stacked against plastic wallets full of worksheets. Nothing like the neatly labelled magazine boxes that characterized every classroom Liz had run. What magazine boxes there were seemed to be repositories for entirely random objects: coloured paper, packs of felt tip pens (lids missing), even in one a spray of peacock feathers. Things seemed to be stuffed: boxes were out of shape, drawers and cupboards wouldn't shut, the big stationery cupboard in the corner looked in serious danger of toppling over.

Maybe, *maybe*, this could have been overlooked if there'd been a certain creative vibrancy to the place. Liz thought of Pat's classroom, never the tidiest of places but always something exciting draped, stapled or hanging somewhere. But this . . . was dull. Faded sugar paper, torn displays, mud brown, olive green faded by the sun to an uninspiring grey. And the displays themselves – autumn leaves, winter poems – were, in late March, well past their sell-by date. But what really settled it for Liz was the planning file. Her heart grieved remembering her own immaculate holly-green tome reverentially set up for her by Topsy at the end of every summer ready for September, with its sections, its labelled pockets, placed prominently in the classroom like a Bible on a lectern. Mrs Bell's file, on her desk under assorted sheets, a battered copy of *The Witches* and a coffee cup, was a Leeds United ring binder, stuffed like every other container in the room, the front cover creased out of shape by the amount of paper sticking out of it. Mrs Bell, for all her talk of spending evenings and nights planning (with bells on), was obviously putting none of that energy into sorting out her classroom. 'Give us a minute, Tracey,' said Mrs Bell and Tracey retreated. Was it Liz's imagination or was there a certain tension as the silent figure left the room?

'Jacob, your grandma's here. And we need to tell her about the choices you made this afternoon.'

'Now then, Jacob.' Liz put a stern inflection in her voice and a scowling eye wavered up to meet hers.

'If you won't tell your grandma, then I'll have to,' said Mrs Bell in tones that were more sorrowful than anything else. 'Because I'm sure your grandma hasn't the time to stand round here waiting for you to speak.'

She launched on an account of the day. A good day to start with, the three emojis (she gestured to a board that looked to be plastered with faded smiley faces – was that what emojis were? Smiley faces? At least she could have had them laminated). He had a go with his writing (hey, that's all I ask, you have a go, Jacob!) – but then came the art.

'The painter of this picture was very proud of it, Jacob. How do you think she felt when you ruined it? How would you feel?' She sorrowfully produced a creased and torn picture, which looked decidedly mediocre to Liz, but who nevertheless obediently sucked in her breath and shook her head.

'Jacob,' she said. Again that reluctant eye contact. 'It's very wrong to damage other people's work. Very wrong.' There was something firm, something final in her tones that seemed to both abash Jacob and satisfy Mrs Bell, who pronounced that tomorrow was another day, and maybe tonight when Jacob had his iPad time

213

withdrawn he could think about his actions and the consequences of those actions. Liz (who had no intention of withdrawing anything) nodded solemnly and led Jacob out the room.

'He's a great little fella,' said Mrs Bell. 'Believe it or not I love him to bits.'

Not, thought Liz. *Very definitely not. And tidy up your classroom, lady.*

On the way out they passed Tracey, who was walking to the classroom with an armful of photocopying. 'Goodnight, Jacob,' she said.

'Goodnight, Mrs Clough,' he said.

Mrs Clough dropped her voice, and looked round to see who might overhear her. 'He's all right is Jacob,' she said. It was all she needed to say.

Crossing the empty playground a hand slipped silently into Liz's.

'Cassidy said I was emotionally dysfunctional,' he said.

'I see,' said Liz. It was all she needed to say and she felt the hand grip a little tighter.

Pulling away from the school, an open-topped sports car nipped out of the car park in front of her, driven by Mrs Bell, blonde hair blowing out in the breeze; she gave a cheery wave and accelerated away. Liz looked at her dashboard clock: three-thirty-seven. She, herself, never normally left school before five. So this was the wonderful Mrs Bell. She could almost hear Mags Preston-Batty's arch tones: 'It's a complete mess in that classroom, but my God the kids love it, and they love her. And my God they learn.'

And everyone thought there was nothing wrong.

Suddenly she felt burningly, tinglingly angry. She looked at Jacob in the rear-view mirror, face solemn as he flicked through the Batman cards she'd given him (obviously the correct choice). She thought of Topsy, lost and forlorn in an overbright cardigan, all her money greedily snatched away from her by someone too lazy to roll up their sleeves and do an honest day's work. 'Right,' she said to herself. 'Right.'

CHAPTER TWENTY-EIGHT

*Numbers are collated, a love life is dissected
and Tolkien's final passing is mourned.*

Driving back up the Borrowby Lane, having collected her car from Thelma's, Pat passed the Celtic poet coasting serenely down the hill through the village, past the perched cottages and high verges. The splodges of purple and yellow crocuses looked almost as if she were trailing them in her wake. She gave a cheery wave, which Pat acknowledged with a smile, but also a stab inside as her worries about Liam came slamming back. Her mind went back to the girl's words: *Social media. It saps the soul.*

Why that frozen look on Liam's face? And just what had Ness been referring to in such a snide way? Pat realized with a sinking feeling that she had to find out, which meant some sort of confrontation when all she wanted was nothing more taxing than assembling the supper to the background of Jules Bellerby on Radio York.

It wasn't hard to think of an excuse to go to Liam's room, but then it never was. In Pat's experience there was always something in the life of a teenage boy that needed washing or ironing or generally sorting. She picked up the pile of washed and folded running gear and made her way upstairs. Classical music was emanating from behind his door, always a sound of concentration and introspection; Pat remembered he had a physics essay to give in the following day. Steeling herself she knocked.

'Enter, Mother of Mine.'

Good, he wasn't in one of his inward monosyllabic moods, though he might well be when she'd asked what she was going to ask. She opened his door – and stopped.

His last Tolkien poster had gone.

Ian McKellen staring crossly into the middle distance had been replaced by a soulful black and white image of that man who played the villain in *Sherlock*. Quite why this should upset her so much Pat wasn't sure but she felt a sudden painful pang for the far-off days when everything had been Tolkien Tolkien Tolkien. How well she remembered and missed the times when she'd walk in this very room with a plate of bacon sandwiches for a group of boys ferociously concentrating over a handful of multi-shaped, multi-coloured dice playing Dungeons and Dragons. She could hear Liam's voice like a half-forgotten song: *I invoke my wand of fireballs*.

Now he was rattling away ferociously on the keyboard. On the screen were at least three Internet sites and a Word document. He could be doing his physics essay, he could be playing some online game, he could be working out how to make a bomb.

'Only me,' she said unnecessarily, putting the washing on top of his chest of drawers.

No comment.

'I was wondering about supper.'

Silence.

'I was thinking maybe the Jamie Oliver sausage thing we had the other week.'

Non-committal grunt. This was not going well and it was evidently too much of a leap to weigh in and mention Facebook and the Internet. She sighed to herself and with a sense of an unpleasant task deferred she turn to the door.

'I'm doing it now.' His voice stopped her in her tracks.

'Good,' she said enthusiastically and then again with less certainty: 'Good.' He turned and looked at her with that half-smile that said they both knew full well she had no idea what 'it' was.

'Your physics essay,' she guessed.

'Your sleuthing.' He waved the photo of the page from Oliver Harney's Filofax, the green, blue and red phone numbers.

'Hardly sleuthing.' Pat felt a bit affronted. The trip that afternoon had left her a bit uneasy about the whole Oliver Harney/Tony Ransom business as if merely by talking about him he might appear and do damage. She had a sudden unsettling image of an almighty scratch on Rod's four by four.

'Oliver Harney.' Liam pressed a key. 'Oliver Harney builder – nul points. Search again using decorator, Oliver Harney – again nul points. Repairs, guttering, plasterer – all a big fat nul points.'

'Well thanks for trying.' She tried to sound grateful now he was communicating but her mind was scrabbling for ways to introduce the subject of the soul-sapping properties of the Internet.

'Whoa, Mother! Where is the staying power of the older generation?'

'If you can't find anything . . .'

'You go back to the proverbial drawing board and you have a jolly good old think.' His tone was almost a carbon copy of Thelma's best explaining voice and she found herself biting her lip in spite of everything.

'And?'

'And I took the numbers you said Thelma got from his Filofax. The List of Mystery. I've been running a sweepstake with India. She thinks they're a pagan cult but I'm tending to the idea they're all brothels.'

'They're numbers of his clients.'

'Aha! Clients!' He put an arch emphasis on the word. 'Oliver Harney: no job too hard. Brings own tools.'

Why couldn't she laugh? If it had been her friend Olga who'd said that, she'd have laughed long and hard. But it wasn't her friend Olga; it was her youngest son and she found herself growing hot round the cheeks.

'If you're going to talk nonsense I'll go away.' The words sounded lame and automatic even as she was saying them, and Liam didn't appear to be listening as he turned back to the screen in response to some ping. She sat on his bed, and Larson peacefully relocated himself into her lap. The bedroom window was open; the sun was beginning to drop down over the Pennines. It was going to be one of the first good sunsets of the spring.

'Oliver Harney, master of the black arts, or just master . . .' Liam gave a final flourish on the keys. Pat tried to understand what was going on.

'So you've entered all the phone numbers into a search engine thing?'

'I put them into "Fetch" – a rather nifty search programme. It's taking the numbers and doing a sweep of t'Internet to see if there's any commonality between them.'

'And is there?'

'It's still processing.' He turned and busied himself at the computer again and she watched him from the bed. The back of his neck was definitely the back of a man's neck. She squinted to try and resolve it back to that of a child but she couldn't. She noticed the drawer on the desk looked slightly lopsided and made a mental note to ask Rod to look at it. She remembered when they bought that desk. It had come in and the old cabin bunk had gone out. Childhood over with one delivery van. You did it as parents: made these the physical changes to rooms and clothes but it was inside your head – the mental changes – where you had the trouble.

It was so peaceful in the room. Pat knew she should ask him what was wrong, but she simply lacked the energy. She thought back again to what had happened that afternoon – Jenny and her mother, the tale of Oliver Harney. And then there had been

218

Thelma, and that thunderstruck look she'd given in the café . . .
What was it she'd been saying? Of course – Lloret . . . the bit of
fun on the slide. But why would that make her look so startled?

'Lloret Whitlaw,' she said out loud.

'What about him?'

'Do you think he's capable of doing wrong?' She'd asked the
question before she could think it through.

Liam looked at her, puzzled. 'It depends what sort of wrong.'

'Criminal wrong. Stealing.'

Liam shrugged. 'It'd have to be someone else's idea.' He turned
back to the PC. It looked like he was doing a Google search.
'He'd do wrong if it was the easiest thing to do and involved
ducking some issue or other.'

None of this sounded like someone who would cold-bloodedly
plunder someone's bank account and then tamper with their
tablets. But what if he was in league with someone else? Someone
who had no such scruples. Like Ness. And if they had been
committing fraud, maybe Lloret had got scared, and yesterday had
been all about him backing out.

'Why this sudden interest in Lloret Whitlaw?' said Liam.

'No reason,' said Pat unconvincingly.

'There we go.' Again Liam spun the screen round. Electronic
chords sounded as an image of clouds billowed across the screen.
Four bars – apricot, raspberry, lime and tangerine – slid hori-
zontally across the clouds.

'Nice graphics,' said Liam. 'The boy done good.' He clicked
and a picture appeared of Lloret, obviously professionally taken,
expensive suit, smart pink shirt, charming, carefree, in control. *E
Titans,* read the title. *Social media managers*.

'So he's running his own business?'

'Looks like it. It also looks like someone else is bankrolling
him. This is all quite sophisticated. Unless he happens to have a
few thousand spare. Which he didn't last summer when I don't
think he bought one single drink for anyone.'

Another chime from the computer cut across his words and suddenly Pat knew now was the moment. She just couldn't face another night of questions and speculation boiling round her head. She had to speak. 'Liam, talking of social media . . . Facebook.'

'What about it?' He didn't turn and look at her.

'Have you been having . . . problems?'

Just as before it wasn't so much that his face moved, rather the shadows did. The planes and shadows shifted, elongated his features into something harrowed and haunted. His voice struggled to be normal.

'What sort of problems?'

'You tell me.'

He took a breath and turned and faced her. It was a mannerism she knew of old, one that always prefaced some weighty revelation – windows broken, biscuits stolen, that time he'd burnt her best copper pan trying to make bonfire toffee.

'Liam. Whatever is it?' she said again, feeling completely unable to cope with whatever it was and wanting to be doing nothing more stressful than collating a sausage pasta.

Another electronic chime made them both look at the computer and all at once the moment had passed; Pat didn't know whether to be relieved or frustrated.

'Don't you want the result?' he asked. She stared at him uncomprehendingly. 'From the database? Thelma's magic numbers?'

She nodded, realizing her hands on Larson's bristly back were shaking.

'And the winner is—' He did a drum roll with his palms on the desktop. 'The *Ripon Gazette* Online.'

'I'm sorry?'

'All the phone numbers from what's his face's Filofax. All linked to names to be found at some time in the *Ripon Gazette*, specifically . . .' he squinted at the screen '. . . the births, marriages and deaths page.'

CHAPTER TWENTY-NINE

Peace is restored between friends, a call is taken and wickedness of various types is contemplated.

At last Thelma looked up from the printed sheets and carefully put them back in the wallet.

'Well done, you,' she said. 'And full marks to Liam.'

Pat felt a flush of pleasure as she put the wallet back in her bag. Despite her weariness she felt a sense of deep and enduring accomplishment. The previous night, after realizing sleep was yet again impossible, she had sat herself at the kitchen table, with an iPad and a what-the-hell coffee, trying to make sense of Liam's search results. And as the first fingers of dawn had slanted long shadows down the Hambleton Hills and made warm patches of light on the flags of her kitchen floor, she trawled through news sites, forums, chat groups and Facebook pages (not Liam's). Certain pages she'd printed out, certain paragraphs she'd highlighted in pink. These were the results she had now presented to Thelma.

'But what do we do now?' she said.

Thelma didn't answer immediately, but knitted her fingers together and looked at the sheets.

'What we need to do,' she said eventually, 'is tell the police.' Her voice was so ordinary, so matter-of-fact, she might have been talking about ordering chubby crayons and powder paint.

Pat looked uncertain. Doing research was one thing . . . but telling the police . . . She thought of those scratches on the side of Jenny-in-a-Hurry's car.

'What if I'm wrong though?' she said uneasily.

Again Thelma didn't answer immediately. Then: 'I'll do it,' she said hesitantly. 'At least . . . the fact is . . .' She stopped herself, again glancing at her phone she'd left out on the table. No missed calls and a full five bars of signal.

Pat looked at her friend. She seemed curiously . . . uncertain . . . Not herself at all. Come to think of it, Thelma had seemed preoccupied ever since they met today. There, but not there. And she kept glancing at her phone. Was something the matter? If it was anyone else she would have wondered if there'd been a row at home but not Thelma and Teddy.

'I've got the number for that DC Donna.' Now she sounded as if she were talking herself into something. 'That she gave to Liz.'

Instinctively both of them looked at the empty chair where Liz habitually sat. Neither of them commented on her absence.

'And in the meantime . . .' Thelma's voice took on a determined energy as she produced her own wallet, bulky and bulging and put it on the table. 'I've been doing some homework of my own.'

Not to be outdone, was Pat's instant thought, a thought immediately squashed down. Thelma lifted a carrier bag onto the table and put it next to the wallet. 'The junk mail from Topsy's. I've been through it.'

'There's so much.' Pat sounded slightly bewildered, looking at the paperwork Thelma was arranging in neat piles across the table.

'There is,' agreed Thelma. 'And this is only a fraction of what must have come.' She picked up the envelopes like a card shark about to deal a hand of poker. 'I've sorted it into three categories. First there's the envelopes.' She pushed a few across to Pat.

The words on the back were instant and eye-catching: *Open immediately*, *Action required*, *Urgent response needed*.

'Note the text. Exactly the sort of wording to make the recipient curious, if not anxious.'

'Especially if they're going doolally tap,' said Pat. If Thelma winced at this casual labelling of the elderly losing their faculties, she didn't show it.

'Then there's the inside,' she said.

Pat scanned the sheets. All had the same type of layout, that of a bill or receipt. Some were salmon pink, some grey, some pale blue: colours of officialdom, colours that said *trust me*. And then there were the promises: in stencil font, in coloured clouds, in strident quotations. Promises of money: *£10,000*, *£15,000* – *Mrs Topsy Joy, your cheque is waiting for YOU!*

Pat sighed. 'And you think Topsy fell for some of this?'

Thelma nodded, remembering the three carriage clocks and the Perspex swans. 'From what I can gather from various Internet forums, people are bombarded with this stuff on a daily basis.'

Something caught Pat's eye. 'There's a mistake here,' she said, scanning another. 'That's not for Topsy; it's addressed to Paula.'

'Paula?' Thelma frowned and took the sheet. Sure enough, Mrs Paula Oldroyd of Gortops Rainton was promised Big Big Prizes. Was it significant in light of what she knew? Or *thought* she knew, she sternly reminded herself. She glanced again at the phone, as if by doing so she could make it shrill into life.

Pat meanwhile was scanning a third pile, which consisted of catalogues, bewildering in their variety. Walking frames, leisurewear, gardening tools. She opened one and saw a rather glamorous silver-haired lady reclined in bed reading a book with a cup rest (tray-te yourself with our no-spills coffee cuddler!) and a book light (read with ease!) and a neck support and shawl. On the bedside cabinet lay a sort of plastic carousel, which automatically dispensed medication (Never forget that night time dose!). *Delights for tranquil nights,* sang out the canary yellow print. *Gifts for your loved ones.* Pat shook her head; her idea of a nice present never had been and never would be any sort of pill dispenser.

'Products all aimed at the elderly,' said Thelma. 'People often alone, maybe confused . . . the promises of money, the endless catalogues . . . Clever but essentially very wicked.'

Pat thumbed through the catalogue, looking at the various images of old age – walking, showering, reading – depicted by groomed models who didn't look a day over sixty and wouldn't know an incontinence pad if it hit them on their stylishly coiffed heads.

'I don't see where this gets us though,' she said. 'There's so many.'

'So many products, but,' said Thelma, 'on the envelopes . . . the return address is the same every time: PO Box 25, Woldfield . . .'

'So *all* these companies are using the same address?'

'They're all the *same* company – a company trading under the name Golden Days Direct. You should see what people had to say about *them* on the Internet.'

Pat scanned yet another sheet, again trying to fight off that snippy feeling of having been outdone. The substance was essentially the same: poor goods, non-existent costumer service, and again and again people being bombarded by junk mail.

'It's disgusting,' she said wearily. 'The whole lot of it.'

'What's disgusting?' Neither of them had heard Liz approach, but there she was, coffee in hand with a bright, almost feverish look in her eye. Pat had a sudden impulse to gather up all the mail and frantically stuff it underneath her jumper. But Liz was smiling, a slightly forced smile, but a smile nonetheless.

'Now then,' she said sitting down. 'I want to hear all about how you got on yesterday, going to Masham.'

'Never mind Masham,' said Thelma. 'How's Jacob?'

★   ★   ★

'There was stuff all over the place . . . The whole room was a complete and utter tip.' Liz set her coffee cup down in her saucer with an emphatic chink. She had been talking non-stop for precisely seventeen and a half minutes.

'There's worse things than a messy room,' said Pat. She was remembering the state her own classroom had got into from time to time.

'It's more than just mess.' Liz struggled to collect her words. 'There's no *system* to anything . . . The books are crammed any old how; the work on the walls is out of date. Jacob says she's forever losing stuff. And yet everyone thinks she's this wonderful, five-star teacher. And she's not. But she has this way with people and they all believe her.' Her voice was brisk and angry. 'It beats me how everyone can go round believing something that's basically not true.'

'People have a tendency to believe anything, if it's said often enough and in the right way,' said Thelma. She wondered who had first given Mrs Bell the epithet 'five-star'; she had a shrewd idea it was probably Mrs Bell herself. Over the years she'd met a fair few Mrs Bells.

'It's what to do,' said Liz. She was seeing Tim and Leoni later on to bring them up to speed on events as requested and at this moment in time had absolutely no idea what she was going to say. She exhaled and for a moment, just a moment, allowed the peaceful bustle of the garden centre café to subsume her anxieties.

'Of course there are always other schools,' said Thelma mildly and matter-of-factly. Liz stared, coffee cup halfway to her mouth.

'St Anne's is very good,' she said. 'Everyone says so.'

'But not for Jacob,' said Thelma.

'And certainly not with this Mrs Bell,' said Pat.

Liz looked at her friends. Every single conversation with Tim and Leoni had been underlined by the unshakeable belief that St Anne's, the Ofsted-outstanding St Anne's, was the best school in the area. She remembered hoping against hope that Jacob

225

would get a place despite living just outside the catchment area. The massive relief and bottle of Prosecco when he had. And yet . . . and yet . . .

She looked again at her friends, her very good friends. 'The other day,' she said. 'At the funeral . . .'

'It was a very difficult day,' said Thelma.

'I reckon we were all a bit bonkers,' said Pat.

There was a pause and they smiled at each other. It was enough.

'Anyway,' said Pat. 'Wait till you hear about Masham.'

Thelma told the story with colourful interjections from Pat. As she did, Liz's frown returned and deepened, mind now obviously taken off Jacob; by the end of the tale she was actually clutching the edge of the table, knuckles whitening. Then Pat produced the results of Liam's online sleuthing and explained what it was the numbers from Oliver Harney's Filofax had in common.

'*The Ripon Gazette*,' she said.

At that moment Thelma's phone shrilled into life. With a tense, set expression Thelma snatched it up and looked at the screen, slopping her coffee in the process.

'Excuse me,' she said, 'I have to take this,' and retreated off to a quiet corner of the Edinburgh Woollen Mill.

'So why has Oliver Harney been ringing the *Ripon Gazette*?' said Liz, frowning.

'He hasn't been,' said Pat, looking over at where Thelma was deep in conversation. 'He's been reading it. The births, marriages and deaths column,' supplied Pat. She took a printed-off article from the *Yorkshire Post* from her wallet and pushed it across the table. *Vultures: the scam tradesmen preying on the bereaved and vulnerable,* read the headline.

Liz felt the beginnings of an icy fist somewhere about her chest; she knew this all meant something unpleasant, she just wasn't sure what.

'What these people do,' said Pat, 'is they look through the death notices, and after a while call round to see the bereaved and reckon on something their dead husband or wife or whoever arranged for them. Rod was telling me last night.'

Liz stiffened remembering Brian's words at the funeral.

. . . almost like the voice beyond the grave. It was about three months after the funeral . . .

. . . I'm very lucky. He said another winter and I could have lost the whole roof . . .

She snatched the paper and began reading with worried concentration as Thelma rejoined them.

'Is everything okay?' said Pat, knowing that obviously it wasn't.

Thelma looked at her friend; sudden phone calls to middle-aged people were so often harbingers of some sort of calamity and she had to say something to put her friend's mind at rest. But neither was she prepared to say what the call had been about. Not yet.

'Garage,' she said. Which was true, after a fashion. Pat looked at her friend. In her experience one didn't retreat to quiet corners of the Edinburgh Woollen Mill to take calls from the garage. But before she could say anything the scrape of a chair made them both look over at Liz. Their friend was standing up, a look on her face that could only be adequately described as terrible, a look that put Thelma in mind of the time she'd seen Dame Diana Rigg playing Medea; specifically the part where she'd murdered her sons to get vengeance against her husband. Pat had only seen that look on her face once or twice in all the time she'd known Liz: that awful time when a dinner lady had hit a child. They both felt a pang of worry; had they done the wrong thing in telling her what they knew?

'I have to go,' Liz said in a voice that allowed no contradiction of any sort. On her way to the café door she paused and looked back at the other two.

'Skel Hill,' she said. The others looked blankly at her. 'The other school in Boroughbridge.'

CHAPTER THIRTY

A dress is admired,
karaoke considered and a cup broken.

Thelma emptied another bag onto the floor of the stock room and made a determined effort to focus on the pastel knitwear and array of slacks. Again her phone was out in view; again she kept checking it to make sure she had full signal. She was glad of her shift at the charity shop, a welcome chance for her to focus her thoughts on something else than the decision she felt she was about to have to make. She began sorting the clothes into the three piles, checking in the pockets as she did. (There was that time when there'd been a £50 note!) That was the good thing about the charity shop – there was always *something* to absorb the attention, always someone you knew coming in, always some interesting bit of news to mull over.

That afternoon there had been no shortage of things to distract her: more news of the executive head teacher at St Barnabus's (apparently setting the PTA targets for fundraising, an action that had caused universal outrage), plus the curious behaviour of the landlord of the Station Hotel (not at all curious to Thelma; in her experience fifty-something men fell in love with twenty-something girls practically every verse end). Plus a flu outbreak at that new care home by the college meant a larger than usual intake of things to sort and although there were nominally three people on shift (herself, Polly and Verna), this was the afternoon where Verna changed the window display.

The window display at the hospice charity shop was Verna's jealously guarded province, something she changed without fail on the third Thursday of every month, unhesitatingly and uncompromisingly delegating all serving and sorting duties to whoever happened to be working that afternoon as she worked on her latest creation. And the results . . .

It wasn't that they weren't eye-catching or even well thought out; it was just that always in some crucial way, the contents of the display somehow never quite managed to gel. Colours clashed; items had some glaring stain or rip or flaw. There was the unforgettable time when a cannabis plant had featured prominently at the centre (horticulture not being one of Verna's strong points). 'Windows by Verna' was quite an ongoing joke with her and Teddy.

It was about four o'clock and Thelma was on the last bag when Verna finally finished, brushing her hands together and stepping back crying 'ta da!' with the sunny self-confidence of one blessed with not a shred of self-doubt. Polly and Thelma dutifully regarded her handiwork. This month green and yellow were the signature colours. A bright green and yellow lettered sign informed the people of Ripon that *Spring Has Sprung*. Three dresses of different shades of green and yellow adorned the three rather battered dummies the shop possessed, in front a collection of objects that Verna obviously thought evoked the essence of spring: a couple of trowels (one rusty), a pair of secateurs (surely pruning was more summer?), some gardening books, a tea service arranged round a cake stand . . . except the greens and yellows didn't quite match and two cups from the tea service were missing and had been substituted with other, mismatched cups. The *idea* was sound enough, thought Thelma, surveying the collection.

'Ooooo,' said Polly with obedient awe, 'I don't know how you do it.'

'Of course I do have some retail experience,' said Verna airily. 'Which helps.'

Thelma, who knew for a fact that this consisted of working part-time at Dunelm Mills in Castleford fifteen years ago, said nothing. 'It's very striking,' she said. She looked at the display again, with a growing sense there was something about the display, some detail, that had brushed against something at the back of her mind . . . some connection with something. She tried to think exactly what but at that moment she heard her phone shrilling in the back. 'Excuse me,' she said.

Five minutes later she came back slowly into the shop. It was almost exactly as she had thought, and she was fervently wishing it hadn't been. Now she would have to decide what to do. Outside in the street the first lights were coming on. It was a time to be thinking about going home, turning on the lamps and shutting the curtains on the day and thinking of nothing more taxing than what to have for tea, and what to watch on TV. Thelma dreaded the thoughts she knew would come throbbing in like toothache once she had some mental space.

She stopped. There, rifling through the children's clothes, was Mandy Pinder-as-was.

She was absorbed in her task and didn't see Thelma. There was a practised but joyless efficiency about the way she was expertly scanning the garments, size and price. She looked . . . worn down. Worn down and weary. What was she doing in a charity shop in Ripon when she lived and worked in Thirsk?

'Hello, Mandy,' she said.

'Oh, Mrs Cooper. Hello, I didn't know you worked here.' There was an unsurprised flatness in her tone, the trademark sound of the weary and worn out.

'I do. What brings you to Ripon?'

'I'm on my way to work.'

Thelma looked puzzled. 'Doesn't the bank close in half an hour?'

230

'Not the bank – Sainsbury's. I do evenings there: Thursday, Friday, Saturday.' Her fingers nervously pleated and re-pleated her scarf and she shot a quick nervous glance out of the window. At that moment Polly asked Thelma about the possibility of a chipped piece of china being worth something (answer: no) and Mandy resumed her looking, squinting at a girl's top and holding it up to the light. There was something very practised about the way she checked the seams, the armpits – this was not her first time in a charity shop. She replaced the garment, and looked at the adult clothes. Her eye fell on one of the few really good-quality garments in the shop, a burgundy dress, one brought in by that nice young wife of that new solicitor from Kaye and Stephens. Mandy held the dress against her and for a second her face went dreamy and Thelma was reminded of that closed-up little girl with the bag of pink, green and blue ponies.

'No,' said Mandy, placing the dress back on the rack. 'No, I must be good.'

She gave Thelma a weary smile that was more of a grimace and left the shop.

'There goes a lady who knows clothes.' From Polly, with her own elegant line in attire, this was praise indeed.

'Has she been in before then?' asked Thelma.

'A few times. Has a real eye for the good-quality stuff. She was showing me a dress she got in the Oxfam: Chanel. And that tan – none of your cheap spray-on. What I wouldn't give for my own tanning bed.' She sighed into a middle distance of Chanel dresses and tanning beds.

'You think she has a tanning bed?' Thelma's mind did a quick spin but she couldn't see how this could be connected with that other matter.

'I doubt it.' Polly brought herself to and began closing the blinds. 'Have you seen the price of them? Not much change from thirty grand.'

As a matter of fact Thelma knew this only too well.

Turning off the lights and locking the back door Thelma thought, Mandy worked in a supermarket? Why, when she already worked in a bank? And why was someone who obviously had money going round the charity shops in such a practised way?

Although it had been a fairly quiet afternoon at the Hotel Da Intereiza, it had not been without its drama. The Rod Stewart tribute act had come down with some unspecified form of food poisoning. Rumour had it that it was the cold buffet but, knowing the performer of old, Carolina – the chief receptionist – thought it was more likely to be vodka-related. She had spent a frustrating hour trying to source an alternative act (someone had said there was a newcomer to the expat community who could do a passable Mark Owen) so when the phone rang in the hotel office she thought it was most probably him.

'Good afternoon, Hotel Da Intereiza, how may I help you?' As she spoke she grabbed for pencil and Post-it Notes.

'Hello.' The line was very faint. 'Hello, my name is KellyAnne Joy; I stayed with you a few weeks ago.'

A complaint. Perfect. 'Good to hear from you, Ms Joy!' With practised ease she made her tone sunny and bright, as if there could be no possibility of any problem.

'I forget which room I was in. I know I had a view of the pool, only I think I left something.'

Joy . . . Joy. A sudden vision of a pink dress and a lot of blonde hair belting out some Madonna song on the karaoke machine.

'Ms Joy, how are you?' Karaoke? There was a thought.

'I'm fine.' She didn't sound fine. Husky voice; one of these colds the English were always getting. On cue there was an explosive cough.

'I've this dreadful cold. But anyway, I feel such a fool. I wonder if I left some pink earrings there. Pink triangles on gold hoops. I've been looking here and I suddenly remembered wearing them at the hotel, and I wouldn't normally bother but they're my favourite pair.' Another cough, or was it a sneeze? 'Do excuse me.'

Carolina brought out the lost property box: any number of phone chargers, a couple of rings, and rather bizarrely what looked like a small metal armadillo. But no earrings. She relayed the news in suitably regretful tones whilst scratching around for the number of the karaoke man in case Mark Owen was a no-show.

'I'm so sorry, Ms Joy.'

'No problem. It was a long shot.'

'I'm sorry to hear you're not well. You must come and see us soon. We'll soon get rid of any nasty bugs for you. Then you can sing "Like a Virgin" to us once again.'

'My love, if only.'

'Did you sort out the problem with your mother's phone? Where you able to get through in the end and tell her to take her tablets?' *Merda,* now the other line was ringing. It had to be Mark Owen. 'I'm so sorry, there's an important call.' Pray to the Lord she wouldn't have to fall back on the karaoke man again, after all, that would make it twice in the last two weeks.

Some 1,492 miles away in Borrowby, Pat replaced the phone, tucking the hanky with which she'd muffled the call back into her sleeve. The smell of No-Shame Savoury Chicken Meatballs (103 calories a pop) filled the kitchen. So KellyAnne *had* been where she said she had. Pat rose to stir the supper. She'd always thought so, and of course, as Thelma said, the police would surely have checked.

The feelings of quiet the thought gave her had been with her most of the afternoon. Since coming back from the garden centre she'd tried ringing Liz a few times, but the calls had gone straight to voicemail. She'd also searched Liam's room (as much as had felt right) and found nothing untoward. He was at school. Presumably everything there was all right otherwise she'd surely have heard. There hadn't seemed much else she could do, and not being able to settle to anything more demanding, she'd taken Larson on one of his favourite walks, on the path that meandered unhurriedly from the lane through the fields at the base of Sutton Bank.

From inside, the skies had seemed threatening, but outside, from the muddy pathways, and despite the approaching rain, they were a gentler scuddy grey, the changing shapes strangely peaceful. With Larson nosing unhurriedly in the hedge bottoms, Pat let herself think maybe, just maybe, everything was all right after all. Maybe whatever it was with Liam was even now sorting itself out . . . and even if it wasn't . . . there was something perhaps bigger than all of her worries, something timeless and peaceful and unchanging. What was that favourite phrase of the school nurse back in Bradford? *Let go and let God.* Even her hip seemed to be improving.

The sudden tinny noise of 'You make me feel like a natural woman' snatched away the moment, giving her panicky images of various worst-case scenarios. *That's what comes of thinking everything's going to be all right, you foolish woman.*

But it wasn't Liam, or the school (or the police or the anti-terrorism squad) – it wasn't even Rod – it was Liz. At last! What had been happening?

'Liz,' she said, 'is everything okay?'

'I've just got back from Northallerton,' she said a bit breathlessly. 'The police station.'

Sitting in the dim stillness of St Catherine's waiting for choir practice, Thelma prayed.

What should I do?

That was the thing about taking action, one could never be totally sure one was doing the right thing. It was never like one of those game shows when a wrong response was met by a flashing red light and a klaxon. She had intended to pray the whole thing through, thread to needle, a sort of spiritual debriefing, but now she was sat here, all she had the mental energy to do was listen to the music and feel vaguely worried. She tried again.

Should I even do anything? What if I'm wrong?

She tried to marshal her weary thoughts, but there seemed so many of them, sifting through them felt like traversing some massive mental obstacle course.

This was no good. Again she tried Liz. Again Liz's formal, strained tones invited her to leave her name, number and a short message.

Somewhere away in the kitchen Maureen and Keith were setting out cups for the Thursday evening prayer meeting – otherwise all was still.

Grant me wisdom; grant me discernment.

She raised her face to the muted dull east window and all at once a thought came to her, a clear, focused image, a slightly expressionless face with wide impassive eyes and silver eyeshadow, looking at children's garments in the hospice charity shop.

And with that image came that chilly knot of fear.

I'm worried about Mandy Pinder-as-was, said Thelma. The thought came as a surprise, so unconnected as it was with that other dilemma that had been weighing her down. But now the thought was there in such clarity, it needed pursuing.

Rather than try and recall the ins and outs of everything to do with Mandy, she tried to make her mind still as years of practice had taught her, letting thoughts about Mandy surface and cohere one by one like bubbles on the surface of water. A series of images of Mandy's face rose into her mind . . . Her face when confronted by Jo . . . seeing the text and leaving the bar, lit eerily in the light of a street lamp, scanning the shadows of the car park . . . looking out of the window of the charity shop. Each image was similar, expressionless, eyes slightly staring . . . but underneath that face? Anger? Defiance?

But then came an image of something else – not her face . . .

Her *fingers* . . . suddenly, with clarity Thelma saw Mandy's fingers nervously pleating and plucking at her scarf – and her mind flew back to 2003 and saw those same fingers, stained with purple felt tip, shredding a list of spellings when she lost Thistledown Pony (later found in Matthew Parry's pump bag).

Thelma realized that Mandy Pinder was not just worried, she was scared. She was more than scared, she was nearly frantic.

About what? wondered Thelma.

'Lord,' she said. 'Lord, come alongside Mandy, bless her and protect her and deliver her from all evil.'

She sat back and thought. So she knew Mandy Pinder was scared, but where did that get her?

She tried to think what she'd learnt that afternoon . . . designer clothes . . . driving an expensive car . . . So why was she going to charity shops, according to Polly on a regular basis?

And there was still that other issue, that course of action. What should she do?

'Grant me wisdom, grant me discernment,' said Thelma again.

And then it came to her – she had an answer, of sorts. Mandy definitely needed help of some sort. And as for that other business, if in doubt – which she certainly was – do nothing.

Despite the darkness, despite the thud of the wind, it was peaceful in the church. She shut her eyes and relaxed, feeling all of a sudden that none of this was ultimately her problem. Someone else was in charge.

A sudden sharp crash from the narthex made her start.

'Only me,' carolled Maureen. 'Only a cup.'

'Don't worry,' called Keith. 'All under control.'

Thelma frowned. It struck her as significant, but for the life of her she couldn't think why.

A shrill noise in her handbag alerted her to her phone ringing. (She could never see the point of a phone sounding like anything else but a phone.) A glance showed her it was Liz. At last!

CHAPTER THIRTY-ONE

There is a confrontation and an image of a warrior queen is evoked.

Earlier that day.

The shafts of sun that did manage to punch their way through the gathering clouds haloed the driver of the black van with occasional bursts of energizing brightness.

Just now he was Oliver Harney.

That morning to the confused lady in Richmond he'd been Tony Ransom, who'd lost his mother six months previously, was still fragile but was finding solace in working All The Hours God Sent. First thing (according to his partner Courtney) he'd been a Useless Tosser who couldn't even remember to pick up a pack of disposable nappies. But now . . . now, speeding down the A1, windows down, heavy beat of something with angry bass slamming through his body, bursts of sun buffeting his face as the bruised greening fields and blossoming trees racketed by, now he was Oliver Harney, with a gifted child whose little finger he was happily wrapped round and a wife who didn't 'get' said child's incipient talent.

Leaving the A1 at Baldersby he slowed as he passed 'his' house (one of several on his various routes round the north-east). This one was nothing special to look at – your average Sixties detached

– but set back as it was amidst pooling fields and trees, the wide white-framed windows promised views from the back that must be really something. For the briefest of moments he imagined himself sat out the back on a warm summer's evening, beer in hand, drinking in that view.

Unloading the van outside Brian's bungalow, he thought again about the house with the vague 'one-day' thoughts that coloured so much of his life. He shouldered the heavy lump hammer he'd 'acquired' from a building site a few years back. This job shouldn't tie him down for too long; he'd knock the wall down in half an hour tops and then maybe see if Yarm Brunette (his latest online hook-up) was Up 4 Sum No-Strgs Fun. He'd come and clear away next week and that'd be it for Brian.

He'd been coming here off and on for almost seven months and he needed to be finding a few new 'clients'. No point in outstaying his welcome. Plus it was a bit close to Rainton, but then the old lady there was dead so he'd reckoned he'd be okay to do this one last job. And then, there were so many lonely old people with their stories about the past willing to believe in dodgy walls and slipping tiles. He made a mental note: he'd need some new burner phones and business cards. He was always the one to contact them; it was a rule he always stuck to. The exception had been that weird old woman in Ripon, but despite the obvious rich pickings there'd been something about her, something that had made him leave well alone.

Brian opened the door. His jumper needed a wash.

'Now then, Brian.' He wielded the hammer. 'Today's the day, my man.'

'It is indeed,' said Brian, following him through the house. 'I've been expecting you.' Normally it was a golden rule of Tony's never to say precisely when he was coming, but with Brian's children all many miles away he felt safe enough.

'Of course once upon a time I'd have been able to take care

of this myself,' said Brian. 'But nowadays, my knee you know.' Oliver did know. By heart.

In his pocket he could feel his phone buzz with another text. Courtney, had to be. Tuning out Brian's account of the fateful 1951 rugby match against RAF Feltwell, he thought reluctantly about nappies and supermarkets. His best bet would be to go to that new Pound Emporium off the A19. He still had a good wedge of cash from yesterday and there was a promise of cash up front from Richmond tomorrow morning. He could maybe even get Courtney something. Quite what Pound Emporium would stock that would stop that sullen disappointed droop of her mouth he wasn't quite sure. Something.

Out in the back garden he braced his legs apart and took a hefty swing at the wall but misjudged and the heavy hammer barely made contact. The next blow was better and the structure noticeably wobbled. He hit the wall again and a big slab on the end broke off like Christmas cake icing. It fell with a surprisingly loud noise and a puff of dust and brick splinters. This was proving a bit harder than he'd thought it would. Maybe more like an hour. Good job he'd not texted Yarm. But then it wouldn't be the end of the world if he didn't finish knocking it down this afternoon.

'Hold on a minute.' A voice cut across his thoughts. A greying older woman. Had he seen her somewhere before?

'Everything okay, love?' He raised the hammer again. 'Better stand back.'

'Just wait a minute before you do any more damage.'

'Damage?' He put the hammer down. Was she some sort of lady friend? A bit on the young side for Brian, but then you never knew. She looked upset.

'I've been employed by Brian to do some work here.' He put on his professional voice. 'This wall's dangerous. It needs to come down.'

'Does it though?'

What was this about? Brian had come out and was watching them, obviously as bemused as he was.

'Is there a problem, love?' He himself was starting to get pissed off and clenched his fingers.

'The problem is . . .' Suddenly, incongruously, the theme from *Wonder Woman* blared out. Without her eyes leaving his face or her challenging expression fading, the woman turned her mobile phone off. 'The problem is,' she continued, 'you're charging £700 to knock down a wall that doesn't need knocking down.'

He felt a bit of an icy lurch in the midriff somewhere. 'It's the going rate.' His voice sounded weedy, even to him.

'Is it though?' Her face was flushed and she looked as if she might be about to cry.

'Look, love, what's this all about?' This was all getting way too heated. He deliberately made his voice calm and matter-of-fact like they'd shown him on that course in the remand centre. 'I can show you the costings if you like. It's all completely above board, love.' He turned to Brian who was still hovering, for once at a loss for words. 'Brian, d'you let all your visitors speak to people like this?' He tried to sound light but his heart was now pounding and he couldn't help some of that coming out in his voice.

'The going rate.' The woman's voice was flinty. She produced a piece of paper from her coat pocket.

He noticed her hands were shaking somewhat. What was this?

'Just as £840 was the "going rate" for Mrs Walker of Masham to replace two lengths of guttering and £970 was the "going rate" for Mrs Cooper of Ripon to replace the roof tiles on her back bay. Or—' and now her voice raised and faltered then took on a hard, determined tone '—or £700 was the "going rate" for Mrs Topsy Joy of Rainton to demolish *her* garden wall.'

Shit.

That was where he'd seen her before.

'I've not got time for this.' His hands (by now also trembling) picked up the hammer. 'Brian, I'll come back when I'm not being verbally slandered by mad old bitches.'

'There's no call for language like that.' Brian sounded genuinely troubled and shocked.

He scanned the ground to make sure he'd got all his tools. No way was he coming back here. Let him sort his own bloody wall out.

'Not only that.' She wasn't still going on? Now she was standing on the path directly in his way. He shouldered the hammer and pushed past.

'. . . I'd be very interested to know why all the people you contacted . . .' She was even following him through the bungalow! 'Why all the people whose houses you turned up at . . . saying you'd been contacted to do work . . . how all those people had recently deceased partners whose obituaries had appeared in the *Ripon Gazette*.'

Shit.

He was running now, down the garden path back to the black van. Where two people were waiting.

'Now then Tommo,' said PC Trish. 'Long time no see.'

'I honestly thought the police wouldn't be able to get there in time.' Liz's hands shook slightly at the memory and she pressed them firmly round her coffee cup. 'When I rang that DC Donna, she said she'd have someone go round but it could be up to twenty minutes. So I had to do something or his whole wall would have gone.' She looked up defiantly. 'So I confronted him. It was the only thing I could think of to delay him.'

It was the next day, Friday, and the three were sat at their usual table in the garden centre café.

'You should have let us come with you,' said Pat. There was a tinge of reproach in her voice as she took a reluctant sip of her tea (lemon and comfrey). 'Anything could have happened.'

'That would have scared him off.' Liz's voice was stronger.

241

'Anyway, I'd no guarantee he would come. Brian was telling me about him at the funeral but I wasn't really listening to what he was saying; I couldn't even be sure he'd even said next Thursday. But I thought, with the brighter weather, there was a good chance. It was all chance.'

She thought just how much chance had been involved: her being there, Oliver (or Tommo) coming when he said he would, DC Donna picking up her call, someone being free to come. It was all something she preferred not to think *too* much about. It could have got very nasty, as the Jan voice had kept reminding her through the small hours of the night. Pat's frown mirrored her own unease. Yes, on reflection, she'd probably been rather foolish. She'd no idea what Derek would say when she told him the full story, which was why she hadn't.

'It could so easily not have worked out.' She sighed.

'But it did,' said Thelma in a voice that had an indefinable quality that made the other two look at her. Pat wondered if it was something to do with that mysterious call from the garage yesterday but there was something in her tone made Liz think suddenly that maybe – maybe – her frantically uttered prayers in Brian's garden had produced something other than a bolt of lightning and a frown on the face of the Almighty.

'He won't prey on any more vulnerable people.' There was something of a pronouncement in Thelma's words.

'He still made a mess of that wall though,' said Liz.

'Rod's going to go over first thing tomorrow,' Pat reminded them.

'You did wonderfully well,' said Thelma. Both she and Pat smiled at Liz.

'Well, it was good your Liam worked his magic with the Internet,' said Liz, deflecting the praise but feeling much better. They all shared a moment of quiet respect for Liam and his search engine gadget. Targeting bereaved people via obituary notices, pretending to have been engaged by the deceased partner!

According to DC Donna, Oliver/Tommo wasn't the first, wouldn't be the last, but was at least on bail with explicit instructions to avoid Thirsk, Masham, Ripon and all points between. 'Your Liam's a clever lad – you tell him from me.'

Pat didn't smile, or rather she did smile but the smile didn't quite reach her whole face. *And* another dull-coloured top, Thelma noticed. Had something happened at home? Dowdy was never a word she'd associated with Pat but all these greens and browns were so unlike her. She'd already registered the dark smudges under her friend's eyes. Pat had told them about her phone call to the Hotel Da Intereiza. Maybe Rod had been annoyed about the phone bill?

'I rang KellyAnne,' said Liz, 'just to keep her in the picture. I'm meeting her here tomorrow to bring her up to speed vis-à-vis Mr Builder.'

'So,' Pat took a final disgusted sip of her tea, which tasted exactly like weak Lemsip, 'do we or do we not think Oliver had anything to do with mucking up Topsy's medication? And was he the mystery man round at the house?'

'I don't know about that,' said Liz doubtfully. 'Knocking down a few walls and then emptying someone's bank account – they're hardly the same sort of thing. And why do all these bits of work if you've got all Topsy's money stashed away somewhere?'

'He could have been in it with someone,' said Pat. 'Working together. Ness.' There was an acidic relish in her voice.

'Or Lloret,' said Liz.

'Or Mandy Pinder,' said Pat. 'I know you saw her in the charity shop but that's not to say she couldn't have spent that 450 grand.' She thought of the bank employee with his drunken grin waving his bar tab. 'It's easily done.' Was there anywhere in Thirsk where you could spend thousands of pounds on a night out?

'Or there's Paula,' said Thelma. She hadn't spoken for some time and again there was that odd note in her voice.

They both looked at her. Thelma looked down at her knitted fingers, as if debating whether to say something.

'Paula?' said Liz.

'Why Paula?' asked Pat.

'When people do wrong,' said Thelma sombrely, 'they usually think of all sorts of reasons to justify their actions . . .'

Her hands on the handle of the pram. Someone need to take care of him. That was obvious . . .

Banishing the image she continued. 'Paula knew, or thought she knew, how Topsy's illness was going. She could have talked herself into believing that it really and truly was a kindness to spare her from all that. We know she knew all about her medication; that she had access to the house.'

'Do you know something that we don't?' said Pat suspiciously, her thoughts going back to that phone call in the Edinburgh Woollen Mill. Thelma appeared to come to an internal decision. 'No,' she said decisively. 'At least—' She looked at them. 'Remember there's not a grain of evidence here. It's just a theory.'

'A pretty nasty one,' said Liz. She looked frankly horrified and even Pat was shaking her head. She had no particular love for Paula but there seemed something peculiarly repugnant in suspecting someone so well known to all of them. Thelma was looking at her, and when she spoke it was as if she knew what she was thinking.

'We don't *know* what happened,' said Thelma and her voice was sombre. 'We don't know and because we don't know we have to think of every possibility. It'd be all very nice and straightforward if it was some criminal like Oliver Harney, but what if it was someone we knew? Someone we've all known for years? *That's* when it all gets messy.' Again there was that quietness in her voice, as if what she was saying was something she'd thought about again and again.

There was a pause. For a moment the three were all thinking more or less the same thing: that they could just finish their coffee, get up and walk away from all of this. Walk away and then meet the following week as they always did and talk about children, grandchildren, bedding plants and book groups. But not one of them moved. Thelma was reminding herself of the upset and heartbreak caused by that evil-minded fraud and again wondering what the right thing to do was. Pat was thinking of what reasons could drive someone – *anyone* – to murder an old lady. And Liz . . . Liz was thinking of that pair of pinking shears lying in an IKEA box in her spare room wardrobe.

It was Liz who broke the silence. 'Anyway,' she said, 'Brian said I was his knight in shining armour. The Boadicea of Thirsk he called me.'

The other two looked at her, noting the resolve in her voice. There was to be no walking away.

'Liz Newsome, you dark horse,' said Pat and for the first time that morning the smile reached her eyes.

CHAPTER THIRTY-TWO

There are two confrontations in Sainsbury's car park, a personal alarm triggered and a resolution reached.

Sainsbury's at twenty to eight on a Friday night, a twilight time when most people were at home and the main shoppers were singletons with their wire baskets of salad-for-one plus bottles of wine or water. A red-faced man carried two boxes of cheap lager, a harried-looking woman dashed from aisle to aisle stocking up on the largest and cheapest and quickest: multipacks of pizza, of juice, of toilet roll.

The evening had seemed to go on forever for Mandy, one of those evenings that whenever she looked at the big wall clock it barely seemed to have moved forward. She felt tired tonight. While walking up and down the aisles, tidying the gaps, moving the nearly-out-of-date packages to the front, her body felt heavy and tingly. There was a grittiness behind her eyes. An effort was needed to rotate the biscuits, the cereals, the herbal teas. Normally it was one of the jobs she not exactly enjoyed – but it was something that allowed her to daydream. Looking at the different packets, the lifestyles promised, the vital, slim people smiling from gyms and cars and scrubbed pine tables with their percolators, their designer jumpers . . . and she'd imagine herself, the girls, similarly glowing and healthy.

And free.

Not tonight. Not after that last text she'd received earlier on. Now the same images mocked her, reminded her of what she'd done. What if they found out at the bank? They were suspicious enough anyway and Jo – dependable, reliable Jo – Mandy could tell she was at the edges of her patience; she'd barely spoken to her since that night in the wine bar. She wouldn't give her away of course, but what if someone else found out?

If only. If only . . .

Finally, eventually, at long last the piped music upped its tempo and Yvonne's leaden tones could be heard announcing the store closing, and after a short conversation with Dawn and Rajinder about *Celebrity Love Island* (totally made up on Mandy's part; she was a good six episodes behind), she looked cautiously out of the back door, scanning the nearly empty car park. Satisfied no one was about, she stepped outside.

'Mandy.' Mandy gave a half-shriek, her hand flying to her mouth, but it was only Thelma, emerging from the shadows, wrapped up against the chilly, damp night.

'I'm so sorry to startle you,' she said. 'It's me – Thelma Cooper. I wanted a quick word about the other night.'

Mandy faced her, that blank mask carefully in place.

'I'm sorry, I shouldn't have jumped out at you like that, Mrs Cooper. It's just like I said, I was upset.' Her face was calm but her eyes were darting from side to side as she spoke. Thelma followed her eyes, but the car park seemed empty.

'It wasn't that. I just wondered . . . if something else was the matter.'

'I was just tired.' Still those eyes darted to and fro. 'Look, I'm really sorry, Mrs Cooper, I've got to go.'

'You seemed . . .' an image of those fingers nervously pleating and re-pleating her jacket '. . . you seemed upset.' Thelma's voice was both kind and strong, the voice that over the years had comforted many a child missing Mummy or with a nasty scraped knee.

The wide blue eyes suddenly brimmed with tears and Mandy did that thing that Thelma, a confirmed hanky carrier, could never understand, which was flap her hands madly in front of her eyes in an effort to dry the tears. Thelma handed her a tissue.

'I was thinking you must be so tired, with two jobs.'

Mandy dumbly nodded as if not trusting herself to speak.

'However do you manage with child care?'

'My mum. And his mum. The girls' dad. He's not on the scene.'

'I do admire you.' Again the eyes brimmed so that the hand flapping and the tissue combined were barely able to cope. 'You mustn't be so hard on yourself.' Thelma paused. She had said all she could say. Any revelation now had to come from Mandy.

'That's not it. At least not all of it.' Mandy looked miserably round.

Thelma passed over another tissue.

At that moment the door opened again, and two shop staff emerged. 'Night, Mand,' said one of them.

'Look, I've truly got to go,' said Mandy and walked away still flapping her hands. Such was the urgency in her voice that Thelma felt as if she had no choice but to watch that lonely figure retreat across the darkened car park. She sighed to herself. She said what she'd intended to say and that seemed to be that. As she turned to walk home she wasn't sure if she was relieved or disappointed.

Mandy was only a matter of yards away from her car when the man appeared with a slick and sickening inevitability. He must have been watching her from the cathedral gardens.

'Mandy Szafranska.'

She couldn't make out his features; he was taking care to stay out of range of the CCTV camera. His voice sounded posh, like someone you might encounter in some antiques shop or country pub, not a shadowy car park late at night. 'Charlie Morton, Forward Credit.'

'I'm in a hurry.' Where oh where were her car keys? She must must must give her handbag a good clear-out. Why was she so lazy and pathetic?

'This won't take long.' And now somehow, he had managed to transpose himself between her and the car. The hand that fumbled in her bag shook.

'My kid's sick. I need to get home.'

'You can't keep putting us off, Mandy.'

'I need to go.'

'Look, love.' The voice sounded reasonable. It could have been that of a teacher pointing out the importance of handing homework in on time. 'This isn't going to go away.'

'I said, I'm sorting it.'

'When?'

'I've got the money.'

'Then let's go to the cash point.'

'Look, I said I'm late. Leave me alone.' Even as she spoke the words she realized how like a child she sounded.

'I can't do that, Mandy.' He sounded sad now, sad and regretful. 'Or if I do I'll have to come back. Maybe to the bank – maybe that's the best place to catch you.'

Her voice rose. 'If you do that I'll lose my job.'

'Not my problem.'

'It will be. How could I pay you then?'

He took a step forward. Again, the weary tone. 'Look, love, it's late. Give me your bank card, we'll go to the cash machine, get enough to keep the management happy and we can all get home.'

He took a step forward, his face oh so reasonable.

'Good evening again.'

Neither of them had noticed the calm figure that now stood a few feet away from them, haloed and assured in the glow of the security light behind the library. 'I'm so sorry to intrude,' said Thelma. 'There was something I forgot to say, Mandy.'

'We're busy, love.' Now a harsher tone had crept into the easy, arrogant voice and Mandy felt a surge of hope. Thelma didn't even look at him.

'I wanted to say to you, Mandy, if you wanted to talk . . .'

'I said we're busy.' Even harsher now with an element of something darker. 'I suggest the best thing you can do is go away.' Hope was replaced by another feeling in Mandy: fear.

Finally Thelma acknowledged him. Her look was steady and calm, a look that had quelled countless playground dramas. When she spoke, her voice was measured. 'I have my phone here on 999. If you come any closer I will call the police.'

Charlie Morton laughed, a confident, knowing laugh that made Mandy wince. 'This isn't *Crimewatch*, love.'

For an answer Thelma held her phone to her ear. Swiftly he moved to take it from her.

Thelma had only ever used her rape alarm once before – 'used' was perhaps an inaccurate term, it had gone off when she was prompting *Run for Your Wife* at the college players, when she'd been groping in her handbag for cough lozenges. That time the theatre had emptied in under five minutes. This time, the noise was even more alarming coming out of the dark. Other super-market staff, people coming from the poetry slam at the library, people having a smoke outside the One-Eyed Rat – all came running towards the piping, insistent sound. By which time Charles Morton, Forward Credit was long gone.

Debate over what to do was loud and vigorous and fell into two camps: those who wanted to call the police, and those who felt there was no point in ringing as by the time they got there whoever the joker was would be in the next county. Thelma kept trying to speak but was no match for the man who said thanks to the Tories, police in Ripon were non-existent and the woman who talked stridently about her campaign to have CCTV installed through the town centre.

'I'm so sorry,' Mandy kept saying, as she steadily worked her way through numerous tissues thrust on her by various bystanders.

Eventually the reality of the cold night won over and Thelma was able to dispatch her off in the company of someone she mentally labelled as A Capable Friend, who promised to follow her home and make sure she got inside.

'Don't take any calls,' said Thelma. 'Not until I've spoken to you tomorrow.'

Mandy gave a watery smile as she got into the car. Watching her pull out of the car park, closely followed by Capable Friend, Thelma reviewed what she had found out. Payday loans, debt collectors . . . it all made perfect sense – of the calls in the bank, of Jo's attitude. Plus it all argued Mandy was in need of money – not £450,000 richer.

Unless . . . more money was needed for some reason?

But as she walked back to 42 College Gardens, she was aware of another feeling. She had been so close to walking away, back home, head safely beneath the parapet. If she'd not waited to see her get into the car, if she'd not seen that figure appear . . . but she had and now she felt . . . not exactly triumph, not as strong as that, but a certain satisfaction about having stood up and righted a wrong. She could now empathise with that warrior-like glint in Liz's eye that morning.

As she pushed open the gate and wondered what (if anything) she'd say to Teddy, she was aware of something else.

Tomorrow she would go to Northallerton Police Station.

CHAPTER THIRTY-THREE

There is an entreaty to move on, plus a vision of feng shui in a seaside room is shared.

The garden centre was busy for a Monday morning, no two ways about it. Was busy and had been busy over a bright weekend that had shown definite spring-like qualities. There were gaps in the various garden tools on sale; there were no white foxgloves to be seen and Liz noted the gladioli bulbs were running low. The year was definitely turning and people were likewise turning their mind to gardens and allotments that had slept through the long soggy winter. Liz was loading bedding plants into her car boot when her phone pinged. She thought it had to be Leoni with news of Jacob's visit to Skel Hill, but it was KellyAnne.

HERE SAT BY THE DOOR LOL X, it read.

She was early. Liz heaved in the last bag of compost, her mind spinning into flustered excuses even though it was over ten minutes before they had arranged to meet.

'It's fine.' KellyAnne graciously stemmed Liz's apologies as she approached with her coffee. 'It doesn't matter, my love.' Today she wore a cashmere top of a deep rich magenta that accentuated her tanned shoulders and cascading golden hair. As she hugged Liz she smelt of something restrained (and no doubt pricey);

sitting down she interlaced and stacked her pink-lacquered nails together like a Jenga tower.

'Now, you relax.' She smiled warmly and looked round the café as if giving Liz the chance to compose herself. For the first time that year the double doors were open and people were even sitting on the patio outside.

'It's busy in here.' KellyAnne briskly stirred two sachets of brown sugar into her coffee. 'I had a job parking.'

'It's a day like today,' said Liz. 'It makes people think of their gardens.' She thought of the begonias in her boot. Would it be overstepping the mark taking some across to Brian?

'I love all that.' KellyAnne raised a forkful of Masham mince slice to her pink lips. 'People buying things for their gardens. Plants and stuff. And garden furniture. And them solar lamp things. Having gardens and doing things in them.' She smiled bashfully. 'Don't laugh,' she said as if confiding a slightly ridiculous wish, 'but I'd like a garden. Only I wouldn't know where to begin.'

'It's easy enough,' said Liz. 'There's no great mystery.'

'If I got a garden would you help me?' KellyAnne smiled shyly and Liz's mind presented her with a vision of her weeding furiously and KellyAnne drifting by from time to time asking if she was all right.

'Of course I would. It's a lot of hard work.' Liz looked at those pristine pink nails.

'I'm fine with that. You know me, Liz, if there's a job to do Let's Get On With It.' She smiled brilliantly and blew into her coffee. 'I was glad when you called,' she said. 'I was going to ring you. We didn't really get the chance to talk at the funeral. Not properly.'

Liz, remembering KellyAnne's snappy outburst, felt herself tensing but the warm smile was showing no sign of fading. 'I wanted to say thanks for what you did. Sitting with Ness, bless her heart. I just didn't feel up to it.'

'Not at all,' said Liz.

'Between you and me,' said KellyAnne, 'she'd had a bit of argy-bargy with Craig.'

'Craig's her—'

'—fiasco, I know.' KellyAnne smiled the term into fond ridicule. 'Honestly, Liz, I tell you – those two! Up and down, in and out and round the houses. I say to them, "You two, at the end of the day, you can't fool me that the pair of you don't love each other to bits."'

Liz was unsure how to reply. Did KellyAnne really know nothing about Ness and Lloret? Or was she perhaps covering up for her friend? If she'd been Thelma or Pat she would have done a bit of digging, but the only digging she wanted to do was bedding in her begonias back at home.

'And then there was me, snapping at you,' said KellyAnne.

'I've forgotten all about that,' said Liz untruthfully. 'Water under the bridge.'

'No, my love.' KellyAnne warded off the comment with a pink-nailed hand and a sombre shake of the head. 'I went home and I thought to myself: *KellyAnne, what were you playing at? That was your mum's very good friend and you had no business taking your stress out on her like that.*'

'It must have been a tough day for you,' said Liz. 'Please, don't even think about it.'

KellyAnne smiled, squeezed her hand again and looked down at the sugar crystals on top of her Masham slice.

'Have you seen or heard from Paula by any chance?'

The careful words took Liz by surprise. 'Not since the funeral,' she said. She could have added 'but we've speculated about the possibility of her killing your mother'. 'Why, is there something the matter?'

'Don't get me wrong, Liz, that woman has been an Absolute Star, no two ways about it. I don't think she likes me very much. But, hey, that's her problem.'

Remembering the conversation at the Shoppers Oasis, Liz could only nod. 'It's just . . .' KellyAnne took a pensive suck of her sugary finger. She looked troubled. 'I've been going through Mum's things, and there's some stuff, I think, has gone missing.'

'What sort of stuff?'

'That's just it,' KellyAnne said almost reluctantly. 'I'm not exactly sure. Things I think should be there but aren't. Mum's floral watch, her charm bracelet . . . a couple of rings. I mean it's most probably me.'

'You think *Paula* might have taken them?'

KellyAnne seemed to come to some sort of inner decision. 'No,' she said decisively. 'I think Mum probably lost them or more likely they're hidden in one of the boxes somewhere.' She smiled, seemingly unconcerned, but there were images in Liz's mind . . . Paula with a key . . . and the things she'd said about KellyAnne . . . and what Thelma had said about the way people justified their actions. But before she could properly pursue the thoughts, KellyAnne took a businesslike bite of the Masham mince slice and said, 'So? You said you had something to tell me about that Bastard Builder, pardon my French.'

Liz dutifully relayed the story of Oliver Harney. When Liz had finished she said a single word.

'Bastard.' No 'pardon my French' this time, but then she was entitled to feel upset, thought Liz as she rummaged in her handbag for the card DC Donna had given her.

'You're to ring this lady. Tell her what happened from your point of view. If you want to. I mean they've probably got enough to bring a case against him.' She paused and then said delicately, 'I was thinking, you could even ask them about the fraud . . . I mean you never know, they may be connected?' KellyAnne didn't take the card but took Liz's hand in both of hers, tickling the palm with her pink plastic nails.

'Liz, you've been a true friend to me.'

Liz made a deprecating noise in her throat.

'No, I'm being dead serious here. You've been a good friend to me and you've been a good friend to Mum, God rest her soul.' She smiled. 'I'll ring this DC Donna, of course I will, but the truth is, Liz, I just want to put it all behind me.' She sat back and smiled fondly at Liz for a long moment before speaking again.

'I had a dream, Liz.' She looked down as if trying to find the right words. 'It was lovely. I can't remember all the details and you know me, I'm not a religious person, but this dream, it felt deeply spiritual. I was on this hill and Mum was stood next to me. And you know what she said, Liz?' Liz shook her head. She could imagine all manner of things Topsy might say but couldn't place them in any category labelled 'deeply spiritual'. 'She said, "I'm at peace, love." Just like that. "I'm at peace. You move on in your life." And I have, Liz. I've moved on. And I want you and your friends to move on as well.' She took the last bite of the slice and smiled beneficently at Liz. The hand gripped hers in a final squeeze before chasing the last of the crumbs with a pink-nailed finger, which she popped into her mouth.

Liz sipped her coffee.

'There's something else you should know.' KellyAnne's tone was again businesslike. 'I'm moving away.'

'From your flat?'

'From the flat, from Ripon, from Thirsk. It's what I need, Liz. A complete change of scene.'

'When?'

'As soon as I can. It'll be a while before I can sell Mum and Dad's, so I'll rent.'

'Have you somewhere in mind?'

'I'm not one hundred per cent sure.' Again that shy, confiding smile. 'But I've a vision, Liz.'

'Oh?'

'Somewhere by the sea. Filey, Flamborough, Bridlington. You're going to laugh at me, but I've this image in my mind . . . I want to wake up overlooking the sea; I don't care how grey it is, I don't care how stormy, I want to look out over the sea.'

'So you've a job you're going to?'

'Social media management. It's a growing market, Liz. I spoke to some experts, I'm like: "Okay – level with me, is this a crock of the proverbial?" And you know what? They all said, "KellyAnne, go for it."' She smiled. 'I'm going to be the lady on the phone. I'm like: "Ringing people up? I can do that."'

'So is this with a company?'

'Someone's expanding something. Watch this space. And you know the real beauty of it, Liz? I can work from anywhere, as long as there's decent Wi-Fi. I've been looking into it.' She looked dreamily out of the window. 'Liz, I'm going to get one room done out as an office. And trust me, there's more than just sticking a desk in there: colour, décor, the feel of a place; it's scientifically proven to be as important as the work itself.' She smiled, looking into a feng-shui-ed future. 'I'm going to have one wall done sunshine yellow. And I'm always going to have lilies, come what may. And at coffee time I'm going to be out there holding my coffee cup and looking out to sea.'

'I'm happy for you,' said Liz, if not one hundred per cent truthful, one hundred per cent hopeful.

'You know what, Liz? I'm happy for me. It's about bloody time.' She smiled happily. 'It's all I truly want, Liz.'

Liz registered the eager tone in her voice; it was one she'd heard many times before as she'd talked about the stables, the beauty salon, the vet from Richmond. She looked at the dreamy smile, the hair, the nails, the top – and felt a sudden pang, a sudden shiver of something as she saw just how vulnerable, how very, very vulnerable in her dreams KellyAnne was.

'I wish you all the very best,' she said. A memory came to her . . . Topsy's indulgent tones speaking out of the past . . . *The little madam.* Liz smiled sadly.

'What are you thinking?' said KellyAnne.

'I was thinking about you,' said Liz truthfully. 'I was thinking about when you were six and painted spots on your face.'

'Oh my God!' KellyAnne gave a snort of laughter. 'I'd forgotten about that. I used Mum's lip gloss and told her I wasn't well.'

'She wasn't fooled.'

'Not for a minute. Knowing Mum I think she'd have been more bothered about her lip gloss.'

'You'd done something you were afraid you'd be in bother for.'

'I remember Mum was worried I'd get a skin reaction. But I don't remember being in bother.'

Liz did. That cut-glass green vase that had been a wedding present from a favourite aunt. And Topsy's soft as the playdough she rolled. *The little madam. I hadn't the heart to be cross with her.*

The thought of Topsy rolling out playdough was one that made her eyes suddenly fill with sharp tears, not just for Topsy but for those warm, safe, lost times twenty, thirty years ago.

'What made you think of that?' asked KellyAnne.

'I've no idea,' said Liz.

Later on, kneeling in her garden planting out the begonias, Liz wondered if KellyAnne really had moved on. She could certainly understand her wish to do so. But would circumstances allow her?

As it turned out, they wouldn't.

By six o'clock that evening the news was all round Thirsk that Rocky Oldroyd had been arrested.

CHAPTER THIRTY-FOUR

An arrest is discussed and there is an encounter in Baldersby churchyard.

The police had come for Rocky mid-afternoon, right in the middle of the tech rehearsal for the Northern Knights' latest set piece (Naked Valhalla). This was according to the troupe's newest member, Jeremy Fairhurst (AKA Sven Hungsten), whose mother was briefly torn between reticence about her son's career and the desire to share the news on her Pilates WhatsApp group. And apparently, Rocky had been shopped to the police by his girlfriend Shell, who'd decided enough was enough when he returned from Redcar with two love bites, which he swore blind were an allergic reaction to a new brand of shower gel. (These details spreading via Phil at the Auction Mart whose stepdaughter was Shell's bezzie mate.)

And so the news spread round Thirsk and Northallerton and Ripon, via WhatsApp and Facebook, via text and tweet, over bars, next to tills and across car parks.

Speculation about the reason for the arrest was rife. The landlord of the Station was of the opinion Rocky must have been responsible for the spate of burglaries in local villages, whereas Hoss the local tractor guru was sure it must have been the theft of farm equipment that had drawn police attention, just like before.

'Paula says it's something to do with his tax and it's all a mistake,' Liz told the others the next day as she sipped her coffee.

'Rod's mate thinks it's probably to do with some fiddle with the money from the Northern Knights,' said Pat.

'I think Paula's more worried that Reuben and Cesca's mother won't let her see the children. Anyway she reckons it'll be all sorted out by tonight,' said Liz. Pat and Thelma exchanged knowing looks, remembering much the same reaction to the Great Top Trumps scandal.

'I don't think it will,' said Thelma. 'Or at least not in the way she hoped.' The other two looked at her. Once again she'd been very quiet; indeed this was one of the first things she'd said. And there was something in her tone, something in the way she lifted her head and met their eyes with a frank, steady look that made both of them tense up. 'I think we'll find that Rocky was the one who carried out the fraud on Topsy.' She stopped and drew a breath. 'At least that's what I told the police.'

In telling her friends about her visit to Northallerton Police Station the previous Saturday, there was a certain amount Thelma left out. She told them of walking into the police station, but she didn't tell them of the way she'd had to ball her hands into fists to stop them shaking, nor of the panicky flutter in her normally calm voice when telling the brightly dismissive woman at the desk why she'd come. She told them about the two and a bit hour wait to see someone, but she didn't mention the number of times she came very close, so very close, to leaving the building. Neither did she say about the lukewarm tea or the room where she was interviewed, obviously not an interview room but some storeroom stacked with boxes of photocopier paper and a harsh neon light.

She said how she'd reported her concerns to a young man who looked about fourteen and who obviously didn't take a word of what she was saying with any seriousness, but she didn't say about the growing relief she felt when she realized he was probably going to dismiss what she'd said the second she'd left the building. In fact, as she said to her friends, the whole visit would have come to nothing if she hadn't happened to meet DC Donna on her way out, who remembering her previous phone call, was curious enough to hear her story again – especially when the name Nigel Oldroyd was mentioned. This time, repeating her story in an altogether more salubrious room complete with comfy chairs and black and white prints of Monkton Abbey, Thelma had sensed a lot more interest in her ideas, but she didn't tell her friends how sick to the stomach that made her feel.

'Why didn't you say something?' Pat tried to sound concerned, not accusing. 'I'd have gone with you.'

'Because I couldn't be sure.' Thelma's tone was grave. 'And because Paula's someone we all know and I'm accusing her son of something terrible. And if I'm wrong, I didn't want you . . .' here she looked at Liz '. . . to know anything about it. It's all down to me, and I'm happy to face the consequences of that.' She didn't mention she'd started using Asda in Knaresborough to rule out any chance of accidentally running into Paula.

'But he's got no money,' said Liz. Her voice was quiet as she pictured that cheery face in the Shopper's Oasis Café, hearing that voice: *Needs must, Mrs Newsome.*

'He *said* he had no money,' said Thelma. 'But when you actually look at the *facts* . . . Suddenly there were all these things being bought – that fancy car you saw Liz, and that top-of-the-range sunbed. You don't afford any of that on a call centre salary.'

'There was that outfit Paula was wearing at the funeral,' said Pat. 'I thought it looked a bit plush for eBay.'

'But he took the car and the sunbed back,' protested Liz. 'He said he couldn't afford them.'

'He took them back *after* Topsy died,' said Thelma. 'When Topsy died it must have been a horrible shock. He'd have known questions would be asked and he could become suspect number

261

one. And then he heard you'd been looking for Paula and had seen the sunbed . . . He must have been horribly frightened. So he got rid of them and made sure everyone knew he'd taken the things back and that he was short of cash. That car he was driving when he collected Paula from the funeral, really, it was a total jalopy, almost conspicuously so . . . He'd never driven a car like that before, no matter how hard up he was. It was like he *wanted* people to notice it.' She looked at them both. 'He paid for both of them in cash,' she said. 'I called both the garage and the sunbed company last week.'

'That was who was calling you back last week,' said Pat.

'And they both told you?' said Liz. 'Just like that?'

'Well,' said Thelma, 'I used a certain amount of subterfuge. I said I was thinking of buying from them, and had a friend who said it would be all right to pay in cash, and could they confirm? And both places remembered a young man who came in a month ago, and paid up front in cash.'

Pat found herself biting her lip, picturing Thelma reclining on a sunbed, or driving a top-of-the-range convertible (as opposed to the mussel-blue Fiat).

Liz meanwhile was thinking things through. 'Hang on though,' she said. 'Didn't Paula take that first call from the fraudster? Surely she'd have recognized Rocky's voice?'

'I rather think that first call *was* from a genuine criminal – if that's the term,' said Thelma. 'Someone trying their luck. One of these career criminals – maybe, as Rocky said to me, not even based in this country. Paula's response would be more than enough to have warned him off. But then having taken the call, what did she then do?'

'Tell Rocky,' said Pat.

'Tell Rocky, and *Wayne*,' said Thelma.

'Wayne explained how these fraud calls work,' recalled Liz.

'Wayne probably told Rocky all he needed to know. Or at least enough so he could then find out the details himself,' said

Thelma. 'Like how to electronically disperse and hide the money that was transferred across to the account he'd have set up.' She looked at Liz. 'When you asked Paula if anyone called Gortops, what did she say?'

'Only Rocky,' said Liz.

'He must have known by and large when she was cleaning and not to call – but he slipped up at least once.'

'Isn't all this speculation though?' said Pat. She thought back to the business with Rod's lock-up. 'I mean it's not very much to go on. A couple of cash purchases.'

'There is one clear piece of evidence,' said Thelma. 'One that clinched it for me and made me sure it was Rocky who did the fraud.' They both looked at her. 'Financial misnomers,' she said. 'One of those phrases that sounds right and people often use without realizing it's wrong.'

'Topsy said it to us here,' remembered Liz.

'And then Rocky used the exact same phrase to me outside the Bay Horse,' said Thelma. 'It's a very distinctive phrase. He must have used it to Topsy over the phone when he rang her pretending to be the bank.'

'He'll have got it from Wayne,' said Liz. 'He said that to me: financial misnomers.'

'I knew then it was more than likely he'd have used it with Topsy. It's too precise to be a coincidence.'

'Unless Wayne was the one to ring Topsy?' suggested Pat.

Liz shook her head thinking of the three houses in Yarm and Thornaby. 'He's got himself sorted financially,' she said. 'Not like Rocky.' She looked at the cars parked outside, thinking of the cheeky chappy grinning down from the wall of Paula's boiler house all those years ago, loving life with wine, women, cars but no pension plan. But was he *really* capable of fleecing his mother's friend?

'It still doesn't seem much,' said Pat.

'That's what the first officer said,' said Thelma. 'That's why it was so fortunate I ran into DC Donna. Seeing how she reacted when I said the name – well, reading between the lines I gather they already had their suspicions, and then of course his girlfriend had already been to them. What I said probably just confirmed what they knew.' She stirred her coffee. That's what she'd been trying to tell herself again and again and again ever since she'd heard the news about the arrest.

She looked up at her two friends to find them watching her. 'I'm truly sorry I said nothing,' she said. 'It just seemed the best course of action under the circumstances.'

'If it *is* true – I mean it's just so . . . callous,' said Liz. 'I know Rocky wasn't close to Topsy, but at the end of the day she was his mum's friend.'

'It all comes back down to what I was saying about people justifying what they do,' said Thelma. 'Rocky would have heard from Paula how much money Topsy had, and how she was fast reaching a stage when she wouldn't have known she even had it – and how KellyAnne didn't deserve it. And there was he, approaching the end of his career as a stripper, working in a call centre, two kids to provide for.'

'Hang on a sec,' said Pat suddenly. 'The night Topsy died, wasn't he off performing somewhere?'

Thelma nodded and from her handbag produced the neatly folded flyer for the Northern Knights: *February 27th The Pier, Cleethorpes,* it said.

'So he *couldn't* have been the one to mess with Topsy's tablets,' said Liz, with something like relief in her voice.

'Just because he carried out the fraud, it doesn't mean he was the one to kill Topsy,' said Thelma. 'In fact his panicked reaction getting rid of the car and sunbed rather argues the opposite.'

'He could have been in cahoots with someone,' said Pat. 'Like Ness.' It took no effort whatsoever to envisage Ness as some avaricious criminal Mrs Robinson figure.

There was a pause and then by common unspoken consent they allowed the conversation to move on. After all, it was all now in the hands of the police who would presumably find out all that needed finding out; there was nothing they could do. Liz talked about Tim and Leoni, trying Jacob at a new school. Pat shared (some) of her worries about Liam. But underneath it all there was a sombre muted tone to their conversation. If Thelma was right then there was a sadness, even a responsibility for what had happened. Rocky was someone they'd all taught, someone each had spent a year of their life showing good ways to live . . . sharing pencils, not pushing in lines, being kind, being generous. Principles shown every carpet time, every PE lesson, every chapter of Roald Dahl read aloud. To see that legacy so roundly, sordidly ignored and rejected . . . It was enough to give all of them pause for thought.

Ordinary evil. Thelma looked round at the people in the café. The young trainee wiping tables for the first time. The woman in the lilac cardigan struggling with the *Ripon Gazette* crossword. The men, the women, the old, the young . . . all with their thoughts, their dreams and plans. But were any of them having criminal thoughts?

The baby, its face one gummy smile . . . the pressure of the pram handle under her hands . . .

And she wheeled the pram away.

It was that easy.

She shook herself and with a mental effort forced herself to focus on what Pat was saying about Liam's predicted grades.

Dusk was falling as Thelma parked up outside the school opposite Baldersby church. On her back seat was a spray of daffodils of much better shape and colour than the ones she'd put on the altar that day she'd sat in St Catherine's. Dusk was falling and the sky was clear, the last apricot sweeps of sunset fading over the Pennines. On Sunday the clocks would be going forward; this time next week it would be light at this time. She wondered if Rocky could see the sunset wherever he was sitting. It was an

265

image that had come to her, off and on, ever since she'd heard the news of his arrest, the strutting figure, woebegone and no doubt in tears. Partly because of her.

Which was why she'd come here, to bring flowers to Topsy's grave and in doing so remind herself of the upset and heartbreak that had come as a result of Rocky's actions.

From some way off came the mournful chorus of cows waiting to be milked, and a faint evening mist was rising as she crossed the churchyard, but Thelma felt no apprehension, only a sense of peace. Rounding the corner of the church, however, she stopped, with a lurching shock.

Standing by the Topsy's grave was a figure, a figure that her startled brain identified as Topsy herself. No, *not* Topsy she realized after a paralyzed second. Of course not Topsy – but KellyAnne. Standing in the half-light she bore a strong physical resemblance to her mother.

Somewhat shaken, Thelma approached. 'KellyAnne,' she said.

'Thelma.' If KellyAnne was surprised to see her she didn't show it. Her voice was flat and uninterested. At her feet on the fresh soil of the grave lay an enormous, almost gaudy spray of plastic-wrapped flowers.

'They're beautiful,' said Thelma.

'I just wanted to come . . . bring some flowers. See . . . Mum . . .' Her voice faltered and Thelma put a hand on her arm. 'You've heard about Rocky, I take it,' she said.

KellyAnne nodded. 'The police called me.' Her voice was flat, drained. Thelma was surprised; knowing KellyAnne as she did, she'd have expected at least *some* strong reaction.

'He had nothing to do with the tablets or anything like that,' said KellyAnne. 'In case you were wondering. That was all poor Mum getting muddled. He just did the fraud.' The words hung in the air. 'They said I might even get some of the money back.' She laughed, a sad, bitter little laugh.

'That's good news.'

KellyAnne said nothing.

Perhaps her apathy was maybe not that surprising. In Thelma's experience feelings seldom followed emotional logic. People had flashes of happiness in the most trying of circumstances and then sadness when there were many reasons to be feeling just the opposite. KellyAnne sighed, a deep sigh that went right down into the heart of something unutterably sad and broken.

'What's it all for, Thelma?' she said. 'That's what I'd like to know.'

Thelma said nothing but put her hand on the younger woman's arm. She didn't have an answer, or at least not one she could easily put into words even after all these years of church services, prayer groups and daily readings from *Walk with the Lord*. If pressed she'd have said something to do with the peace of the graveyard, something in the noise of the trees, the distant cattle, the sight of the first stars sprinkling the mauve skies over the hills.

The pressure of the pram handle under her gloved hands as she wheeled the pram away . . .

The beep of a text sounded and KellyAnne snatched out her phone with a sudden energy.

'I have to go,' she said. 'Do you need a lift or anything?'

'I'm fine,' said Thelma. 'I'll stay a moment.' KellyAnne sighed again and turned to go. 'KellyAnne,' she said, 'if you ever need anything just call me.' The girl smiled sadly, and disappeared round the corner of the church.

Thelma stood in front of the grave and thought not so much a prayer as a wordless burst of sadness and affection for Topsy. The flowers KellyAnne left really were spectacular, easily eclipsing her own.

Of course! The daffodils! Still on the back seat of her car. Tutting she retraced her steps round the church – and stopped.

There stood in the lych gate was KellyAnne. There was a man with her, obscure in the shadow. All Thelma could see of him was some darkish jacket and a beanie hat. KellyAnne had her arms tight round his neck and her head was flung back and even in the dim light it was clear she was looking into his eyes with an expression of such . . . *intensity*. Into Thelma's startled mind came words from *A Streetcar Named Desire*. The words of doomed Blanche Dubois to a youthful delivery man who takes her fancy . . . *young man . . . young young man*. It wasn't so much the man's age that brought the words to her mind – though from what Thelma could see he had a youthful air – it was the look on KellyAnne's face, a look of passion, of love and of hope. A look that was uncontrolled.

Dangerous. Certainly nothing at all like the look she'd given the vet from Richmond in front of the ice sculpture and the string quartet.

CHAPTER THIRTY-FIVE

*Tourists are shocked in Thirsk marketplace
and there is a revelation over brunch.*

Thirsk marketplace the following day; a warm brisk day with white clouds marching across a textbook blue sky. For the first time that spring Pat had had to dig out her sunglasses from the glove compartment. For the first time that year the tourists looked like tourists, free from their camouflaging raincoats and fleeces, their pastel jackets and polo shirts and knitwear blooming like so many spring flowers, their audible tweets of delight at seeing the Darrowby Arms.

It felt wrong to be worried on such a lovely day, but crossing the cobbles Pat was worried, horribly worried. If there had been a thought bubble bobbling above her head like a birthday balloon it would have said one word: *Liam.*

Things had not got better as she'd hoped; in fact they'd got worse, much worse. The previous day he'd come home from school, gone straight up to his room and shut the door admitting no one, not even Larson, who had spent the evening lying on the landing outside with a puzzled expression. And that'd been it; he'd not had any supper, not been down to watch the football with Rod, had only used the bathroom when no one else was around and any questions, queries, plates of Lamb Henry

269

and mugs of Horlicks had all been met by the same concrete, curt refusal.

'What gives with old Face-Ache?' Rod had asked, and of course Pat had had to say she didn't know. And it was that – that not knowing – that was driving her frantic. Something to do with Facebook but what? His Facebook page was the same as ever; in fact it had not been updated for a few days. So what?

Her thoughts had been (and still largely were) a sort of constant trolley dash of worry, from illegal pornography to terrorism and back again via scams, drug addiction and accidentally hacking into the Pentagon website. Her latest black thought was mental health problems. Her mind spooled back through the years to Rod's Auntie Janet who ended up having to go somewhere. How had that all started? How she wished she'd watched all those worthy mental health documentaries she'd passed over in favour of *Come Dine with Me*. And then there was what had happened in the middle of the night: 3.12 a.m. to be precise; the cherry red digits of her alarm clock were branded into her memory like the time code on a crime scene CCTV still.

She'd been lying half immersed in the sort of dream that you know is a dream; Rocky was back in her class again and she was trying to teach him but he kept blowing out clouds of purple smoke into her face . . . and then Thelma had come in and Pat knew with a chilled heart she'd come to take Liam to the police. The sound of their bedroom door opening broke into this unhappy doze and with all the presence of mind twenty-four years of motherhood brings she'd instantly sat up, her sleepy brain reeling off a list of possibilities: bad dreams, chicken pox, vomiting, wet beds . . .

'Liam,' she'd said as Rod, equally befuddled, had groped for the bedside light. Her son looked young, despite the *I'm not shy, I just don't want to talk to you* T-shirt; in the dim light from the lamp his features had tumbled back some ten, twelve years as he stared fixedly and glassily at a spot on the wall behind their bed.

'What gives?' Rod had said as Pat had simultaneously hissed, 'He's sleepwalking.'

At the sound of their voices Liam had gasped, a truly heart-clutching intake of breath, and woken up, coughing, doubled up, one hand groping for the bedhead.

'Sorry,' he'd said, retreating. 'Sorry, sorry.'

Rod had been all too happy to dismiss it as 'exam stress' and had fallen back asleep almost straight away. Pat, however, had gone and sat on the landing outside Liam's bedroom door. Larson had joined her and the two of them had kept vigil for over an hour; it had been many, many years, she reflected, since she'd listened to one of her sons cry himself to sleep.

And that next morning, it was as if nothing had happened.

After a long talk with Rod – or more accurately at Rod – she'd been all ready to sit Liam down with a cooked breakfast and punch at that concrete response no matter how bloodied they'd both got in the process. But Liam had come downstairs, if not exactly full of the joys of spring, then perfectly normally, asking Rod about last night's match, wrestling with Larson and telling Pat she should think about opening one of those lay-by food stands. When Pat had asked about the sleepwalking, he merely said, 'Did I? Sorry about that.'

'See,' said Rod as he went to drive him to the school bus, 'I told you not to worry.'

But coming back down Millgate from the Polish deli, Pat knew she was perfectly right to worry. She knew with a cold feeling that was totally at odds with the bright optimistic day that she still needed to sit him down and find out exactly what was going on. If only to stop that horrendous mental procession of possibilities. (Online gambling? Olga knew someone whose son had lost £25,000!) But what if he didn't answer then? What if he simply refused to say? He was more than capable of clamming up completely and shutting the world out when it suited him (just like his father). Somehow she couldn't shake off the

271

thought of Thelma reporting Rocky to the police like that. Of course she knew it was the right thing to do . . . *but* . . . what if Liam was involved in something illegal? She stopped, the bag of shopping cutting heavy lines into her hand. What sort of a mother was she to let her son get into this mess and not even know what the mess was? She could hear Ness's taunting words: *I've often thought Facebook must be a nightmare. I keep my two off it.*

Hang on a minute.

Ness knew.

She realized she was standing almost directly across from Green Grass Properties and without giving herself time to think, she began looking for a gap in the traffic. She wasn't at all sure how Ness would be after the performance at the funeral, but to be quite frank she wasn't worried. For all she cared, Ness could have split noisily and messily with Captain Implosion ten times over as long as she was in a position to help her find out just what this horrible black cloud overpowering her son was about.

She'd just reached the other pavement (after a near miss with an Austin Reed lorry) when the door to Green Grass Properties was opened and Lloret propelled himself out, gym bag over his shoulder, Ness following behind. Neither saw Pat as they strode to the marketplace. No, Lloret strode to the marketplace and Ness trotted along next to him, a proprietorial hand on the gym bag, talking (and laughing) brightly. And Lloret . . . he looked . . . she tried to put one of her titles to it . . . cornered . . . 'Cornered of Thirsk'. Looking at his darting eyes and uneasy expression she saw the truth of Liam's words: Lloret went out with people because he didn't like to hurt their feelings by not doing so.

What else might Lloret do if the correct pressure was applied?

The pair came to a stop near the marketplace map; Ness now appeared to be reasoning with him as he looked in every direction but at her, unwilling to stay, unable to go. Cornered.

The kiss took Pat (and the people coming out of Yorkshire Pound Warehouse) by surprise. One minute Ness was talking brightly, the next she had Lloret in what could only be described as a clinch. It wasn't so much that *that* shocked Pat, as the air of something . . . *abandoned* in the way the older woman was holding him, holding onto him, stroking his back, desperately, totally giving herself up to the kiss.

It took Pat a moment to place the stocky bearded man in a beanie hat striding purposefully towards them; indeed it was only when she heard Ness say 'Craig' sharply that Pat registered here was the fiasco, last seen supporting Ness across the car park of the Bay Horse. She was shocked and surprised by the speed and anger with which Craig moved, shoving a terrified Lloret sharply in the chest and grabbing him in a headlock, from where he proceeded to pummel the lad's face as the gym bag and its contents went flying across the pavement.

A cross-section of the Monday morning Thirsk market crowd watched: two young mums, mouths agape, a couple of grinning men from one of the stalls, disapproving older people including a man in a cap who kept shouting 'now then, lads' – plus a whole posse of tourists clearly not sure whether to move on or film the whole thing on their mobiles. In all, the scuffle could only have lasted some thirty seconds, Craig wrestling and pummelling Lloret as Ness yapped shrilly round, raining her fists on Craig's back. With a final snarl of 'stay the f**k away from my fiancée' he strode off, Ness dancing angrily round his heels after him, leaving Lloret on the pavement amongst a collection of pants, protein shakes and what looked like junk mail.

Pat knew instantly that the hard part for Lloret wouldn't be the pain of the bruises blossoming on his face but the attention of the crowd that was fully on him as he lay sprawled by the James Herriot Country map, gingerly feeling his nose and phone to presumably check if either were broken. The market men saw something to laugh about, the older people something to frown over at their coffee mornings, the tourists an example of the fabled British hooliganism – but Pat, neither a market man, pensioner nor a tourist saw none of these things. She saw a teenage boy, sprawled and upset, no different from the thousands of boys she'd seen sprawled and upset in playgrounds over the years, and she was not about to see him reduced to even more of a public spectacle.

'Lloret,' she said in friendly but firm tones. 'Hello.'

He looked up as he feverishly stuffed the last of the mail into his bag, looking infinitely sad and lost. 'Hello, Mrs Taylor,' he said dully.

'Come on,' she said. 'Let's get you sorted out.'

Afterwards, thinking back, Pat was a bit surprised at just how passively he went with her; but then she was offering the quickest and simplest of getaways. In the minute it took Ness to dispatch Craig, Pat was negotiating her way out of the marketplace parking space as he slumped down in the seat, presumably to avoid being seen.

Years of dealing with hurt, angry, upset children had taught Pat to say nothing — well, nothing about what had happened. She knew that what they wanted and needed more than anything else was space and time and quiet to allow their own roaring feelings to subside. In days gone by she'd been used to getting out a big blue IKEA box with all the leftover pencil crayons and giving the child a sharpener, so they could sharpen and sort the lime green, the sunshine yellow, the crimson lake, whilst she marked books and made bright comments about holidays and school dinners. Now, driving back to Borrowby (to get that face seen to), she made similar inconsequential conversation about the weather, about the daffodils, about the chances of Rievaulx 1st XI this season.

She fully expected Lloret to take refuge in monosyllabic responses but, instead, bright nervous eyes blinking, he gave cheery, brittle answers. As they arrived back at the house he began asking her question after nervous question, about her, her retirement, about Liam, her friends, the age of Larson (regarding them both suspiciously from under the settle) – anything other than what had just happened whilst she tended to his nose (not broken) and face (a bag of frozen peas – she could always do a risotto).

After Pat had finished tending his wounds, it seemed the most natural thing in the world to cook him brunch. In her experience teenage boys were invariably ravenous and there was something about Lloret that brought all her maternal instincts roaring to the fore. In her fridge were tuna steaks, mozzarella, smoked turkey breast; by instinct she ignored all of these and began frying Farm Shop pork and sage sausages, two rashers of their sweet cured bacon and two of their large brown eggs, each a great aurora of white with an unbroken dollop of glowing amber in the middle.

Aside from the sizzle of fat and the tick of the clock, there was a peaceful silence in the sunny kitchen. Lloret left his phone alone, switched off; Pat suspected the second he turned it on, it would explode with communications from Ness. Instead he had taken the G2 section of her *Guardian* and attacked the puzzles section; he'd devoured the crossword and was currently frowning over the Sudoku.

As Pat cooked, she thought. Thelma had, of course, been right: whatever was going on between him and Ness was obviously now over and the scene in the marketplace suggested who wanted it to be over and who didn't.

So what now? She looked at the bruised, forlorn figure frowning over the paper, so different from the confident, smiling figure on the E-Titans website. She could ask him about Ness, she could ask about Rocky or Mandy Pinder or even Oliver Harney. She could certainly ask about Liam but flipping an egg she realized for the moment she lacked both the will and energy to do any of these things; besides, the lad had been through enough without her pumping him for information. She put the warm plate of food in front of him.

He blinked nervously and she suddenly noticed how rich the brown of his eyes was, with an almost amber quality.

'You must let me give you something for this,' he said.

'Don't be daft.' She topped up his coffee and he fell on the food, eating ravenously. How long since he'd had anything proper to eat? Pat automatically poured herself a coffee, realized what she had done, and pushed it to one side, totally lacking the will to make a mint tea.

'I saw your website,' she said, more for something to say.

'Cool.' He looked up eagerly. 'I need people to see it. I need to improve my online footfall.'

'Of course.' Pat hadn't a clue what that meant but nodded wisely. Without thinking she took a sip of the coffee she'd pushed to one side. The sudden rich explosion of taste was like a slap of cold common sense; her eyes watered and her glands tingled as she felt both will and energy stirring back to life.

'Liam was telling me how much it costs to set up a business these days,' she said, taking another blessed sip. 'Even online. It's frightening. I'm guessing it's been the Bank of Mum and Dad, like it is with our three?'

'Actually no.' He frowned. 'Dad's not around. Mum isn't really in a position to provide any backing. It's a shame for her – it's a golden opportunity, and I'm always looking for new backers.' He looked at her with an earnest flash of those amber-brown eyes and Pat smiled noncommittally, trying and failing to picture Rod's face when she told him she'd invested in a nineteen-year-old's web business.

'I see,' she said. 'I'm guessing Ness is a backer?'

'She's one.' He finished the last piece of bacon, his tone decidedly less confident. 'But for various reasons she was unable to commit much.' Reasons like Craig the fiasco maybe, thought Pat.

'How's the nose?' she asked.

'Sore.' His manner was now drooping by degrees, but she sensed he was not unwilling to talk.

'He was a big man – he must have packed quite a punch,' she prompted.

And then the words came in a semi-coherent rush. 'This is God's honest truth, Mrs Taylor, I didn't know he and Ness were together, not like that. I swear it on my mother's life. I mean I knew they had *been* engaged but Ness said . . . she said it was over in all but name and they lived independent lives, like brother and sister.'

Brother and sister. How many times had she heard that one before?

'Well now you know different,' she said not unsympathetically.

And bit by bit the tale came out, about him helping her set up her website, about 'one thing leading to another', about the evenings in the office of Green Grass Properties (presumably on those dove-grey carpet tiles with the track lighting turned off), about how Ness was looking for a place of her own, and how she wanted Lloret to move in, and how at the funeral he'd told her he didn't think it was such a good idea. And today he'd just been over to collect some things he'd left behind, and Pat knew all the rest.

'It's not even like we're together any more, that's the stupid thing. The last thing I want to do is come between them. I tried telling him that but he wouldn't listen.' He looked at her with those eyes with their long dark lashes and Pat had to take a further hasty gulp of her coffee. No wonder Ness had embarrassed herself outside Yorkshire Pound Warehouse and Lucy Beesborough thrown her knitted beret over the windmill. She allowed herself a moment of pity for Ness, but only a moment.

'I mean don't get me wrong, she's a very special person,' he said earnestly. 'I wish her all the happiness in the world. But she's on, like, a journey and while she's on that journey I don't think long-term commitments are right for her.'

Claptrap.

Pat took his plate to the dishwasher, feeling a pang of annoyance at Ness or whoever it was who had been stuffing this lad's head full of half-baked psychobabble when it should have been full of, well, nineteen-year-old stuff.

Instantly, insistently, her mind flew back to Liam and that old lump of ice was right back there in her chest and she knew whatever she asked, she had to ask him about that. But as she was assembling the words to ask him, he spoke again.

'KellyAnne says she's just using me to make a statement to Craig.'

And then she had one of her lightbulb moments, an idea so sudden and strong it verged on conviction.

'Would KellyAnne be another one of your backers by any chance?'

'Sure, she said she'd put in some money . . .' His tone had changed to one that Pat, well versed in the ways of teenage lads, instantly clocked as evasive. 'She even said she'd come in on the business with me. Partners.'

'Tell me to keep my nose out,' she said neutrally. He was now staring at the table, tracing the lines of the grain with his finger; she could tell he knew what was coming.

'Are you and Kelly Anne . . . perhaps a bit more than business partners?'

He didn't look up. The business by the sea. How come she'd not thought of it before?

'It's eighty per cent professional.' He sounded as if he was trying to convince himself.

'Does KellyAnne see it like that?'

And then as Pat rinsed plates and filled the dishwasher, a second story came out. About helping KellyAnne set up her laptop, about the connection they felt, about him giving her a shoulder to cry on through that truly terrible time, about his guilt at cheating on Ness with her best friend, and about KellyAnne's proposal to invest in his business, and for them to relocate and set it up somewhere together. He sighed and looked down at the table.

'It's one of those awkward things you get into,' he said.

One of those awkward things you *get into,* thought Pat, scouring her beloved copper-bottom pan.

Of course, looking at it all made total sense, she thought; one of the first things KellyAnne had said when she was sat with them at the garden centre was about finding her prince. She sighed, thinking of KellyAnne's happy smile, knowing from Lloret's tone that this particular prince was about to turn back into a frog – or at the very least hop off into the distance as fast as his legs could carry him. What a mess. What a sad, broken mess.

A succession of buzzes and pings seemed to echo her thoughts: Lloret had turned his phone on. He stared miserably down at the screen.

'Ness,' he said. 'And KellyAnne.'

She gave the pan a final scour and put it in the dishwasher and turned it on; it came to life with an infinitely reassuring hum.

'Maybe,' she said, sitting back down at the table, 'I mean tell me to neb out, Lloret, but maybe it's time to have a talk with KellyAnne. If you're not comfortable with how things are. If you don't feel the same. I mean better now before things go too far.'

'That's not everything.' His voice was so small she wouldn't have heard it if she'd not happened to be looking at him. What now? Was he seeing a third person? Where did the young find the energy? He was staring fixedly at the phone. She sat down at the table and closed a hand over his.

'Lloret,' she said in her gentlest voice, the one she used to use with really severe five-star infant school meltdowns. 'Whatever it is, you're much better telling someone. It doesn't have to be me, but it needs to be someone.'

Again he didn't look at her. 'That night . . . the night KellyAnne's mum took those tablets by mistake.'

'Yes?'

'They said they thought someone was there. Someone was seen round the house.'

'I remember.'

'There was.' He looked at her and his face crumpled. 'It was me.'

CHAPTER THIRTY-SIX

A wedding day is remembered and a bad decision regretted.

'You get a real sense of the venue in this one.' Mandy turned over the page of the padded white album, the protective tissue crackling softly.

Thelma looked at the photo. Radiant, she thought, was an oft-misapplied term, but here it was spot on. Mandy was stood on an artificial-looking stone bridge over an equally artificial-looking pond; a cascading white dress pooled around her feet and she brandished a bouquet of fat snowy roses in the same way she had once presented Thelma with Thistledown promise pony. At her feet sat two grinning little girls in rich purple dresses; beside her stood the groom, her ex-husband, wearing a slightly startled grin as if surprised at the situation he found himself in.

'Pav was so good-looking.' There was something in Mandy's voice and look that reminded Thelma of the way she had judged the burgundy dress that day in the charity shop. 'Plus he knew how to have a good time.' She sighed. 'Nights out in Leeds, weekends in spa hotels.'

Thelma might have said something along the lines of 'Who paid for all the good times?' but she didn't need to; the sheaf of envelopes with their red markings stuffed behind the lamp on the coffee table told their own story.

She was sitting in the front room of Mandy's house (rented), a bleak little shoebox of a thing that was one on an estate of bleak little shoeboxes that had sprung up mushroom-like in the fields beyond St Barnabus's, where buttercups used to proliferate. Where, so many moons ago, the Reception class used to have their annual teddy bears' picnic. The room was sparsely furnished but there were the indelible signs of children: pink dolls, Elsa from *Frozen*, iPads. There seemed to be no expense spared in that department. Yet the room was more than slightly chilly.

'You don't mind?' Mandy had said. 'I keep the heat off as much as possible.' Thelma didn't mind, of course she didn't, but surreptitiously rubbing her hands she wished she'd kept her coat on.

'There's a fountain in the pond,' said Mandy, still looking at the album. 'You have to pay a bit extra but they switch it on at night and it goes red and green and blue.' Thelma turned the page and Mandy smiled at a close-up of herself, her face framed in improbable-looking ringlets and for a second her expression was identical to the one in the photograph. Radiant.

'How lovely,' said Thelma. She looked at Mandy; in the chilly March light the tan looked distinctly pallid. She flicked through more pictures, more arrangements of the dress, by bowers, bushes, on a bank of snowdrops.

'It only lasted the year,' said Mandy, a muted regretful note in her voice, as if describing a pet that, in spite of everything, had died. 'But it was a lovely day.'

Thelma carefully handed her back the white leather-padded album. Equally carefully Mandy put it back in its white box and replaced it in the wall unit with all the reverence of the dean placing the King James Bible in the lectern at the cathedral.

'That was what really started it all,' she said. 'All the debt and stuff.'

'Paying for your wedding?'

281

'We had all the bills but we were paying them off over time, like you do.' Mandy sighed and looked weary, far wearier than someone of her age should look.

Like you do, thought Thelma compassionately. She thought of the dress and the album and the fountain playing red, green and blue. She thought of the car and the Michael Kors scarf and the cost of the Zumba class that Pat still mentioned in scandalized tones. And she thought of her and Teddy, their wedding reception in the church hall at home, her mother and Auntie Irene organizing the buffet between them. She thought of her and Teddy as newly-weds sitting in three jumpers apiece to save turning on the heating, and the taste of that awful cheap margarine. She said nothing but sent up a quick angry prayer about a society that pushed every consumable going but had made it impossible for young people to even get on the property ladder.

Mandy sighed again. 'And then when he pissed off – sorry, Mrs Cooper – when he went, there was still over half to pay, and everything else you need to pay on top of that and it's like your money's halved. So you miss one month and you think it's all right but of course it isn't because there's the next month and there's still last month to pay and so on.' She sat down and began pleating the edge of the cushion in that familiar way. 'I took on the Sainsburys' job, extra to the bank, but it didn't help – not really. There's the kids for a start. You're always shelling out for them; you can't find everything in a charity shop . . .'

They both glanced at the two bright little buttons smiling cheekily down from the sideboard in their purple St Barnabus's Academy jumpers. A quick look inside their book bags at their spellings and reading records had told Thelma they were as bright as they looked. And no matter how tough things got, no matter what the world threw at her, she had them in her life and would have them, and when she got old . . .

'I hadn't a choice,' said Mandy. She shook her head, shutting her eyes. 'I know payday loans are a stupid idea, Mrs Cooper, I do, of course I do – I work in a bank. If you'd come to me and said, "I'm thinking of taking out a payday loan," I'd have said, "Don't be so daft." But at the end of the day I had no choice.'

I had no choice.

The old familiar memory smacked Thelma like a sudden throb of migraine . . . Walking through Ripon feeling drugged and slow and lethargic from the tablets . . . Seeing the pushchair, outside what was then Osbaldistons the stationer's, a rather scruffy pram. From within she could hear a contented burbling and she found herself peering in to see the child, in a grubby lemon-coloured cardigan. The smell, the stains, the chocolate mark on the mouth told her this child, for whatever reason, was not well looked after but what hit her like a bolt to the heart was the sudden, gummy smile, the hands reaching out in recognition and before she had time to process it her hands were on the handle of the pram . . .

She'd felt . . .

She'd felt like she had no choice . . .

She stifled the memory and with a mighty effort turned her attention back to the matter in hand.

'So . . .' she said.

'Yes, go on.' Mandy turned her blank stare towards Thelma.

'I spoke to Citizens Advice this morning . . .' after being put on hold for twenty-seven and a half minutes at premium rate, Thelma might have added but naturally didn't '. . . and it's slightly complicated.'

More than slightly. The system was different, *way* different, from the days when Teddy ran a debt counselling service for St Catherine's. Successive funding cuts had left the service the merest shadow of its former self and now it seemed, according to the fraught-sounding woman she spoke to, the only way to get any sort of appointment was to turn up in Harrogate on one of three given days, stand in a queue and hope to be seen. To stand any sort of chance to get counselling 'that day' meant being no more than tenth in the queue. And, to ensure that, it meant being there when the queue started forming. Usually round the six thirty mark.

'Six thirty?' Mandy's face froze over with its habitual blankness.

'I know, I couldn't believe it. In days gone by you could more or less just turn up. The woman, to be fair, did sound apologetic. And you need to take with you as much information as you can. Details of all your accounts, bills, especially details of all the loans.'

'Six thirty.' Mandy was obviously having trouble moving on from this fact.

'How will you manage with the children?'

'They can stop at my mum's. They'll have to.'

'And have you heard from the debt people?' Thelma asked.

'Like you said, I've kept my phone turned off unless I've needed to use it. But they haven't, not yet. They operate like that, I've found. Get really nasty, then go away for a day or two, give you time to sweat.'

'If they do call, you're to tell them—' Thelma unfolded the paper from the file '—tell them you're taking legally accredited debt counselling and will contact them in no more than three working days' time.'

'I just hope they don't come into the bank. That's what really bothers me. If the bank find out, I lose my job, and then no one's any chance of getting anything.'

'Mandy, I've been meaning to ask. And please tell me to mind my own business. But surely you could have gone to someone in the bank for help?'

Mandy laughed mirthlessly. 'Then I would definitely one hundred per cent have lost my job.'

'Don't they offer some sort of debt counselling?'

'Only to say don't do it in the first place. Anyway, who would I ask?'

'Is there some sort of human resources department?'

'If there is I've never heard of it. It's not that sort of place; everyone's just busy getting on with it.'

'Surely there's some senior managers.' Thelma thought of Mr Riley back when she and Teddy were buying College Gardens. Always ready to listen.

Mandy snorted. 'There's a manager. He's shared between three branches. And he's younger than me. It's a joke. I tell you, Mrs Cooper, that day when Mrs Joy lost her money, when her daughter found out and came in kicking off big time, no one had a clue what to do. We didn't even know we had to tell her to go to the police. Everyone was rushing around like headless chickens and the manager's kid was ill with chicken pox so there was no sign of him. We were more or less told to ring the fraud department and let them get on with it. And there was her daughter, kicking off in the middle of the branch for the whole world to hear. I felt sorry for her, truly I did, but I'd no idea that there were such scams going on.'

'Surely you'd had some sort of training?'

Mandy shook her head. She looked around furtively as if someone behind the wall unit was listening and lowered her voice. 'We were all told to *say* we had. And we did get some the week after. But what good was it then? We all knew by then.'

Soon after, Thelma took her leave. Pausing on the doorstep of the bleak little house, looking out at all the other bleak little houses, she was aware it was distinctly warmer outside than within.

'Remember,' she said, 'six thirty tomorrow.' She wasn't at all sure Mandy would in fact go.

'Yes.' Mandy's less than committed tone confirmed her thought.

'Will that be all right? With the girls I mean?'

'That won't be a problem. Mum loves having them, thank God. And just as well, Mrs Cooper, I'd be well and truly stuck without her. You can't be in two places at once, can you?'

Thelma smiled to herself, knowing that – actually – your

average primary school teacher, retired or not, could achieve exactly that effect.

She suddenly frowned.

Mandy paused, scanning the street for any sign of Charles Morton, Forward Credit. Nothing, thank goodness. She turned to Thelma but she seemed to have gone into a dream, staring across the bare pocket-handkerchief lawns of the estate. 'Mrs Cooper?'

Thelma recovered. 'I'm so sorry,' she said. 'Something just occurred to me.'

CHAPTER THIRTY-SEVEN

Revelation follows revelation and more than one person ends up crying into a table.

Lloret cried like a, well, like a nineteen-year-old: convulsively, a series of embarrassed snorts and shudders, face pillowed in his arms on the kitchen table. Pat knew better than to do anything other than sit in silence, a single hand gently resting at the top of his spine. When he eventually sat up, she wordlessly handed him a folded wedge of kitchen towel.

'KellyAnne said it'd be all right but it's how it'd look if people knew . . .'

'How what would look?'

'I'm really really scared, Mrs Cooper.'

'Whatever is it, Lloret?'

Lloret tried to compose himself, breathing and shaking his head and wiping his face with the kitchen towel. 'Money,' he said. 'I'm setting up this new business, or rather we are, me and KellyAnne; she's one of the backers like I say and anyway I need some cash because there was some stuff I needed to pay for up front, some tech stuff.' He shuddered again. 'Only I needed the money there and then to get this deal, but Kel – KellyAnne – she was away for the weekend. And I knew she'd say "do it". She said if I ever needed money up front I should do it . . .'

'Do what?'

'Take money from her mum's account.' He took a deep shuddering breath that reminded Pat of Liam. 'It wasn't nicking it because KellyAnne said it was okay – and I knew she kept her card in her purse and her purse on the side, and I knew she never locked the back door.'

He paused, breathless, and Pat topped his coffee up. He took an enormous gulp. 'I should've just knocked on the door but I knew Mrs Joy didn't like me. KellyAnne said it was her illness, but she was always off with me. There was this one time, just after the fraud, and Kel, she was upset and sounding off . . . and she said she wished her mum was dead . . . I thought Mrs Joy was asleep but she wasn't, and ever since then . . . No way would she have let me go in her purse.' He closed his eyes. 'Anyway I just thought it'd be easier if I snuck in and took the card and went. So I looked in through the kitchen window and I could see she was on the phone. She had her back to me.'

The phone call with Paula presumably.

'So I tried the back door and it was open. Like I say I knew she always forgot to lock it. So I went inside and stood in the kitchen, waiting for her to go back into the living room. I knew exactly where the purse was: in the hall on the telephone table. And she goes back into the sitting room, so I took the card from the purse . . . and then this smoke alarm goes off. It scared the shit out of me . . .'

'Was something on fire?' she asked.

'I didn't see nothing, but I thought maybe a kettle or the toaster. But then it sounded like it was in the sitting room – anyway I didn't wait to find out. I went back out the side door. And then the next day I went to the cash point at Tesco, and then KellyAnne rings me and says what's happened . . . I swear to God I was gutted . . . I didn't know what to do and ever since I've been going out of my mind, Mrs Cooper.' He dissolved into fresh sobs and again she patted his back and supplied kitchen roll, only this time she was thinking furiously.

When he finally sat up she said, 'D'you think anyone else was there, when you went round?'

He frowned. 'I didn't hear anyone, but then I suppose they could have been in the sitting room. I wouldn't have seen them there.'

'Did you happen to see any cups?' He looked at her blankly. 'On the draining board?' she said.

'No?' He sounded puzzled but decisive. 'No. I was thinking I might have to climb out of the kitchen window, so I looked on the draining board and I remember thinking there was nothing there I'd have to move out of the way.' He wiped his blotchy face and Pat thought some more.

If Lloret was telling the truth, the cups weren't on the draining board at that time. But they were there the next morning, when KellyAnne had come round. Perhaps they were already set out in the sitting room? Maybe someone else was even sitting there waiting for Topsy to get off the phone.

'And you didn't see or hear anyone else?'

'No, just Mrs Joy. She had the telly on. I panicked when the alarm went off. And that's the God's honest truth.'

'None of that sounds so bad,' she said. He shut his eyes and shook his head as if rejecting the comfort she was offering.

'What if there was a gas leak and that was why the alarm went off? Or carbon monoxide or something?' He put his hands to his face. 'And suppose that's why she died and I could've done something about it if I'd not run off?' For a technical wizard he was surprisingly unversed in the ways of household emergencies.

'Lloret,' said Pat. 'That wouldn't have set the smoke alarm off. Anyway, they'd have found out if she'd been killed by carbon monoxide.'

'Anyway then I heard the police had traced the payment and KellyAnne thought it might be Paula, so I told her what happened.

289

And she told the police it was her . . . said the best thing to do all round was to keep quiet.'

'Why would she say that?'

'In the past . . .' He drooped again. 'In the past, Mrs Cooper, there were things I did. Mistakes. Nothing that serious. But KellyAnne said they'd question me and that they have a way of twisting things. She had a cousin once . . . and something happened and it wasn't him but he copped for it. And they were bound to want to find someone to pin it on. She said she'd look after me. And that's all. I swear to God.'

Was he telling the truth? He blinked miserably at her. He was certainly scared and upset, but was he being truthful?

He blinked again. 'It was really good of her to cover for me. But ever since then . . .' His voice tailed off.

And ever since then, thought Pat, *she's had a hold over you.*

'I mean when she first said about the business, before all this . . . I was like "okay" but now I'm not so sure,' he said miserably. 'I mean I love her. Of course I do, I wish her all the good in the world.'

Again he dropped his head into his hands and wept. When he'd sat up and yet another wodge of kitchen roll had been dispatched, Pat took his hand. 'The only thing to do, Lloret . . .' She used her best calm teacher voice, the one she used to use to talk down children having meltdowns. 'The *only* thing for you to do is to go and tell the police. Tell them what you told me.'

'Really?' His eyes widened.

'It's by far and away the best thing. If it's as you said it was, then it'll be all right.'

'What'll happen?'

'You'll probably get a bit of a telling-off. But they're not going to charge you, not for that.' She emphasized her words with a reassuring squeeze of his hand.

He didn't look convinced.

'The alternative is carrying this around with you.' And carrying KellyAnne around with you as well, she could've added.

He sniffed and blew his nose. He didn't exactly nod but looked at her from under those long lashes. Was there an element of calculation in that look? Liam's voice came into her head: *He'd do wrong if it was the easiest thing to do.*

The sudden click and creak of the back door seemed almost accusatory; without realizing quite why, Pat snatched her hand away (almost dashing the cafetiere to the flags in the process).

It was Liam, still droopy, still unkempt, framed in the doorway looking tired, school bag over his shoulder as if it contained rocks rather than an iPad and two ring binders. Pat realized with some guilt she'd mostly forgotten about him in the light of Lloret's revelations. There was a pause during which Larson ambled unconcernedly across the kitchen to him as if picking sides and Liam's whole face transformed into a question.

'Liam.' Pat realized she hadn't a clue what to say. 'You know Lloret. From cricket.' She could hear a tone in her own voice, which was uncomfortably like the one she used to use to welcome new children to the class. But then, what else could she say? She could hardly tell the truth.

Fortunately Lloret took control. Thinking about it later, Pat surmised he'd had a fair bit of experience in awkward situations. Standing up he began chatting, much like he'd done earlier in the car: easy, unforced chat about Rievaulx XI, about the commitment he wasn't sure he could make this year, about the team's chances now Dribble had moved on to pastures new in Darlington.

Liam responded equally easily, neutral pleasant answers, and Pat marvelled, not for the first time in her life, at the male capacity for compartmentalization as two young men, one beaten up on his way to the police station and the other with goodness knows what going on his life, chatted about the wicket at Pateley Bridge and the absolute joke that was the scoring at Thornton Witless.

She drove him to Northallerton. She wanted to go into the police station with him but Lloret said no, so quietly and definitely, without so much as a flash of the brown eyes, that she didn't even attempt to argue. He could, of course, be planning not to go at all, bunk off round the corner as soon as she pulled away, but Pat rather thought not. Could it be Lloret was finally learning to stand up for himself? She was glad to see his resolve and also, truth be told, she was glad not to be part of whatever was coming next for him. 'Thank you, Mrs Taylor.' He leant into the open window.

'You've got my number.'

'I'll let you know what happens. I promise.' And how many times had he said that before?

'And . . .' A sudden awkward blurt, not calculating, not emotional but genuine. 'I'm sorry about Liam. That twat – excuse my French – that Luke . . . I mean, what he posted on Facebook, it was way out of order.' Pat stared at him. 'Honestly, Mrs Taylor, that guy's a real nasty loser. Liam deserves so much better than him.'

It was a selfie from the title page of Luke's Facebook account, screenshotted and forwarded to her by Lloret. It looked, as all selfies do, that mix of the exuberant and haphazard. Liam, blue polo-shirted and decidedly kempt, was the one taking the photo; his face loomed large at the front . . . . Alive. That was the word Pat chose to describe her son's expression – alive, lit from within by something that was all too obvious for the world to see. Behind him was Luke, sharp face, assessing. There was something as cold in his eyes as there was bright and optimistic in Liam's. Underneath, in bold, pink font were the words *I am what I am*. *Sneaky* was the word that came to her. Nothing plain, nothing spelt out, nothing that could get Luke into any sort of bother – he was way too crafty for that, she thought with a jolting burn of anger, but the meaning was as obvious as if Luke had posted 'Liam Taylor is gay' in pink vibrating letters.

Gay.

How on *earth* hadn't she realized, guessed, intuited? When it all made such clear perfect sense? It was like the first time she'd read *Murder on the Orient Express* – the solution was in retrospect so obvious, yet leading up to the denouement she'd had absolutely no idea. It really and truly had never crossed her mind. Or rather, it had crossed her mind in a faintly academic way, devoid of any import, in the same way it crossed her mind Rod might have an affair or this week's lottery ticket be a winner – but it had kept on crossing her mind and gone right on out the other side without stopping. All at once her fears of the trailer park in Boroughbridge seemed as remote and naïve as belief in the tooth fairy.

Pat's fingers were white around her mug of liquorice and rosehip, as she surveyed the ingredients for lamb with chicory with neither energy nor enthusiasm. The earlier sunshine had long since dissolved into scudding grey clouds with the certainty of rain. She tried to raise the energy to do something – turn the light on, empty the dishwasher – something. But she sat. In the background, the rhythmic thud of the tumble dryer finishing off Liam's bedding. Larson lay snuggled against her feet like he'd done that time when her dad had had his first angina attack.

And inside she fizzed and roared with rage, as you do when someone you love has been hurt.

Her thoughts had not progressed much beyond all this when the sound she simultaneously dreaded and yearned for made her tighten her grasp on her herbal tea: Liam's bedroom door opening and his steps on the stairs.

She fully expected him to move wordlessly to the fridge and take an energy drink, but instead he stood framed in the doorway, much as he had been earlier. He was looking straight at her.

His words, however, took her by surprise.

'Mum, what was Lloret Whitlaw doing here?'

She felt almost impatient at what she saw as an irrelevancy.

293

'I *said*. He got into a bit of bother in Thirsk. Hence his face. I was cleaning him up.' She steeled herself. 'Liam . . .' she began.

'What about?'

'Sorry?'

'What was the "bit of bother" about?'

What to say now, without going into the whole Ness/ KellyAnne scenario?

'Some falling-out,' she said vaguely.

'It wasn't . . .' She realized he was struggling with the words in the exact same way he used to when he was little and got overexcited. 'It wasn't my dad he fell out with, was it?'

What?

'No,' she said, a second before the realization hit her like a burst of caffeine. Liam thought she was another Lucy Beesborough! 'No!' In spite of everything, she laughed.

'I'm glad you find it so funny,' he said coldly.

'Liam love, Lloret was hurt and upset. I happened to be passing and brought him here. End of.'

But he was still frowning, as he had when reading aloud in assembly age eight. 'It's just you've been so funny lately.'

'Have I?'

'Yes, you have.' His words had a bewildered ring and Larson pricked up his ears and whined.

'In what way funny?'

'Going to Zumba.' He said the word like it was akin to a wife-swapping party. 'Wearing weird clothes. Drinking that *stuff*.' He gestured to the liquorice and rosehip like it was neat vodka.

'I've been trying to lose a bit of weight, that's all,' she said lamely.

'Lloret's bad news, Mum. You need to stay away from him.'

Pat couldn't think of one thing to say to him. Her son thought it was entirely possible she was carrying on with a nineteen-year old. A very attractive nineteen-year-old. In the midst of the foggy tangle of embarrassment, shame and laughter, a bright gold nugget of ego gleamed.

Liam turned away.

'Liam.' He stopped but didn't turn back round. 'Liam,' she said again.

This time, when he turned, he saw the turned-round iPad showing the picture of him and Luke. He said nothing but just like the other night, his face changed. He looked so tired . . . and yet so young. He took that heaving great breath of his as if to speak but the words didn't come.

'Liam,' she said.

And for the second time that day she had a teenage boy sobbing into her kitchen table.

CHAPTER THIRTY-EIGHT

There is a moment of clarity in St Catherine's Church.

That evening, around seven o'clock, found each of the three sat in different places, thinking.

Liz was sitting on the bed in the spare bedroom. On the quilt beside her was the blue plastic box of Topsy's things that she'd collected from Gortops all that time ago. Since seeing KellyAnne, Topsy had been on her mind. Not in any particularly intrusive way, not in a way that gave rise to feelings of grief or worry, more of a presence, solid and doleful, as she had been in life. Like with Jacob's visit to what would indeed be his new school. Holding the pinking shears, Liz could imagine Topsy listening to his solemn voice describing the classroom . . . 'Everything has a laminated label on it, Grandma, *everything* . . . and everybody has to sit in the same place and you all have to have a drawer to keep your things in and the drawer has to be kept tidy.'

Leoni had had her doubts. Mrs Franklin had seemed to her slightly old-school – 'a bit of a schoolmarm' had been her words – and was that what Jacob needed? Liz, however, had been sure that that was exactly what Jacob needed, and thinking of the laminated labels and tidy drawers, she was sure that was what Topsy would have thought as well.

She replaced the pinking shears and took out the shiny steel whistle. In her mind Topsy's voice called out across some long-ago September playground . . . 'Boys and girls, stand STILL.'

'She's at peace.' That was what KellyAnne had said, and with something of a jolt Liz realized she didn't agree. She didn't know whether Topsy – if Topsy still in some way existed – was at peace or not; it was more that she didn't feel KellyAnne believed her own words. More that the words were ones she *wanted* to believe. She pictured KellyAnne's grey, rather indeterminate eyes, that face, slightly saggy under the make-up. She thought of what Pat had told her about KellyAnne and Lloret Thing (how old was he?) – and the sudden shining sense it made of all that stuff about a house by the sea. And again she felt how very vulnerable KellyAnne was to those around her . . . to Lloret, to Ness . . . to Rocky.

Especially to Rocky.

She was still not sure how she felt about Thelma reporting him like that. She'd heard via Paula's sister that he had Gone To Pieces. Liz remembered similar collapses when he'd been caught out doing wrong, not least the Great Top Trumps scandal . . . She could see that cheerful face convulsed with noisy, helpless sobs and stuttered promises never to do wrong again . . . Liz shook herself. He'd done a wicked, wicked thing and caused KellyAnne a lot of heartache . . .

KellyAnne.

She could hear those words . . . *It's all I truly want, Liz.* She sighed slightly. How many times, how many, many times had she said them or something very like them over the years?

She remembered the pouting youngster in a strop about her pony; putting on those spots to try and get out of trouble; the affair with the married vet. And Topsy's indulgent tones: *The little madam. I hadn't the heart to be cross with her.*

This was getting her nowhere. Book group tomorrow and she had to have read at least another four chapters of *Broken Biscuits* to have a hope of holding her own in the conversation.

Sighing, she reached up to put the box back in the wardrobe but something prevented it from sliding all the way back to the wall. She reached up and in her hand was her mother's old Dossette box; it must have fallen out from her last box of things. She remembered the Dossette box she'd seen at Gortops . . . Topsy's fingers carefully counting out the pills . . . What was it she'd said? *So we're back on this again?* And something about a gizmo, Liz couldn't remember exactly what.

Surely a curious choice of phrase, implying she'd been on something else? Liz shrugged impatiently. She needed to stop her mind wandering and wondering.

She was still sitting there, fingering the Dossette box, when her mobile buzzed. Thelma. What could she be wanting?

Pat was sat in her car, parked up in a gateway on Moor Road, looking out at the lights coming on across the valley. It was noticeably lighter since the clocks had gone forward. It was gone seven but the sky over the Pennines was still streaks of grey and apricot. The year was moving on.

She had said she was going to the Shell Garage for milk but instead she'd come to this secluded pull-in, as she did from time to time when she needed space and peace. Lights were glimmering amber and white across the Vale of York, and she thought of how, behind the lights, whole lives were going on: filling dishwashers, *Emmerdale*, ironing shirts. Maybe people were rowing, maybe people were making love (less likely at 7 p.m. but you never knew); maybe people were staring out into the dark like she was, staring and thinking.

They had, herself and Rod, on the face of it been model parents. She had hugged Liam and told him she loved him and whatever choices he made she'd always be there for him and Rod had sort of shuffled his feet, thumped him on the back and said a more garbled and much shorter version of the same. They'd been onto the school, who promised to follow the matter up. She understood that Luke's post had since been taken down from Facebook.

Only . . .

She knew Rod was shocked and uneasy; she could tell that by his bewildered wide-eyed look, and as for herself, there was this cold feeling just below her chest. Her son. *Her son*. She could see those two faces, the radiant one and the sly one, staring out from that Facebook page . . .

The trailer park had gone for good.

With an odd little pang she realized she quite missed it.

She shivered. Her Country Casuals top was a bit on the thin side but it wasn't her sensible blue or her 'it'll do' green; it was one she'd found in the wardrobe that had somehow missed her earlier cull. And, shamefully (or not shamefully depending on how you looked on it, Pat wasn't at all sure), somewhere deep inside her was that golden thought Liam had actually thought it entirely possible that she had a toy boy. And though the thought was to be squashed away, unvoiced . . . first chance she got she was going to that new place by the cathedral in Ripon to see what they had in the way of summer tops.

Then of course, there was Lloret, the would-be toy boy himself. She'd not heard from him. She wasn't at all sure he had gone into the police station. Or maybe he had and was even now sitting in some cell or other, those big eyes of his staring reproachfully out of the barred window. (Did they have cells with barred windows at Northallerton these days?) She'd debated calling him but Thelma had advised not to. And Thelma, she'd been so lovely when she'd told her about Liam. So matter-of-fact, no platitudes or easy words. The comfort of those supportive silences.

She sighed and started the engine, feeling a twinge of envy for all those ordinary lives going on across the valley, with nothing more momentous than whose turn it was to empty the dishwasher. But then she remembered the couple in the teashop in Masham, Mr and Mrs Bland. When it came down to it, did anyone have an ordinary life? Her phone buzzed. Thelma. What was she doing texting, when they'd spoken not an hour since?

Earlier on, Thelma sat in the slightly chilly peace of St Catherine's, left-hand side, toward the back. She'd arrived a bit early for choir practice and was listening to the organist practising 'Jesu, Joy of Man's Desiring'. The cool fluting cascade of notes filling the church, with the occasional pause as he scribbled a note on the sheet music. She felt tired. She felt as though she'd been paddling and paddling a canoe against a tide, which had grown stronger and stronger until it had broken over her with an inevitable force of muddle and confusion and worry.

Rocky. *Had* she done the right thing?

She looked up at the dark east window in silent prayer, and her thoughts went back to that other time a few weeks ago when she'd looked at the daffodils. What *had* KellyAnne seen? She'd never go to the bottom of it.

She thought of what Rocky had said that day in the Bay Horse car park . . . *bad things happening in that house* . . . A lie to deflect from the truth . . .

Truth. Pat knew the truth about Liam. Thelma sent up a quick prayer for the family. She herself had suspected for some time. Liam had reminded her so strongly of someone from college days (now a successful theatre director). She'd always felt slightly guilty at not sharing her thoughts with Pat, particularly when her friend was stressing about the Celtic poet, but she'd had no shred of evidence. Her friend had assumed one thing – when something different turned out to be true.

Like with the five-star Mrs Bell. This, of course, had been more deliberate. Everyone believing a lie deliberately nurtured by someone.

And then there was Mandy.

She sent yet another quick prayer about the visit to Citizens Advice tomorrow, hoping against hope it would all work out for her. And for those beautiful girls of hers. Still, whatever happened, Mandy had those girls and they had her, and when Mandy got older, like Topsy, she would hopefully have their support.

And then Lloret and Ness . . . and KellyAnne. She thought again what Pat had told her earlier that day. Really just like that unfortunate business with the last youth group leader but one a few years back.

She had a sudden image of KellyAnne's face haloed in the lych gate lamp, that upturned passionate face, alive with need, that dangerous need that made her so vulnerable. What was it she'd said to Liz?

It's all I've ever wanted . . .

And her mind spun back some thirty years. It had all seemed so clear and easy: she would wheel the pram away, take the child home, wash the cardigan, clean the face . . . The tasks had shone out clear in her mind, the only clear thoughts that had, amongst the murky grey cotton wool that had been her existence ever since that awful, awful day when the bleeding wouldn't stop . . .

It was as she approached Boots to buy what she needed that the shock hit her. It had been like that time she'd touched that faulty electrical socket, the realization of what she was doing. No, it had been more, much more than physical. There had also been heartbreak in there as she knew the one thing she wanted more than anything else was to be denied to her . . .

The wicked had sorrows, but then sorrows could make people wicked.

The music abruptly stopped and was replaced by the repeated hitting of what sounded like top E.

'It's all right,' the organist called. 'It's not a fire alarm. The note's sticking.'

But it hadn't reminded Thelma of a fire alarm.

It had reminded her about something else.

She stopped, sat upright, her hand clutching the side of the pew.

What was it Mandy had said that morning . . . about being in two places at once? And hadn't Liz said something similar?

A tsunami of thoughts smashed and crashed through her head . . . smoke alarms . . . cups on the draining board . . . Paula's tales of Topsy wandering across the fields . . . Lloret . . . Ness . . . and money. Lots and lots of money.

It all made sense.

It all made brutal shining sense.

She reached for her phone and texted her friends: WHEN WE MEET TOMORROW I HAVE SOMETHING I NEED TO TELL YOU.

CHAPTER THIRTY-NINE

At the garden centre, Cleopatra is brought to mind more than once.

Both Liz and Pat knew that this was not to be just any old meeting of their Thursday coffee club. They had known it from Thelma's text the previous night but thinking about it later they both felt they could have guessed anyway; the events of the previous few days had left them both with the strong feeling of something brewing, something coming to a head.

Liz was eleven and a half minutes late. First thing that morning Jacob had phoned her, just before setting off for the first day at Skel Hill with precise and detailed instructions about his Friday tea (Arkham Melts and spaghetti hoops – *not* the Batman hoops but the regular ones – the hoops on one side of the plate *not* touching the Lunar Croquettes on the other, with *one* slice of unbuttered white bread). These instructions had been repeated to her twice (and would have been a third time had Leoni not taken the phone off him) and Liz had had to make a lightning dash to Tesco's; the meal components were now safely stored in her freezer.

Pat was fourteen minutes late. That morning's breakfast had been strained, as had been the previous evening. She had read about families who had faced difficult revelations and subsequent conversation where all the right things had been said and generally everyone came through with flying colours. But what about the conversations after that . . . ? Breakfast with Rod and Liam, despite a mega fry-up of the best the Farm Shop had to offer, had been a largely silent meal punctuated by her bright trying-too-hard efforts at chat and a growing fear that here was a potentially insoluble issue that no number of conversations could address.

The chilly atmosphere (and her private scenarios involving Liam relocating to Soho and cutting all ties with the family) had been abruptly interrupted by Larson. He had suddenly limped into the kitchen with a bloodied glass-embedded paw, which he presented to them with a pained, affronted air. This dramatic appearance had been followed by a panicked melee of towels, hot water, disinfectant and snapped orders, culminating in Pat holding a basin of hot water and Dettol, Rod removing the offending shards and Liam holding Larson in a comforting tight embrace that somehow seemed to include the whole family.

By the time Rod and Liam were loading Larson into the Land Rover for a frantic dash to the vet's, it was almost as if things were – not exactly normal, but definitely moving in that direction. And then as Rod was starting the Land Rover, she heard him ask Liam in non-committal tones if he fancied catching the match on the widescreen at the Wheatsheaf and Liam had said okay in equally non-committal tones at which point Pat had had to retire to the utility room for a private weep.

Pat took her coffee (no cake – she had that trip to the new boutique earmarked for later on) and joined her two friends at their favourite corner table. Today was different again from yesterday's sunshine. It was cool and grey and the patio doors were firmly shut as if to say: 'That was spring; you've had your lot.'

Thelma got straight to the point.

'I think I know what happened,' she said. 'To Topsy.'

They both looked at her.

'Was she murdered?' said Liz. (Again the word came out, just like that.)

Thelma nodded. 'I believe so.'

Pat realized she was holding her breath. She felt exactly as she had on the Pepsi Max ride that awful time, the moment before the carriage plunged down into what seemed like infinity. 'Go on,' she said. 'Who?' She suddenly wished she had gone for that slice of cake after all.

'Before I say,' Thelma spoke both calmly and firmly, 'I want you both to think very carefully. Do you really want me to tell you?'

'Of course we do.' Pat braced herself for the plunge.

'No wait.' Thelma held up a distancing hand. Unbeknownst to each other, both Liz and Pat had the same image of their friend in her M&S winter coat reporting Rocky at Northallerton Police Station. 'If I tell you,' she said, 'then you'll both be involved, both of you. And I want you to think what that means. Statements to the police, hours of questioning – and that'll be the very least of it. Potentially even a trial, where you could be called as witnesses. Press attention.'

'But surely that'll be the case anyway,' said Liz.

'But it won't have come from you. You won't have been the one to have gone to the police in the first place. I'm the one the culprit will know spoke out.' Pat thought Thelma definitely had a point. To drive away from here secure in the knowledge that someone else would do what needed to be done and say what needed to be saying.

'Are you all right with that though?' she said.

Thelma nodded. 'Absolutely,' she said. 'I'm the one who Topsy spoke to about someone wanting to kill her.'

'No.' Thelma and Pat barely recognized Liz's voice (neither did Liz come to that). 'If someone murdered our friend, our very

305

good friend, I want to be a part of bringing that person to book. We owe it to Topsy and we most definitely owe it to KellyAnne.'

'Totally,' agreed Pat, ashamed of her earlier thought.

'Well,' said Thelma. 'If you're both sure.'

'One hundred per cent,' said Liz.

Thelma paused and gathered her thoughts, lacing her fingers together as she did so. 'I made a phone call this morning,' she said. 'To a certain catalogue company about an order that was placed there a few months ago.' She reached in her bag and Pat recognized one of the catalogues from the stack of junk mail they'd looked at a few days back.

Thelma sighed. 'It all goes back to Rocky and that awful fraud,' she said. 'That awful, awful fraud.'

She broke off, for at that moment she realized Liz's attention was not on her but someone else, someone across the room. Gone was her resolute expression, she was smiling and there was tension and uncertainty in that smile. Thelma turned her head and saw standing in the entrance by the Bring'n'Swap bookshelf was KellyAnne.

Today she was in shades of purple: maroon jacket, lilac blouse, mauve skirt. The effect was more sombre than the customary pink. And her face – definitely not Blanche Dubois, more Cleopatra when she'd been brought the news of Antony's marriage. These thoughts flashed in and out of Thelma's mind and she barely had time to offer up a quick prayer for support and brace herself for the confrontation she felt sure was to come.

However, it was not to Thelma but Pat that KellyAnne spoke.

'I've just one thing to say to you.' Her voice thrilled round the garden centre coffee shop, making staff and customers alike turn. 'And that's stay out of people's lives.'

Pat made the beginnings of some comment (indeed kept on trying to make the beginnings of some comment or other) but KellyAnne carried on. She obviously had a lot more than just one thing to say.

'Are you proud of yourself, that's what I want to know? Talking to a vulnerable young lad, badgering him to get himself into trouble? Do you get off on that? And does your husband know what you've done? Three hours! Three hours I've just spent in a police station. And Lloret, even as I speak, he's being interviewed under caution. A nineteen-year-old boy, Pat! Are you happy with that? I can't believe you would do such a thing. I thought you were my friend.'

Part of Thelma appreciated the sheer artistry of the whole thing: the poised body, weight slightly on one hip, the contemptuous gestures, the thrilling voice – the rest of the coffee shop were openly staring and she realized KellyAnne was well aware of the fact. Whatever emotions she was going through, she went through them the better for having an audience.

'This woman.' Now she was acknowledging said audience and sweeping a challenging gaze round the room. 'This woman—' a pink-nailed finger pointed at Pat's heart '—takes a vulnerable young lad, beaten up, in one helluva bad place, and she manipulates him into going to the police and getting himself in a whole heap of trouble he did not need to be in.'

The voice dropped and abruptly she turned her attention to Liz.

'Didn't I ask you? Didn't I sit with you yesterday in this very place and ask you to stop interfering?' The anger was now replaced with something softer, more sorrowful, more vulnerable. 'You can't know, you cannot begin to know, how painful all this is for me.'

'KellyAnne.' Something in Liz's voice made her stop. There was no attempt to talk over Liz, as she had with Pat. 'KellyAnne, sit down. Thelma thinks she knows what happened to your mother.'

Her face went completely blank, uncomprehending. She seemed to lose all her animation and sank down.

'I don't understand,' she said. 'What are you saying?'

'Your mother, KellyAnne.' Liz's voice was so gentle, yet there was an undercurrent of steel.

'Thelma thinks she knows what happened to her that night.'

'An accident.'

'No, not an accident.'

'The police said it was an accident, Liz.' Her voice rose from its bewildered tones, strengthening. 'That's what the police said. A tragic accident. Look, I can't be doing with this . . .'

'KellyAnne . . .'

'It's what the police said; it's what's in all the reports.'

'KellyAnne.' Liz's tone was one that had brought round many a sobbing child. 'We think your mother was deliberately killed.'

KellyAnne thrust up a pink-nailed hand as if warding off the words.

'No.' She was firm. 'No, I can't take this. Look.' She dropped her hand and looked round at the group, speaking low, passion-ately (Joan Crawford now, thought Thelma). 'I wasn't going to say, but I've not been well. I've been feeling very tired, not just tired, wiped out. Exhausted. I thought it was the grief, but I've been to the doctor's. And, anyway, to cut a long story short they've been doing tests. I've been to the Friarage for scans.'

'I'm sorry to hear that,' said Thelma wondering what on earth to say next.

'There's something there.' KellyAnne looked at the three, her eyes crystal with tears, her voice no more than a choked whisper. 'They say there's something there.'

The three looked at her.

'I'm not well,' she said, 'I'm really not well.'

Thelma sent up another quick prayer for guidance, whilst Pat braced herself in case she should suddenly turn on her again. But it was Liz who spoke. 'KellyAnne.'

For the second time that morning Thelma was put in mind of Cleopatra. Not by KellyAnne this time but Liz.

'KellyAnne,' she said again. 'How could you?'

Pat looked at her friend uncomprehendingly, but Liz was looking directly at KellyAnne. Her expression had gone from concern to anger.

'How could you kill your own mother?' she said.

It was Pat's experience from books and television that when people were confronted with an accusation of murder they tended to act in one of three ways.

1) By trying to laugh it off as a joke, saying that the accuser must be mad.

2) By attacking their accuser (and often being restrained in some way by, say, an officer of the law).

3) Making a spirited, but ultimately doomed, attempt at escape.

KellyAnne did none of these things (not that the garden centre café was really conducive to them, certainly not 2 and 3.) Instead her face froze, quivered for an eternal moment and then something inside seemed to break and she burst into noisy sobs and pillowed her head in her hands, her golden hair spreading out across the table. (They all noticed her roots needed doing but none of them mentioned this later, not even to each other.)

Pat was aware of two thoughts: one was something along the lines of what was it about people crying into tables, the other, squashed deep inside and barely even voiced, was along the lines of *her too . . . she thinks it perfectly possible I could have had a toy boy.*

Quite how Pat took control of the situation Thelma wasn't sure, looking back. The next thing she realized was that she and Pat were supporting KellyAnne into the manager's office (a peat-smelling cubbyhole, half filled with what looked like shrink-wrapped ceramic turtles). Here she sat holding the weeping woman's hand whilst Pat tried (and tried) to get through to the police and KellyAnne talked (and talked). Over the years Thelma had encountered many children (and adults) who, when faced with the evidence of their wrongdoing, would flatly deny the most overwhelming evidence. KellyAnne was not like that. She spoke repeatedly about a terrible, terrible accident, about the horrendous mental strain (and the need to see a psychiatrist or new-age healer or both) and how she was ultimately relieved she had been given the chance to explain what had happened.

DC Donna's phone had gone to voicemail but eventually Pat had got through on 101. She now seemed to be arguing, like someone trying in vain to order a taxi, rather than someone reporting a murder. KellyAnne convulsively clutched her hand; the talking seemed to have come to a stop for now, but she kept up a steady wall of sniffs, sobs and occasional wails, almost as if she didn't dare stop.

Only Liz took no part in all of this. She stood with her back against the door, seemingly staring at box files . . . 2015, 2017, 2018 (what had happened to 2016?) – but the look on her face was no longer Medea or Cleopatra but Liz, indefinably, indelibly Liz.

Thelma's thoughts went back to that day in the garden centre toilet . . .

It'd be better all round if she was dead . . .

How long ago that now seemed.

She remembered that day, the familiar emotions that it stirred . . . staring into the mirror wondering who would take care of her. Wishing she'd had a daughter like KellyAnne, wishing she was part of a family unit.

Wheeling the pram back across the market that long-ago day she had spotted the group huddled round Osbaldistons, a scrawny girl with bleached blonde hair a hysterical focus of the concerned people. Seeing Thelma with the pram, her face collapsed into relief and she threw herself on the baby in the grubby lemon-coloured cardigan. Thelma said she'd found the pram down the ginnel by Woolworths, she thought she'd remembered seeing it earlier on – the fluency and conviction of her words was one of the many, many things that shocked her, both then and now some thirty years later. Sitting on the bench outside the cathedral – no way could she face going in – she hugged herself, shivering as if she'd never stop.

And watching KellyAnne now gabbling on about chemicals affecting one's reason she thought . . . I understand . . . I *know* . . .

As if divining her thoughts, KellyAnne gave a fresh wail and dissolved anew into protesting sobs.

Thelma looked outside. In a wooden planter was a single celandine (baby daffs as Teddy persisted in calling them) and in the sunlight the colours were so bright, almost enamelled, and as she watched, a sparrow perched on the edge of the planter, a wonder of beige and brown, burnished beak and tiny perfect claws . . . And then all at once, in a way she found hard to recall in any detail afterwards, she found herself somehow *beyond* the immediate moment . . . It was almost as if she could hear a voice; certainly there was a feeling of words deep inside her and those words said: 'I will always, *always* look after you.'

In the event it proved quicker and easier to drive KellyAnne straight to the police station themselves. Thirsk was apparently 'an office only', whatever that meant, so for the second time in two days Pat found herself driving to Northallerton. Thelma sat in the back still holding KellyAnne's hand and Liz sat in the front staring out of the window, that same bleak terrible expression on her face.

They supported her into the station between them, KellyAnne volubly demanding water, solicitors, the need to talk, startling the officer on the desk and generally putting Thelma in mind not of Blanche or Mildred or even Cleopatra, but a spoilt, frightened child.

CHAPTER FORTY

A story of ordinary evil is recounted by three people.

'It was when she said she was ill,' said Liz, industriously scrubbing at burnt bits of Arkham Melts from her favourite baking tray. 'That's when I knew.'

'How?' said Derek. He was sitting at the kitchen table and had one eye on the door, they both had. Jacob was in bed and supposedly asleep, but you never could tell when he would decide he wanted juice or a biscuit or even just a hug.

'It was just like when she was a little girl. Putting spots on her face and making out she was ill. Saying anything to get out of being in bother.'

'So KellyAnne wasn't in the Algarve?' said Teddy, puzzled. They were sat in their favourite alcove at Valentino's awaiting the arrival of their food. It had been very late by the time Thelma had finally got back from Northallerton but they'd managed to book a table just before the restaurant stopped serving. 'Oh no,' said Thelma. 'She was in the Algarve all right.'

'So how does that work then?' asked Rod. For once the flat-screen was off, he and Liam were looking at Pat, curled up in her favourite chair, large glass of glorious rich velvety Merlot in her hand. Only Larson (paw heavily bandaged), asleep in Liam's lap, seemed unconcerned.

'Murder by remote control,' said Pat.

'You can get these devices,' said Liz, carefully drying the baking tray.

'Devices?' Derek regarded her uncertainly.

She showed him the advert from the catalogue. The smiling lady in bed. *Pill Mate! Never forget your dose again!*

As she knew he would, he put on his glasses and earnestly scanned and rescanned the advert. She knew better than to comment until he'd finished. At last he looked up.

'Okay,' he said in a non-committal tone.

'She saw the catalogue amongst all that junk mail Topsy was receiving,' said Thelma. 'And that must have put the idea in her head. So she ordered one. She used Topsy's name and Topsy's credit card; then she could always claim she knew nothing about it. But to muddy the waters she also ordered one or two things in Paula's name. Then, in the unlikely event of questions being asked, suspicion could be thrown on somebody else.'

'You load them up for a week at a time with tablets,' said Liz, replacing the baking tray in the rack. 'And at a set time a wheel inside rotates, an alarm goes off and a new set of pills pop out. The alarm sounds very much like a smoke alarm.'

'We heard one going off that day we went to Masham to see Mrs Walker,' said Pat. 'I thought it actually was a smoke alarm, but it wasn't, it was the pill thingy. Anyway all KellyAnne had to do was load the thing up with an overdose of Topsy's heart medication, and then toddle off to the Algarve. She tried to set it up for a time when no one was likely to be at the house but when it did go off both Lloret and Paula heard it. Only they thought it was a smoke alarm. Presumed overdone toast, not overdose.'

'I should've realized something wasn't right,' said Liz. She was now sat at the table, wiping cutlery before putting it in the drawer.

'How?' asked Derek.

'When I went round, and KellyAnne handed her the Dossette box with the pills in, and Topsy said, "We're back on this are we?" Implying she'd been on something *else*. And then of course she referred to a gizmo . . . I should've known then some machine or other was involved.' She shook her head sadly, her mother's silver serving spoon in her hand.

'Go on,' said Derek.

'Well,' said Liz. 'It was important KellyAnne tried out the machine to make sure it would work with Topsy. And she kept making a great point of how Topsy muddled her pills – but we only had her say-so for it. Like with how bad Topsy was getting, walking across the fields at night. A few people told us about it – Paula, Ness – but they were only repeating what KellyAnne had told them.'

'Are you saying she wasn't confused?' Derek looked puzzled.

'Oh she was,' said Liz, 'but not nearly as bad as KellyAnne made out. The over-sixties lot knew that, but most people only had KellyAnne's word on how bad her mum was getting, even Paula. And if you say something enough times people begin to believe it. Just like with Jacob's teacher. And then, of course, there was KellyAnne giving her the tablets in front of me.'

'What about it?'

'It was only *eleven o'clock* when KellyAnne gave them to her. But her usual time was much later, teatime. Paula told me. So why did KellyAnne move the tablet time? So I could be a witness to how muddled she was getting.'

She shook her head and looked grim. 'Whatever she might have said to the police, she had it planned to the hilt.'

'So KellyAnne set the dispenser up with an overdose of heart medication. If someone found it, she could always say Topsy had been meddling with it. She told no one she was going away and when she came back all she'd have to do was hide the dispenser and muddle up the tablets in the Dossette box. She waited until a weekend when she knew Paula would be busy, set up the machine, and off she flew to the Algarve.' Thelma took another sip of her wine. 'It really was the perfect alibi. She seemed beyond suspicion. A few people mentioned being in two places at once and it struck me as important, only I wasn't sure why.'

'A word from upstairs?' said Teddy as their starters arrived (calamari for her and deep-fried mozzarella for him, as per usual).

'She rang Topsy from the hotel,' said Pat. 'The receptionist told me. But there she hit her first snag. Because of the call blocker Lloret had fitted, she couldn't get through. But she had to pretend she had.'

'Why?' said Liam.

'Because if she couldn't get through, people would wonder why she hadn't rung someone else – Paula, Ness – asked them to check on her mum – which of course was the last thing she wanted. And when I rang the hotel and the receptionist said she'd had trouble getting through, it seemed odd. She'd made a great point of telling people about ringing her mother, but had never mentioned there being any problems.'

'And Topsy took the tablets,' said Thelma. 'And she died.'

'Eat your supper,' said Teddy.

★ ★ ★

'KellyAnne came back home and she found Topsy dead.' Liz's eyes filled. Derek was holding her hand. His grip tightened and he stroked the back with his thumb. He didn't say anything; he didn't need to.

'At least she was in her chair,' said Pat. 'You could almost say a quality death.'

'Don't be morbid, Mother,' said Liam.

'So what was all that about KellyAnne sensing something was wrong when she came to the house?' asked Teddy.

'KellyAnne told us when she came to the house she immediately knew something was wrong.'

'Did she see something?'

Thelma shook her head. 'Absolutely nothing. But she *knew* what she was going to find, which must have been pretty unnerving.' She took a sip of her house red. 'When I asked her about it at the funeral she pretended to be trying to remember – and then called everyone's attention to Ness, using her as a distraction.'

'A way of diverting attention from her lie?'

'Partly. But also Liz had mentioned the *smoke alarm* and KellyAnne couldn't let there be any conversation about that.'

'So what was all that about the brown cups?' asked Derek.

'I should've realized there and then,' said Liz. 'All that about brown cups appearing on the draining board, and because of that people thinking someone had been round.'

'Hadn't someone?'

'No, absolutely not. It was KellyAnne's way of making people think someone had, a sort of back-up plan if people asked questions. Like sending off for those catalogues using Paula's name, and then hinting she might have been stealing.' She shook her head and looked grim. 'But I should've realized all that about cups was all made up.'

'How?'

'The cups on the draining board were brown. Topsy herself said she used the green cups for visitors.'

'Typical KellyAnne,' said Pat. 'Never really listening to anyone other than herself. Topsy said about the cups to Liz and Thelma, but KellyAnne didn't listen to what her mum was saying. Like that day in the garden centre when she bought us all cakes, never stopping to ask if we actually wanted them.'

'That was KellyAnne's tragedy,' said Thelma sombrely. 'She'd been brought up as the golden-haired princess, every whim indulged. People like that have a sense of entitlement, which muddies their moral sense. If they want something – really want it – they think it's rightfully theirs and they get it or they take it.'

She paused a moment, thinking into the past, of a young woman walking away from a pram.

'You say "tragedy",' said Teddy. 'Surely a curious word to use?'

'It's absolutely accurate,' said Thelma. 'Because of how she was, how she'd been indulged by her parents, always getting what she wanted. She couldn't be happy if she didn't. She never made her own way in the world, just took the easy option every time. And we both know that's not where happiness lies.'

'And was that what KellyAnne wanted?' asked Teddy. 'Her mother's death?'

'No,' said Thelma. 'She wanted money. Lots and lots of money.'

'She'd always relied on Topsy and Gordon for money,' said Liz. 'How many times did Topsy tell me she was shelling out on this that and the other for her. And KellyAnne, she'd grown to rely on it.'

'The Bank of Mum and Dad,' said Pat, looking pointedly at Liam, who smiled sardonically.

'I thought the money had all gone,' said Rod. 'I thought Rocky had made off with it all.'

'Topsy's savings had gone,' said Pat, 'but not the money tied up in the house. It's worth easily half a million. But there would likely have come a time when all that would have needed to go on Topsy's care – possibly years and years of care – with nothing left over for KellyAnne. She only had to listen to Paula banging on about how it had been with *her* mother to see how it could go.'

'But why?' said Teddy, cutting into his calzone. 'Why go to those terrible lengths? Was she in debt?'

'Oh no,' said Thelma, and there was something about the way she said it that made him look at her.

'Then why?'

'Love,' said Thelma, and there was something about the way she said the word that seemed to resonate in the air and suddenly remind Teddy of her performance as Blanche Dubois all those years ago.

Thelma paused, not seeing her salmon carbonara; instead she saw a figure under the lych gate, an upturned face haloed by golden hair looking with such fixed intensity.

Young man . . . *young young man.*

'Love,' she said again.

'She was nobody's fool,' said Pat. 'She knew she was on the wrong side of forty, and having seen what had happened with Lloret and Ness, she knew she'd need more than just herself to keep Lloret. She may have already seen signs of him getting cold feet. That's why she needed the money and lots of it, to bankroll his business and keep him with her. Though of course after Lloret told her he'd been and taken Topsy's bank card, she had even more of a hold over him. That was probably what gave her the lever to get him to finish with Ness. Yorkshire

Coast here we come.' She looked sombre but inside she was picturing the blouse she'd seen in the boutique window and tomorrow was going to buy.

'So would it have worked out?' asked Derek.

Liz remembered the eager face outlining plans, the house by the sea, the wide windows, the light rooms.

It's all I truly want, Liz . . .

More images came before her: the studio in Richmond, the vet, the ice sculpture and the string quartet playing 'My Heart Will Go On'.

Then another image came to her, a young man lying on the floor, distracted by his phone, and that bleak look on KellyAnne's face . . . the moment she knew to keep him she'd have to kill her mother.

'No,' she said.

'Maybe it wasn't nasty as it sounds,' said Pat. She was on her second glass of red. India was coming for dinner (braised artichokes) and Andrew had rung to say he was coming home for the weekend. She felt she could afford to be charitable.

'The woman murdered her mother,' said Liam.

Pat thought of Thelma's words about self-justification. 'She probably persuaded herself she was giving her an easy way out. Sparing her a horrible illness. But, of course, the ironic thing was that actually Topsy's life wasn't that bad, not yet. She was still in the early stages of the illness.'

'She had many good days left,' pronounced Thelma. 'Many good, happy days.'

'KellyAnne couldn't see, or didn't let herself see, the good life Topsy still had, with things like the lunch club,' said Liz. 'But then I don't think she even knew Topsy went. All she knew was what Paula told her was going to happen. And Paula could only see everything in terms of how it had been with her own mother.'

'And of course when Rocky was caught, she realized the awful truth . . . She needn't have killed Topsy after all. That's why she was so devastated when I saw her that night. She realized she'd killed her own mother for nothing.'

Teddy shook his head. He'd just ordered a second half carafe of wine.

'The whole thing strikes me as so . . .' He frowned, searching for exactly the right words. 'So cold-blooded. The planning, the lying.'

'Maybe,' said Thelma, remembering that stricken figure in the graveyard. 'Maybe the planning of it . . . but not the execution.'

KellyAnne had seen love and thought of a way she could have it. She remembered a young woman sat shivering on a bench outside the cathedral knowing if she thought she could have got away with it . . . she would have taken someone else's child.

She looked at Teddy. Lit in the ambient light of Valentino's, it was possible to see the earnest blond rugby player she'd met all those years ago. God had been very good to her.

'It all comes back to what you were saying that night after the play,' she said. 'Ordinary evil.'

EPILOGUE

Six months later, a bright, sunny September afternoon.

The phone stopped ringing just as Liz managed to snatch up the receiver, panicky mind flashing up various terrible scenarios (Derek taken ill, Tim in a car crash, Jacob in trouble).

'If it's important they'll call back,' said the Jan voice patiently, even slightly patronizingly, but then there'd been something about the insistent ringing of the phone in the sunny hallway that had unnerved her and another voice whispered on (Tim did drive too fast, what if Leoni's cold turned out to be sepsis, Derek's gripey tummy could herald all manner of nasty things) as she gathered up the shopping from where it had spilled out of the bags across the hall floor.

She was running late. It was Paula's afternoon to clean and she wanted to tidy round and be out in the garden when she came. It wasn't that she exactly wanted to avoid her, but the constant tales of how well Rocky was doing at HMP Wayland – like it was a sixth-form college or something – were always a bit hard to take. Plus Jacob and new friend Ezra were coming for tea and she'd been delayed in Tesco following Jacob's precise instructions (gluten-free cheese and tomato pizza, Grandma, because Ezra's gluten intolerant and when you cook it, can the cheese be brown the colour of toffee but *not* black, not even in tiny weeny spots).

Before that she'd been at Brian's getting his garden in shape for the winter, and then she'd been to 'Sing for the Brain', which she'd started going to every second Wednesday. It was held in the empty Royal York Bank building (empty for some three months now, though there was a persistent rumour Starbucks was interested). Sing for the Brain was a singing group, for those who were living with dementia (living with, not suffering from, as Jan kept on reminding her). The singing was meant to reinforce memory patterns; whether it did or not was beyond Liz but what she did know, beyond a shadow of a doubt, was that it helped those who attended by simply being a lot of uplifting fun. That day, singing 'Yellow Submarine', looking round the old banking hall, early autumn sun streaming through the windows, she'd seen smiles: smiles and energy and optimism. Thelma had been there and Pat – and Pat's son Liam (all set to go to Durham) – and that nice friend of his, who Liz could only remember as the Celtic poet.

Over plastic cups of tea (not such a cause for cheer), she'd heard from Thelma the latest on KellyAnne, a subject she normally avoided. Apparently (after a lot of to-ing and fro-ing) the case was going to prosecution and a new bezzie mate had set up a supporters' web page complete with petition – as Pat said: Free the Rainton One. The bezzie mate (Gabz – 'the wind beneath my wings' according to the web page) had approached both Pat and Thelma to sign the online petition.

Liz had received no such request.

Unpacking the shopping, Liz remembered KellyAnne's face as she'd planned her dream office by the sea. With her best friend's teenage lover.

Ness had relocated with Craig the fiasco. She'd sold Green Grass Properties and had moved to Scunthorpe where, according to her Facebook page, *it was all happening!* And Lloret was now safely working for Rod (it really was an excellent web page he was creating apparently) and seeing a barmaid from Topcliffe, so things seemed to have settled down there. For now.

Putting pizza on a baking tray, Liz reflected that she wasn't really sure how she felt about the way things had turned out. What would Topsy have wanted? Certainly not KellyAnne in prison. She remembered her indulgent face as she recounted the story of the faked illness. Would that indulgence have extended to her own murder? She thought of those words Thelma had heard in the toilets, which rang round her own mind as clearly as if she'd actually heard them herself . . .

They say I'd be better off dead.

Oliver Harney (or Thomas Blair O'Connell) had received five years and there Liz had no ambivalence of feeling. Plus Brian had been taken on as treasurer at the over-sixties (as he told her, bursting with pride as she weeded his border) so that was good.

Good. She paused at the word. Three people in prison, one friend dead. But, the sun was shining and Jacob was settled at school and was coming to tea.

The phone started ringing again.

'Hello?' she said, apologetic, mind once more spooling back through possibilities of catastrophe.

'Mrs Liz Newsome?' The voice, with its slight north-east burr, sounded somehow warm and reassuring.

'Who is this please?'

'My name is Neil Griffin. I'm from the anti-fraud department at the Royal York Bank.'

'Fraud?' Had Jacob somehow got hold of one of her cards again?

'*Anti*-fraud. It's probably nothing, certainly nothing to be unduly worried about, but we have noticed some irregularities on your Platinum Plus Savings account.'

Her savings? She felt a stab of fear.

'What sort of irregularities?'

'There's a chance—' his voice was calm and invited trust '—just a chance that someone may have been withdrawing money from your accounts.'

'Withdrawing? How much money?' She sank down, the bright afternoon suddenly a hostile place. 'I've not noticed anything.'

But when was the last time she'd even opened one of her bank statements? Her eyes flew to the Torquay letter rack, where she could see at least two stuffed amongst the sheaf of letters stuck behind the faded blue of Torbay.

'You wouldn't notice, Mrs Newsome. These guys are clever. And it makes me so angry to say this, but there's a very good chance that it could possibly be bank employees.'

Bank employees? Was nothing safe? Her hand holding the phone shook slightly. Their savings. The static caravan at Bempton Cliffs. Derek's stricken face.

'But there's no need to worry, Mrs Newsome, I want you to know that. They may be sophisticated, but so are we.' So calm and trustworthy the voice sounded. 'All we need to do is put your money somewhere where it's safe and these people can't get at it.'

'How do we do that?'

'I need you to authorize a transaction to move your money into a secure account.'

'Move?'

'It's a standard procedure. We just need you to pop along to your local bank and make what's known as a CHAPs payment.'

'You want me to transfer my money out of my account into another?'

'Just to ring-fence it so it's one hundred per cent secure, whilst I do a bit more digging.'

'I see. And when should I do this?'

'In a case like this, speed is of the essence, Mrs Newsome. Is there any way you can get down to your bank today?'

'Maybe.'

'And can I stress – and I can't say this enough – that it's vital you tell no one about this. Especially no one in the branch. Just until the security side of things is sorted out. Have you got a pen and paper? I need you to take down some details.'

A minute or so later Liz looked down at the account number and sort code written in her own neat print.

'I'll call you later, Mrs Newsome, just to check in.'

'Before you go.' Her hand was no longer trembling.

'Yes?' Was there a tinge of impatience in the oh so trustworthy voice?

'I've been out this afternoon. In fact I've been out most of the day. You only just caught me as I got back. I've been doing the garden of a friend. And then I went to a singing group, which is meant to help people with dementia . . .'

There was the puzzled beginning of a comment along the lines of 'that's nice' with more than a tinge of impatience but Liz was carrying on.

'And I've my grandson and his friend coming for tea. What I'm saying is, when I go, when I die, that's it. That will have been my life pretty much. Gardens and groups and whatnot. Nothing very earth-shattering but I'm all right with that . . .'

'Mrs Newsome—'

But he stood no chance.

'And I'm asking you, young man, to think of when it's your turn to go. And believe you me, it comes quicker than you could possibly imagine. I want you to think of your legacy. What you'll have done in your time. Lies. Fraud. Helping yourselves to other people's money. And the misery and heartbreak that causes. Other people's misery and heartbreak. That'll be you. Your place on the planet. And I hope when your time comes that knowledge is sharp in your mind.'

And she put the phone down.

ACKNOWLEDGEMENTS

The journey from enthusiastic writer to published author is one that's exhilarating and sometimes a touch overwhelming. On that journey you find yourself helped at many stages along the way and it's those people I want to acknowledge.

First of all, thanks to Sharon Oakes, writer and chair of Script Yorkshire, who took an interest in the story and recommended that I try and get myself onto the Writers Block Northeast Writers course. Then there was the course itself, run with energising expertise and enthusiasm by Laura Degnam and James Harries; their teaching and support were massively helpful for me and my emerging manuscript. A shout-out as well to the group itself, the class of 18-19. Being a part of you people gave me insights and inspirations I'd never have had otherwise - plus that priceless feeling of not being alone in the struggles with writing. Particular thanks to Victoria who put me in touch with Tony Hutchinson. His advice about police procedure was invaluable; thanks again (and again!) Tony!

Big thanks too, to the team of early readers for the feedback and insights they gave as the story moved from notebook to sprawling typescript. Thank you to Maureen at church, Joyce across the road, to my wonderful Auntie Lee, to Catherine

Johnson, the evergreen Audrey Coldron, to Nick Quinn and to Sandra Appleton, my former English teacher from secondary school, still wielding her red pen some forty years on.

A major turning point in this journey was meeting Stan, who became my agent. Thanks to him for seeing something in me, something in my writing – and then helping me find and sharpen that something. And thanks Stan for your tireless efforts sending the novel round various publishers – and in being so expert at getting me to see the bright side of the various rejections along the way.

Huge thanks to the people at Avon Books: Katie, who first read and liked the manuscript, and then to Cara, Becci, Ellie and Helen. 'Thank you' feels a bit inadequate when I think of the work you all put in, plus the cheerful enthusiasm and patience with which you took a rather bewildered writer through the various processes of publication.

Equally patient have been my niece and nephew, Conor and Caitlin, as they worked with me on the mysteries of Instagram and Facebook to publicise the book, reminding me so much of the times when I showed my late parents how to work a video recorder back in the day. Thanks to you both. And a special thanks to Louise Fletcher, not only for her help with social media but her belief in me which was on so many occasions much needed fuel in the tank.

I also want to say a special thanks to the people of Ripon and Thirsk, who were there with my family's difficult journey during our dad's final illness and showed me a world richer and funnier and more compassionate than one I could ever hope to create. Thanks to the Reverend Susanne Jukes, to Martin and Jill Fish, the people of Rainton, the staff of Elderflower Homecare and Hambleton Grange – and of course Thirsk Garden Centre. These latter will perhaps never fully realize the haven they provided to my sister and myself, and the jolt they provided for my creativity right at the very start of this journey.

And throughout – at every stage – thanks for the support of various family and friends: Niall, Jess and Andy, Sally, Trevor, Maisie and Elyse, Babs and Tracey, Auntie Catherine and Ruth – and of course to Sally and everyone at work.

And of course, Simon, for his constant solid-gold reminders that there's more to me than a manuscript.

And finally, to my sister Judith, whose idea it was to write the story in the first place.